FIRE
THE
SKY

Book Two of
Contact: The Battle for America

W. MICHAEL GEAR AND
KATHLEEN O'NEAL GEAR

Pocket Books
New York   London   Toronto   Sydney   New Delhi

Pocket Books
A Division of Simon & Schuster, Inc.
1230 Avenue of the Americas
New York, NY 10020

This book is a work of fiction. Names, characters, places, and incidents either are products of the authors' imagination or are used fictitiously. Any resemblance to actual events or locales or persons, living or dead, is entirely coincidental.

Copyright © 2011 by W. Michael Gear and Kathleen O'Neal Gear

All rights reserved, including the right to reproduce this book or portions thereof in any form whatsoever. For information, address Gallery Books Subsidiary Rights Department,
1230 Avenue of the Americas, New York, NY 10020.

First Pocket Books paperback edition September 2011

POCKET and colophon are registered trademarks of
Simon & Schuster, Inc.

For information about special discounts for bulk purchases, please contact Simon & Schuster Special Sales at 1-866-506-1949 or business@simonandschuster.com.

The Simon & Schuster Speakers Bureau can bring authors to your live event. For more information or to book an event, contact the Simon & Schuster Speakers Bureau at 1-866-248-3049 or visit our website at www.simonspeakers.com.

Cover illustration by Gregory Bridges

Manufactured in the United States of America

10   9   8   7   6   5   4   3

ISBN 978-1-4391-5392-5
ISBN 978-1-4391-6707-6 (ebook)

To Marianne Szamraj, Angela Cole, and the Spring Arbor, Michigan, News Group Midwest. Thanks for everything!

ACKNOWLEDGMENTS

We couldn't write the Contact: The Battle for America series without the support of our publisher, Louise Burke. Her enthusiasm and encouragement helped bring this story about our national heritage to print.

Our agent, Matt Bialer, at Sanford Greenburger Associates, has believed in the project from the inception. Thanks, Matt. Your faith is deeply appreciated.

Our editor, Jennifer Heddle, has given a critical eye to ensuring that we don't lose sight of the forest when all we can see is a bunch of trees. She endows clarity to us myopics.

We would like to acknowledge Katherine Cook, under whose care the "granddogs" are left when we're on the road. She also labored through the manuscript, catching misspellings and mistakes in grammar. Any mistakes that remain, of course, are ours.

Finally, to Mark Janus, the southeastern Simon & Schuster sales rep: Mark, you're one of the very best. After all these years, it's a pleasure to be working with you again. We hope you enjoy the story.

HISTORICAL FOREWORD

FOR THE MAJORITY OF OUR READERS *Coming of the Storm* and *Fire the Sky* will be an introduction to an intriguing and long-forgotten chapter of American history. As anthropologists and archaeologists we've been fascinated by the sophisticated and complex cultures that thrived in the southeastern United States at the time of European contact. We call them Mississippian mound builders, and they were remarkable.

The people you read about in *Fire the Sky* are ancestral to the Cherokee, Creek, Seminole, and Chickasaw—what would become known as the "five civilized tribes." If you have this ancestry in the family genealogy, this is *your* forgotten heritage.

In 1539 Hernando de Soto landed the most sophisticated military the world had ever known on Florida's shores. He marched his army through the center of what we now call Mississippian cultures; they amazed him with their artistry, courage, and sophistication—even if he despised them as "damned" pagans.

What really surprised de Soto was the fiercely independent spirit of the people he encountered. His winter-long battle with the Apalachee was fought to a draw. The stubbornness of their resistance induced him to change his strategy. De Soto might have been a monster, but he was a very smart one. As he led his *entrada* north in the spring of 1540 he learned how to use the Mississippian concept of "white peace" to manipulate the native nations. By the time the Mississippians figured out they'd been duped, the rulers were in chains, and Spanish soldiers were in possession of their capitals. As soon as de Soto and his men looted the tombs of their ancestors, consumed their stores of food, and raped their women, his army was on the move again. Only when de Soto stopped for any length of time—as he did at Cofitachequi and Coosa—did the population turn against him. Faced with being savaged by war dogs, mutilated, or burned alive, his captive rulers were generally motivated to suppress and disperse the rebellion.

Archaeologists tend to call Mississippian polities "chiefdoms" and sometimes "paramount chiefdoms" depending upon the geographic extent and number of subordinate towns under their control. In the novel, we use the more general term "Nations." Many of these were as complex and stratified as feudal kingdoms in Europe and, but for historical legacy, should be viewed with a similar appreciation.

Most of the nations you will encounter in *Fire the Sky* spoke a Muskogean tongue ancestral to the Creek, Seminole, Choctaw, and Chickasaw languages. There were, however, regional dialects. To simulate ethnic identity, we have employed different spellings. Hence the Muskogean term for a ruler might be "mico," "mikko," or the western "minko."

The names of nations, towns, and leaders are those of real peoples, places, and individuals recorded in historical documents. As much as we'd like to make things easier for our modern readers—and avoid the tongue-twisting pronunciations—we're stuck with the facts. If you really get flustered by pronunciation, just sound it out: Cofitachequi = *Koh-fee-ta-check-ee*.

Is the story of Hernando de Soto's *entrada* important in the twenty-first century? One-fifth—20 percent—of modern Americans claim some sort of Native American ancestry ranging from imaginary to full-blood. But what do Americans really know about their Native American heritage? Southeastern peoples weren't just unsophisticated forest hunters. They built cities, alliances, and nations that—despite inferior military technology—finally defeated de Soto.

It was hard fought. In the span of American history, including all the wars, treaties, and blunders, nothing had an impact on this nation's original inhabitants like de Soto's *entrada*.

Later events, including Chivington's Sand Creek massacre, Connor's Bear River massacre, Wounded Knee, and Custer at the Washita, are often mentioned as atrocities. There, hundreds died. At Napetuca, de Soto killed over five hundred Timucua men, women, and children. At Mabila, on October 18, 1540, he killed *thousands*. The Gentleman of Elvas estimates twenty-five hundred dead. Rodrigo Rangel claims three thousand. Luys Hernandez de Biedma states that five thousand Indians were in Mabila, and the Spanish "killed them all, some with fire, others with swords, others with lances." The verbose and unreliable Garcilaso de la Vega places the number of dead at *eleven* thousand. Such casualty rates would not be seen again on American battlefields until the Civil War.

Put in perspective—and depending on whose figures are used—this amounts to either a Pearl Harbor, a 9/11, or both combined.

The importance of Mabila should be assessed not by the body count, but by what it tells us about the courage, spirit, and determination of the people who fought there. For the native peoples—and for de Soto and his army—it was a turning point. One that would shape the future of America.

The Balance

She stared at the roaring fire. Yellow-white flames shot up from the logs and sent sparks dancing toward the high tchkofa roof. Around her, people's faces reflected in the leaping light.

As her souls swayed in time to the flames, the old woman felt a tightening in her gut. In that moment, she drifted back, losing the present, only to find herself on the plaza at Mabila. Heat made her skin shrivel; her souls filled with horror.

When she opened her eyes the image faded into the past, replaced by the Chicaza's great log-and-earth tchkofa. Where the dead had been, living people, smiling, laughing, filled the room.

She could no longer tell dream from reality. It hadn't always been so. Looking back through her memories it was clear that once, long ago, she had been able to separate this world from that of the spiritual. She had known the difference between war and peace, male and female. The red Power of chaos, disorder, creativity, and innovation had been distinct from the white Power of harmony, peace, tranquility, and order. Defeat and victory had stood separate and inviolable, sharply defined by pain, death, and loss.

Over the long years, however, the separation had blurred, blending red and white, male and female. Even war and peace had merged; the boundaries between them grew hazy and indistinct. When had disaster become triumph?

As they so often did, images of the past rose to dominate her souls, entwining themselves into her recognition of now until she lost the place and time in which she was actually living.

Was it simply a life lived too long? Or had wisdom finally settled on her shoulders like some great bird of prey to observe the silly actions of the younger people who now surrounded her, worshipped her, and catered to her needs?

They think I'm a hero.

The thought amused and annoyed her. She knew what she was. She'd lived it. Now her life was the subject of stories, her deeds recounted by men who were not yet born when she performed them. They hadn't lived the events, suffered the desperation, or known the soul-crushing fear.

But I did.

The Chicaza chiefs, priests, nobles, and warriors around her feasted on deer, quail, catfish, and corn boiled in sassafras root. Delight shone from their tattooed faces as they laughed, eyes glinting, teeth shining. The incomprehensible din of their raised voices as they shouted over each other to be heard sowed chaos in her souls.

She sat in the place of honor beside the high minko—the great head chief of the Chicaza people. They had done this for her: a celebration to honor her role in the battle against de Soto so many years past.

But the food before her remained untouched, flavorless.

The balance between present and past shifted, the images of those long-gone days growing clearer in the eye of her souls. The great council house around her dimmed, the people crowding the large log-and-earth structure no more than fading shadows.

She stood, and her feet moved of their own will as she walked to the fire. Extending her palm to the blaze, she knelt on the hearth stones. Figures danced in the flames: people writhed and burned, leaping and vanishing. She squinted against the radiant heat, her hand trembling with the pain as she reached out for the fire.

Around her, the room had gone silent, people watching in awe.

During that terrible year, Black Shell and I lived defeat after defeat . . .

She felt herself falling into the past, screaming as the fire burned and roared . . .

2

ONE

THE URGE TO HUNT LURKS DEEP IN THE BONES. IT pulses with each beat of our hearts and jets with our blood. To hunt—be it for food, for sport, or as an act of war—causes body and souls to thrive at the height of existence.

We are not the only ones enchanted by the hunt. So, too, are the invaders. And on that cold and rainy day, I watched them from a vantage point high in a live oak. I am Black Shell, of the Chief Clan, of the Hickory Moiety—an outcast from the Chicaza Nation. I am *akeohoosa,* or "dead to my relatives."

The Kristianos had come to collect wood; they'd chopped it the day before with their *hierro* axes. The distinctive sound had carried across the forest and betrayed their location.

Kristianos needed a lot of wood, and not only for fires.

They were busy fortifying the captured Apalachee city of Anhaica.

Their leader, *Adelantado* Hernando de Soto, had reason to add to the city's defenses. They'd forced the Apalachee people—to whom it rightly belonged—out into the forests. Predictably, the Apalachee considered such behavior to be intolerable. The monster and his invading army had been under constant harassing attack since. And the Apalachee had fought Kristianos before, having defeated another invader called Narváez but eleven summers past.

Where Kristianos went, they went in force, knowing that every thicket, swamp, and patch of timber harbored Apalachee warriors—all of whom were thinking up creative ways to kill them.

The woodcutting party I watched had come in strength and armed for combat. Having run out of daylight the day before, they were back, seeking to collect the remainder of what they'd cut and drag it back to Anhaica.

Thirty of them—accompanied by twenty slaves and ten cabayos—entered the clearing just north of my high perch. "Cabayo" is their name for the great animals they ride. Larger than an elk, the cabayo has rounded hooves, a hornless head, and a long-haired tail.

We try to kill them at every opportunity.

The slaves were a mixed lot of Timucuans, some from the south, others having been but recently captured in the Uzachile lands. The Uzachile captives looked the healthiest, having only starved and camped in the open for three moons. The others, those enslaved most of the year, looked like walking death. Their flesh wasted by hunger, they were hollow-bellied, their ribs protruding. Their eyes, now deep-set, stared dully out of skin-wrapped skulls. Two were staggering and would no doubt be killed before the day was out.

Alert for an ambush, the Kristianos inspected their stacked wood, anxious to see if it had been tampered with. Talking in low voices, they stared suspiciously at the surrounding brush, crossbows at the ready, while their slaves began tying up bundles of wood for the cabayos to drag away.

Several of the *soldados*—Kristianos who fought on foot—edged toward the brush, hands on sword handles, searching for any sign of ambush. I eased behind the thick bole of the live oak. Having been raised as a forest warrior, I knew how to merge with my high perch to avoid detection.

Then the hunt began.

The woman appeared on a trail just back from the clearing. She seemed oblivious to the sounds of the working men, and her path would screen her from the majority of the wood party. A thick tumpline ran down from her forehead to the bulky pack resting on her hips. A tumpline doesn't allow free movement of the neck, but restricts vision to straight ahead, so she didn't see the soldados off to the side.

The Kristianos, however, definitely saw her as she stepped negligently past an opening in the brush. One immediately raised a knotted fist; at the same time he placed a finger to his lips: the signal for silence. Men placed hands over the noses of the cabayos, others grabbed metal chains to keep them from clanking or threatened the slaves into stillness.

Hunters—though delighted by the chase itself—relish taking a trophy as the ultimate measure of their worth.

And the woman was a trophy indeed. Long-legged, tall, and muscular, she was young, with glossy black hair hanging down past her buttocks. A fabric skirt had been belted at her thin waist, her breasts bare despite the chill.

As she approached my hiding place, I admired her triangular face, the thin and straight nose, and the fire that flashed behind her dark eyes. Oh, yes, a beauty in any man's eyes—especially a Kristiano's.

I watched five soldados take up the woman's trail. In single file—like two-legged wolves—they hurried forward, slipping through the band of brush separating the trail from the clearing. They kept hands on their weapons, bearded faces lean, eyes intent. The ones in the clearing settled down to wait, watching the spot where their companions had disappeared.

I hunkered down against the bark, curious as to how their pursuit would play out. Had they the wiles and skill to sneak up on and overtake the unsuspecting woman? Or would their foreign clumsiness betray their presence?

The invaders were not of our world, but alien, coming from a terrible land beyond the seas, the likes of which I couldn't even conceive. I'd followed the Kristianos since they first landed down south in the Uzita lands. I'd tracked them, studied them, even captured one once. For the most part they had limited forest skills, though they fought and killed with vicious ferocity.

The five I now watched didn't make the usual mistakes. They didn't clump along in their heavy boots and were careful to keep branches from rasping on their shirtsleeves or their thick, cotton-and-metal batted vests. Those with swords kept a hand to the hilt to keep them from rattling in the scabbards. The man in front—a burly and grizzled fellow with a gray-streaked beard and close-set blue eyes—held his loaded crossbow sideways so the staves didn't knock against the leaves and stems he eased through.

They're learning.

Three moons ago, before Napetuca, these five would have just charged after their quarry, seeking to run her to earth like a rabbit. Oh yes, grand sport that. But the Kristianos were changing. At Napetuca they had kicked the beating heart out of the Uzachile Nation and destroyed the best Timucua warriors in the world. Then they'd marched west through the thicket country that separated the Uzachile from the Apalachee—and smack into a different kind of war.

Adelantado de Soto might have taken the Apalachee capital, Anhaica, his invincible *soldados* and the cabayeros on their terrible mounts driving the Apalachee High Mikko Cafakke—the divine ruler—into exile. Capturing the capital was one thing. Controlling the country? That, my friend, was something entirely different.

Kristianos never traveled out from Anhaica alone and rarely in groups as small as the one I now watched. Had the gray-bearded leader not caught sight of the woman, he would never have left the security of his woodcutting party.

But the hunt is bred into our very blood and bones. In the presence of prey our muscles tighten, the pulse quickens, and our senses narrow and sharpen.

The woman continued striding down the trail toward my tree. Not thirty paces behind, the five slipped along, eyes gleaming. As much as they feared ambush, the hunt proved irresistible. Risk only added to the thrill and the value of the prize.

My curiosity was piqued. Could the Kristianos close the gap without betraying themselves? I judged the shrinking distance and craned my neck to see the woman's goal: a small, thatch-roofed house. It lay no more than two bow-shots to the south. Surrounded by trees, thick sumac, honeysuckle, and vines of greenbrier and grape, the clearing was little bigger than the house itself.

Will she make it before they catch up?

The woman passed directly below my high vantage point, her hips swinging to the stride of those long legs. I couldn't help but wonder how she could look so unconcerned, oblivious to the closing threat.

My urge was to hiss, call a sibilant warning. I desisted; she mastered her own fate. My duty was to watch, to study.

I eased behind the live oak's curved trunk, making myself small lest one of the Kristianos look up. Heedless, they passed in single file, trotting as though to a silent cadence.

The woman was almost to the clearing, the Kristianos no more than ten paces back. The grizzled leader evidently caught sight of her, for he ducked down, scuttling forward in a crouch. The others mimicked his bent-backed scurry.

With firm strides the woman walked into the clearing. Stopping before the doorway, she swung the big pack from her hips, rolling her neck at relief from the strain. She turned her head as a mockingbird landed on one of the grape stems off to the right—and immediately launched itself skyward with a panicked chirp.

"I'm home," she called in Mos'kogee, no hint of alarm in her voice.

The Kristianos had frozen, still screened by the brush at the end of the trail. The grizzled leader hunched like a porcupine and peered through a screen of yaupon leaves, the crossbow held low before him.

When no one answered the woman's call, she shrugged and ducked through the low doorway.

The Kristiano gestured for his men to fan out, surrounding the house. He darted forward—still in a crouch—to take a position beside the door. His ear was pressed to the wall, listening. He raised an index finger—perhaps indicating a single occupant? The surrounding men looked at each other, grinning.

Ah, the hunt!

The graybeard laid his crossbow carefully on the ground; working his fingers, he spread his arms for the capture. He took a small step . . . and charged headfirst through the door.

I tensed, heart hammering. This, after all, was the essence of the hunt: that moment when the prey has nowhere to go, that split instant of realization, the widening eyes, the sensation of disbelief and panic.

The woman's scream—muffled by the house—mingled with a blunt male bellow. I shot a glance back at the distant wood party. Evidently they heard nothing; the rest of the soldados were alternately watching the brush—alert for the return of their companions—or keeping an eye on the working slaves.

In the house clearing, the four Kristianos were grinning, eyes flashing with delight. In his imagination, each was sliding his shaft into her, pumping his loins empty.

I saw an arrow flash from the honeysuckle and grape where the mockingbird had fled. One of the Kristianos whirled, his arm pierced by Walking Thunder's arrow. Terrified, the man yanked it free, blood spurting.

A Kristiano in a faded red shirt staggered sideways, head cocked, an arrow striking at an angle below his jaw. He grasped the shaft with both hands, a stunned expression on his face. He had to be Corn Thrower's victim, given where the latter had secreted himself beneath the sumac.

I watched a third man drop to his knees, hands to his belly where a crossbow arrow had miraculously missed the metal plates sewn into his batted jacket and driven deep into his gut. Wide Antler—a warrior from Ahocalaquen town—liked using captured crossbows in ambushes where he could pick his target and aim carefully.

The fourth man jumped as a war arrow thudded just below the collar of his shirt. The armor stopped it cold. Frantically, he jerked the shaft free, throwing it angrily to the side. His armor stopped yet another, coming from the side. I could hear a third clang off the man's helmet. Then he was running, charging straight for the trail.

Oh, the hunt! I lived for it. As I reached for my bow I caught a glimpse of the woman. She emerged from the doorway of the little house, black hair swaying, a long Kristiano sword in her hand. Across the distance, I could barely make out the bloody sheen on the blade. She would have struck just as the grizzled man stuck his head through the door.

I had my own work to do and clambered down through the branches. This time there was no doubt that a Kristiano was on the trail. I could hear the thudding of his boots and the whipping of vegetation as he burst through.

I settled myself on the lowest branch, grinning as I

nocked a war arrow and drew it to my ear. I shifted my aim as he emerged from the brush, arms pumping, panic in his eyes.

"*Alto!*" I shouted. "*En el nombre de dios!*"

Stop! In the name of god! That last bit about god always did the trick.

He slowed, pulling up. I waited until his searching gaze met mine. The eyes were an odd mix of green and brown. Remarkable—like so many Kristiano traits.

My souls thrilled at that final instant, echoing sensations that go back to the Beginning Times, to when the drives and emotions that make us human were instilled. Then I watched my arrow flash across space.

It happened so quickly that his curious green-brown eyes had only begun to widen, his lungs to draw that final breath. His hands had barely started to rise when my hardwood arrow drove into the hollow at the base of his throat.

I'd made spine shots before. This was another. As if an invisible cord had been cut his body crumpled, limp as fabric. The man's metal helmet popped off his head and bounced hollowly across the damp soil.

I dropped to the ground, nocked another arrow, slipped to the side of the trail, and waited.

Any other fleeing survivors would stop at my victim's body. In that instant, I'd have my shot. Or so I hoped. Hunting Kristianos—with their impenetrable armor— took skill, patience, and perfect aim. An arrow had to be placed under the armpit, at the face or neck, in an arm or leg or other vulnerable spot.

The tweeting of a warbler carried on the air. I whistled back, imitating the winter call of a robin.

I glanced up as the woman appeared on the trail, her long legs imparting a sensual sway to her hips. I grinned as her flashing eyes met mine, then followed her gaze to the dying Kristiano, facedown on the trail.

She stopped short, the long metal sword in her hand. Over the death rattle issuing from the Kristiano's pierced throat, she asked, "Did the others hear?"

I glanced in the direction of the distant wood party. "No. But they'll be on the way as soon as they decide these fools are overdue."

Pearl Hand gave me a grin, flipping back a wealth of gleaming hair before she bent down and ripped the sword from my victim's sheath. "He didn't even draw his weapon."

"He was preoccupied. Running for your life will do that." I rolled him over, wondering if we could salvage his padded armor shirt, but gave it up. My arrow had sliced clear through him and stuck in the armor behind. Stripping it would take too long given that the rest of the Kristianos were just a couple of bow-shots away.

I watched Pearl Hand's quick fingers as she searched the man's body, finding a sack of the little round metal pieces they all seemed to carry. It jingled as she tossed it to me. From the dead man's belt she drew a long dagger made of the metal Kristianos call *hierro*. Her delicate hand clenched a fistful of his hair, and she tugged, skillfully running the knife around his scalp, separating the connective tissues, and with a jerk, popped it free.

My wife's dark eyes flashed as they met mine, and a crafty smile curved her full red lips. She whirled the scalp—what we call *íhola'ka*—to sling the blood off. "You planned it perfectly."

"It wouldn't have worked without you. Nothing even hinted that you knew they were following." I paused. "Have any trouble with the graybeard?"

She grinned saucily and tossed me the Kristiano's sword. Then she inspected the scalp dangling from her delicate fingers. "The graybeard? I screamed as soon as his head poked in. He froze like a gopher, the back of his neck exposed. He never knew what hit him."

"Let's get out of here." I trotted past her, heading down the trail. "I doubt the Kristianos will pursue once they figure out what happened. Losing five . . . all at once? They'll be spooked, convinced it was a large party of Apalachee."

Pearl Hand gave me a thoughtful glance as we walked into the house clearing. True to form, my Orphans had stripped the dead and taken their ihola'ka. Since the Beginning Times, ihola'ka had been taken from the vanquished. Beliefs differed among peoples, but most thought that different parts of a person's spirit, or souls, occupied different parts of the body. The head, being the highest and filled with the most senses, was believed to hold the Life and Dream souls. The top of the head was closest to the Sky World. Higher was better, and even our chiefs built their palaces on raised ground.

By taking a vanquished enemy's ihola'ka, a warrior took a part of the dead man's soul—a piece of him that he could possess and control or offer to the Spirit World, sacred ancestors, the sun, red Power, or even white Power.

But to take ihola'ka from Kristianos? To do so was rapidly becoming the greatest of honors, ripe with Power. Not only that, but so many of them had interesting hair colors, ranging from brown, to yellow, to black, and even red. They'd become the most valuable of trade goods.

Back in the clearing, the dead Kristianos had been stripped of clothing, armor, weapons, and jewelry. This the Orphans had bagged in fabric sacks and would be given—along with the ihola'ka—to the Apalachee high mikko, Cafakke. Or whoever succeeded him, since he'd been captured by the Kristianos.

Call it tribute if you like. Neither I nor my Orphans cared. Why were we called Orphans? We were survivors of the massacre at Napetuca. Our purpose was to hunt Kristianos. As to Cafakke, his problems were his own. He'd given permission for us to hunt in his territory a couple of days before de Soto snatched him for a hostage.

The Orphans were waiting, grins on their faces. We didn't always have a day like this. Ambushes had a habit of going wrong—which is how Long Arrow had been killed less than a moon earlier. The Kristianos—with their deadly mixed weaponry—weren't always as obliging as they had been today.

For those of you who have never fought Kristianos, mixed weaponry means that thunder-stick shooters, crossbowmen, and pole-ax spearmen provide protection for each other, like a woven defense. And finally, should the *soldados* actually be threatened, a single trumpet call would bring the cabayeros on their armored beasts to shatter any formation of Apalachee warriors, no matter how well disciplined.

I grew up as a Chicaza noble, literally suckled on the art of war; but until the arrival of the Kristianos . . . Well, I never would have believed anyone could be so deadly. They brought a kind of combat beyond our comprehension. Even the mighty Apalachee—who would have been a serious threat to my own native Chicaza—were smart enough to avoid an open fight.

"Black Shell?" Blood Thorn asked.

I turned to where my friend lifted a clanking sack of armor looted from the dead. Among his Timucua people he had been an *iníha,* or ranked noble, if you will. Of medium height and muscular, he had a square face, and his upper body was tattooed with stars on the breasts and zigzag lines on the shoulders. White scars ringed his neck, compliments of a Kristiano slave collar. At Napetuca the Kristianos had murdered his betrothed, his family, his friends, and his community—and most of his reasons for living.

He asked, "Which trail do we take?"

"The one to the southwest." I pointed. "We need to be out of this area as fast as possible. It will take them a while to figure out what happened. Then they will proceed cautiously, but quickly, back to Anhaica. After that the *Adelantado* de Soto will send cabayos out to sweep this entire area."

Blood Thorn squinted his right eye and jerked a nod. He gestured to the rest of my little band of Orphans and took the lead. Pearl Hand and I followed as Blood Thorn pushed through the honeysuckle and onto a narrow trail that led through long-abandoned fields, now surrendering to forest.

Past that we emerged under old-growth canopy, the trail vanishing under last fall's thick brown leaf mat. Our way led beneath spreading oaks, hickories, sweet gums, and occasional maples. High overhead the winter branches were interlaced, roofing the world a bow-shot above. I could see the first buds beginning to swell on those high tips, the promise of spring to come.

Once I'd had a soul-deep fondness for the dim openness under the great trees. To walk under the high canopy gave one a sense of ancient peace—a place where the white Power of tranquility pervaded. For the moment, however, the open forest floor set all of us on edge. While the massive tree trunks provided some cover, Kristiano cabayeros could charge, wheel their mounts, turn, and strike. Anyone fleeing would be run down and lanced from behind.

Blood Thorn broke into a distance-eating trot, his feet thrashing through the leaf mat. I followed behind, watching the fabric sack full of booty bounce on Blood Thorn's wide back. His thick-muscled legs weren't those of a runner, but Blood Thorn was a driven man.

So were we all.

TWO

THROUGH THE LONG DAY WE RAN, THE PACKS HAM-mering our backs as we took the roundabout path back to our camp above the river. We ran through mottled shadows, keeping to the thickest of brush and trees, avoiding the trails.

"*Peliqua?*" Blood Thorn hissed, pointing ahead through the maze of trees and vines. "Someone is at our camp."

We stopped, easing behind cover. I craned my head to see past the thick-boled trees. Our camp lay atop a high bluff overlooking the White Heron River. The location was remote, away from routes that would be traveled by either the Kristianos or the local Apalachee. Being away for two days, we'd left our belongings under the guard of my dogs—four of them—each a large beast, trained to the protection of our packs.

Through the gaps in the trees I could see the visitors

were Apalachee warriors, at least four of them. They stood, as if waiting, in a clear space overlooking the river and perhaps a bow-shot north of our camp.

For the most part we avoided the Apalachee. My Orphans were Timucua: ancient enemies of the Apalachee. Granted, we faced a common threat from the Kristianos, but why irritate wounds that had been festering for generations?

While we had Cafakke's permission to be there, it didn't mean that a small group of Apalachee wouldn't take an opportunity to pay back old grievances. And in the confusion of the Kristiano invasion, who'd be the wiser?

As we eased closer, weapons were checked, quivers shifted into position. Individually we slipped from tree to tree, keeping a wary eye on our surroundings. The forest seemed unusually foreboding.

Overhead I could hear the wind blowing up from the gulf; it hissed through the winter-bare branches. Wind is a manifestation of Power, sent across the world by the four giant ivory-billed woodpeckers that live at the edges of the earth. It can blow fair or foul.

Blood Thorn rearranged his heavy sack of Kristiano armor, patting his war club with his right hand, as if to ensure it was ready.

I hurried on ahead of the rest, hearing Pearl Hand's feet patting in the leaf mat behind mine. She had unslung her crossbow and had it cocked and nocked.

Four Apalachee warriors stood under the trees; they'd dressed in leather breechcloths, feather capes over their shoulders. Unstrung bows were in hand, full quivers resting across their backs. Tattoos were barely visible on their lightly greased skin; their faces had been touched with dabs of white paint—a sign of peaceful intentions.

"Stay alert," I called, "at least until we know what they want. And remember, no matter what, we're here to make trouble for Kristianos, not Apalachee."

"And if they make it first?" Blood Thorn asked.

"You let Black Shell handle it," Pearl Hand told him bluntly. "High Mikko Cafakke gave us permission to be here. No matter what, be polite. All of you."

The Apalachee watched us approach with stoic expressions, their black eyes hard and unforgiving. Each had shaved the sides of his head, leaving long roaches in the center, and the forelocks dangling down their foreheads were decorated with shining white shell beads.

With my left hand I gestured for the Orphans to slow. I led the way, Pearl Hand just to my right and slightly behind. Blood Thorn had taken a position to my left. The rest followed, their feet barely rustling in the leaves.

"Greetings!" I spoke in the Apalachee dialect of Mos'kogee. "I am Black Shell, of the Chicaza. I am here under the Power of trade and with the blessing of High Mikko Cafakke."

A muscular man stepped out from the rest. At first guess I'd have said he'd barely passed twenty summers, but the eyes in that youthful face would have been at home in a much older man.

"Greetings, Black Shell." He shot a glance over his shoulder toward our camp. "Your dogs are superbly trained. They won't let us into your camp. Your packs, it seems, are well guarded."

"That is their duty. To whom am I speaking?"

"My name is A'atehkoci, nephew of High Mikko Cafakke, of the Chief Clan, of the White Moiety. I serve as usinulo to the high mikko and come to you under his authority."

I bowed and offered my hands, palms up, in a token of respect. A'atehkoci, in the Mos'kogean tongue, translates as "Little Pot." Like so many Mos'kogean peoples, the Apalachee divided themselves into two moieties, or groups: the Red and the White, representing the two forces of creation. Color itself has Spirit Power, and red is emblematic of chaos, creation, art, innovation, reproduction, and struggle. White signifies peace, tranquility, wisdom, patience, acceptance, inner harmony, and virtue.

Within each moiety were several clans. In the Apalachee's White Moiety, the Chief Clan held the greatest prestige, having been established in distant antiquity. The great mikkos were descended from it, mothers passing the sacred leadership down to their sons and maternal brothers, sometimes to a nephew or perhaps even a daughter in dire circumstances. Such leadership, most Mos'kogee believed, had been instituted in the Beginning Times by Breath Giver himself and reflected the divine ordering of the universe and all of creation.

The honorific of *usinulo* indicated that A'atehkoci was the chief's maternal nephew, and hence most likely to succeed Cafakke as high mikko. As first heir, the usinulo's responsibilities included calling and orchestrating council sessions, advising the high mikko on policy, implementing edicts, taking responsibility for the Green Corn Ceremony, supervising the ritual ball games, mediating disputes, and acting as liaison between the clans and the Red Moiety.

I began to understand the stress lines around the young man's eyes. Like a certain akeohoosa trader, A'atehkoci had spent his entire life being trained, tested, and prepared for his eventual ascent to the high mikko's panther-hide chair. Then, just as the pieces were falling into place, the Kristianos appeared, captured the capital, and precipitated the most terrible warfare in Apalachee history.

I could sympathize.

"What service might we do the high mikko or his usinulo?" I asked, straightening. "We heard that Cafakke was captured by the Kristianos and taken to Anhaica. If this is so, our hearts are both saddened and worried."

"He was," A'atehkoci replied, watching my face for any telltale expression. "Power, however, has helped him to escape. He is once again reunited with his people."

"For that we are thankful and deeply grateful. May Breath Giver bless him," I replied, forming my tongue around the awkward Apalachee dialect. "The accursed Kristianos don't usually turn loose any of their captives, let alone great rulers." This would be a story to hear. "What service might we perform for you, Usinulo?"

"By the order of the high mikko, I am sent to escort you to Cane Place town. Our great and most holy hilishaya—the priest called Back-from-the-Dead—wishes to speak with you, Black Shell." A'atehkoci gave me a serious inspection, then glanced past me at my companions.

His gaze sharpened at the sight of Pearl Hand—a normal reaction for any male . . . assuming his heart was still beating. When she smiled at him, a faint flush rose along his white-dabbed cheeks.

It went away as he cataloged my Uzachile companions, taking in their Timucuan dress, the way they wore their hair tied up in a warrior's pom that jutted up from the top of the head, and the bristling weapons—many of them Kristiano—in their hands.

For those of you who might have missed the last three hundred years before the coming of the Kristianos, the Uzachile and Apalachee had been in a constant and brutal state of war.

"These are the Orphans, honorable Usinulo."

"Orphans," he mused, struggling to keep his expression blank. That he did so was a mark of his self-control. When Pearl Hand and I had originally broached the subject of Uzachile warriors, the Apalachee response had been volcanic. Cafakke, however, had seen the logic of accepting any allies he could find—and that was before he'd been captured.

Behind A'atehkoci, his three warriors shifted uneasily, gripping their bows and resetting their arrow-packed quivers on tense shoulders. They kept glancing out at the forest. I followed their gaze, seeing nothing.

Why? What's out there? And the renowned spiritual leader Back-from-the-Dead wanted to see me? A sudden premonition ran down my spine on icy feet.

I took a moment to study A'atehkoci's companions. Young, muscular, and lean, they reminded me of stickball players, the kind that are fast on their feet and not easily winded. The wolfish look in their eyes belied the white daubs of paint on their cheeks.

"I would not have believed it," A'atehkoci said softly. "When the high mikko said he had given you permission to fight the Kristianos as you would, we had our doubts. Meanwhile, we've kept an eye on you, Black Shell. No food has ended up missing. None of our women have been molested." He grinned. "And you've killed a great many Kristianos."

"Not as many as we'd have liked," Pearl Hand muttered ironically.

"Agreed," I added, casting sidelong glances at the forest. What was out there that interested A'atehkoci's warriors so? "Just this morning, we managed to kill some more." In Timucua, I said, "Blood Thorn, please step forward and deposit the results of our morning's work at the usinulo's feet."

Blood Thorn never lowered his eyes from A'atehkoci's as he advanced and dropped his heavy sack onto the ground. The metal inside clanked. One by one, the others did the same.

I raised an arm. "A gift from the Orphans to the high mikko and the people of Apalachee. May it please the great Cafakke and his council."

One of A'atehkoci's warriors stepped forward, opening the drawstring on one of the sacks so A'atehkoci could see the contents. The usinulo lifted an eyebrow; then he shot a curious look my way. "The other bags are the same?"

"Weapons, metal, cloth, some jewelry, and Kristiano leather from five *soldados*. Oh, and we'd better not forget the ihola'ka. Horned Serpent blessed us with a good day." To emphasize the point, I touched the pouch at my breast, a gesture not lost on the usinulo. His gaze sharpened. He'd obviously heard rumors of my talisman—a *sepaya*, a piece of Horned Serpent's antler.

"These spoils would be worth a fortune in trade up north," A'atehkoci said reasonably.

"We are here under the Power of trade," Pearl Hand replied. "High Mikko Cafakke allowed us to hunt Kristianos unmolested in return for what we captured from them. We honor our word and Power." She made a face. "Unlike the Kristianos."

"What is being said?" Blood Thorn asked, shooting a

wary glance at the Apalachee. I could feel his rising tension.

"I'm not sure yet," I replied in Timucua. "We're still in the preliminaries."

"Trouble?" Walking Thunder asked.

"No." A'atehkoci replied in atrociously accented Timucua. He smiled at the Orphans' surprised expressions. "My . . . how would you say . . . caretaker? Yes, perhaps that is the best word. The slave who attended me as a child was Uzachile, captured on a raid. She taught me some of your tongue. I was encouraged to keep enough of your language to understand prisoners."

Prisoners? Wrong word, Usinulo. The Timucua were stiffening, grips tightening on their weapons. I managed a placating grin. "Walking Thunder raises a point. What are your instructions regarding us, Usinulo?"

He glanced at the sacks of spoils on the ground, then slowly met our eyes, taking his time, looking at us one by one. Coming to a decision, he said, "My uncle, the high mikko . . . *requests* that you come. The hilishaya would have counsel with you, Black Shell. Given the current conditions, we will not feast you as we once would have, but there will be enough to fill your bellies." In Timucua, he added, "You will all be welcome and honored at the high mikko's camp. This I promise on the White Arrow."

On the White Arrow. Thank the sun, moon, and stars. Tension began to ebb from my Timucua. Everyone on earth—except the stupid Kristianos—understood the White Arrow and its promise of safe passage.

Blood Thorn placed a hand to his breast, nodding his head respectfully. "On the White Arrow, Usinulo, we accept and appreciate your offer. In return, we ask what we could contribute. Perhaps a deer? Or will music from our flutes be sufficient?"

A wry smile played along A'atehkoci's lips. I got the feeling he hadn't enjoyed much real humor since de Soto's arrival. He kicked one of the sacks; metal clanked. "This is worth more to us than four deer and all the flute music in the world."

The deer and flute music made reference to the traditional way of peacefully approaching an enemy. Unlike the filthy Kristianos, we had long-established rules of conduct. Enemies wishing to meet in peace sent their adversaries a white arrow, followed by four deer carcasses, and finally arrived in procession, playing flutes. All was in accord with white Power, and for the most part, no one violated the truce. Those who did found themselves shunned for the rest of their lives, many even by their closest kin.

At a gesture from A'atehkoci, the Apalachee warriors stepped forward, rearranged their quivers, and lifted the heavy sacks of armor and weapons.

Together we walked the rest of the way to the bluff. Our camp there consisted of makeshift structures erected in a half circle around a central fire pit. The limbs of an old oak, its branches festooned with long streamers of hanging moss, spread overhead. On the west, a drop-off fell four body-lengths to the swirling waters of the White Heron River.

Pearl Hand and I shared a small cabin consisting of cane walls daubed with mud to keep the wind out. Our roof was a gabled affair over which cattails, cane, and tall river grass had been laid and then lashed together. Atop it we'd placed a layer of bark and then earth. While not as snug as a regular trench-wall house with a thatch roof, it was better than the lean-tos the Orphans had thrown up.

The central fire pit—now filled with cold white ash—had been dug into the ground. Logs had been dragged in for seating, and a wooden rack could be placed over the fire for roasting meat, hanging cookware, or drying food.

My dogs were waiting anxiously, tails wagging, eyes bright. Bark, of course, couldn't stand it and began telling us how happy he was to see us return. Squirm, his paws pattering, ignored my signal to stay and came at a charge. When one goes, so do the rest. Gnaw let out a low howl and came slinking along in the rear, tail flaying the air, his head down, snout curled in that tooth-bearing grin some dogs adopt.

Pearl Hand dropped down to wrap her arms around Bark. As the big black dog wriggled like a fish, she ruffled up his neck and ears, all the time seeking to avoid his sloppy tongue. Bark isn't the brightest of my dogs, but he and Pearl Hand had forged a special bond. Maybe because they both savored a good fight?

Skipper managed to knock Squirm out of the way with a body block, which earned him first ear-rubbing rights. I told him what a good dog he'd been. Joy filled his odd eyes, the right brown, the left a sky blue. Then I shoved him away and made sure that Gnaw and Squirm got equal time.

Gnaw was the biggest. He's gray with a white-tipped tail. I swear he had the endurance of a beaver and would go from dawn to midnight.

Squirm, well, he was a problem. He'd never met a trade pack yet that he liked, let alone one he couldn't wiggle out from under given enough time. Since he was a dark brown in color, his white bib and the blaze marking his face were quite distinctive.

Dogs are central to a trader's life, and I'd had mine for quite some time. They were big animals, sturdily built and muscular from years of bearing heavy packs. A trader can go through a lot of dogs looking for the right one. Such an animal must be not only strong and loyal but smart enough to learn the rules. And, oh, are there rules!

First is never to bother the trade packs or chew on the leather, a failing Gnaw managed to outgrow just as I was about to turn him into stew. A trader's pack dogs must not pick fights with town dogs when we're guests—though if attacked first, all bets are off. Immediate and complete obedience is essential, not only for their survival, but also for a trader's. Finally, they must stay and guard a camp to the point of starvation or death from thirst.

In return, they eat well, even if it means sharing my last morsel. At times I've gone hungry to keep a bit of something in their bellies. Because they are family, I'll kill to protect them. People among all the Nations understand the value a trader puts on his dogs. And, for the most part, they are universally well treated and often allowed into the palaces of the high minkos, *tishu* minkos or second chiefs, *hopayes* or priests, and other elite rulers.

Blood Thorn had dropped to his knees and was telling Gnaw what a good dog he'd been and how perhaps later there would be a special treat for him. He and Gnaw seemed to have come to some sort of understanding.

I'd always appreciated that about Blood Thorn. He liked dogs; he'd had one back home in Uriutina. After the Kristianos occupied it, the animal was never seen again. Not only that, we all owed our lives to my dogs. They'd thwarted an attack by de Soto's war dogs at Napetuca, bought us time to flee, and saved countless lives.

And finally I must mention Fetch.

A Kristiano—our sworn enemy, Antonio Ruiz y Gonzales—killed him down in the peninsula. Pearl Hand and I had left food and supplies for Fetch's soul-journey to the Land of the Dead, but Fetch came back. At Napetuca—in the heat of the battle—he'd appeared as a Spirit and led Blood Thorn and me to safety. And then, later, in the Spirit World, as I was dying, he came again.

Oh, yes, my dogs are special.

What A'atehkoci made of all this, I couldn't tell. His warriors, however, watched with condescending amusement.

Not all people share my affection for dogs. In some Nations, dogs are a nuisance tolerated only because they clean up garbage, they bark an alert at the approach of strangers, and puppies end up in the stew pot. Among other peoples, dogs are considered part of the family, honored, cared for, and even buried in special tombs when they die. As I hope mine will be.

And the Kristianos? Now, keep in mind, I've never spent any time socializing with them, but I've never seen them treat a dog as anything but a tool. First off, they don't think dogs have souls. Can you imagine? Who'd want to die, send their souls to the Land of the Dead, and not have dogs around? What kind of afterlife is that? Kristianos call their afterlife *paraíso,* and there are no dogs allowed! Perhaps because of this, they have bred their dogs for war and use them to execute slaves when they run or grow too weak to work.

You heard me right. I've witnessed it with my own

eyes, been threatened by the beasts myself. I've seen them literally rip men and women apart, even tear the bowels from their victims' living bodies. No wonder Kristianos think their dogs have no souls.

Our dogs cared for, we led the way into camp, and I asked, "Usinulo, can we offer you anything? Corn cakes? Ache bread? It's fresh; we collected the cattail roots for it but two nights past." I pointed to a brownware pot. "We have tolocano to slake your thirst." *Tolocano* is made from groundnuts, dried persimmons, and blueberries, then boiled and allowed to steep.

"The drink would be fine." He looked around at our snug little camp. "You're far from the trails."

"The better to avoid any Kristianos," Pearl Hand told him as she picked the tolocano pot from its place and handed it to A'atehkoci.

The usinulo lifted it to his lips and drank, then offered it to one of his men. The others swung their loaded sacks to the ground and took their turns emptying our tolocano pot. As much as I hated to see it go, it was for a good cause.

"Blood Thorn? Could you, Bear Paw, and the others collect the rest of our spoils for the usinulo?"

"More?" A'atehkoci asked.

I shot him a grim smile, fully aware the dogs were now shooting glances out at the trees, too. What was out there? "Not every fight has been as productive as this morning's, but we've chipped away at them."

"Why are you so successful?" A'atehkoci murmured.

"Killing Kristianos is not a game for the fainthearted. Each attack must be carefully planned, patiently executed." I shrugged, watching as my Orphans returned with the rest of our loot: another six sacks. "They are like a great tree, and we carve off but a splinter here or there."

He nodded. "We know. It's the why of it that bothers so many of us."

"The why?" Pearl Hand asked.

"Why Breath Giver ever allowed them to exist in the first place. And why he would allow them to come here. That question preoccupies our greatest holy men." He stared right at me, eyes darkening. "And, perhaps as a means of answering that, the hilishaya requires your presence."

I shot Pearl Hand a quizzical look. "Let us put together our packs, feed the dogs, and collect our things. Is it far? This Cane Place town?"

"Two days' walk."

"Then we'll pack our bedding. Give us a finger of time and you can lead us where you will." I paused. "Under the White Arrow, of course."

A'atehkoci just gave me a smile, but it didn't reach his eyes.

THREE

OUR WAY LED THROUGH OCCASIONAL STANDS OF old-growth forest but mostly wound through second-growth that had sprung up in old burns or patches where gulf storms had laid down swaths of timber. There the trail turned difficult, snaking through deadfall thick with saplings, brush, and thorny vines.

Why the difficult route? The reason, of course, was that Kristiano patrols avoided them. They had learned that dense foliage provided perfect cover for an ambush. Tens of arrows could be shot before the invader could recover. By the time they did, the archers would have slipped away in the tangle. Kristianos preferred open territory where they could better use their cabayos, dogs, and weaponry.

A'atehkoci slowed his pace to match mine. He shot me a measuring look, then inclined his head toward where

Blood Thorn walked just behind Gnaw. "He seems to have the respect of the other Uzachile. Do you trust him?"

I gave him a knowing squint. "Let me tell you about Blood Thorn. He was an iniha, a subchief, received in great Holata Uzachile's council. Being a young man of increasing political stature, he'd been prepared to marry Water Frond, heir to the chieftainship of Ahocalaquen town. Blood Thorn was terribly in love with her, but their marriage was postponed by the arrival of de Soto. Blood Thorn found her raped body tied to a palisade post in Napetuca. De Soto left her for the flies, crows, and vultures."

A'atehkoci's expression tightened.

I continued. "Blood Thorn went a little mad after that. But his one-man war against the Kristianos didn't end so well. They captured him, used him as a beast, carrying heavy boxes, food, *hierro,* and other supplies. He got to see firsthand how Kristianos use war dogs to enforce order and obedience among the slaves. He was beaten, whipped, and half-starved."

I couldn't help but finger the scars on my own neck. I'd been there, once, back in Uzita town. I glanced at Pearl Hand where she walked ahead of us, forever thankful that my wife had dared to free me. I owed her my life as well as my happiness.

"But he got away?" A'atehkoci mused.

I nodded. "He used a piece of sandstone, ground away at his chain, and managed to escape during the confusion when the Kristianos overran your town of Agila. Fleeing south, he ran smack-dab into me and my Orphans—just in time for us to kill his pursuers."

I didn't tell A'atehkoci the rest, how Spirit Power—that essence of the Creator that flows through our world—led us to rescue Blood Thorn. Power echoes from the Beginning Times, lurks in rocks, springs, rivers, and the winds. It rises with the sap in trees and hums in the blood coursing through our veins. Power resides in colors, shafts of sunlight through the clouds, and the souls of the dead. It fills our world, ebbing, rising, and shifting with the actions of men and the mythical Spirit Beasts of the Beginning Times. Power is the life-breath of our world.

At the thought, my sepaya warmed against my breast. Horned Serpent is my personal Spirit Being.

Not everyone has one of those.

No sane person would want one—especially one as Powerful as Horned Serpent. Believe me, being chosen by Power isn't conducive to peace, contentment, carefree dreams, or long life. I'd trade all of my obligations to Power for a quiet little forest farm beside a river and happily grow corn for the rest of my life.

Why?

Because Horned Serpent is a Spirit Creature who rules the Underworld—a great winged snake with rainbow-colored scales and large crystalline eyes. Crimson antlers spring from his forehead, and rattles the size of melons tip his tail. With his feathered wings he flies up into the summer sky and guards the Path of the Dead. As old as Breath Giver's creation, Horned Serpent dates back to the Beginning Times.

He frightens me down to my bones.

When I died at Napetuca . . . Well, that's a story for later.

"And the one who follows just behind us? Who is he?" A'atehkoci asked.

"Walking Thunder," I told him, "a blooded warrior

from Napetuca town. He lost everything to the Kristianos: family, clan, friends, and future—all dead in blood."

"Does he fight well? He seems all lanky legs, and that short trunk and arms don't look like a warrior's."

I chuckled at the description. Sometimes I thought of him as the human version of an oversized blue heron. "He fights well, Usinulo."

"And the muscular one behind him? He looks like he could twist a man's head right off his neck or uproot trees."

"That's Corn Thrower, once an adviser to War Chief Rattlesnake. He looks like a squat bear because he is. I don't think he'd twist a man's head off. Built the way he is, he'd just pop it off like plucking a crabapple from its stem. He grew up just outside the capital city of Uzachile." After leaving his native land behind, he'd taken to completely shaving his head, giving it the look of an oversized hickory nut atop a stump.

"And the one off to the left?" A'atehkoci asked, indicating Bear Paw. The warrior's keen eyes continually studied the shadowy forest depths around us. His tattooed skin appeared mottled in the dappled forest shadow. He was long limbed and lean, with a somber expression behind his eyes.

"Bear Paw is the quiet one, forever watchful, competent, and absorbed by his own nightmares." We all had them. After Napetuca, who didn't? "Bear Paw's best friend was a fellow called Long Arrow. A Kristiano killed him last moon. Since then Bear Paw's been even more withdrawn, but get him in a fight, and he's smart. To a Kristiano, he's as dangerous as a water moccasin."

A'atehkoci's expression flickered. "A curious analogy.

What about that one, the one who keeps looking at you with those gleaming eyes?"

"Wide Antler?" The gleaming eyes said it all. Average of height and build, he was the believer. He'd caught a glimpse of my sepaya after I'd escaped the lake outside Napetuca. Seeing that, hearing the story of how Horned Serpent had carried me to the Sky World and what had happened there, Wide Antler had bound himself to me and our cause.

"If there's trouble among us, it's him," I told A'atehkoci. "After Napetuca he exists only to serve Power and kill Kristianos. He's the glowing stone in our firepot, the one who has only a single fear: that if he cools off, loses his ability to sear meat, then his existence will become meaningless."

"Like a blade that can only cut in one direction." A'atehkoci glanced up as a flock of passenger pigeons exploded from an oak off to our left. "Then we had better keep him focused on Kristianos, don't you think?"

"Oh, yes."

He smiled wryly. "Black Shell of the Chicaza . . . and his Orphans. So fitting."

"We've all forsaken family—any that haven't been murdered—home, and Nation. Me, I started out akeohoosa." In the Mos'kogee tongue it means "dead to one's kin." A better term might be "outcast."

"And Pearl Hand?" A'atehkoci arched an eyebrow.

"Chicora. From up north. She was sired of a Kristiano father and birthed by a Chicora mother. Being born to a matrilineal people, she's fully Chicora—but that didn't stop them from selling her as a 'bound' woman to the highest bidder. She's had an interesting but tough life, living among the privileged—until I managed to win her from a disgusting Timucua chief down south."

"Yet you married her?"

I grinned at him. "How many men do you know who have gambled for their wives and won, versus those who gambled on them and lost?"

He chuckled.

"I thought so."

Pearl Hand was one of the most physically beautiful women I'd ever seen. The first sight of her on a southern trail had piqued my very male interest. Her wit and poise had sharpened it even further. That she turned out to be clever, smart, talented, and unbelievably brave? A miracle.

To her previous owners, she'd been a prized sexual possession, passed from chief to chief as their fortunes waxed and waned. She'd been traded across half the country. A woman in such circumstances who kept her ears open and used her wits could learn a great deal about governments, trade relations, warfare, religion, and the wielding of authority and military might.

That she could love me with all of her heart? There, my friends, lay the greatest miracle of all.

I stepped over a fallen log, helping A'atehkoci with the treacherous footing. "Last spring, Usinulo, in spite of all Pearl Hand's vociferous warnings, the Kristianos captured me down at Uzita. They'd just come ashore from their floating palaces, and I'd been determined to see one in the flesh. I'd have been better off had Pearl Hand just broken a war club over my thick head to dissuade me."

"The scars on your neck?" he asked.

"After they ran me down with a cabayo, they clamped a collar around my neck and began the task of working me to death. I hauled boxes, containers, packs of every sort, furniture, huge metal pieces, you name it. This was done in a state of constant terror. Any who hesitated were whipped. Those who stumbled were bitten by the war dogs. And when one's body finally failed?" I glanced at him. "They turned the dogs loose, allowing them to tear the poor wretch to pieces. Once dead, the slave's head was lopped off to free the collar. Then work resumed, the bloody, empty collar jangling on the chain to remind the rest of us in line what our fate would be."

He said nothing, no doubt thinking about his own people who had been taken captive. For a time we walked together, then he said, "I think I understand, Black Shell. At least as much as anyone could who has not lived what you have."

At that he trotted ahead, taking advantage of a section of open trail to catch up to the lead warrior. I could see them talking in low voices, each staring out at the trees. Talking about us, no doubt, and what we'd been through. Kristianos are always sobering.

As a trader, I had been among some pretty savage people. Nothing had prepared me for the Kristianos. Not even a person's worst nightmares could hint at their arrogant brutality. Shocked and horrified by my captivity, I had come down with some illness, possessed of the fever and shakes.

The night before I would have died, Pearl Hand sneaked into Uzita. She seduced the guard, cut the man's throat with his own knife, and literally carried me out from under the Kristianos' noses. Only later did I begin to understand the courage she'd mustered and the sacrifice she'd made to free me.

Pearl Hand hates Kristianos. And, yes, her father *was* one. Perhaps "father" is too misleading a term. The man's only role was capturing and impregnating Pearl Hand's mother. The woman understood she was to be carried off as a slave and worked to death. At the last moment, as the Kristianos loaded their great ship, she escaped. Her Chicora, however, weren't welcoming when she returned—and grew big with a Kristiano brat. For reasons I still don't understand, when she heard the Kristianos had landed five years later, Pearl Hand's mother tried to find the man who captured, raped, and would have enslaved her.

Thus, as a child, Pearl Hand spent some time among the Kristianos. She came to speak their language and learned a little about them. She hates them and is just as dedicated to destroying them as the rest of us. She's killed more Kristianos than I have, and even High Mikko Cafakke paid attention when she addressed him.

She dropped back now that we didn't have to travel single-file.

"Interesting talk with the usinulo?"

"He may be a bit less suspicious of us."

Still, I couldn't help but notice that A'atehkoci's warriors, as well as the dogs, kept glancing off to the sides, and more than once I thought I detected movement paralleling ours.

"Someone's out there," Pearl Hand said, aware of my sidelong glances.

"They move too well to be Kristianos."

"Who?" she wondered.

"Apalachee, I suppose," I answered. "We're being watched, judged."

"Still?" She arched an eyebrow.

"It's all a test. We outnumber A'atehkoci's party. If we were intent on mischief, what better time than now?"

"Is Cafakke always this suspicious?"

"He just escaped the Kristianos. Wouldn't you be?" I glanced at A'atehkoci's broad back, thinking about what he'd said. "The renowned hilishaya Back-from-the-Dead wants to talk to me."

"I've heard of him. And none of it good. What does he want with you?"

"The Kristianos are changing the Power, ruining the balance. If you were a priest, what would you think?"

"That something was amiss." She paused, then asked, "What if Back-from-the-Dead doesn't like what you have to tell him?"

I fingered the bit of Horned Serpent's antler that lay in my medicine pouch. "Our likes and dislikes aren't the issue. The Kristianos are here . . . and nothing will be the same again."

"And you think, dear husband, that the Apalachee will be looking forward to hearing that from a stranger like you?"

My stomach tightened, and I shot another uneasy glance at where the mysterious strangers paralleled our course. Maybe we had more enemies than just the Kristianos.

We camped that night in a stand of pitch pine, listening to the breeze whisper through the long green needles above. The wind had changed, blowing down out of the northwest. High clouds rolled across the sky, lighter bands illuminated by the waning moon. The temperature continued to drop.

Two low fires provided the only light; it reflected on our somber faces. My Orphans circled their own fire, each reclining on an elbow or sitting cross-legged, some with chins braced. Others held their hands out to the warmth.

Pearl Hand and I sat with A'atehkoci and his three warriors, having roasted two turkeys we'd managed to shoot during the day's travel. The dogs had feasted on opossum and porcupine—the latter obviously skinned by Pearl Hand before the dogs received the fat-rich carcass.

My pack dogs lay sprawled in the darkness, already lost to dreams. They deserved it. They'd had the hardest day, jumping over logs, crashing through brush despite their heavy packs. Still, it was good for them. They'd grown too fat while lazing around our river-bluff camp. Now I wondered if we'd ever see it again.

"I suppose you are curious about why the great hili-shaya wishes to speak to you?" A'atehkoci asked from where he crouched, a feather cape drawn tightly about his shoulders.

"A little," I replied with disarming mildness.

"There is talk about you," A'atehkoci said. "Some of the stories . . . Well, they defy easy credibility. At least when applied to a trader such as yourself."

I smiled as he gave my hunch confirmation. "Journeys to the Spirit World will do that."

"Then you don't deny them?" From his expression I could see that A'atehkoci was fishing.

"I'd have to hear what story is being told to know whether to deny it or not."

"It is said that four times you went to the Spirit World."

"That part is true," I replied. I held my peace as the silence stretched. A'atehkoci hoped, no doubt, I would fill it with something.

His three companions had straightened, watching me with anticipation.

Pearl Hand used a stick to stir the fire, rolling what was left of the turkey carcasses, most of the bones now burned to a reddish white. We had all offered pieces to the fire with a prayer of thanks to the souls of the birds. A knowing smile bent Pearl Hand's perfect lips, and she shot me a reassuring glance.

"That is all you will say?" A'atehkoci finally asked.

I made the "pay attention to this" hand sign. "Usinulo, the things I experienced were the result of Power. One does not speak lightly about them. What happened to me during my Spirit journeys is not for the entertainment of others. I make no secret that my souls traveled to the Spirit World. The details, however, I have shared only with a select few."

I smiled at Pearl Hand. "After the stories have passed from mouth to mouth, I cannot imagine the direction they have taken." I cocked my head. "What have you heard, Usinulo?"

A'atehkoci smoothed his cape. "That you have been given special Power. That you know how to crush the Kristianos."

"Sorry. I cannot gather the lightning and hurl it at the invaders. I cannot call the winds to blow them away or entice the great serpents to pool the waters to drown them."

I let him stew on that, then said, "But I do know how to destroy them."

At that the Apalachee warriors straightened again, eyes glistening with anticipation.

"Just as we are doing," I answered flatly. "Grinding away at them, killing a few here, a few there, never letting them rest. Any attempt to crush them with one blow will end in death, defeat, and sorrow."

"You're not very encouraging," A'atehkoci muttered.

"Good. Heed my words: You cannot defeat the *Adelantado* in an open fight."

Pearl Hand tucked her long hair behind her shell-like ears. "Usinulo, if you learn nothing else from us, please learn this: In massed battle, the Kristianos are invincible."

"We know." He sighed. "Narváez taught us that when he passed through years ago. We were just hoping that something had changed, that you'd learned a weakness."

"Napetuca proved just the opposite," Pearl Hand whispered, and I nodded.

"What happened there?" A'atehkoci asked.

I spoke softly. "The chiefs went to de Soto, seeking to gain the release of hostage chiefs and captives taken for slaves. De Soto refused." I gestured at Pearl Hand. "She speaks the Kristiano language, overheard them planning to take the great Holata Uzachile hostage. Pearl Hand told the Uzachile chiefs exactly how the Kristianos planned to betray them in the end."

Pearl Hand shot him a sober look. "Once the Uzachile learned the extent of the Kristianos' treachery, they laid a trap of their own. War Chief Rattlesnake offered to trade other chiefs for the ones de Soto had already taken captive. The *Adelantado* agreed to the exchange, willing to meet them with a small party upon his arrival at Napetuca. Rattlesnake laid out an elaborate ambush. Hundreds of his warriors, their weapons hidden, would attack de Soto's small party, killing him no matter the cost."

"What went wrong?" A'atehkoci asked.

Pearl Hand's eyes narrowed. "Some of de Soto's slaves—Southern Timucua—accepted the Kristianos' god, probably thinking to better their position. They told the Kristianos of the ambush."

I nodded, making the hand sign for futility. "Betrayal upon betrayal; the Kristianos played it perfectly. They hid their cabayos, kept their soldados under cover. De Soto came out with a small band as he was supposed to." I added, "He brought war dogs with him, knowing their demoralizing effect. And he brought four cabayos. One, he mounted at the last minute, turning the war dogs loose and using a horn to blow the attack signal."

"Our dogs saved us," Pearl Hand said, waving toward where my pack lay sleeping. "They met the war dogs head-on. War dogs are trained to hunt and kill people. A trader's dogs, on the other hand, grow up fighting other dogs." Her face softened. "Usinulo, treat our dogs with reverence. They saved a great many lives that day."

"But not everyone's," I growled, making a dismissive motion. "The Uzachile warriors didn't have a chance. They formed up, fighting with as much courage, skill, and desperation as anyone could. Even my own Chicaza." And no one had a reputation for war like the Chicaza. "Within moments, hundreds were killed, the rest running for their lives."

"You ended up in one of the lakes?" A'atehkoci asked.

I could see Blood Thorn listening, picking up some of the words. I pointed. "The iniha and I were led to the larger by Fetch, my Spirit dog. Had we escaped to the smaller . . ." I smiled wistfully. "Just accept the fact that we wouldn't be here now. Those were the ones the Kristianos were able to drag out after a day or two."

"We heard they were herded into Napetuca," A'atehkoci said softly. "Made slaves."

"Essentially, yes." I nodded. "Apparently War Chief Rattlesnake and the captive chiefs couldn't stomach the notion."

Pearl Hand narrowed her eyes. "The day after Horned Serpent returned Black Shell to us, the captive Uzachile rose in revolt. They grabbed up anything they could and attacked the Kristianos. The fighting was brutal, but they were mostly armed with bits of firewood and what they could grab from the Kristianos. We think someone came close to killing de Soto. Even from a distance we could see him wiping blood from his nose and mouth. But the Kristianos crushed the desperate warriors."

She paused, and her face reflected the memory, firelight playing in the hollows of her cheeks. "De Soto was so angry he ordered all the survivors—men, women, and children—tied to the palisade posts. Then, perhaps to bind his converted slaves, he ordered them to kill every last prisoner."

She looked up. "The dead in Napetuca were piled in the plaza. Those killed in the main battle were left where they lay. So, too, were the murdered ones, their corpses tied to the posts where they died."

"They're still there," one of A'atehkoci's warriors whispered. "Or so we've been told. The Uzachile think the dead at Napetuca are somehow polluted. That nothing else could explain a disaster of such magnitude."

"They're wrong," I replied, seeing Napetuca in my head. The countless bodies were staring at me through death-clouded eyes. The smell of them hovered behind my nose, cloying as they swelled in the hot sun, flies buzzing in columns. I could hear the gurgle and hiss as gases escaped the bloating bodies.

"Wrong how?" A'atehkoci asked.

"The pollution doesn't lie with the dead at Napetuca. It hovers on the shoulders of de Soto. It marches with his soldados, scurries around the *puercos* his workers herd, and perches on the shoulders of his cabayos. The Kristianos are the pollution, and they will remain so until we destroy the last one."

"Akasam," they said in unison. "May it be so."

"Akasam," I added, as if the dead haunting my memories could hear and be cheered. Their faces—twisted with death—lingered behind my eyes. Staring, longing, and wondering why.

Left thus, their bodies unattended, they would never make the journey to the afterlife. Instead they would remain forever in the vicinity of Napetuca, until their screams and terror vanished into eternity.

That night, despite sleeping with my body curled against Pearl Hand's, the dead pursued my souls as I ran, naked, cold, and weeping, through the fetid stench of Napetuca.

I kept crying: *"I have no answer."*

They didn't seem to hear, but continued to wail after me in horror.

FOUR

THE SUN WAS SETTING ON THE SECOND DAY. WINDING along high ground where tall oaks, maples, and hickories crowded the sky, we descended to a swampy bottom filled with palmettos, water oaks, gums, and bald cypresses. Here we began to encounter people: local Apalachee going about their business.

The mystery of our curious followers was dispelled as well. Warriors appeared as the land narrowed, a line of ten of them paralleling our path. I trotted up to where A'atehkoci led the way.

"Friends of yours?" I gestured to the closing warriors. "They've been paralleling our course all the way from our camp on the river, haven't they?"

"Consider them an escort, protection, if you will. It would not have been pleasant to encounter, shall we say, surprises."

I gave him a flat stare of reproach. "We take the Power of trade seriously."

"I am aware of that." He paused. "But the hilishaya warned us to be careful."

"Why?" Suspicion laced my voice.

"Consider the stories told about you, Black Shell. An exiled homeless trader? Granted Horned Serpent's Spirit Power? Really? Or perhaps you had bargained off your souls to some other Power, one not conducive to the continued Spiritual health of my people?"

Sorcery! Even the thought of it sent a shiver down my back.

"And now?" I asked. "Do you believe me to be a witch?"

"A witch wouldn't willingly come to face the greatest hilishaya in living memory."

Even the slightest suspicion of witchcraft could get a person killed. To learn that Back-from-the-Dead—whose very name inspired awe among the Apalachee—suspected me of something as heinous? I fought my shiver, about to protest.

A'atehkoci, however, waved me back and continued down the winding trail to a canoe landing, such as it was—a track-pocked, muddy bank lined with sixteen dugout canoes in various states of repair. These looked more like local fishing craft impressed into High Mikko Cafakke's service.

I glanced around, taking in the depths of the surrounding swamp. Cafakke had learned his lesson. No force of Kristianos would surprise him here; it would take de Soto's entire army to force its way across the water to Cafakke's remote island.

And I was about to set foot in Back-from-the-Dead's lair?

A single thought echoed between my souls: *Run!*

But where? And how?

I glanced at the Orphans, who all looked equally nervous.

Come on, Black Shell. You've stood face-to-face with the West Wind; been threatened by Piasa, the water panther; and sat at Old-Woman-Who-Never-Dies's fire. You've shared Corn Woman's embrace and been carried to the Sky World by Horned Serpent. What's an Apalachee priest after that?

When necessary, I can even lie to myself with convincing authority.

We were all transferred to the dugouts, each to be paddled by one of A'atehkoci's warriors. I placed one of the dogs in each boat, cautioning them to be still. Behind us, the twenty warriors remained in a semicircle, as if to cut off any attempt at escape.

"What do you think, Peliqua?" Blood Thorn was watching the warriors through slitted eyes. "Are we truly guests? Or was the talk of the White Arrow only so much empty breath?"

Already unnerved, I considered that as our packs were being loaded into canoes. Several of the accompanying warriors stepped forward to paddle them into the swamp.

"The usinulo himself gave his word." I glanced at the somber faces around us. Pearl Hand had that curious half smirk on her face. She, too, was uneasy. "But there's more to this than just a friendly visit. Be smart, Blood Thorn. All of you, make no trouble. Understand?"

My Orphans nodded, then cast suspicious glances at our supposed hosts.

Pearl Hand and I rode with Squirm and A'atehkoci himself. I glanced around at the tupelos and bald cypresses. The great trees rose like giants from the calm water. Occasional cypress knees stuck up like fingers, and true to form, anhingas rested upon them, watching us pass with keen brown eyes.

"Go and tell the Underworld we continue the fight," I called to one bird who let us pass perilously close. "And tell the Piasa I haven't forgotten our trade."

The bird dove neatly from the moss-covered knee, entering the water with barely a splash. Only widening rings remained in his wake.

I turned my head, giving A'atehkoci a humorless smile. "Never speak rashly around an anhinga. You never know what story they'll tell . . . or in which world they'll tell it."

The question hovered unspoken behind his lips, wariness in his eyes. Finally he said, "Anhingas are special among the Power birds. Is one your Spirit Helper?"

"Among others," I whispered, turning my attention back to the swamp. A'atehkoci didn't need to know that Anhinga was even now swimming down to the Underworld to tell the Piasa what I'd said.

The Piasa, you ask? That's Water Panther, another of the Spirit Beings from the Beginning Times. Imagine a great panther with giant falcon wings rising from the middle of his back. Each of his four legs terminates in a scaly yellow eagle foot with long, grasping talons. A long snake's tail, thin and graceful, flips back and forth. The face is pure cougar, but the three-forked eye pattern of the Underworld surrounds his fierce yellow eyes.

Water Panther and I have the problem of an unfulfilled trade lying between us. He wants my life—and would have taken it after he dragged me under the lake at Napetuca. Unfortunately it was pointed out to him that trade goes two ways: I needed something in return. And, until I received it, he couldn't go about slowly ripping my body into chunks of Water Panther meal. Meanwhile, the promise that someday he and I were going to have to conclude our deal hung heavily upon my conscience.

And I was worried about a skinny Apalachee priest?

A'atehkoci led our small flotilla toward a rise of high ground deep in the swamp. The shore was lined with lotus pads and the cane stands for which the town was undoubtedly named. Tupelos, bald cypresses, and water and pin oaks, spiced with occasional sweet gums, towered over the island. Winter-bare vines laced through the high branches.

"Let me guess," I said. "The new capital of the Apalachee people?"

"Temporary, we hope. Cane Place town sits on an island," A'atehkoci told me. "The Kristianos will not come here . . . even if they capture and torture some of our people into telling them where the high mikko has fled to. No matter what, we will have ample time to evacuate our leaders." He gestured. "The swamp runs in all directions. We have a great many options."

Even before the canoe landing came into sight, I caught the odor of wood smoke on the air. Faint shouts and children's laughter carried across the water. Overhead a V of ducks winged past, turning to give the island and its human population a wide berth.

I looked up through the winter-stark branches to the gray and leaden sky. It still threatened rain. Ahead, the landing consisted of trampled soil, and perhaps ten canoes had already been beached and inverted to keep rain from pooling inside.

Back under the trees I could make out buildings,

mostly rude huts with makeshift roofs of bark and hastily procured thatch. Ramadas had been built along with simple raised storehouses. Beyond, among the larger trees, I could see more substantial dwellings.

A man rose from a fire to one side of the landing, peered at us, and then turned and trotted away under the trees. Almost immediately people began to appear along the trail he'd taken.

As the canoe slid into the mucky bank, Pearl Hand and I stepped out, gesturing for Squirm to stay. We grabbed the gunwales, pulling the craft ashore as A'atehkoci hopped off the stern and pushed. I gestured for Squirm to get out, and he rose, trying to shake under his heavy pack.

Then I lent a hand as the other craft landed, all the while keeping an eye on the dogs as they started sniffing around, lifting legs on canoes, and so forth. Meanwhile, from long habit, I withdrew my trader's staff from my alligator-hide quiver. This is a carved pole, bent over at the top and festooned with white heron feathers. It serves as the badge of a trader and helps to keep the dogs in line.

"Where are we?" Blood Thorn asked as he and the rest pulled flutes from their possessions. A'atehkoci might have said they didn't need them, but why tempt fate? I was pleased to see the Timucua take seriously my suggestion that they be perfect guests.

"Our new capital," A'atehkoci remarked without humor. Then he and his warriors bent to retrieve the packs. The approaching people called greetings; they gave my Timucua reserved glances and barely a smile. A'atehkoci gave crisp orders, and posthaste the packs were borne away.

I called the dogs to me and, with the Orphans following, set off in A'atehkoci's tracks. Numerous Apalachee paralleled our route; excitement filled their eyes as they spoke among themselves in low voices. The lilting sound of flute music rose as the Timucua followed.

"Have the Kristianos even tried to find this place?" Pearl Hand asked from behind.

A'atehkoci said, "Despite the high mikko's escape and our knowledge of de Soto's treachery, the *Adelantado* continues to send out requests for a meeting with our mikkos, priests, and clan leaders."

"Which the high mikko is smart enough to ignore," I added hopefully.

"Cafakke is no one's fool. He barely got away last time." A'atehkoci led us through a maze of hastily constructed houses. Pestles and mortars for milling corn had been brought in along with baskets, ceramic ware, and wooden boxes of personal goods.

"Also, we learn from those of our people who have been lucky enough to escape captivity: Kristianos have no honor."

"No. They don't," Pearl Hand stated sourly, then snapped her fingers when Bark began growling at a local dog. He backed down, trotting closer to her heel, a chastised look on his fight-scarred face.

The people stood either before their houses or along our route, smiling and pointing, or waving, awed by the Orphans with their Timucua hairstyles, dress, and lilting flute music. Many were signing, their hands making the inquiry, "Trade?"

I kept calling back in Mos'kogee, "If the high mikko agrees, we will be more than happy to trade."

We crested a low rise, and I almost stopped in amazement. The center of the island had been cleared; new buildings rose around a freshly packed rectangular plaza. What obviously served as the high mikko's palace dominated the north side, while temples and clan houses had been raised around the east, south, and west to create a serviceable square. In its center stood the council house. In Apalachee, it was called the *kukofa*. I knew it as the tchkofa in the Chicaza tongue.

A curious warmth rose within me when I realized—after all I'd been through—how comforting it was to step into a Mos'kogean town. The sensation was as if I were coming home again. People followed along behind us, calling and laughing. Others rose from beside their fires or emerged from the buildings. Children ran up, many chased by dogs.

I gave my pack the "desist" signal that told them we were entering a town and they were to behave. They, of course, had pricked their ears, eyes focused on the approaching dogs. I brandished my staff—a reminder to the dogs and the approaching people that we didn't want trouble. Several of the adults detailed children to keep the local dogs back.

The sound of Timucuan flutes rose in a trilling melody that reminded me of chickadees in spring. All in all, we put on a pretty good show.

A'atehkoci led us ritually, marching three times from west, to south, to east, to north around the plaza. I was amazed to see that a chunkey court had been laid out, the packed clay surface carefully smoothed and graded. Cafakke was addicted to chunkey. He'd been a dedicated player as a youth—before his body had been afflicted by a wasting disease. Figures he'd have a court made forthwith. Even with his capital occupied, a deadly invader stalking his lands, and despair in all directions, Cafakke let nothing interfere with his enjoyment of chunkey.

After the third round, A'atehkoci stopped before the palace and I gave the structure a quick inspection. Obviously constructed posthaste, it stood only a story and a half, with a high gabled roof. Instead of thatch, the roof had been covered with bark over matting. None of the traditional carved totems rose from the ridgepole. The walls were cane, interlaced with vines. Normally they would have been sealed with white clay; instead only tightly woven matting had been hung to defeat wind and rain.

I glanced back at the plaza. Cafakke had hauled in clay for a chunkey court, but his palace walls were sealed only with mats? Ah, the curious priorities of leadership.

A'atehkoci walked boldly to the palace doorway and turned, raising his hands. People around us went still, and I signaled for Blood Thorn and the rest to cease playing.

A'atehkoci's voice rang out. "By order of Cafakke, son of Matron Pahlko, of the Chief Clan, of the White Moiety, and high mikko of the Apalachee nation, these guests come among us under the White Arrow of peace."

The speech went on for considerably longer, and I've omitted all the ancestors, honors, and platitudes referred to by A'atehkoci in his role as usinulo. Suffice it to say that it was long, flowery, and but for the ritual significance, boring.

My take on this has always been that such long-windedness is antithetical to keeping the peace. Rather than listen to all the endless speeches, which—believe it or not—can go on for days, it's easier to say, "Forget the endless droning nonsense, let's go to war. It's easier on the ears."

Besides, who ever fell asleep in the middle of a battle?

Actually, I should not be so snide about the droning ritual. It actually served a purpose in allowing the other participants time to get properly dressed, clean up messes, arrange for food to be delivered, and attend to any last-minute details.

I glanced at Pearl Hand as she wrapped her fingers around mine. Back in the old days, before I won her away from Chief Irriparacoxi, she'd been on the other end, rushing to get dressed, fix her hair, grease her skin so it shone, and present herself as the most beautiful female adornment ever to grace a leader's bed.

Head high, I stepped forward, Pearl Hand beside me. Back arched, I took a position by A'atehkoci's side and faced the crowd-filled plaza. "I am Black Shell, of the Hickory Moiety, of the Chief Clan, of the Chicaza Nation. Beside me is my wife, Pearl Hand, of the Chicora. Those who accompany me are the Orphans: warriors who have dedicated their lives to the destruction of the invaders."

I watched as individuals in the audience stamped their feet and shouted, "Yaa, yaa," in approval.

I continued. "Under the Power of trade, the high mikko willing, we offer some goods that we have brought from the south. Under an agreement with High Mikko Cafakke, we offer our war trophies, ihola'ka, and Kristiano armor in return for the opportunity to kill Kristianos in Apalachee territory."

I shot a glance at A'atehkoci, then indicated the bags of plunder. He was a little slow but got my meaning, upending one and spilling out the contents.

People pushed forward, uttering sounds of awe.

A'atehkoci turned to us, stating, "The high mikko would see you now."

Backed by the shouting crowd, we marched forward to the makeshift palace. I pointed to the side, next to the wall, and ordered the dogs to stay.

The palace interior was nothing like the one Cafakke had been forced to evacuate in Anhaica. That one had been spacious, opulent with wood carvings, artistic weavings, polished copper reliefs, furs, and war trophies. This was little more than a large house overstuffed with prize pieces salvaged during the pell-mell escape from the capital.

Four men—all resplendently dressed, with feather sprays at their shoulders, copper breastplates, leather forearm cuffs, thick layers of shell necklaces, and clean aprons—stood just behind the central fire. These were the subchiefs, the tishu-mikkos.

One old woman, her face tattooed, her skin sagging, and wearing a white cotton dress, stood to the right of Cafakke's bed. Several middle-aged females—Cafakke's wives—waited along the sides of the room, all wearing different-colored dresses indicative of their clans.

Three men stood just to Cafakke's left and wore beautiful feather capes that mimicked wings, and each had the forked-eye tattoo, their faces painted in red and white. Their left hands held large wooden rattles. In their right, they clutched ritual maces in the shape of turkey tails: They were the hilishaya, the high priests of Apalachee.

Back-from-the-Dead was easily distinguished. He was the older one, lean of face, tattooed, and watching me with gleaming black eyes that seemed to slice right through to my souls. I swear, I could feel his antagonism like radiated heat.

I ignored him, my heart skipping.

The old woman in the white dress I knew as Cafakke's mother, Pahlko. The other women were his various wives, all dressed as befitted their station. Like most Mos'kogee, Apalachee were required to marry outside of their clan. Cafakke had taken a wife from each of the five subordinate clans he ruled.

Against the back wall, in a raised bed, lay High Mikko Cafakke, supreme ruler of the Apalachee. The construction of his bed was difficult to discern, covered as it was by a giant buffalo hide that had been overlaid with cougar pelts.

I approached as far as the fire pit, dropped to one knee, and offered my palms. Pearl Hand followed suit, and I could sense the hesitation among my Timucua. Offering obeisance to such a foe ran against the very grain of their souls. Nevertheless, they lowered themselves, hands palm up. I could imagine, if not hear, the grinding of their teeth.

I shot Blood Thorn a sidelong glance, seeing the shock and confusion on his face as he finally got a good look at Cafakke.

Years back, either disease or witchery had attacked Cafakke's joints. The man's hands appeared mangled, the knuckles huge; his fingers—like short roots—were twisted and withered. His feet bore similar affliction, making them lumpy and curled; the gnarled toes jutted this way and that. Arms and legs, thin from disuse, contrasted to the swollen burls that were his knees and elbows.

Cafakke's gut bulged out like an overinflated deer hide.

Being high mikko, Cafakke ate well, but unable to walk or use his hands, he had no way to temper his intake with exertion.

The man's moon-face was dominated by a broad nose, wide mouth, and fleshy cheeks. His face had been tattooed in the pattern of a Mos'kogee chief: The forked-eye design was prominent in black; a bar ran across his nose from cheek to cheek. Depending upon circumstances this could be painted to indicate his predisposition. For the moment it was white, indicating peace. For war, he would have painted it red, black for mourning, yellow for healing, and so forth. A pattern of lines surrounded his mouth, adding emphasis to his smile or frown. His hair was pulled into a bun high atop his head and held in place by a series of white swan feathers poked through his thick black locks. Finally, large polished copper ear spools filled his elongated earlobes.

"Rise, Black Shell of the Chicaza," Cafakke said wearily.

"Thank you, great High Mikko." I stood. "We have offered prayers of thanks upon hearing of your escape from the Kristianos. I would offer a fine skein of buffalo wool just to hear the story."

"I am here by chance only, good trader. Power was with me." He gestured at his misshapen body, a grin matching his suddenly sparkling eyes. "Kristianos, it seems, underestimated my ability to crawl. And they were foolish enough to carry me out from Anhaica in hopes I would order my people to stand down from their attacks. No sooner had a couple of their guards fallen asleep than I started my crawl. Just past their pickets I found a party of my warriors sneaking up in anticipation of a dawn raid."

He shot us a beaming smile. "They carried me away. It

is, however, my understanding that the *Adelantado* was displeased with those who were guarding me."

"May he remain so," I said, touching my chin respectfully.

"And these Uzachile?" he asked.

"My Orphans, of whom you already have been apprised." I turned, gesturing at my Timucua.

In passable Timucua, Cafakke added, "Be welcome, warriors of Uzachile. Your presence here honors the Apalachee people and makes your ancestors, the Creator, and the Sacred Sun in the heavens proud. Rise and be received as the heroes you are. Know that among the Apalachee Nation, your names will be remembered, honored, and cherished. And after you have passed from this life and joined your ancestors, may our songs of thanks bring smiles to your lips for generations to come."

With expressions of disbelief, my Orphans stood. Blood Thorn, keeping his hands in the supplicant's position, said, "We thank you, High Mikko, and offer our heartfelt gratitude at your escape from the Kristianos. We regret only that we could not have brought more warriors to help in your battle against these despicable people."

Cafakke pursed his lips, a sadness behind his gleaming eyes. "Only now, to our peril, do we learn that there are more terrifying threats than those represented by our petty animosity toward each other. If there is a benefit to be reaped from our years of war, it may be that we are better prepared to face the threat. We have kept each other strong and fierce. Let us hope that serves both of our peoples now."

Blood Thorn smiled sadly. "It did us little good at Napetuca, High Mikko. The Kristianos butchered us by the hundreds. I have heard that my people are so horrified that the bodies have been left where they lay . . . deemed accursed."

Cafakke's voice softened. "No matter what your people may think, the Apalachee honor those who fell at Napetuca. Iniha, we shall pray for their souls."

Back-from-the-Dead, however, didn't seem to think much of the proclamation. His thin lips bent sourly, his eyes thinning. But they never strayed from me. Not even a glance.

The other Orphans gasped, staring, struggling to believe an Apalachee ruler would say such things.

Cafakke raised his misshapen right hand, saying, "Usinulo, please escort our honored guests to the eternal fire in the kukofa and provide them with what food we have. Assemble our people, and, if you would, find someone to translate as each of these nicoquadca tells his story."

Nicoquadca. The Apalachee term referred to only the greatest and most honored of warriors. The extent of the honorific didn't pass unnoticed given the expressions of amazement around the room.

"You would do that?" Cafakke asked, eyes on Blood Thorn. "Honor my people by telling the story of your battles with the Kristianos? Share what you have lost? Explain to them why you fight as you do?"

Blood Thorn dropped to his knees once again and offered his upturned palms. He lowered his head in humility. "We are made humble by your request, great High Mikko."

I watched as A'atehkoci stepped forward and offered his hand. Blood Thorn took it and was pulled to his feet. With his feathered staff of office held high, A'atehkoci called for attention. Walking regally, he gestured for Blood Thorn and the rest to follow and started from the room.

In Mos'kogee, Cafakke added, "Stay, please, Black Shell." His eyes shifted toward Back-from-the-Dead. "There are matters we need to discuss."

I turned as the Orphans filed out to the clapping, whistling, and cheers of the watching Apalachee.

Back-from-the-Dead, however, continued his stare. And behind it I could see a festering resentment. Whatever he wanted, it wasn't going to be good.

FIVE

"PEARL HAND STAYS WITH ME," I SAID, GRABBING HER arm as she turned to follow the others. "We live as one, sharing thoughts and responsibilities."

Cafakke shot another look at the waiting hilishaya, then he gave the two of us a long and thoughtful appraisal. Finally he said, "When you first came here, I thought the woman little more than an affectation. Do you truly trust her that much, Chicaza?"

"With my life, High Mikko. And more. Power joined us for a reason."

Pearl Hand cocked an eyebrow and added, "Do you always underestimate women, High Mikko?"

He chuckled, amused at the tone in her voice. "Only those who arrive in the company of scurrilous traders like Black Shell. Have you ever considered giving him up to become a high mikko's woman?"

In the driest voice she could manage, Pearl Hand replied, "I've been one. There's not much to be said for it."

I shot a glance at Cafakke's wives. Their reactions ranged from shock to amusement.

Cafakke just lifted a skeptical eyebrow as Pearl Hand gave him a wicked smile. She added, "With Black Shell, I am more than an evening's diversion. As proven by the ihola'ka in those bags we brought."

"You make your point with precision and skill, *Mankiller* Pearl Hand. I stand corrected . . . and humbled." At his words the people in the room shifted uneasily. He waved them down, saying, "I've followed your actions since you arrived here. Your successes surprised even the tastanaki."

Tastanaki? That was the supreme war chief and Red Moiety tishu mikko, Fire Falcon.

Hands on my hips, I called up every bit of courage I possessed and said, "You didn't call us here to be congratulated by your war chiefs." I glanced at the priests. "The usinulo said something about the great hilishaya wishing to see us."

Back-from-the-Dead's smile tightened, his eyes like polished obsidian.

Cafakke replied, "He shall have his chance. Meanwhile, I have news. You are aware that more Kristianos have come from the east? A party of perhaps one hundred or more? They arrived here muddy, travel-worn, and exhausted, having moved faster than word of their approach could have been sent. Do you know who these men are or where they came from?"

Pearl Hand gave me a knowing glance. "Muddy and travel-worn? The ones de Soto left behind in Uzita?"

I considered it. "If he's evacuated his base camp at Uzita, the *Adelantado* is obviously not planning on returning south."

"No, he's not." Pearl Hand shot a look at Cafakke. "Generally, Kristianos raid for a season, then leave. That or they try to build a permanent town. In the past these have always been on the coast, where their ships can deliver supplies or they can evacuate if fortune turns against them."

Cafakke made a futile gesture with his misshapen hand. "The other news I have is that the invader's great boats have arrived off the coast to our south and are sheltering in one of the bays. An expedition of another hundred Kristianos and cabayos has marched off to meet with them. As we speak they are returning with supplies and additional men."

He paused, staring at the two of us. "I spent but a few days with them. You are said to know them even better. Are they planning on staying here? Fighting a war of attrition to drive us out of our country? Or is this just reinforcement before they go somewhere else? How do I tell?"

Pearl Hand asked, "What are the slaves doing?"

"Dying." Cafakke shifted his bulk. "The Kristianos are working them to death. From dawn to dusk they labor building fortifications around Anhaica. They receive little food and are made to sleep naked in the open. Rain, snow, wind, it makes no difference to the Kristianos. To keep the slaves from giving up, they turn dogs loose on them. Terrible dogs that literally tear a human being apart. Then these vile animals the Kristianos brought with them—"

"*Puercos,*" I muttered.

"Yes," Cafakke said. "*Puercos.* They eat the bodies of the dead slaves. And then the Kristianos eat the *puercos.* It is disgusting. Inconceivable."

He gestured his futility. "The Kristianos look like men: two arms, two legs. But they act as if they have no souls, no responsibility to the world around them." He shook his head, brow furrowed. "As high mikko, I have passed judgment on the criminally insane. I've interrogated and executed evil sorcerers. Such individuals appear when Power has been abused, or due to witchcraft or the violation of taboos. But an entire army of them?"

I nodded. "That's what the Kristianos are: a vile, invincible army of pollution, rolling across our world."

Pearl Hand crossed her arms. "I've never heard it stated so succinctly."

Cafakke gave a weak smile, glancing at the waiting hilishaya. "I worry now that the monster plans to stay in Apalachee. In addition to the fact that he has no respect for Power or the ways of decent men, working his slaves to death indicates that he isn't concerned about transporting all of his baggage anywhere else."

Pearl Hand frowned. "Are they building great palaces? Large buildings?"

"No. Mostly digging fortification ditches, cutting and setting palisade posts. That and replacing the buildings we've managed to burn."

"Burn?" I asked.

"On occasion we've been able to sneak close and set fire to the buildings in Anhaica by throwing firebrands over the walls at night. And periodically an archer lands a pitch-fired arrow in something burnable. Last time, with the wind right, we managed to set fire to half the town. It keeps them busy, off balance, and, we hope, wishing they were someplace else."

"Hence the endless woodcutting parties." Pearl Hand looked thoughtful. "But how many of your people have the Kristianos captured?"

Cafakke gave her a flat look. "Perhaps a hundred. Not as many as they would have liked. We've learned to keep out of their reach. Some Apalachee were captured, then managed to escape. The stories they tell have passed from lip to lip. Most of my people now believe an immediate death is better than a lingering one in a Kristiano collar."

"If they were planning on staying," Pearl Hand mused, "they would be marking off land, adding to the palaces. At least, that's how they acted among the Chicora. And, after following de Soto all these months, we know he leaves as soon as the food is eaten."

I added, "I think he'll go when the weather warms. More than anything, Kristianos desire gold. It obsesses them. That doesn't mean, however, that he wouldn't leave some Kristianos here as he did at Uzita. Especially if the floating palaces are in the bays." I frowned. "But it would mean splitting his forces."

"Gold?" Cafakke adopted an incredulous expression. "Would someone explain its value? They asked me about it over and over, even showed me pieces just to make sure I knew what they were talking about. It's a worthless metal."

"Not to them," Pearl Hand said. "Think of how we value copper, then increase its worth by a factor of ten, and you might begin to understand how the Kristianos lust for it."

Cafakke's puzzled look deepened. "But there's no gold.

I told de Soto that to his face. Every now and then some-one wears a nugget for decoration. Otherwise it's just a rock. Mica has more reflection, and copper has Spirit Power. It can be worked and polished. What possesses these idiot Kristianos, anyway?"

"A red rage of chaos," I muttered, noticing A'atehkoci as he entered discreetly. He gave Cafakke a nod that all had been taken care of.

"Even red Power abhors abomination," Back-from-the-Dead announced, eyes unblinking. The effect re-minded me of an owl's fascination with a caged rabbit.

Pearl Hand added, "High Mikko, when the Kristianos begin to clear and plant fields it will be a sign they're stay-ing. This they did among my mother's people when they sought to build a permanent town. If they are not farming they will most likely move on this spring."

"Provided they have anyone left to carry their supplies," Matron Pahlko growled from the side. "The dead slaves are just left in a rotting pile, food for crows and those hid-eous and hairless little *puercos* they brought with them." She made a face. "The whole thing is an affront to Power."

"Abomination," Back-from-the-Dead growled again.

Cafakke looked at the man, then at Pearl Hand and me. "In addition to my questions, the great hilishaya has his own curiosity." He made a gesture, encouraging the priest to step forward.

As I met Back-from-the-Dead's glittering eyes I expe-rienced a tickle of unease. Medicine and Power people have always unsettled me. They concern themselves with forces and teachings that would make anyone nervous.

"I am known as Back-from-the-Dead," the great hili-shaya said. "I speak with Power, hear the Song of the Spirits, and chant with the souls of the dead. Curious stories are being passed about you." He pointed the turkey-tail mace in his right hand at me. "And about this woman. And about the Timucua who follow you. Even your dogs are spoken of. One is said to belong to the Spirit World, but I saw no such animal upon your arrival."

How do I describe the way he talked? It was as if each syllable were alive and every word weighted with a meaning that went beyond the here and now. And the control in his voice was an eerie thing, as if it contained a perfectly choked threat. One that, if let loose, could lash a man's soul.

He hadn't received his name by accident. Only the most Powerful of hilishaya could send their souls to the Underworld, Sky World, or Land of the Dead and return. The stories I'd heard claimed that Back-from-the-Dead's souls turned themselves into serpents when they traveled to the Underworld, thereby becoming a match for the tie snakes, piasas, and other creatures of the lower realm. When he flew to the Sky World, his souls supposedly turned themselves into an eagle that could outmaneuver lightning, buck the winds, and perch atop the rainbows.

Most frightening of all, he had died many times. When the souls leave, a person's heart stops and the lungs cease to fill. The eyes go vacant, and the skin grows cold. During this time the physical body is in great danger. If left too long, the corpse begins to decompose, and the souls will be unable to reanimate the flesh when they finally return. Or the flesh might be witched, infected, or otherwise "occupied" by other Spirits. Sometimes, by mistake, the corpse is burned, buried, stripped of flesh, or otherwise processed for a funeral, leaving the desperate souls nothing to return to.

As to the traveling souls themselves, a host of things could go wrong: They could become confused, disoriented, and might lose their way back from the Spirit World. Even worse, they could be captured or devoured by Spirit Beasts. They might become enamored, tricked, or otherwise seduced to stay in the Spirit World. But whatever happens, if they don't return in time, death is final. Even the most Powerful of priests, shamans, and sorcerers approach such journeys with trepidation.

Believe me, I knew.

Back-from-the-Dead apparently had few such fears. According to the stories, his souls had spent as long as a quarter moon roaming the Spirit World while his abandoned body lay clay-cold and limp. It was said his own assistants shivered when in his presence and feared his Power, authority, and temper.

I began to understand why. In his eyes was a hollow emptiness—a dislocation from the world around him that seemed to suck at a man's souls.

"I am Black Shell of the Chicaza, great Hilishaya. I cannot be responsible for the stories told about me."

"You are, however, responsible for the ones you tell about yourself." His voice—ever so precise—seemed to create a shimmering in the air.

This could go very wrong. "Stories? Those I tell during trade serve as entertainment in exchange for hospitality. Stories are accepted as what they are: beings with lives and an existence of their own. They have their own Power, the whole being more than just the combined parts. Some exist to create laughter, others, sorrow. We teach and learn through stories. They explain the world . . . or expand it. Through them, we touch other peoples' souls, lives, and imagination."

At the narrowing of his eyes, I hurried to add, "You, however, are interested not in stories, but in Power and what it wants with me."

As his gaze invaded mine, I flinched from the sucking sensation it created. His tone became more precise, vibrating between my souls. "It is said that you are Horned Serpent's being."

The effect was as if cold air had filled the room. Something unseen, like a ghostly hand, caused a constriction around my throat.

He's testing, seeking to intimidate me. Why?

I ground my teeth, clenched my fists, and stepped closer to Back-from-the-Dead. He apparently hadn't expected that, for his lips bent in a slight smile. At the same time he raised the turkey-tail mace as if ready to counter a blow.

Looking into his black eyes, I saw the layers of his being, partially haunted, yet driven by a thrilling ecstasy I could barely perceive. There, too, lay a deep hunger—that of a predator too long denied a kill.

I gave him the slightest of smiles. "Horned Serpent chose me long ago."

"Why?" The question sliced like an obsidian blade.

"I am akeohoosa. Dead to my family."

"A curious fate for a Chicaza noble, don't you think?"

"Horned Serpent told me it was a gamble."

"Why would Horned Serpent have wagered on you when so many others could have been chosen?"

I could feel his Power, reaching out, trying to wrap

around my own. Like being smothered with a sooty blanket, the sensation wasn't pleasant.

Ever try to flex your souls, like tightening muscles? I tried as I replied, "I asked the same question."

"Where did you ask it? And of whom?"

That threw me. "High in the Sky World, great Hilishaya. At the entrance to the Path of the Dead. I asked Horned Serpent."

He cocked an eyebrow ever so slightly. "You flew to the Sky World? Or did you jump through the portal—the constellation we call the Seeing Hand?"

Sensing the trap, I managed a dry chuckle. "Neither. I was carried."

"From this world?"

"No, from the Underworld."

"And how did you get there?"

"I was dying in a lake outside Napetuca. The Kristianos chased us into the water. For two days I paddled around with the others. The water felt warm at first, but after two days? The chill ate into us, sapped us of warmth and hope. Others surrendered, but Blood Thorn and I held out. On the second day, most of the Kristianos had left, and we tried to make our way to shore."

The rest of the room was hanging on each word, but I kept my eyes locked on Back-from-the-Dead's. In a way I couldn't comprehend, we were wrestling, grasping, struggling against each other.

"I remember sinking," I said softly. "That's when Water Panther reached up and dragged me down to the Underworld."

"Why would the Piasa bother himself with a trader?" The words were ever so soft.

"I'd made a trade the first time I traveled to the Underworld. Anhinga and Snapping Turtle were witnesses."

Slyly he asked, "What did the Piasa want out of your trade?"

"To kill me."

"Yet, here you are? Alive in this world?" His words were poised to strike, sensing the coming of a lie.

"Even Spirit Beings are bound by the Power of trade," I answered with invincibility. "Water Panther wants my life but has offered nothing in return for it . . . yet."

"How does that make you feel?" The black pool of his eyes seemed to expand, sucking me in. The faintest smile lay on his thin lips.

"No one makes a bargain with a Spirit Being and isn't scared soul-sick. Not if he has any sense anyway." I paused. "The Piasa wasn't exactly happy the last time I saw him."

"That doesn't explain how you got to the Sky World." Back-from-the-Dead had retreated, seeking another path of attack. "Carried, you said?"

"After the Piasa left, I was talking to Snapping Turtle and Anhinga. Horned Serpent grabbed me from behind." I shrugged. "He carried me through the tunnels, past the roots, then out, across the gap between the edge of the earth and the Sky World. He leaped through the Seeing Hand. The rest was a frightening blur."

"He carried you in his hands?" Back-from-the-Dead asked with a softness that belied any threat. "Or did you ride on his back?"

"Horned Serpent has no hands. He pins you in his jaws with long and deadly fangs."

"And that is when you asked why he chose you?"

At my nod, Back-from-the-Dead's voice dropped to a whisper, as if in that misleading feint that comes before a surprise attack. "What was his answer?"

"'A priest,' Horned Serpent told me, 'would have been blinded by the Spirit World.' Preoccupied with the ways of Power. Unmoved by the realities of war with the Kristianos."

I took another step, my face but a hand's breadth from his. I met his haunting, soul-sucking look, battling it, imagining I was seeing it through Horned Serpent's great crystalline eyes. "By priests, he spoke of Spirit Dreamers like you, Hilishaya. You're absorbed by the Spirit World. Even as we speak, it fills your souls and stares out of your eyes, sharing your vision. But against the Kristianos and their weapons, war beasts, and heartless god, you are impotent."

For long moments, we stood, toe-to-toe, locked in a silent struggle. His Power coiled and rolled, trying to slip between my souls, to find a hold that would give him domination. Against it, I had only the hard shell of certainty, tempered by my own ordeals in the Spirit World.

"How did you return from the Sky World?" The words coiled around me.

"I don't know."

Victory clung to the corners of his mouth where little lines deepened. "You don't know?"

Just tell him the truth, Black Shell. "The last thing I can recall"—the callous act failed me, and I couldn't stop the soul-deep shiver—"was terror. Numbing, consuming terror."

Back-from-the-Dead's eyes enlarged as if they'd fill his face.

I knotted my fists, took a deep breath. "He bit me,

crushed me . . . The sensation of my bones snapping, my body compressed and breaking . . . Dying. Eaten alive . . ."

"Eaten alive?" he said mockingly. "Did he spit you out, perhaps finding lowly traders distasteful?"

The warmth came from my medicine bag, as if that fragment of Horned Serpent's brow tine had taken on the heat of a hearthstone. I let the sepaya's Power roll through my chest, swelling my souls as my gaze bored into his. "Distasteful? I wouldn't know. My last memory is of my neck popping like an old root. I remember the sensation of my head being pressed through my chest . . . the snapping of my ribs, the bursting of my heart. And after that? Only blackness until I came to, lying in cattails and covered with mud." I pressed closer. "You doubt me? Look into my eyes, read my souls, Hilishaya. Truth is there."

Uncertainty weakened his voice for the first time, and he backed away. "Why were you devoured?"

I straightened, willing strength back into my sagging souls. "I was given a choice: I could walk away, follow the Path of the Dead to my ancestors. I was already there, having only to pass Eagle Man's challenge where the road forks. Or I could go back and undertake the seemingly hopeless battle against the Kristianos."

"And you chose . . . ?"

"Pearl Hand remained behind. I love her. More than life itself. And the Kristianos must be fought . . . no matter the cost." I smiled, perhaps out of partial delirium. "And even as I made my choice, I saw Fetch—the Spirit dog of whom you've heard—telling me it was right."

"You knew Horned Serpent would devour you?"

Bitterness laced my laughter. "Had I, I'd have chosen

to stroll on down the Path of the Dead. Nothing, and I mean nothing on earth or in the Spirit World—can prepare you for the terror, pain, and horror of being eaten alive." *Want to try me on that, you spooky hilishaya?*

The twirling worlds behind his glistening eyes must have read my souls, because his expression changed. His gaze lowered, fixing on my chest. Slipping the handle of his rattle into his waist sash, he reached out with his left hand, palm toward me, fingers straight. As it neared the sepaya hanging on my chest, I could feel the energy. It seemed to burn, like a white-hot cooking stone.

Back-from-the-Dead's hand hovered above the little leather bag. How long did we stand so? I couldn't guess, but finally he pulled back, working his fingers as if they were covered by something oily.

"I will speak with you again," he whispered hoarsely. Then he turned and plucked the rattle from his sash, shaking it as he began to sing, voice booming in the too-quiet room. The words, the lilting melody, were unlike anything I'd ever heard. Invisible fingers stroked my skin.

The other hilishaya began shaking their rattles, their voices rising to join his. As Back-from-the-Dead headed for the door, the younger priests followed in single file. All eyes were upon them as they ducked out one by one, leaving the room in absolute silence.

I swallowed dryly, drained, as if I'd been balancing for days on the knife's edge of disaster. A cold shiver ran through me, slightly countered by the dying heat from my medicine bundle.

A man could get into such trouble over the love of a woman, a dead dog's blind faith, and loathing hatred for de Soto and all he represented.

"What just happened here?" Pearl Hand asked nervously.

"I'm not sure." I managed another dry swallow and felt sweat trickle down my neck. When had it gotten so hot? Only when I puffed an exhalation did I realize it hadn't. My breath fogged in the cool air.

"You've been tested," Cafakke declared, but his usual insouciance was missing. "And whatever the great hilishaya expected, it was not what you just told him."

I grinned, desperate to cover my unease. "Somehow, I don't think he gets many invitations to supper or social gatherings."

Blood and pus, I hate fooling around with Power.

SIX

I AM OFTEN AT THE CENTER OF ATTENTION. IT'S WHAT
traders do: create attention. But for once I really wished I
could have just faded into the wall matting and vanished.
Every eye was upon me, expressions ranging from disbelief to amazement.

Pearl Hand's eyebrow arched skeptically. Cafakke and
A'atehkoci had adopted expressions of uneasy curiosity.
Cafakke's wives were looking at me as if I'd just peed in
the fire.

Then Cafakke laughed. And laughed again, even
harder. Through slowly ebbing chuckles, he finally said,
"You don't think he gets many invitations to social events?
After what we just saw and heard, Trader, you may not either."

I grunted, hoping for once that it might be true. Better
to be out in the forest, hunting Kristianos.

Cafakke made a gesture with his shriveled hands, his dark eyes alight. "A man doesn't speak lightly about being eaten by a Spirit Being, let alone Horned Serpent." He paused, gaze going distant. In a lower voice he said, "Only the greatest survive such a thing."

I adopted a pained expression and flipped my hand in a mild gesture, hoping to defuse the tension. "We live in perilous times. The monster de Soto has come to our world. It's up to us to defeat him. If we can drive him off, broken and beaten like Narváez—or this Ayllón who landed among the Chicora—the Kristianos may finally give up the idea of coming to kill and enslave us."

Cafakke gave me a pensive look. Like I said, his body might have been a mess, but there was nothing wrong with his smarts. "As you point out, we drove off Narváez. But they keep coming back stronger, Black Shell. De Soto didn't make the same mistakes Narváez did. If we beat him, what makes you think that my children won't face an even larger force of three or four thousand? What if there is no end to them?"

I fingered my chin, pacing lightly across the cane-mat flooring. "Horned Serpent told me this is just the beginning, High Mikko. Prepare your children. Prepare your people."

Pahlko snorted irritably. "We beat them before. I was a young woman at the time, nursing him." She inclined her head toward Cafakke. "They didn't impress me then, and they don't now. They couldn't even keep a crippled high mikko captive."

With knobby knuckles she thumped her sternum. "Power hears our hearts and souls, it heeds our prayers, and it will lead us to destroy them again. They are an abomination in our world, and Breath Giver will call down the Winds. The Thunderers will smite them. Earth herself will rise against their polluted feet, sucking them down to suffocate in the very dirt."

I met her angry gaze, reading defiance in her eyes. Of course she believed it. Way down in the bottom of my soul, I did, too. We'd been raised that way. People were part of Power, as much as the earth, wind, water, plants, animals, and rocks. Power flowed through everything, interacted with everything. It was revealed and acted through the forces around us, from sunlight and storm to the life of forests. It filled the air we breathed and surged when we fought, made love, ate dinner, danced, or sang . . . were born and died.

How, then, could Breath Giver tolerate a pollution like de Soto and his soldados and cabayeros? That the monster existed at all was counter to the underlying assumptions we all made about the universe. As a violation of those basic laws, why didn't the universe rise up and destroy him?

"Nothing is as it was," I whispered softly. "I'm sorry, Matron, but Power now looks to us. We must save our world."

"And if we can't?" Cafakke asked.

It was Pearl Hand who said, "Then there is only death, great lord. And abomination inherits the world."

I emerged, emotionally exhausted, from Cafakke's make-do palace and stared up at the evening sky. The clouds were scudding low, the breaks here and there cast in golden light from the slanting sun. Exhaling, I could see my breath.

I'd left Pearl Hand locked in conversation with Matron Pahlko. Me, I just wanted to get away. The interior of Cafakke's refugee palace was suffocating with fumes of despair and hopelessness.

Instead I stood in the cool air, smelling the pungent odors of swamp mixed with hickory, pine, and cedar smoke. Someone was cooking hominy, and somewhere fish roasted over a bed of coals. The muffled sound of voices, the *thunk-thunk* of a woman pounding corn in a wooden mortar, and the distant chopping of wood with a stone ax were reassuring after Cafakke's palace.

I needed only look to the north. There, hidden by trees, swamp, hills, and distance, waited the monster and his army. I could feel them, like a malignant darkness eating at the soul of the land.

And one day, Black Shell, you will look de Soto in the eyes again. And when you do, life will stop for either you or him.

The dogs slept beneath one of the ramadas. The packs had been piled beside them, safely under their guard.

I took a moment to study them. Gnaw's ribs swelled, then shuddered as he vented a sigh. Bark stretched out on his side, grunting as he tensed, then went limp.

As I approached, Squirm opened an eye, thumped his tail a couple of times, smacked his jaws, then went back to sleep. They weren't concerned with Power, potential death, or impending doom.

Ah, dogs.

Turning to my familiar use-scarred packs, I pondered our situation. Cafakke wasn't ready to let us go; he was waiting on Back-from-the-Dead. That and Tastanaki Fire Falcon was due back the following day with a report on the Kristianos—one I wanted to hear.

I propped a hand against the ramada pole, the wood smoothly polished and graying from exposure. Old cut marks indicated that the pole had served different purposes over the years and had been reused over and over. Now it had been carried here. End of the line. Was it the end for the Apalachee, too?

Desperate to engage in anything except reliving that confrontation with Back-from-the-Dead, I pulled my chunkey lances from inside the alligator quiver. From Skipper's pack, I retrieved my chunkey stone. What was the point of Cafakke hauling all that clay in if not to provide me a place to play?

A chunkey stone—for those of you who grew up in impoverished cultures that lack truly inspiring games—is a disc. The sides, depending upon tradition, may be flat, vaguely convex, or, like mine, smoothly dished out. The diameter varies—again depending upon the people—but mine was shaped to fit snugly inside a cupped hand. Made from red granite, the concave sides were polished to a mirror sheen, the outer rim rounded and rough from rolling down countless chunkey courts.

I stepped to the head of the court and inspected my lances. Both were short specimens capable of easy transport. Most lances were longer than a man was tall and kept in the local temple, clan house, or palace. I preferred a longer lance but had grown proficient with my short ones. The wood was polished from years of handling, the points fire hardened and blunt.

From the rudimentary kukofa I could hear a roar of applause. Which one of the Timucua was finishing his story?

As I fingered the blunt tip of my lance, I gave Cafakke

credit. Because he allowed the Timucua to tell their tales, Cafakke's Apalachee were learning just how vicious de Soto's Kristianos could be. The Apalachee would be wondering if the horrors of Napetuca could happen here.

I set the shorter lance to one side and hefted the remaining one in my left hand while bouncing the stone in my right. Then I slipped the lance under my armpit and seated the stone into the curve of my right hand. The familiar, cool weight felt reassuring. How many clay runways like this had I stood on during my life?

Uncle's voice came from the past: *Take your time, boy. Chunkey is won by those who allow the Power of the game to flow through them. Become one with the Power. Surrender to it. Shut the world from your thoughts and share the Spirit of the stone, the soul of the wood. Breathe deeply, and see it in your mind.*

Choosing the Power I would play for, I prayed, "White Power, come and grant me serenity. Endow me with peace and harmony as I make this play."

A feeling of ease and familiarity slipped through me like smoke on a still morning. Opening my eyes, I charged forward. My right arm went back, elbow straight, and I dropped my shoulder as I bowled the stone. It left my hand, gently kissing the ground, rolling forward like a shot.

Without missing a stride, I shifted the lance to my right hand, and two paces later, I whipped it forward, casting it after the rolling stone.

I pulled up with a slight hop at the mark and watched the lance arc up, spinning as it arrowed toward the slowing stone. Chunkey was about anticipation. A good player cast his lance, knowing full well where his stone was going to finally stop. Judgment and timing were everything.

Along with the quality of the court. My stone bounced on the uneven clay. As it slowed, it hit a final irregularity, curved to the right, and flopped onto its side as my lance impacted a body-length off to the left.

"Perhaps you should have called upon the red," an eerily familiar voice said behind me.

I turned to see Back-from-the-Dead.

Not you again!

His stony gaze was fixed on my lance where it had stuck in the ground at an angle. He carried a lance in one hand, a beautifully polished stone in the other. I'd figured he'd be back in the temple, casting bones, butternut seeds, or some such in an attempt to scry my true purpose here.

"The white suits me today," I replied warily. He waited while I trotted down to recover my lance and stone. I could see the little lump of clay, clearly visible in the track my stone had made. With the ball of my foot, I mashed it flat, trying to smooth the track, before walking back.

"Might I join you?" His voice could have been a caress.

"More testing, Hilishaya?"

He gave me a humorless grin and surveyed the course. "When the older boys have time, the usinulo tries to get them to rake the clay." His shoulder lifted. "Generally there are more important things to do."

"With Kristianos tearing up the country, I can imagine." I turned to watch him take his stance at the start of the course. His tattooed face lined with concentration as he hefted his stone. With a smooth stride he started forward, ducking, bowling his stone, and, two paces later, casting with good follow-through.

I cocked my head as the stone shot down the alley, Back-from-the-Dead's lance seeking it like a thing alive.

His stone jumped and hopped, deflected by the irregular clay. The lance impacted within an arm's length as the stone toppled.

"Well done," I remarked as he went to fetch his lance.

"Wager?" he called as he plucked up his pieces.

"I'd offer a small wooden carving of Eagle Man. One I picked up down south. Timucua made. After de Soto's rampage, I'm not sure there are going to be any more. Not from the Ocale lands. Those the Kristianos didn't enslave or kill are scattered like rabbits."

His eyes expressed anything but understanding. "I would offer a pressed copper piece. A relief of Falcon . . . no longer than my hand. It polishes nicely, and a person can sense the metal's Power when he rubs his fingers over it."

"Done. Best out of twenty? Ten up, ten down? Isn't that how you Apalachee play?" They scored chunkey by twisting a twig into the ground with each win up to ten. Then one was taken out with each point until none were left standing. The first person who ran out of sticks won.

"After you." He gestured. "You have called white, I call red. May Power bless the player with truth in his heart."

"If it's truth over skill, you've just lost your copper."

The look he gave me would have shriveled a water moccasin.

I stepped forward, gripping my stone, feeling the cool surface. How many games had I rolled with this stone? And for what stakes? When played as Back-from-the-Dead and I were now playing, chunkey became the living representation of the struggle between Powers, or the Hero Twins in the Beginning Times, or the forces of life and death; it settled questions of justice, disputes, or anything else that required the invocation of Spirit Power.

My hand hadn't seriously touched my stone for over a year. To say I was mediocre during those first few throws would have been a kindness. Back-from-the-Dead easily took the first five, but I was starting to regain the feel. My body began to remember, and I loosened up, actually winning the sixth cast by little more than a finger's length.

We'd played to ten; he was seven ahead. Then he stopped, fingering his lance, glancing down the court. "You do not have the manner of one who has been touched by Spirit Power, let alone devoured."

"What manner is that?"

"Humbled, quiet, with a profound peace behind the eyes."

"And what am I?"

"Bitter, possessed of an ironic sense of humor. When you should be on your knees with humility, you stand, hip cocked, making flippant comments. As with any trader, it is difficult to pin you down. You treat Power as if it were a bargaining trick, a way to bring you more pretty shells and copper."

"Then maybe, Hilishaya, you read me wrong."

I watched him cast, his lance landing close to the stone. I'd learned the court now, and a faint track marked the route of my previous releases. I bowled my stone down the same line I'd used before, took two paces, and released. My lance spiraled and arced, landing a hand's width from my stone. My point.

He said, "Your trip to the Sky World has done little to dampen your arrogance."

As we walked down I replied, "You mean trips. Four

times I went to the Spirit World. The first I ended up at the edge of the world, along the trail of the dead, looking across the abyss at the Seeing Hand and wondering if I should jump. The West Wind turned me back."

"Having met you, I'm surprised the West Wind didn't just knock you over the edge instead."

I ignored the sarcasm. "The second time I wandered up a ravine to a hidden spring guarded by a tie snake. That time I ended up in the Underworld. That's when the Piasa thought he got the better of me."

"You're telling me you passed a tie snake? How?"

"I climbed over his scaled body, and as he began to swallow his tail I fell into the spring he was guarding."

"You could have heard that story from any holy person who made the trip."

"If I'm a liar, Power will make me lose this game." I met his glare with my own.

"And the third time?"

"That time I found myself by a great river and walked to Old-Woman-Who-Never-Dies's house. She fed me, cured me of the Kristiano disease that was killing me. Old-Woman-Who-Never-Dies explained the threat we face and how it has to be fought. If you don't like it that this has to be fought out by men, take it up with her."

"And that was all? She just told you that men must decide the future? Nothing else?"

"I met Corn Woman, her daughter. She delighted me right down to my bones, so to speak." I grimaced. "Just before she scared the liver out of me."

"So, you are arrogant because you are scared?"

I glanced at him as I plucked my lance from the

ground. "If I'm arrogant, it's only when I'm in the company of men who do not understand the stakes."

"And you think I don't?"

I sighed. "Hilishaya, in your place, not knowing what I know now, I'd be clinging to the old ways, too."

Back-from-the-Dead gestured that I should cast. I couldn't read the expression on his face.

I took my mark, cleared my head, and sent my stone down the track. I followed it with a good cast, the lance impacting no more than the length of my forearm beyond.

Back-from-the-Dead flexed his legs, rolled his shoulders, and sprinted forward. I watched him bowl his stone, shift his lance, and launch it. The man had good form, but without the second nature that comes of endless practice. His lance stopped a pace beyond and to the right of his stone. My point.

We started down the track and he asked, "What do you get in return for fighting Kristianos? Status among these Timucua? Is that what Power promised you? The Timucua will make you a chief?"

"I get the satisfaction of killing Kristianos."

His lips bent skeptically. "You expect me to believe that? You fight them . . . expecting no reward?"

I gave him a disgusted look. "This isn't about status or prestige. It's not about advantage or advancement. It's not about Timucua, or Apalachee, or Tuskaloosa, or Chicaza. It's about saving our world. If we don't destroy the monster his kind of Power will overwhelm our own. Do you understand?"

For long moments we stood, gazes locked: I to make him comprehend, he to divine my hidden purpose.

Finally he asked, "What induced you to accept this challenge, Trader?"

"Hilishaya, until they make you prisoner—clap that collar around your neck—you cannot understand. I *survived* the horrors of Napetuca."

"Kristianos are still men."

I gestured with my stone. "It doesn't matter if a person is Yuchi, Apalachee, Chicaza, Cherokee, or Timucua, we share the rules of behavior given us by Power. Everyone honors the Power of trade and understands that when a person is taken as a slave, it's because Power deserted them for its own reasons. When we fight, it is with the knowledge that we are extensions of Power, that ultimately we are balancing the red and white, chaos and order. Are we brutal at times? Yes. Because the red Power demands it. Do we take captives and torture them to death as a means of testing their courage? Yes. Those who bear up and demonstrate fearless resolve are often released. Slaves are often adopted or allowed to buy their freedom."

"Yes, yes, and the sky is blue," he growled. "What is your point? For all the ways we have of making war, of feeding the red Power, we have just as many, or more, for promoting the white: making peace, trade, alliances, and harmony."

"That *is* my point! Kristianos have *nothing* in common. They come from a different Creation, a different Beginning Time, one governed by greed, lust, and murder."

His eyes narrowed. "I have traveled to the Sky World, to the Underworld . . . sent my souls to the Land of the Dead, sought out and retrieved the lost souls of others. I have stared down from the sky and looked upon this land.

I have flown over it with Eagle Man. I would have seen these Kristianos. One of the Winds, or the tie snakes, or the Little People would have told me about them."

I shrugged, taking my place, setting my feet. "Kristianos are from another world, a place beyond our ability to comprehend." I took a deep breath, charging forward, bowling my stone. At the release, I shifted the lance, balanced, and cast. It felt perfect, and I watched my stone slow, the lance slamming into the clay just ahead of it. The stone rolled just to the right and flopped on its side. Again, my point.

As we walked to retrieve our pieces, Back-from-the-Dead seemed oblivious, lips pursed, dark eyes in turmoil. "Another world? Where? Why can't I see it from the sky?"

"I don't know."

"You expect me to believe that these Kristianos are not subject to the laws of Power when such laws permeate all of Creation? You tell me they come from another world— one that not even the Spirit Beings know? All this from you, an outcast trader? An akeohoosa?"

"Fine. Maybe I'm a fraud." I tapped my medicine pouch. "Perhaps I stole the sepaya. Just understand the stakes for which we fight."

"Yes, yes, the end of our world. What gave you such an insight?"

I took my mark, grip firm on the stone. I had my rhythm now: two steps, bowl; two steps, cast. I finished with a flourish just shy of the penalty mark. My lance, almost anticipating the stone, thudded to a stop a hand's distance to the left.

"They have a translator: Ortiz. You may have heard of him. He spoke Uzita but learned bits of a Timucua dialect.

When they captured me, he chained me to a post. I kept telling him over and over that I came under the Power of trade. Can you get any more basic than that?"

Back-from-the-Dead frowned. "Everyone knows the Power of trade."

"Ortiz looked at me with blank eyes. I might have told him that I came under the Power of dust."

"That's nonsense."

"And the Power of trade was nonsense to Ortiz. So were the offers of peace, made under the White Arrow, by the Uzachile prior to Napetuca. At the peace council, Pearl Hand overheard the Kristiano chiefs talking about how best to use the Power of peace to capture Holata Uzachile. To us, treachery under the White Arrow is an affront to Power. Kristianos spit on the notion."

Back-from-the-Dead cast, his lance landing a full pace beyond his stone. My point. We were tied.

"You make dangerous accusations, Trader. Power brought the Kristianos here for a purpose. Perhaps we have offended Power through even the simplest of things, like eating the wrong food, or touching a woman's menstrual possessions, or mixing fire and water? The Timucua are a lesser people. Perhaps Power sent the Kristianos to destroy them?"

I gave him a disbelieving stare as we retrieved our pieces. "Haven't you heard a word I've said? Stop looking at this through the eyes of an Apalachee. Stop telling yourself 'Of course the Timucua were crushed. They didn't have the right Power. But the Apalachee do, and we'll win in the end.'" I gestured futility. "The problem is, *priest*, that we're playing chunkey as refugees within one of the most powerful of Nations. The monster de Soto is sleeping in Cafakke's palace, and his soldados travel where they wish. Why? Because this has nothing to do with the inherent superiority of any people—or their humble piety. It's about military might and nothing else."

"Power will favor those who surrender to it."

"Then"—I poked a finger at his breastbone—"as the matron asked inside: Why hasn't Power already struck them dead?"

He was fuming as I took my mark, feeling the Power run through me. I charged forward, bowled my stone, cast, and pulled up, watching my lance spear the earth a hand's width from the stone. *Beat that!*

He cast, his lance going wide. Maybe Power was trying to tell him something?

"So I am to believe that you, Trader, know something that all the generations of hilishaya do not? Horned Serpent gave you this great revelation just before he ate you?"

I pulled my lance from beside my stone. "Kristianos have their own form of Power. It's something alien, given to them by a god they call *dios*." I shook my head, fingering my stone. "Kristianos believe that the soul—they have only one—goes to a place called *paraíso*. There are no dogs, deer, birds, or other creatures. No plants. Just Kristianos serving other Kristianos . . . Oh, and they sing."

"Animals and plants"—the look Back-from-the-Dead gave me might have been reserved for the insane—"we are all one. All part of Breath Giver's Creation. Everything, even the rocks and air, shares Spirit Power."

I shrugged, taking my mark. "One more time, Hilishaya: Kristianos come from a different Creation. Their Power is in that long-tailed cross they leave everywhere."

My cast was good but not great.

He cast, pulling his release, his stone hitting another of the lumps of clay and veering right. That put me two ahead.

"Who told you these things?"

"We took a Kristiano, Antonio, captive. The way Antonio explained it, *paraíso* is about as featureless as the inside of a brownware bowl. They don't even get to take all the gold they are so desperate to find here."

"Then what's the purpose of living?" Back-from-the-Dead sounded confused instead of hostile.

I glanced over at where my dogs were sleeping. "Who'd want to spend eternity without animals?"

"What do they eat in this *paraíso*?"

"Antonio told us there is no food in *paraíso*. Maybe they don't have bodies? No bodies, no need to hunt in the afterlife?"

He gave me a pensive look. "No feasting with ancestors and friends? No hunting? No animals? Just a soul in a brownware bowl? For eternity?"

"And endless Kristianos," I said, reminding him. "None of whom have the faintest idea of how to behave politely, respectfully, or peacefully."

"Do they lay with their women in *paraíso*?"

"We didn't think to ask."

"Surely they must lie with their women. Without feasting, hunting, pets, and the other things, coupling would almost make up for it. Maybe in *paraíso* a man's shaft never softens, and his seed is endless." He nodded, as if in understanding. "We know they have a huge appetite for women. Those of ours who have been captured and escaped tell how they were chained and served a line of men for most of the night."

I fingered my stone. Endless coupling? That could make up for so many other deprivations. "Wait. If they don't have bodies, how can a man's shaft . . . ?"

"Oh, come, Trader! Surely a man like you has sent his souls dreaming beyond the body. And somewhere in your dreams, you've slipped your shaft into a voluptuous and willing woman."

I cast. My stone bobbled at the last moment as it veered slightly wide of its track and hit a lump. I looked at the priest. "I may have only dreamed it, but the evidence was plain in the morning."

Back-from-the-Dead took his mark. He was preoccupied with the conversation; I beat him by half of a hand's distance.

Retrieving our pieces, I said, "Antonio was fixed on Pearl Hand when we had him captive. He kept staring at her breasts as if he'd never seen a woman before. At the time I thought it was odd, but now, well, you might have finally discovered why Kristianos follow *dios*. Perhaps, once dead, he supplies unlimited women?"

I plucked up my stone, adding, "When you think about it, that giant wooden cross they set up is sexual. The long end is the hard penis driven into Mother Earth. The cross piece represents the testicles."

It explained why they didn't have bodies in *paraíso*. I'd seen a naked Kristiano. He was anything but attractive, having dead-corpse-white skin and patches of thick black hair. No doubt that's why they insisted on covering their bodies from head to toe.

Back-from-the-Dead won the next cast, and I took the following, leaving me two ahead.

He stated, "You seem very sure of yourself, Trader."

I cast, satisfied with the lance's impact beside my stone. "I learned the hard way. In the end, we kill them. Or they kill us."

"Power will not abandon us, Trader."

I took down a peg with my eleventh point. "Let me ask you this: You're the greatest of the Apalachee hilishaya, right? Since the arrival of de Soto, you and the others have been making medicine, channeling Power against them. Perhaps you are even consorting with witches and sorcerers . . . anything to harm them. But your most virulent charms, curses, and witchery remain ineffective. Why?"

He expressed a scathing mix of irritated frustration and downright loathing. "That is not a trader's concern."

"I'm not your enemy."

"Then what are you? A sorcerer possessed of some Power I cannot perceive? Is that why our Spirit attacks against the Kristianos don't work?"

"Forget it," I muttered. "Let Power decide. Here, with this game. I'm playing for white. If I'm deceitful, Power will ensure that I lose."

I won by four. But somehow, looking into his seething eyes, I didn't think Back-from-the-Dead was convinced.

SEVEN

"HE STILL HASN'T SENT THE COPPER YOU WON?" PEARL Hand asked, her warm body snuggled against mine. We lay on one of the sleeping benches in the kukofa. They had been built into the walls, the space beneath filled with wooden boxes, baskets of dried fruits, ceramic jars of hickory oil and bear grease, rolls of blankets, and other supplies.

Our dogs were camped on the floor, lying in a semicircle around the packs. Periodically Bark made grumbling noises as he scratched at fleas. The only other sounds were the soft snoring of Bear Paw, two beds down, and the gentle patter of rain on the thatch roof. I could hear it dripping just beyond the thin cane wall.

Thinking about de Soto's slaves sleeping naked and miserable in the mud, I grabbed Pearl Hand's arm and snuggled it over my shoulder. "For a renowned hilishaya,

Back-from-the-Dead doesn't seem to take a hint. I was playing for the white, he for the red." I grinned. "But, to tell the truth, I hope he's a better Spirit Dreamer than he is a chunkey player."

She punched me playfully in the back.

I stared out at where the central fire had burned down to coals. Feeble flickers licked up from the smoldering logs and cast faint yellow light through the room. Just as quickly they'd die back to glowing red. "What did you hear today?"

She whispered, "Matron Pahlko can't seem to get it into her head that nothing will ever be the same. She's positive that Cafakke is going to recognize the right moment to launch a surprise attack and crush the Kristianos. She already sees them fleeing south to the coast, mucking around in the swamps and mangroves as brave Apalachee warriors pick them off one by one from the bushes. Then the few pitiful survivors build boats and make the same exit as Narváez. Swallowed by the sea."

"And Cafakke? Does he see this, too?"

I felt her shake her head. "I had a long talk with his wives. The high mikko is just thankful to have escaped the Kristianos. He has no illusions about beating them in battle. His wives want him to rally the warriors, incite the hilishaya to draw an immense Power and unleash it upon the bumbling Kristianos. After the stories of atrocities told by the escaped captives, and the fact that Kristianos have committed blasphemies in the temples, not to mention profaned shrines, people really can't see how Power would hold back."

I felt impotent. "Sure. Power will always balance in the end. It's what we believe. Even me—and I've been told different by no less than Old-Woman-Who-Never-Dies. Some part of me desperately hopes that a great whirlwind is going to drop from the sky and suck them up. Or lightning is going to blast them. Tie snakes are going to pull down one of their bridges as they march across and drown them by the hundreds."

She ran fingers over the back of my neck, tangling them in the fine hairs. "Their god-and-cross may be like a poison thorn, paralyzing the Spirit World, but it hasn't made them invincible, husband. As you told Blood Thorn so long ago, they are just men once you get them peeled out of their armor."

"You always bring me back, wife."

"Good." She pulled free of my grip, her hand sliding down my arm, over my waist. Her fingers slithered snake-like under my breechcloth. "Now that I've brought you back, let's see if I can coax you up."

I turned so I could run my hands over her smooth skin. She sighed as I cupped her full breasts, massaging them as I knew she liked. I tensed as her grip tightened and stroked.

I've never gotten over the perfect way her body conforms to mine as I settle onto her. Then the magic begins. She is the master, leading the way, tensing, tightening, only to slow, as if she can sense my anticipation. When it fades, she begins to move again, hips rotating, her sheath gripping and teasing.

Finally her muscles flex and her back arches. She locks tightly around me and, loins pulsing, we shudder in delight. As we gasp for air, the tingle drains from nerve, bone, and muscle.

"I've missed you," she whispered. "It's been too long."

I counted in my head. "Five days."

"Way too long. You'd think we'd grown tired of each other years ago."

"We had Kristianos to kill, and then we had to travel here."

"And that's an excuse?"

"Well . . . no."

"You haven't started staring at other women, have you?"

I chuckled. "Maybe every once in a while. That youngest wife of Cafakke's . . ."

"You'd lose interest the first time she opened her mouth. Nothing worthwhile comes out of it."

"Not all men are interested in what a woman has to say." I've often heard it said that men think with more than their heads.

Pearl Hand wiggled suggestively and tightened her arms around me. "You are. That's one of the things I love about you."

"How's that?"

"Remember when you first won me from Irriparacoxi?"

"Talent with a bow and arrow is not his most outstanding ability. And it wasn't fair. I tricked him into thinking I wasn't very good. What's your point?"

"You could have taken me that first night. You won me fair and proper."

"We had other concerns. Like getting away before that fool declared me a witch, smacked me in the head, and took you back."

She rubbed her nose against mine. "You waited for me to make the first move. Remember?"

Remember? Oh yes, every blissful moment, from the

patterns of rain trickling down her perfect body to the way she'd reached out, grabbed me by the shaft, and dragged me helplessly to the bedding. "I didn't dare fight; you might have broken it off."

In the darkness of the kukofa we stared into each other's eyes, and I ran my fingers along the sides of her head, smoothing her silky black hair.

"I knew then that you were different," she said. "I still can't believe that you're not some dream."

"A real dream man would be taking you off to someplace far from war, slavery, and Kristianos."

Even in darkness, I caught the white flash of her teeth as she laughed. "We were born to this, Black Shell. If we ran, tried to forget, it would eat us alive."

"One day, maybe tomorrow, or a moon from now, or next year, one of us won't duck or run fast enough, or we'll make a mistake."

"That's why every heartbeat we have together makes the blood run warm in my veins, husband. We can't waste a moment. Each one has to be savored, lived at a full run, because there may not be many left."

She pulled my head down, kissing me passionately. Her hips began twisting slowly against mine, her sheath working rhythmically, bringing me to complete awareness.

Savored, and lived . . .

The next morning Pearl Hand and I were eating breakfast under one of the ramadas. Our repast consisted of fish that we'd laid on a willow rack to roast above a bed of coals. These were gifts given to the Orphans by grateful Apalachee.

Odd, isn't it, how the world changes? I thought of that

as I plucked flakes of steaming fish from the bones. Prior to the arrival of de Soto, any Apalachee worth his spit would have considered "entertaining" an Uzachile warrior to be torturing him to death. Now, after the massacre at Napetuca and the destruction of the Uzachile Nation, they were honored warriors worthy of receiving gifts. That they were killing Kristianos made them that much more wonderful.

But what really struck me that morning was the arrival of a party of Cafakke's warriors. We were throwing the last of the fish to the dogs and respectfully tossing offerings to the fire, the latter an act of thanks offered to the Spirits of the fish. Calls brought us to our feet, and we walked down with the rest to see the warriors. The canoes landed, bearing twelve Apalachee warriors—three badly wounded. Two of the unfortunates, their arms bound in cloth, were helped out, obviously in pain. The third man lay on his back in the canoe. I couldn't see the extent of his injuries.

How radically had the world changed? We were once a people constrained by ritual. Before de Soto, any war party would have stopped at least a hand's travel away. There they would have dressed in finery, painted their faces, and stuck swan feathers into their hair. Only when perfectly prepared would they have come, dancing and singing, the center of great panoply and ceremony.

The men I watched pull their weapons and packs from the canoes looked weary, hard faced, a grim resolve in the sets of their mouths. When they smiled at friends and family who greeted them, it was with thankful reserve. Warriors were always supposed to strut, a reflection of their personal Power. Instead seriousness cloaked them, accented by the spare and precise movements they made. An image of tired cougars came to mind, as if they had been chased by dogs and barely escaped. Predators turned suddenly wary and unsure.

"What's happening?" Blood Thorn asked, appearing at my elbow.

"War party," Pearl Hand replied. "But they're not acting right."

"They've got wounded," Blood Thorn noted softly. "The Power was wrong for the raid."

I considered that. "Perhaps, but they're not exactly sulking either. Nor are they singing the death songs as they would if they'd lost a man."

"No ihola'ka," Pearl Hand muttered.

I noticed other things: None of them wore traditional badges of honor—swan-feather plumes or miniature white arrows—in their hair. The only distinguishing features were their tattoos, now mud smeared and dappled with forest grime. With a start I realized that the muscular and grizzled man in the middle was Fire Falcon, tastanaki—or war chief—of the Apalachee Nation. He also served as the tishu mikko, or second chief, leader of the Red Moiety, placing him second in authority to Cafakke. His city, Ivitachuco, was the seat of the Red Moiety clans. We'd heard that Fire Falcon had abandoned the town and burned it to the ground before the monster could capture it.

I watched the tastanaki slip his war club into the sash at his waist, sling a turkey-feather cloak over his shoulders, and slip an arm through the strap on his quiver. Six fletched arrows and the stave of his bow protruded.

I'd met him years before on my first trading venture to the Apalachee. Then he'd been dressed in finery, washed, with a shining copper falcon pinned to his hair bun. A magnificent feather cape had draped his shoulders. He'd looked out with the studied arrogance of a man born to privilege and authority. A retinue of fifty nobles had surrounded him, attending to his every need.

The man before me now might have stepped out of another world, hardened, shaken, and half-desperate. It lay in his eyes, in the way he looked at his fellow warriors and the tension in his jaw. I couldn't help but think of a trapped badger: dangerous, fierce—with no way out.

A'atehkoci appeared, trotting toward the canoe landing with his staff of office in hand. Obviously he'd just heard of Fire Falcon's arrival, otherwise he would have been dressed for the occasion, his face painted, feathers and apron immaculate. Instead the usinulo looked slightly disheveled.

Pearl Hand and I were close enough to hear A'atehkoci's greeting, filled with flowery language and all the ritual welcomes for the leader of the Red Moiety.

"Spare us, Usinulo," Fire Falcon said as he raised a weary hand. "We appreciate your concern and respect, but I have men in need of healers; their wounds must be tended first. After that, hot food would be appreciated for the rest. And me, I must see the high mikko immediately. Can these things be done?"

People were watching wide-eyed, awed and unsettled by the frank reply.

"Immediately, Mikko." A'atehkoci didn't even blink at the callous breach of protocol. He pointed at the crowd with his staff. "You people, help those wounded warriors to the temple. Someone find Back-from-the-Dead, make sure he has the healers ready. You people from Eagle Clan, fix these warriors food. By order of the high mikko, do these things!"

The canoe landing exploded into activity, some rushing forward to help the wounded, others scurrying off in different directions. I watched Fire Falcon, his head bent close as he shared some confidence with A'atehkoci. The latter was nodding, lines deepening in his young face as he stared at the wounded man still supine in the canoe.

A'atehkoci grabbed a passing young man by the arm, whispered something into the lad's ear. The young man nodded, gulped, and left at a dead run for town. To do what? Alert Cafakke?

Only then did I realize that the warriors surrounding the wounded man had put together a litter, running poles along the sides of a hammock. Now, with great care, they lifted the man, and I could see all four of his limbs were bandaged—and much too short. Someone had carefully wrapped a heavy feather cloak around his middle, and another was tied around his shoulders in an effort to keep him warm.

"Blood and pus," Pearl Hand muttered darkly, "his arms and legs . . ."

Four warriors lifted the man, using the hammock as a litter. A'atehkoci led the way up the muddy incline. As they drew even with Pearl Hand, Blood Thorn, and me, the usinulo shot us a glance, considered for a brief instant, and said, "If you would join us, Black Shell?"

I glanced at Fire Falcon. He was staring at A'atehkoci as if he'd lost his mind. "Usinulo? I have important business with the high mikko."

"I know," was all A'atehkoci replied. He pointed his staff at us and gestured that we should follow.

Fire Falcon shot us a glance over his shoulder. I saw nothing pleasant in those hard black eyes as he surveyed me from head to toe. Perhaps it was a sign of exhaustion or stress, but he barely glanced at Pearl Hand. When he fixed on Blood Thorn with his Timucua hair and dress, Fire Falcon's expression hardened like flint.

"Who are you?" he asked stiffly.

"Black Shell, of the Chicaza," I replied.

That brought the barest of smiles to his lips. "Is there a chance we might have an ally in this fight? Perhaps, with the Chicaza at our side . . ."

"I am only a trader, Tishu Mikko. Pearl Hand is my wife. Blood Thorn here was iniha among the Uzachile."

The hope in his eyes flickered and died. His face had been tattooed with the forked eye and a prominent black bar across his mouth. Now, combined with his irritated scowl, the man looked positively fierce as he said, "You'd better have a very good reason for asking these people along, Usinulo."

"The high mikko will explain," A'atehkoci said smoothly.

I hoped so. Back-from-the-Dead already had reservations about us. We didn't need Fire Falcon's enmity as well.

We found a place at the rear of the litter bearers, and I was able to see that the warrior they carried was a young man of perhaps twenty summers. Both arms ended at the elbows, the stumps bound in bloody cloth. More bloody rags encased the stumps where his knees should have been. How could he have lost both arms *and* legs?

I glanced at Pearl Hand, who arched an eyebrow.

"Fighting Kristianos?" I wondered.

"We've seen sword wounds before," she said, reminding me. "This is something different."

"Maybe he was cut by four of those spear-ax things?" Blood Thorn suggested. "You know how deadly they are."

We'd seen them in action at Napetuca, where soldados reached out with the long spear-axes and hooked, chopped, and sliced club-bearing warriors with impunity.

I kept catching glimpses of the young man's face; his expression was haunting: a mixture of pain, disbelief, and horror. I could tell that he'd been crying; tear tracks lined his dirty cheeks. From his tattoos, he was an Apalachee *tascaia,* or blooded warrior. They weren't the sort who cried over wounds received in battle—not even when they were as hideous as this.

Then I realized that what I'd thought was dirt were bruises crisscrossed with welts and fresh scabs. The closer I looked, the worse off he was.

A'atchkoci was ordering onlookers out of the way as word spread and people arrived to see what the commotion was. Fire Falcon stalked along, his shoulders hunched, hands working as if in rage. Periodically he'd reach to his belt, resting a palm on his war club, as if desperate for a reason to use it.

"Tough man," Pearl Hand whispered.

"He's been orchestrating the fight against de Soto," I murmured back. "And, from what we can tell, doing a pretty good job of it."

"Oh?"

"There have been no Napetucas."

"Yet."

"That's my wife: always thinking on the bright side."

We were approaching Cafakke's make-do palace.

Whatever the import of Fire Falcon's visit, A'atehkoci didn't stop to make the customary declarations before the high mikko's door. Instead he just pushed the flap aside, helping Fire Falcon hold it as the litter bearers maneuvered their way in.

We followed, taking a place in the rear. The wounded man was lowered gently to the matting before the central fire. Only after Fire Falcon checked the man did the tastanaki rise, take two steps toward Cafakke's bed, and drop to a knee, his palms offered.

"Rise, my friend," Cafakke said, struggling up in his bed to stare first at Fire Falcon and then the wounded man. "The usinulo's messenger said that your arrival was urgent."

"High Mikko." Fire Falcon straightened, the muscles in his thighs rippling. "I have come straight from the forests around Anhaica." He pointed at the maimed man. "This tascaia is Singing Tail, of the Bear Clan, of the White Moiety. Two days ago, during an ambush, he was captured by the Kristianos." Fire Falcon looked down, features softening. "Can you tell the rest, Tascaia?"

Singing Tail's mouth worked, and in a fragile voice, as if hoarse from screaming, he added, "They ran me down with cabayos, High Mikko. I was too stunned to run or fight. Otherwise I would have chosen to die right there, doing my best to kill them in the process."

"You lost your souls for the moment?" Cafakke asked.

Singing Tail tried to nod, barely managing. "When I came to I was chained, a metal band around my neck. I was the only captive; the others were dead or escaped back to the forest."

For a moment he struggled for composure. "That night

I was chained to others inside Anhaica. They brought another captive who spoke Apalachee, and a Timucua. Then one of the Kristianos asked a question of the Timucua, who asked the Apalachee, who asked me, 'Why do you fight? The *Adelantado* wants peace.'"

"And what did you tell him?" Fire Falcon asked.

Singing Tail squirmed as if to sit up and winced, gasping. Through gritted teeth he managed to say, "I told them I was Apalachee, a tascaia. I said that I would fight them until the last one ran screaming from our land. That they would end just like Narváez. That tascaia like me would see to it." He swallowed hard, jaw trembling. "They asked many things, High Mikko: Where you were hiding; were the people scattered or in hidden towns; how many warriors were there. They wanted to know if Fire Falcon was still tastanaki of all Apalachee or if they'd managed to kill him. They wanted to know if any of his relatives or friends were captive."

"Why?" Cafakke asked.

When Singing Tail tried to shrug his bafflement, Pearl Hand called out, "To use as hostages against the war chief, High Mikko."

Fire Falcon turned on his heel, angry eyes on Pearl Hand.

"Go on, Tascaia," Cafakke prompted, rolling onto his side so he could look down at the wounded man. "What did you tell them?"

Sweat was beading on Singing Tail's cheeks, and he looked feverish. "I told them nothing, High Mikko. I am Bear Clan, and my uncle was nicoquadca, a high warrior. He trained me, hardened my souls to torture. He showed me the path to Power and how to call upon it. I am Apalachee, my lord."

He said it so proudly, and I knew—as did everyone in the room—that whatever had happened, Singing Tail had acted with unsurpassed honor and courage.

"That night"—Singing Tail swallowed hard—"we were raided. Torches were thrown over the palisade. With the wind, half the town was burned. By chance I was upwind of the flames. Others chained downwind to the walls were not so lucky and many burned to death."

"I'm sorry," Cafakke said softly. "But it is war."

"They died shouting their defiance at Kristianos," Singing Tail replied. "Even as the fire roared down on the captives, the Apalachee cheered it, calling on Power to burn every Kristiano alive. You would have been proud of them."

"I am," Cafakke told him.

"The next day, the *Adelantado* himself came at the head of the Kristianos. He looked at me and then at the half-burned town. He shouted a question that went through the line of translators. 'Why do you people not give up? I am here in peace, but you do not know when you are beaten!'

"'We are Apalachee,' I told him. 'We will give up when the last Kristiano's severed bones are trophies in our temples.'"

Singing Tail smiled then. "They beat me, High Mikko. And they lashed me with whips that flay the skin with each stroke. Filling my lungs, I sang to Power, to my ancestors, and to Breath Giver. Let them beat me; I would die as an Apalachee."

The room was silent, his words so passionate that we were seeing it in our minds.

Singing Tail continued. "The *Adelantado*, through the

translators, he told me that he was finished with us. That there would be one last chance. Either the high mikko Cafakke would surrender himself and his people, or from now on we will pay the price for our disobedience."

Grumbles sounded through the room. I was fascinated by the expression on Fire Falcon's face, as if he were struggling to keep from bellowing in rage.

Cafakke sighed, a sliver of sad smile on his face. "Brave Tascaia, as you have no doubt guessed, we will not surrender. That being the case, what is this price we have to pay?"

Singing Tail cleared his throat. "De Soto himself called the orders. They dragged me out, fighting the entire time, and tied me down. Then one of the men came with an ax. Blow by blow he chopped off my arms and legs, and another man ran up with hot metal and burned the stubs to seal them."

Around the room, faces were ashen. I winced, almost able to smell seared human meat.

"And then they took my manhood," Singing Tail whispered hollowly.

Fire Falcon bent, lifting the feather cloak from Singing Tail's crotch. The rest of the room couldn't see, but Cafakke's eyes glittered with rage, and his expression turned to chiseled stone.

"What happened to me . . . this"—Singing Tail's voice shrilled in the room—"will be the price paid by any who carry the fight to the Kristianos. Further, if the attacks do not stop immediately, another demonstration of the *Adelantado*'s wrath will occur the morning after the new moon. And they will continue until the high mikko surrenders himself and the Apalachee pledge peace. That is what I was told to tell you."

Silence lay like thick smoke. Pearl Hand had crossed her arms as she translated for Blood Thorn. Fire Falcon knotted his fist around the handle of his war club, half drawing the copper-headed weapon from his sash.

Singing Tail took a breath. "I was carried out and left where Apalachee warriors could find me, High Mikko. And now I have been carried to you. I have given you the *Adelantado*'s message."

Cafakke's jaws ground in anger, his eyes darkening. Around the room people clenched fists, shifting as if to mollify their rage.

Swallowing hard, Singing Tail met Cafakke's gaze. "Now, if a single tascaia may, I will give you my own message: We are Apalachee. High Mikko, before you so much as surrender a single stick in the trail . . ." His voice broke. "Kill them, High Mikko! *Kill them all!*"

The only sound was the popping of the fire. Then Cafakke slowly sat up, propping his withered arms on his round belly. "I am honored to hear your message, Tascaia. Why? Because you are the best of us. The monster's threats shall become lost upon the winds."

Singing Tail gasped a pain-filled sigh. His eyes sought out Fire Falcon as he whispered, "I ask you for your promise, great Tastanaki. I have kept mine."

Fire Falcon smiled grimly. "In a bit. I must attend a final task before I fulfill my promise." Fire Falcon straightened, his war club now clenched in his right fist. He shot a look at Cafakke. "High Mikko, as tastanaki of the Apalachee people, I look upon this tascaia but do not see him."

"What do you see, War Chief?" Cafakke asked.

"I see a nicoquadca."

"As do I," Cafakke said in agreement. "Singing Tail, from this moment on, you shall be known as a nicoquadca of the Apalachee people. Let all who know you do you honor."

Singing Tail gasped, mouth working in disbelief. Shouts of acclamation broke out, warriors stamping their feet.

"That's cruel," Blood Thorn whispered as Pearl Hand translated. "Maimed like that? What kind of life can he have?"

I was about to respond when Fire Falcon took a half step, turned, and—with a whistling blow of his war club—caved in the top of Singing Tail's skull.

We stared in disbelief at the quivering body. Fire Falcon dropped to his knees, carefully dislodging the pointed head of his club from the young man's skull.

Fire Falcon's soft voice carried in the sudden silence. "Nicoquadca Singing Tail, as much as it wounds my souls, I have kept the promise you made me swear to."

With that, the war chief rose to his feet and started for the door. As he passed, I could see the muscles bulging from his locked jaws, the seething anger in his eyes.

EIGHT

FIRELIGHT FLICKERED ON THE KUKOFA ROOF AND walls. At Cafakke's order, a good load of dry wood had been carried in. While it would have been nice to think he'd done it on our behalf, it was actually for Fire Falcon and his warriors.

Pearl Hand and I sat on one of the sleeping benches, the rest of the Orphans lined up to either side while the dogs lay happily on the matting at our feet. Our packs were stowed safely under the pole beds. We'd been fed a stew of duck, catfish, and hominy, backed by freshly baked yellow-lotus bread. A bowl of tolocano had been sent by Cafakke, and this we passed back and forth, sharing.

Across from us, the Apalachee warriors had set up their own quarters. Normally they would have made themselves at home in the Men's House. Unfortunately, Cafakke's refuge in the swamp was too new for such a structure—let alone the complicated ritual that went into selecting its location, blessing the ground, ritually "hunting" the trees used in its construction, and all the necessary rites that attended the roofing, dedications, and final occupancy.

The Apalachee warriors across from us appeared uneasy with the arrangement. Normally, upon returning to the city, they'd be sequestered by the hilishaya, forced to fast, take sweats, drink button snakeroot and black drink, purge, and undergo ceremonial cleansing to rid themselves of the red chaos of war. Power needed to be balanced. But here, in the turmoil of de Soto's invasion, they were still literally on the battle walk, following the rules of a war party.

For that reason, they didn't socialize, ate only the food Fire Falcon's second provided, and didn't sit upon the earth out of respect. Nor would they lean against a post or tree. They sought to do their best to ignore the fire, since it hadn't been kindled by the second or fanned with their eagle wing. I'm sure that deep down, they knew that no matter how hard they were trying, they couldn't help but break the taboos of the war trail. Such things weren't meant for city life.

"I think we should leave Cane Place town." Wide Antler interrupted my thoughts, his eyes fixed on the central fire. "Our job is to hunt Kristianos."

"Food's better here," Corn Thrower retorted, rubbing the thick bicep on his left arm. "And there's a pretty young Apalachee girl who's been making eyes at me."

"That's just my point," Wide Antler growled. "We're getting soft, losing our edge. Hot food every night . . . sleeping in a warm, dry council house like this? It makes us lazy, Corn Thrower. So what next? You and the girl will slip away, and next thing you know, she'll be on her back. From then on, you'll be dreaming of how soft she is, how she made you feel. Your mind won't be on smarter ways to kill Kristianos."

"I can do both," Corn Thrower muttered defensively.

"No, you can't." Bear Paw shook his head. "As to being here? I have to say, I was ready for a little luxury. Maybe we need this every once in a while. It reminds us of what we lost."

"I don't need anything to remind me." Blood Thorn crossed his arms. "Every time I close my eyes, I see it, relive it. She's staring at me with those death-gray eyes, flies on her lips."

He meant his dead wife-to-be. I wound my fingers into Pearl Hand's. She was staring thoughtfully at the fire, flames mirrored in her dark eyes.

"We'd just killed five," Wide Antler said. "Why? Because we were out there, breathing as one with the forest. Power was working through us. Each day we're here, it's draining away. Making us weaker."

Walking Thunder hadn't had his say yet. "And . . . what? If we stay here for a couple of days, we're going to forget? Maybe become childlike and stumbly? I'm with Corn Thrower. Every now and then it's all right to have a rest, eat something besides what we've shot that day." He grinned. "Besides, I traded a Kristiano knife for an Apalachee war bow and better arrows than I could ever make."

Corn Thrower nodded sagaciously. "That's a good point. Things like that compound bow Walking Thunder traded for, we couldn't make the like, not while we're hunting Kristianos. The same with the hardwood war arrows."

"Then let's do our trading and leave," Wide Antler said insistently. "I can feel my Power fading by the moment. We've got to stay pure, focused, and dedicated to the task."

"Or?" Bear Paw asked. "We'll forget, marry Apalachee women, and decide to grow corn?"

Blood Thorn snorted. "This will not last forever. Enjoy a warm dry bed while you have it and eat all you can. Sometime soon you're going to be looking back on this kukofa of theirs with real longing."

"The sooner, the better," Wide Antler said stubbornly.

I figured it was getting too thorny. "Quiet, all of you. We'll take the time we can get here. Blood Thorn and Wide Antler are both correct. Yes, town life makes people soft, but to keep the edge, we've got to have both rest and a chance for our souls to replenish. We do have to refit our weaponry, trade for clothing and food. We need to be reminded of what we still stand to lose."

"These are Apalachee comforts," Wide Antler grunted.

"Uzachile? Apalachee? We fight for all peoples. But more than that, you're all forgetting something: We're here at the high mikko's request. We're not leaving until he says we can."

"But he'd let us go if you asked, right?" Corn Thrower asked suspiciously.

I agreed, not really sure. "He would. But I'm not ready to leave. Something's happening, and the maimed warrior—the one Fire Falcon brought in—has my interest up. De Soto has never chopped up captives and sent them back as warnings. It says something about how he and his Kristianos are doing."

"And how's that?" Pearl Hand asked dryly. "He's got the

hundred soldados and cabayeros he left in Uzita to augment his ranks. His ships are in contact and resupplying him. The Apalachee might have burned half of Anhaica and enraged him, but it's not as if he's suffered any debilitating defeat. He's stronger now than ever."

"Maybe. On the other hand, you can't exactly say he's grabbed Apalachee by the balls. He doesn't have the high mikko or Fire Falcon under his control. And they're both smart and capable adversaries. The Apalachee won't stand and fight, but they're not fleeing like panicked quail. De Soto and his captains are probably concluding that this is going to be a long and drawn-out affair."

She was framing her response when A'atehkoci strode in, shot me a smile, and beckoned from the doorway, saying, "Black Shell? Pearl Hand? The high mikko requests your presence."

Blood Thorn mumbled, "Have fun."

I didn't like the increasingly suspicious look in Wide Antler's eyes. He might have been the believer, but he really wanted to be out stalking rather than warm and cozy with a full stomach. It was something to think about.

We followed A'atehkoci across the small plaza, the cold air prickling my skin. As I exhaled, my breath frosted. This wasn't a night to be sleeping out unprotected. I wondered how many of de Soto's miserable captives would be feeding the *puercos* come morning.

I asked A'atehkoci, "More news?"

"Not yet."

Then we ducked through the doorway and into Cafakke's warm palace. A cheery fire illuminated the interior and sent sparks toward the high roof. Singing Tail's body had been removed, the bloody matting replaced.

Fire Falcon sat on the edge of Cafakke's bed. The Red Moiety mikko wore a tanned buckskin hunting shirt decorated with a falcon design on the front. He'd taken a bath, washing the grime of the war trail from his skin, and donned fresh clothing. His hair was pulled back and pinned with copper. Polished ear spools gleamed in the light.

Matron Pahlko perched birdlike beside him. She glanced up at our entry, her expression turning sour.

Back-from-the-Dead immediately pinned me with his unsettling gaze. The hilishaya wore a long cloak, striped lengthwise with broad red and white bands of cardinal and swan feathers. The thing would have traded for a fortune in copper. The priest sat on a large wooden box carved with images of Mother Spider carrying fire down from the Sky World. I tried to read his expression but gave it up as a lost cause.

"The traders, High Mikko," A'atehkoci announced, lifting his staff of office.

"Thank you, Usinulo." Cafakke sat in the middle of his bed, his back propped. He gestured us forward with his disease-mangled hand. "Find a seat. We are discussing how to respond to the monster."

Fire Falcon was giving Pearl Hand a skeptical appraisal, his tastanaki's mistrust of female Power evident. Don't get me wrong. Women often went on battle walks, even among the Apalachee. Fire Falcon, however, didn't know her.

Cafakke, to the contrary, was smiling as if we had just made his evening. It went away the moment we seated ourselves on the foot of his elevated bed.

He said, "The story of what the Kristianos did to Singing Tail is spreading like pollen on the wind. Those who hear are enraged—even more than they already were. People are ready to throw themselves upon the Kristianos and rip them apart with their bare hands."

"Not advisable," Fire Falcon replied. "I've been fighting them for three moons now. As was the case at Napetuca, it would be a massacre."

Pearl Hand and I both nodded, not really knowing our status. Cafakke had called the four most important people in the Apalachee Nation to his bedside, apparently for an informal discussion of the situation. And here we were, two foreign traders, admitted to the inner circle?

"With the proper preparation," Back-from-the-Dead said, "Power would swell and drive the people. Even the Spirits of the sky and earth would rise to devour the pollution in our midst. This is not a matter of warriors, High Mikko, but of sacred Power. This is a time to sacrifice, to purify our bodies, souls, and thoughts. If we attend to the rituals, spiritually prepare ourselves, Power will favor us. Cleansed of pollution, we cannot lose."

"Yes, you can," I said softly, fighting the urge to wince. I didn't want to oppose the priest. But he was dead wrong. He gave me the same look he'd have given mold on fresh acorns.

"That's right." His voice turned hollow, sultry with threat. "Black Shell, the Spirit Flyer—the lowly, outcast trader that Horned Serpent himself carried to the Sky World. I remain in awe, barely able to comprehend the immense knowledge the Spirit World must have poured into you. Myself, I have dedicated my life to the study of Power, its ways, and how it ebbs and flows through all of life and Creation. I have charted the fortunes of people and Nations, watching how their piety and compliance to the rules of Power have determined their success, survival, or ruination. But now, just at this time of trial, you have come to finally set me—all of us—straight. All those years of study by me, my predecessors, and theirs before them were but a waste of time. I stand corrected and humbled by your mastery."

Pearl Hand was biting her lip, fists knotted, eyes lowered. *Good girl. You can rip his balls off later . . . when doing so won't get our heads bashed in.*

In as even a voice as I could muster, I replied, "Great Hilishaya, I am not here to humble you. Nor would I presume upon your vast knowledge. What I've been told by the Spirits is that we're engaged in a battle between men, that Power is helpless. Why? I cannot say. That is a question for skilled hilishaya, such as yourself, to investigate and answer." I met his hard glare with my own.

Cafakke and Fire Falcon were staring back and forth between us, Fire Falcon with a wary curiosity, Cafakke with a pensive pout on his lips.

A'atehkoci broke the impasse. "Power aside, let's get back to the Kristianos. Should we back off on the attacks? Disengage our warriors? Perhaps create a buffer zone to decrease the risk?"

"No." Fire Falcon was adamant. "Doing so would send the wrong signal. The monster would think he'd found a tool to use against us. He would assume we were afraid . . . that by additional mutilations, we could be intimidated."

"Is that something we can use against him?" A'atehkoci asked. "Perhaps lull him into a false sense of security, make him careless?"

"Red Power would understand, High Mikko." Back-from-the-Dead shot me a sidelong glance, as if daring me to disagree. "To mislead the enemy before striking, that is a legitimate use of Power as long as it is atoned for in the end."

"We have to keep the pressure on," Fire Falcon said stubbornly. "As it is, they haven't had time to catch their breath. They are constantly harassed, rebuilding what we burn, guarding their animals, and moving around only in strength."

"You don't want them getting comfortable," Pearl Hand said in agreement. "You've already told us that their slaves are dying by the tens. If they feel it is safe, they're going to start making sweeps to capture more slaves. I don't think you want that for your people."

"No, we do not," Pahlko stated fiercely. "Already families are scattered, people disheartened. They look to us for a solution. That we cannot drive the invader out is bad enough. If they hear that we've ordered the warriors back, and the Kristianos start raiding for slaves with impunity, people will lose all hope."

"Tastanaki"—Cafakke's expression hardened—"continue to fight them as you think best. You are there, watching and evaluating. You see the spirit reflected in the eyes of our warriors. You know their hearts."

"Then we will continue to pick away at them." Fire Falcon stared thoughtfully at his hand, as if trying to read the future in the lines of his palm. "If we make them miserable enough, they'll fondly look back at the Uzachile lands and return there."

"Some option." Pahlko smoothed her mulberry-fiber dress with a wrinkled hand. "Like having a den of piasas next door. You never know when they'll creep over in the middle of the night, murder you, and drag off your family."

"We need them to leave," Fire Falcon declared. "Convince them that the fight will never cease as long as they covet Apalachee lands. Seen that way, perhaps they will go inflict themselves on someone far away."

Cafakke looked at Pearl Hand and me. "You have followed them from the beginning. What are the chances of this?"

"Good, I think," Pearl Hand answered. "But you have the richest land they've yet seen. Compared to the peninsula, your fields are fertile, your woodlands more productive, and the weather is better."

I added, "The best thing would be if you could burn all the granaries. As soon as they run out of food, they leave." I frowned. "Is there any chance that could happen?"

Cafakke studied me through narrowed eyes. "If we get the chance, yes. But it may be too late. As we speak they are looting the surrounding towns, carrying back all the corn they can find."

"And there's no gold," Pearl Hand pointed out. "They obsess over gold."

"Oh yes." Cafakke cocked his head. "You remember the trader White Mat? Did you know that Kristianos caught him?"

This was a surprise. "White Mat? I've known him for years, traveled with him a couple of times. He would have walked up to the first Kristiano he saw, trader's staff in hand, and formally announced he'd arrived under the Power of trade."

"And Ortiz would have clapped an iron collar around his neck," Pearl Hand finished. "Why do you bring it up, High Mikko?"

"He had a youth with him, Periko." Cafakke frowned. "I

was introduced to the boy while I was held captive. He's a northerner, speaks with a Guale accent. White Mat was teaching him the ways of trade." He paused. "Periko told the *Adelantado* that a great deal of gold could be found in Cofitachequi. He said that the statues of the ancestors were covered with it, that war axes were made with it, and that pearls were everywhere."

"Copper maybe," I snorted derisively. "But gold? I've been to Cofitachequi. Seen the statues . . . all painted wood. There's no gold. How old is this Periko?"

"Maybe fifteen summers." Cafakke shrugged a round shoulder. "You should have seen the Kristianos. They crowded around, showing the boy rings and jewelry, saying something about meesmo."

"*Lo mismo,*" Pearl Hand said. "'The same.'"

"The boy kept saying yes." Cafakke made a gesture with his hand. "Why would he say there's gold in Cofitachequi?"

"Maybe an occasional nugget," I said, imagining the scene through the eye of my souls. The Kristianos would have been falling all over Periko. The stupid kid probably ate it up like forest honey on a corn cake.

"High Mikko, I was born Chicora," Pearl Hand added, "but sold to Cofitachequi as a girl. De Soto will find no gold."

"But we will not tell him that," Back-from-the-Dead said insistently. "Perhaps Power has sent this gullible young man to lead the Kristianos away."

"What this boy Periko can convince Kristianos to believe may or may not be important." Cafakke stared wistfully at the fire. "Our more immediate concern, and the actual reason I called you together, is that Singing Tail gave me a message from de Soto. The monster said that if the attacks didn't cease, he would demonstrate his wrath just after the new moon."

"That's four days from now," Back-from-the-Dead said, a distant look in his spooky dark eyes.

"The attacks will not stop," Cafakke stated bluntly. "Neither I nor the tishu mikko is surrendering." He glanced at us. "You two know de Soto best. What could this demonstration be?"

"Expect something terrible." I made a face.

"At Napetuca it was to murder anyone who fought against him," Pearl Hand added. "It broke the spirit of the Uzachile. People fled like terrified deer. But that didn't stop the attacks."

"How many Apalachee captives does he hold?" I asked.

"Maybe eighty or ninety," Fire Falcon replied.

Pearl Hand glanced at Cafakke. "What would the reaction be if he marched them out and executed them?"

"Anger," Cafakke and Pahlko said in unison. Fire Falcon nodded his agreement. Back-from-the-Dead's scowl darkened, his forehead lining, as if he could see it in his mind.

"When de Soto was at Napetuca," I mused, "he had some of the Southern Timucua on his side. It gave him an advantage in understanding the Uzachile." I remembered "Ears," the guy who wanted Pearl Hand so badly. Ears had converted to the Kristiano god, taken to wearing a little wooden cross hung on a thong about his neck.

Fire Falcon's gaze narrowed. "We're *not* Uzachile."

"That's my point," I answered. "He doesn't have any fawning Apalachee to advise him. He can't know your hearts. But his slaves are dying off?"

"Three to four hundred over the last moon alone," Fire Falcon said after reflection.

"That's *half*!" I marveled.

"But he's taken maybe ninety Apalachee as replacements," Pearl Hand said.

The look Fire Falcon gave me was cold enough to have frozen water. "In the coming days, another two hundred captives will be dead of starvation, exposure, or disease. By the end of the moon, double that."

Pahlko fingered the wattle of skin under her chin. "If the beast doesn't care about the lives of his slaves, if they are worthless to him, perhaps it's because he's not planning on leaving." She glanced at Cafakke. "Why else would he just let them die? He's here, has found our land. Maybe the need for porters is over."

Back-from-the-Dead mused, "In the Beginning Times, Breath Maker watched the earth overpopulate, and the hero Morning Star was instrumental in the origins of death. But death must have a reason, be it war, illness, old age, soul theft, or justice. To murder masses through neglect is unthinkable." He made a face, blanching. "I hate to think of the Power building against him. We need but wait. Like a dam, Power will burst and flow over him, sweeping away all but the memory of these Kristianos. And finally, that, too, shall fade."

"We should be so lucky." Pearl Hand flipped her long hair back.

Back-from-the-Dead continued. "And in the meantime, our people must fast. The strictest observances on the separation of Powers must be maintained. Men and women must not lie together. The dietary laws must be scrupulously obeyed: Fish must not be cooked in the same pot that once held a bird's flesh. Roots like cattail and yellow lotus cannot be mixed with arboreal fruits like mulberries or nuts. No one must so much as allow water to drip into fire. Women's things must be kept separate from men's, even to the point of drawing a line down the middle of a house, men's things on one side, women's on the other."

I watched their expressions, each of the Apalachee nodding, eyes sober. Cafakke said, "Usinulo, issue the hilishaya's order. Make sure that no one violates any of the taboos. If they do, punish them."

They still think Power can save them.

In as meek a voice as I could muster, I asked, "Isn't there a problem?"

"And that would be?" Cafakke asked.

"De Soto landed almost a year ago. Power has had ample time to be insulted, polluted, and profaned by his actions. Yet he remains unpunished. Meanwhile, the Apalachee, one of the most devout peoples I know, are hiding in the forests. Their temples have been desecrated, the remains of the ancestors ignored, and the most sacred of ground is abused. For three moons now, the hilishaya, even the sorcerers, conjurors, and witches, have been casting their Power against the invader."

"And your point?" Back-from-the-Dead grated out, loathing in his eyes.

"According to our beliefs, Power should already have swatted the Kristianos down like the vermin they are."

"It *will*!" Back-from-the-Dead snapped back.

"When?" I asked reasonably.

"When it's *ready*!"

Cafakke's jaw was clenching. Pahlko's expression had

gone stiff. Fire Falcon had crossed his arms defensively. Pearl Hand reached out, laying a hand on my arm, silently requesting that I desist. I needed say no more.

"The tastanaki will be headed back to his camp in the morning. You and the Orphans may accompany him." Cafakke shot me a look from the corner of his eye, no doubt grateful to get me away from Back-from-the-Dead.

He lifted his right hand, the disease-knotted fingers barely moving as he waved down Fire Falcon's protest. "No, good Tishu Mikko. I trust Black Shell. Perhaps he and Pearl Hand will see something we do not." He smiled. "And maybe he and his Orphans can kill a few more Kristianos."

"We are in your service, High Mikko," I added, and touched my chin in a sign of respect. "Any ihola'ka we obtain will be sent to you."

Back-from-the-Dead was giving me that hollow look that communicated threat. I could tell that he, for one, would be just as happy to see me gone.

And so will the Orphans. Otherwise Wide Antler will end up causing some sort of trouble.

That was the problem with believers: They just *knew* they were right.

NINE

MORNING FROST LAY THICK ON CANE PLACE town's thatch roofs, grass, and ramada tops. It outlined branches and coated the canoes and paddles; hoar made patterns on the frozen mud. A delicate rime of ice girdled the shore; it cracked as we pushed long dugout canoes into the water.

I climbed into the rear of one, calling Gnaw and Squirm in with me. Then I placed the packs as my shivering wife handed them in. Pearl Hand had a feather cloak over her shoulders and wore a thick fabric dress beneath it. They didn't seem any too warm given the quick way Pearl Hand was moving, almost hopping in her buckskin moccasins.

Around us, other canoes were being loaded. Locals were standing in the background, arms crossed, looking cold as they huddled in their blankets. Fire Falcon's warriors went about packing and clambering into various crafts, stubbornly headed back to the war.

The Orphans were tossing their packs into the canoes allotted to us, settling in, wincing as the frost on the paddles melted in their hands.

Skipper and Bark both climbed into Blood Thorn's boat, snuggling down between their packs. Of all parties concerned, the dogs looked the happiest, tails wagging, eyes gleaming, as they sniffed the cool north breeze blowing across the swamp.

Men spoke in soft voices, interrupted by the hollow clunk of wood against wood or the scuffing of a pack against the hull. Shell necklaces clicked softly as men shifted.

Fire Falcon settled in the bow of his boat, a fluffy feather cape around his shoulders. The tattoos on his face stood out, the forked-eye design falconlike in intensity. He glanced at me, but I couldn't read the dark-eyed, stern expression.

"Ready?" Pearl Hand asked as I picked up one of the frost-thick paddles and seated myself in the stern.

"Always," I muttered, thankful the frost covered only one side of the paddle.

She climbed in and found her seat. The local, whose craft this was, pushed us out through the broken ice and jumped aboard to take the forward paddle. We backed out, turning, waiting as other canoes were pushed out. The warriors, hunched against the cold, took up paddles. Vees of wake rippled the calm water.

I bent my head back, looking up at the cold and cloudy sky. When I puffed my breath out, it rose white and full. Definitely not a good morning to be a naked Kristiano slave sleeping on the ground.

I snapped my fingers, pointing at Squirm as he tried to

wiggle past Gnaw to a better position on the packs. With a hand sign I made him lay down where he was, uncomfortable or not. He gave me that dog look—the sad-eyed one that told me I was a horrible human being.

Fire Falcon took the lead, paddling back toward the trail head. We let his warriors line up behind him, and then my Orphans and I dipped our paddles, sending us in silent pursuit.

Blood Thorn guided his craft beside ours, a thin smile on his wide lips. "I have to tell you, Peliqua, leaving that place behind is a load off my souls."

"They didn't treat you well?"

He gave a faint shrug. "They're Apalachee. Like being surrounded by a city full of friendly bears. No matter what they profess, a person never knows when they might drop pretenses and become bears again."

"Well, you'd better be used to them, because we're traveling with this party of warriors for the next couple of days."

Blood Thorn's smile bent slightly. "But that's on the war trail. I guess it's more like a fair fight."

I glanced at Wide Antler where he sat behind the local fisherman. "You feeling better now that you're on the war trail again?"

"Yes, Peliqua." Wide Antler grinned. His hands rested on the gunnels as if he expected rough water. "We're back in the hunt again, and without having our Power seriously compromised." He lowered his head, adding, "And perhaps the food, warm quarters, and hospitality were just enough to refresh."

"Uh-huh," I muttered, "I thought you'd figure that out when I rolled you out of that warm kukofa."

Pearl Hand took a quick look over her shoulder, winking at me. It wasn't fair. My bed was always warmer than the Orphans'. But then if any of them could recruit a woman as good at killing Kristianos, they could have warm beds, too.

"Where are we off to?" Blood Thorn asked. "Anhaica, truly?"

"Truly," I said. "De Soto is going to be demonstrating his anger to the Apalachee on the new moon. We're there to watch and see who gets madder afterward."

"Us or the Apalachee?" Blood Thorn asked.

"I was thinking about de Soto or Cafakke, but I'll bet you're righter than I am."

"And then?"

"Then we go back to killing Kristianos."

"About time," Wide Antler said under his breath.

Still, as we landed I kept glancing off to the northeast. There, a couple of days' run from where we stood, lay Anhaica. Pearl Hand noticed and nodded as she pulled the last pack from the canoe and began lacing it onto Squirm.

"Whatever he's planning, it won't be pleasant," she said, warily.

"Got a sense of foreboding like I have?"

"From the moment those two-footed slime stepped on our soil, have they done anything, anywhere, for anyone? Or have they just inflicted misery as a means of serving their own petty cravings?"

"Point made."

I slipped my trader's staff inside my quiver, knowing I would have no use for it anywhere close to Kristianos. Taking up my bow, I shouldered my quiver and checked Bark's heavy pack. Blood Thorn had done a thorough job fitting it.

"Trader?" Fire Falcon called. "Are you ready?"

I waved. "Go ahead, Tishu Mikko. With the dogs we cannot travel as fast. We'll be behind, coming as quickly as we can."

"Will you get lost?"

I laughed. "We're the Orphans, Tishu Mikko. How much more lost can we get?"

He actually shot me a grin, waved to the cluster of warriors around him, and started off up that trail at a jog.

"All right," I called to my people as the locals shoved off. "Let's go find trouble."

Later I would recall how cheery my voice sounded when I said that.

The following morning, with the Orphans slipping along behind, Pearl Hand and I followed one of the trails leading toward Anhaica. Of this, there could be no doubt: the cabayos had cut the damp soil, churning it as if their hooves functioned as field hoes. Here and there, the Kristianos had cut wood. Their *hierro* axes left a clean, beaver-fine cut, unlike our stone axes, which leave a stump almost fuzzy looking.

How did they end up blessed by such wonderful tools when they are such despicable creatures? For the life of me, I couldn't figure it out.

The approach to Anhaica is dangerous. The closer one gets to the Kristianos, the greater the danger. Unlike some remote farm village, Anhaica was the capital. It had been home to thousands, a center for trade, food storage, and the manufacture of ceramics, art, textiles, and other prestige goods. Half the Apalachee Nation went to its central plaza to celebrate the Busk, or Green Corn Ceremony.

The country surrounding the capital was dotted with

villages, clusters of farmsteads, fields, clearings, and hundreds of crisscrossing trails. Thousands of people had lived in these outlying areas, but like the city, the farmsteads were abandoned and lonely.

For generations deadfalls had been immediately scavenged for wood, so patches of old blow-downs had become fields instead of tangled thickets. Brushy areas peripheral to the nut forests were burned periodically to keep the forest back and the understory of fruit-laden bushes producing. The old-growth forests had been maintained for their nut crop—a major source of food and oils. Unfortunately the forest floor was open, meaning the cabayeros could sweep through unhindered.

The only safe approaches were along drainages and brushy corridors, and the Kristianos had learned to patrol them. The other option was to sneak in at night. Kristianos didn't like staying out after dark. They'd been taught better by Cafakke's warriors.

I considered that as we eased along in the falling gloom of twilight. The only reassurance came from watching the dogs' noses testing the breeze as it blew down our shadowed trail.

"You look nervous," Pearl Hand remarked from my side.

"We're headed for Anhaica. Cabayos? Kristianos? De Soto? Then there's Antonio, your old friend Ears, capture, torture, death? Any of these things worry you?"

Her teeth flashed as she shot me a grin. "Planning on living forever now, husband? Or is this just a momentary softening of the backbone?"

I watched her long legs, her swinging hips, as she walked along. "How about you and I wait until full dark?

We'll leave the rest of these fools to fight, and you and I will run like panicked deer for the north. Maybe we'll find some little creek up from the Tenasee River, hack a farmstead out of forest, and live quietly forever?"

Despite the poor light I could see an amused smile playing at the corners of her mouth. "Just forget Power? Forget the Piasa who dragged you down to the Underworld—even when he knew you were fighting for his world, too? Or have you forgotten your Spirit Dreams?"

"Nothing's forgotten." I gestured futility, glancing back to where Blood Thorn and the Orphans followed. "I keep thinking back to yesterday. It was a close thing. We did everything right, and they still almost killed Blood Thorn. If that hickory tree hadn't been there, those two cabayeros would have ridden him down, speared him, or knocked him down and captured him."

"But they didn't, and after killing two cabayos, we had squash for dinner." A pause. "You've been around most of the country now. How many people have you met from the Beginning Times?"

"Well, there was Old-Woman-Who-Never-Dies, her daughter Corn Woman—"

"What I meant was: How many people are alive from your grandmother's grandmother's day? You know, the ones who actually lived at Split Sky City? How many people have you met who saw Old White and Green Snake? What about those who once walked the plazas of mighty Cahokia?"

"Why are you bothering me with this?"

"No one lives forever," she said simply. "We were chosen to fight. It's the bargain we've made. You, me, the Orphans, the Apalachee, we all have surrendered ourselves in the hope of destroying the Kristianos."

It's not that I minded defeat at her hands; it just irked me when she did it with my own arguments. "That doesn't stop me from wishing things were different on occasion."

I heard her gentle chuckle. "Oh, I know. I wonder sometimes what it would have been like to have had you without the Kristianos' shadow looming over us. But, Black Shell, remember why you headed south in the first place? Or are you purposely forgetting why you arrived at Irriparacoxi's that day?"

"I wanted to see the bearded men from the sea."

"And would you have traveled all that way down the peninsula had there been no rumors of the Kristianos to lure you?"

"No, wife. I'd have stayed in the north, carrying trade from the Caddo to the Cofitachequi and all points between."

"And I would have been passed to Ears when Irriparacoxi grew tired of me. And—assuming I wasn't hunted down and killed after murdering him—from Ears to some other man." She tilted her head back, spilling long dark hair. As she stared at the lacing of branches overhead, she added, "Since the day you won me from Irriparacoxi, I've been free, Black Shell. Would I ever have known freedom had you not come south? Perhaps. And even if I had, what are the chances it would have been with someone I trust?"

"As rare as flying turtles," I replied.

She reached for my hand. I warmed at her tight grip, as if she were binding herself to my flesh. "So, we'll fight until we die, husband. And if I go first, I'll be waiting for you at the entrance to the Path of the Dead. I actually look forward to meeting Horned Serpent. He and I will have many things to discuss."

That brought a flicker of enjoyment to my souls. "Uh, he's not exactly warm, sympathetic, or compassionate—let alone a sparkling conversationalist. My last memory of him is one of abject terror. You know . . . the sort inspired by one's bones being crushed."

"And, after that, you still fear dying at the hands of the Kristianos?"

"Perspective again, correct?"

She squeezed my hand. "Only on occasion, my love." Her voice dropped. "At other times, watching you, I see something else."

"And that is?"

She gave a toss of her head. "I'm not sure, but it's not of this time and place—as though the Spirit World is seeing through your eyes. In those moments you are someone different, a stranger, unfathomable and unapproachable."

"When am I like that?"

She shot me a shadowed glance. "The last time? In Cafakke's palace, when you met Back-from-the-Dead. He started out as one of the most powerful priests alive, obviously scornful of anything you had to say. Then, all of a sudden, you changed, seemed to swell, your voice growing deeper, echoing as if out of a tunnel. He saw you as you are, Black Shell, and it frightened him. It changed everyone in the room."

"He never sent me my winnings from the chunkey game."

"He didn't have to. You'd already taken everything from him that you needed."

I stared with resignation at the dark trees around us. The evening gloom was deepening. I could hear the soft murmur of Timucua as the Orphans talked softly among themselves. Gnaw's tail was flipping back and forth, the white tip painting the dusk.

"Back-from-the-Dead's going to be trouble."

Pearl Hand rubbed her thumb on the back of my hand. "I know."

"He's got half the Apalachee fasting, turning their lives upside down to purify themselves—all in the belief that Spirit Power is going to make them invincible against Kristiano armor."

"They know no other way."

I raised her hand as I gestured my frustration. "But I explained it. Over and over. Why did they ask for our advice if not to hear what we've learned about the invader?"

"You can't change a lifetime with a single lecture."

"What if they can't figure it out, Pearl Hand?"

"Then the *Adelantado* will destroy them."

A new voice from the side said, "*That* remains to be seen, woman."

We looked over, startled. The dogs, too, were caught entirely by surprise given the direction of the breeze. They immediately began to bark.

Back-from-the-Dead seemed to float above the screen of holly, dogwood, and sumac off to our left. Then the first of his warrior escorts stepped out of the brush, followed by three of his assistants. Back-from-the-Dead rode on a litter chair, its poles resting on the shoulders of eight burly young men. The hilishaya fixed me with his otherworldly eyes, his expression reminiscent of someone who had just discovered something smelly and rude sticking to the bottom of his foot.

Back-from-the-Dead's voice slipped through the heavy air like a snake. "Trader, I can dismiss your scorn of me and my abilities. Your doubts about Power, however, are offensive. Fortunately the combined faith of the Apalachee people is mightier than your doubts . . . or the polluted arrogance of the invaders. I, Back-from-the-Dead, have sent my souls across the worlds to battle Spirit Beasts. Now I will face the invader . . . and destroy him."

A sick premonition rose in my stomach.

TEN

I WAS IN A SOUR MOOD AS WE FOLLOWED BACK-FROM-the-Dead and his retinue. The well-trodden trail we traveled wound along one of the streams. While rough and unwieldy for Back-from-the-Dead's litter bearers, the encroaching brush, vines, and overhanging trees provided excellent cover. From the looks of the fresh-cut stumps of saplings, the route had been recently widened and "improved" for easier travel. No wonder, given that the main trails now belonged to the Kristianos.

I cocked an eyebrow as I watched Back-from-the-Dead's lofty perch sway and lurch as his carriers negotiated a particularly treacherous section. You had to admire their balance and stamina as they bore their priest along a route more suited to deer than a wide litter. Sometimes hanging vines or low branches entailed lowering, twisting, and fancy maneuvering to get the litter and its occupant past the obstacle.

Where fallen trees had been laid across drainage channels, however, there was no other solution but for the chair to be lowered. Back-from-the-Dead would step off, walk serenely across the crude bridge, and wait while his men manhandled the litter chair across. When it was lowered on the other side, he'd carefully seat himself, arrange his apron and cloak, reset his headpiece, and with a gesture, be raised again to their shoulders.

"Can you see the tension in their faces?" Pearl Hand asked after one such crossing. "Those poor fellows are scared stiff. How'd you like to be the man who dropped the most Powerful priest in the world?"

"He's not the most Powerful priest in the world. Just the most powerful *Apalachee* priest. But, to your point, my bet is the guy who finally drops him will simply bow down, open a vein, and, as he dies, pray that Back-from-the-Dead won't curse his souls to eternal wandering."

"Why doesn't he walk?" Blood Thorn asked. "Being carried thus, along a trail like this, it smacks more of arrogant stupidity."

"You got the arrogant part right," I murmured.

"Part of maintaining authority is projecting an image," Pearl Hand replied. "He wants his people to believe he's going to beat de Soto with his Spirit Power. Maybe he needs to believe it himself."

I chewed my lip, then said, "I'd gratefully gift him with everything we own if I thought he could do it."

"Apalachee have strong Power," Wide Antler said. "We have often suspected they were sorcerers given the successes they had against us."

I met his solemn gaze. "No matter what his reputation,

our spooky friend is headed for a grave and life-changing disappointment."

"But, Peliqua—"

"I've looked Horned Serpent in the eyes, my friend. I have eaten from Old-Woman-Who-Never-Dies's pot. Shared her fire and—"

"Drove your peg into her daughter?" Pearl Hand interjected wryly.

"—heard her say this was a battle between men, not Spirit Powers." I was trying to make a point, but Pearl Hand's remark hit the Orphans with the impact of a thrown rock.

"Corn Woman?" Wide Antler asked. "You did *what* with Corn Woman?"

I winced, shooting an irritated glance at my wife. "I thought you weren't jealous of Spirit Beings."

She gave me a cool gaze. "I was—after a fashion—part of it, remember?"

Embarrassed, I struggled with that hot feeling at the base of my neck. Giving a slash of my hand, I growled, "This conversation is over. Come on. Our self-important hilishaya is vanishing into the forest, and we don't want to miss seeing how he's going to destroy de Soto."

I scampered my way across the latest bridge, watching to make sure the pack dogs followed without mishap. If Pearl Hand had slipped and tumbled into the muddy water below . . . ?

Well, just deserts and all.

All right. Perhaps not. One of the things I truly loved about her was that lack of humility, her wry ability to find humor when we were in desperate straits.

As we entered a stand of red and post oaks, the way

opened and we managed to make good time; the hilisha-ya's bearers almost moved at a trot. His priests apparently hadn't had much forest training; they made a lot of noise: their packs clattered, they talked loudly, and I was sure that they passed no stick they didn't snap with a poorly placed foot.

The escort warriors were unimpressed.

After one of the priests tripped over a mossy log and fell crashing through dry brush, I opined, "Well, if there's any saving grace to this, it's that the Kristianos aren't any better at reading the forest. Even if they heard, they wouldn't know what it means."

"We'd better hope," Blood Thorn replied, his attention on the dark gaps beneath the trees. "But then, perhaps his Power protects us?"

"Really?" I arched a skeptical eyebrow.

Blood Thorn snorted, following behind Pearl Hand as we trotted down the trail. "What do you expect to happen when we arrive at Anhaica, Black Shell? What is this thing de Soto is planning?"

"Something involving death and misery," I answered. "He knows no other way."

Pearl Hand agreed. "So true. But then neither does Back-from-the-Dead. He sincerely thinks Power will protect him."

"Somehow," I mused, "we have to find a way to dissuade him."

"And if we don't?"

"Then he's going to get a lot of people killed."

That night, in a thicket a couple of hands' hard run from Anhaica, we established camp in a grove of pines, chinquapins, and sassafrases. Pearl Hand had dug up some of the root from the latter, softening it with a stone hammer and setting it to boil as we prepared a supper of boiled corn, dried pawpaws, persimmons, and currants. Corn Thrower had killed a low-flying swan with a thrown stick. It now sizzled just above the coals.

Our camp was no more than fifty paces from Back-from-the-Dead's. We could hear them talking, occasionally laughing, and the gentle singing as the hilishaya blessed their food. The escort warriors, of necessity, had their own fire a stone's throw beyond the priests. Bound by ritual, both were following their prescribed behaviors when on the trail.

I kept glancing their way as I poked at the fire with a broken branch, stirring the coals, keeping the dripping swan's grease from catching fire and charring the bird. What was the purpose of ritual in a world turned insane by de Soto's abominations?

Pearl Hand hunched beside me, hair pulled back, her attention on the stew pot with its bubbling contents. The glow from the fire pit turned her smooth skin into glowing copper, accenting the hollows of her cheeks, gleaming from the angle of her jaw. I enjoyed the faint shadows it cast along the sides of her straight nose and how the light emphasized the sleek lines of her forehead. Pearl Hand just grew ever more beautiful. Were we to last a thousand years, I would never grow bored with her looks.

As if she felt my gaze, she tilted her head; an electric tingle ran through me as her dark eyes met mine and began to sparkle. Her lips curled into a smile, teeth shining.

"Want us to leave?" Blood Thorn interrupted my thoughts from across the fire.

"What's that?" I looked up. He and the rest of the Orphans ringed our fire, each grinning at Pearl Hand and me.

"We were feeling intrusive," Walking Thunder said dryly. "Like a grandmother staying too long at a newly-wed's house on the wedding night."

I narrowed an eye, ready to say something unkind, but Pearl Hand beat me to it. "When Black Shell and I reach the point where we're about to explode, we'll be the ones to leave. It's a cold night. You all will need the warmth." She gestured at the flames and gave them a pantherlike grin. "We'll have our own source of fire."

The Orphans laughed at that, nudging each other with elbows. Skipper lifted his head, his oddly colored eyes curious.

After we'd eaten and made our food offerings to the fire, Pearl Hand and the Timucua wended their way down to the dark creek to wash the cooking bowl and clean their greasy fingers.

I sipped at the sassafras tea remaining in my cup and studied Blood Thorn, who had remained behind nursing his own tea. His attention was fixed on the fire, the expression on his face wistful, distant, and pained.

"Does it ever bother you? Pearl Hand and me?"

A sad smile turned his lips. "No, my friend. Just the opposite. Seeing the two of you is a reminder that even now, with the monster loose among us and terrible suffering everywhere, love can flourish. But I wonder how you dare to love with such passion." He paused. "You know that none of us will live through this, Black Shell."

"Death motivates with remarkable ferocity."

Blood Thorn nodded, brooding at the fire.

He looked up. "So does hatred. What they did in Napetuca, and to the woman I loved . . . the way I was treated, and all those others they've brutally murdered . . ." He gestured futility. "Then we come here and find nothing but misery among the Apalachee. There are little things, too. You and the woman you love can never have the life you deserve. I see such things, and to my amazement, I can hate them even more. So I wonder, just where is the final limit of hate? Or does it go on, endless, like a great swelling flood?"

"Even a flood must eventually dissipate. There is only so much water on the earth. Only so much air."

He grunted absently, then said, "Hatred I can understand. I cannot, however, figure out the Kristianos."

"Figure them out how?"

"How can they be human?" He looked up. "Kristianos look for gold, true, but they remain oblivious to the misery and suffering they cause. This lack of comprehension defies reason. Even the most revenge-filled war party understands the pain and misery it inflicts upon captives: It is to repay them for their own suffering. But the Kristianos? They seem unconcerned."

He frowned at his hand, watching as he curled and extended his fingers, as if fascinated by their movement. "You took one captive once. This Antonio. What did he say? How did he explain what they are doing?"

I shrugged. "To them we are soulless, worthless things. Like wiping rags they can use until worn out, then dispose of."

"Perhaps. But until I can understand, my hatred will

continue to grow. And eventually, it will burst my skin like an overinflated bladder."

I nodded, wondering if my own would do the same.

"Trader?" one of the priests called from the darkness. "The hilishaya requests you to come."

"Excuse me," I told Blood Thorn, getting to my feet. "I am being summoned. Good little camp dog that I am."

Blood Thorn fingered his chin. "I wonder if he has the foggiest notion of how dangerous you really are, Black Shell."

"I hope not. And I would prefer to keep it that way." Only then did I realize that while I was making a joke, Blood Thorn certainly wasn't.

I turned, blinking, trying to adjust my vision to the darkness after being fire-blinded. Fortunately the path was flat.

I heard the stealthy padding of paws and glanced back, making out Squirm's white blaze and bib as he followed along behind me. I'd acquired him in a Yuchi town, so I warned him in that language. "Careful, old friend. You'd better hope they're not hungry for dog."

Or for a trader's soul, my internal voice cautioned.

I was led not to the priest's fire but back from there, into the darkly shadowed recesses under a spreading magnolia. My guide stopped, touching his forehead respectfully, saying, "The trader, as you requested." Then he turned and left.

I lowered my head, squinting at the blackness beneath the tree. Squirm stopped by my side and I could feel his tail whipping back and forth. Someone was certainly there.

"Sit," Back-from-the-Dead ordered in a wooden voice.

I bent, felt around, and lowered myself to the leaf mat. Then I pulled Squirm down beside me, relieved to have him close. Hopefully his senses would give me an edge if anyone came sneaking up.

"What can I do for you, Hilishaya?"

Silence stretched.

I was entertaining the notion of leaving when he said, "For generations my ancestors have lived with Power. It runs through the living like braids—strands of human and Spirit Power interlaced so thoroughly that they become one. And incredibly strong. My grandmother, herself a sorcerer and conjuror, caught me as I was born. A newborn's vision is foggy, unfocused, but I recall her expression as my slick body was expelled into her calloused hands. After she used a cloth to wipe my face, I looked into her knowing black eyes. She smiled, exposing that gap between her teeth, and said, 'You are a fine one. Filled with Power, boy. It runs through you like a thick rope.'"

My vision had adjusted. Back-from-the-Dead sat on his traveling chair, a darkness within the darkness.

He remembers being born?

Myself, I couldn't remember anything further back than the beating Uncle gave me for walking into the Women's House and dragging out Mother's menstrual cloths. I was only four at the time, but so strict is the male-female taboo among my Chicaza that only after I'd been washed, ritually smoked, scrubbed with button snakeroot, and painted white did Uncle dare to take a willow switch to my young hide. Believe me, it worked. I've never set foot in the Women's House again—and never, but never, touched a menstrual rag.

As I petted Squirm's long head, Back-from-the-Dead

continued. "In the memory of the people, no one advanced through the training as fast as I did. Grandfather and father agreed that I was ready for initiation at the age of six. At six, you hear? Why? Because I knew the sacred healing roots, could tell them apart by sight, smell, and taste. When the holy words were spoken, they became part of my souls, locked away as if kept in a pot. When I needed them, I had only to reach into that soul pot and pull them out again."

I waited as the breeze rattled the waxy leaves over my head.

"I was seven when I cured a woman who was dying. From the smell of her urine, I recognized the type of witchery used to make her sick. With a sucking tube I removed the bit of vulture bone that had been shot into her. It caused her to bleed from the sheath."

"She was lucky to have such a skilled healer," I said diplomatically, and wondered why he'd called me here.

Perhaps to settle his debt from the chunkey game? Okay, maybe not.

He said, "The first time I sent my souls to the Underworld, I was eight. My training allowed me to avoid the traps. Once, while diving, I saw the Piasa, watched him swim obliviously past, his wings beating."

Wait till he grabs you by the neck. At the memory I rubbed my throat. "He always seems to be waiting when I show up."

He ignored me. "I have flown to the Sky World. Taking the form of an eagle, I have ridden the winds to look down upon the land."

"Hilishaya, I've been to these places. Old-Woman-Who-Never-Dies made me supper and healed the disease I'd caught from the Kristianos. Her daughter, Corn

Woman, took me to her bed and, well, you wouldn't believe how *that* turned out. In the Sky World I was eaten by Horned Serpent and apparently shit out at the edge of a muddy lake outside Napetuca. In short, you aren't impressing me."

He was silent, and I could imagine the expression on his tattooed face.

Finally, he said, "On the day the Kristianos try to teach us our lesson, I am going to walk into Anhaica and defeat them. Not drive them out, not sicken them, but kill them. Do you understand?"

I pursed my lips, trying to stare through the darkness. "All right. But if I were you, I'd try to witch them from a *long* way away."

"I have walked unseen among our enemies. Among all the Apalachee, no one can recall a hilishaya as powerful as me."

"Did you hear what I said about keeping your distance?"

"The skepticism of foreigners is not my concern. I *know* the Kristianos can't hurt me. I've used Power to kill people before, many of them accomplished sorcerers. This time—"

"You'll be dead before you make it to the city gates. Or worse, a captive."

He laughed, the idea clearly amusing. "My body shall be invisible to them. Wrapped in Power, I walked through the middle of a Tuskaloosa war party. Only when I appeared before Tuskaloosa himself did I drop the Power."

"Kristianos aren't Mos'kogee. They're not Albaamaha, Hichiti, or Koasati. They don't have the same Power. Ours doesn't work on them, theirs doesn't work on us. It's different."

"Enlighten me, Trader."

"As best I can figure, it all comes out even. Like two trees of equal weight that fall to lean against each other."

"One will eventually rot out at the bottom and topple to the other."

His words were sobering. "That's literally the root of this entire battle, Hilishaya. The strength in our tree must come from our faith in ourselves. It's only when we lose it that the rot begins."

I felt rather than saw his smile. "Perhaps. But they come with lures, things to drag us away from our ways. Their metal chisels, cooking pots, colorful beads, needles, and knives, all these things tempt us, lead us to covet."

"You need not explain that to a trader." I rested my chin on my fist. "But if you try to fight them directly with Spirit Power, you will lose."

"Your lack of faith disturbs me."

"Faith has nothing to do with it. I've been told, face-to-face, that this is a war between men. Not Powers. I can't be more blunt."

I could feel the intensity of his gaze. We waited a long time; Squirm finally settled his nose on his paw and went to sleep.

"Black Shell, why do you oppose me? What difference will it make if I try?"

"A great deal, if they kill you."

"I have already died many times. I have no fear."

"It's not you I'm thinking about."

"Oh?"

"How will the people react when their greatest hili-shaya is killed by Kristianos?"

He didn't reply.

"Your death would be a blow to their hearts and souls. They would ask, 'How can we fight an enemy Powerful enough to kill our most holy priest?' And their will to resist will drain away like water through sand."

"When I walk out, the Kristianos will not see me. The Power I wrap around me will deflect their arrows and lances. My song will carry me unseen to the center of them, and once there I shall call down a tornado. With its mighty winds I will break them, sweeping the ground of Anhaica clean of their pollution."

I took a deep breath, smiling wearily. "Hilishaya, since you haven't heard a word I've said, I might as well go back to my camp and get some sleep."

I prodded Squirm awake and stood.

"Black Shell, what would you take in trade for your medicine pouch?"

The request stopped me cold. I could feel the sepaya begin to warm through its bag. In reply I snapped: "I was being eaten, *priest*. In my terror I grabbed on to the brow tine of Horned Serpent's antler. I remember the feel of it breaking off. One doesn't trade a Power object like that. Not for any price."

"Yet you say that Power doesn't matter when it comes to Kristianos."

"The sepaya matters to me."

"I could order you killed and obtain it that way."

That sent a chill down my back. "I serve Horned Serpent. How do you think he would react?"

Back-from-the-Dead sighed. "Forgive me. That night in the high minko's, I felt the horn's Power. When we played chunkey, it allowed you to win. When I walk out to do battle with the Kristianos, it could be the deciding factor."

"Hilishaya, I don't—"

"My people are depending on me. You, and your Orphans, need me to win. It's not just the Apalachee but all peoples who hang in the balance. The future, thousands of lives, our very existence, depends on what happens when I walk out to face them."

"If I thought you had the faintest chance—"

"I am begging you, Black Shell. Pleading. At least let me borrow it."

I reached up, clasping my hand around the leather. I could feel the bit of red horn quivering like an anxious mouse.

"I'm sorry, Hilishaya. You'll have to get your own sepaya."

"If I fail, it will be upon your head. My souls will be waiting for yours in the Land of the Dead. There, Black Shell, you shall face not only me, but your ancestors as well. How will you explain that based on pride, you allowed the world to be butchered?"

His words cut like a chert knife. I reached up again, on the verge of removing the thong from my neck.

"Sorry, Hilishaya."

I turned, making my way back through the dark. My only comfort was the sound of Squirm's padded feet on the fallen leaves behind me.

Meanwhile, the sepaya seemed to burn through the leather sack.

ELEVEN

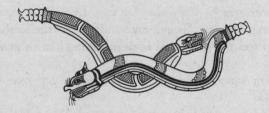

THE BROKEN COUNTRY AROUND ANHAICA LITERALLY teemed with Apalachee warriors. In ones and twos, fours and sixes, they riddled the country like worms in a sack of acorn flour. Patches of timber, the sinuous but brushy stream banks, and shrubby thickets hid them from the Kristianos. Like cunning foxes they slipped through the understory, ghosted along deer trails, and peered out from beneath the hanging vines of grape, honeysuckle, and greenbrier. Individuals perched in tall trees, their forms obscured by streamers of hanging moss and patterns of branches. They waded up streams, leaving no tracks.

But let a Kristiano drop his guard—perhaps stepping behind a bush to lower his pants and squat—and an arrow would seemingly fly out of nowhere. More than one ran screaming, trying to hold up his pants, a feathered shaft protruding from his pale white bottom.

Often they'd lose track of themselves while plucking fruits. A man need only wander from his companions' sight for a moment. In that instant he might have the slightest warning as an arrow hissed in his direction. Most weren't aware until a sharp Apalachee point sliced through their skin or thunked into their armor.

Even the large, heavily armored columns, moving where they would with impunity, suffered a constant irritation of arrows. They need but pass a screen of brush, a tangle of wood, or a copse of trees, and an Apalachee or two would take his time, pick his target, and loose an arrow. Most shots were completely ineffective, stopped cold by armor, clanging off a helmet, or rattling off a shield.

But we could see it: a subtle change in the Kristianos' expressions. After Napetuca, unbridled arrogance had burned behind their eyes. A smirk had hovered around their lips. They'd half slouched in the saddle, disdainful of the crushed and scattered Uzachile. Thus, too, had they clumped their way into Apalachee.

But that had been months ago.

The change was in the furtive darting of their eyes as they tried to mask anxiety. Now their mouths were drawn thin, lines deepening in faces pulled tight. They rode warily, backs straight, shields close against their bodies, heads swiveling as they searched for the ever-present threat.

For Pearl Hand and me, seeing them so brought the tingling sense of hope. Here, for the first time, we could see proof that perhaps in the end we might actually win. Assuming they stayed in Apalachee and tried to fight it out.

Come spring, their dwindling supply of slaves would have to take to the fields, clearing, hoeing, and planting. When they did, the Apalachee would be there. They'd free those they could, kill those they couldn't. And in the end, unless the Kristianos patrolled field after field, come the fall harvest, they'd have no crop.

At least, it would be that way assuming that another couple of thousand Kristianos didn't arrive in their floating palaces. Were that to happen, the end might be just as sure, but the time needed to achieve it could well stretch into years.

I considered this as we—and the hilishaya—were led to Tastanaki Fire Falcon's camp deep inside a briar patch of raspberry, thorny walking stick, and rosebushes. The place was a tumble of old, rotting trees uprooted by either a tornado or a hurricane and completely impassable to a cabayo. Nor could soldados storm the dense thicket with its narrow winding trails. Their armor and weapons would snag on the brush, the stickers catching their cloth garments. By the time they blundered their way into the depths, Fire Falcon's stealthy warriors would have ample notice to melt away.

To our amusement, Back-from-the-Dead's porters were unable to bear his elevated chair into the mess. Despite numerous attempts, the hilishaya finally gave up in despair, ordered the thing hidden, and began the ticklish passage of snags and thorns on his own two feet.

We followed behind the rest, stepping over logs, enduring scratches on our bare arms and legs. The dogs panted as they clambered over deadfall, crashed through branches, and ducked beneath vines.

In a central area—no more than a bow-shot across—Fire Falcon's warriors had erected lean-tos and ramadas.

Fire pits were dug deeply into the ground to mask their glow. A single trail led down to the creek three bow-shots distant where water could be procured. And in the rear a towering beech tree provided scouts with an unimpeded view of the approaches—and best of all, Anhaica in the distance.

As we emerged, warriors rose, touching their foreheads respectfully and dropping to their knees, palms out. Back-from-the-Dead strode forward, head up, as though he were the high mikko himself. Fire Falcon waited under one of the ramadas. As the tishu mikko, he made no obeisance, but met Back-from-the-Dead as an equal.

The area had been beaten down, and while it was criss-crossed with logs, cramped camping space was available.

We watched as Back-from-the-Dead was received, given a seat in the warm winter sun, and offered food and drink.

Meanwhile we unpacked the dogs, chopped out some of the more offensive prickly bits, and raided the food packs. Blood Thorn immediately began to excavate a fire pit, following the example of the nearby Apalachee.

Of course the arrival of the Orphans created a sensation. Pearl Hand and I were continually translating as different warriors introduced themselves to the Orphans. Most had never even seen a living Uzachile warrior before, let alone one admitted to a war camp.

More than a hand of time later, Fire Falcon picked his way to our corner of the camp and squatted, hands resting on his knees. Whatever his actual thoughts concerning the Uzachile, his expression remained controlled.

"Welcome to our camp. I am pleased to see that you made it without trouble." He glanced around. "The accommodations are nowhere near as pleasant as Cane Place town's, but it's the best we can do."

I gave a polite nod. "We'll take security over comfort any day, Tishu Mikko. What is the situation with the Kristianos? Any new developments?"

He smiled thinly. "I heard that Iniha Blood Thorn killed a couple of cabayos the other day. For that we honor him." He touched his chin in a sign of homage.

I translated to Blood Thorn.

"I was honored to do so," Blood Thorn replied, touching his forehead in a sign of even greater respect.

Fire Falcon stood, hands on hips, looking off toward Anhaica. "As to the Kristianos, there's not much to report. Several of their scouting columns have returned; others are still beyond our borders to the west and north. The pile of dead slaves is taller, and the *puercos* that feed on them even fatter. Oddly, however, the Kristianos are stacking up strange piles of wood here and there outside the city. We can't make sense of it. They erect a single wooden pole, and around it the wood is piled. Have you ever seen that before?"

I glanced at Pearl Hand and she shook her head. "New construction?"

Fire Falcon looked perplexed. "Some of our people have slipped up at night and inspected the wood. Much of it is old, pithy, not much good for anything. The rest seems to be the charred wreckage cleared out from the structures we've managed to burn inside the palisade."

"Signal fires?" I guessed.

"To whom?"

I glanced at the towering beech tree. "Can we see them from up there?"

He followed my gaze. "Please take a look. See if you can figure it out."

Pearl Hand and I followed the trail to the smooth-barked trunk. A pole ladder had been placed to allow access to the lowest branches. It was a one-at-a-time affair and wobbled and bobbed as I climbed to the first of the limbs. Then I waited as Pearl Hand followed.

From there we worked up branch by branch, careful of slipping on the shiny-smooth silver-gray bark. Near the top we encountered a young warrior perched atop a pole platform spanning a vee in the branches. Hanging moss had been draped to camouflage the location, the poles tied securely to keep them from shifting.

"Greetings," he called softly. "Welcome to the land of the eagles. I'm Sharp Nose, of the Deer Clan, White Moiety."

"Black Shell, of the Chicaza. This is my wife, Pearl Hand, of the Chicora."

He studied us curiously. "From the Orphans?"

"That's us," Pearl Hand told him with a smile. "The tishu mikko asked us to take a look at Anhaica, perhaps to figure out what the Kristianos are doing."

He squinted off into the distance. "So far today they are staying pretty close to home. I've seen slaves guarded by other slaves go for water. The cabayos are being herded over on the other side of the palisade. For a while, when the wind was right, I could hear someone chopping wood and caught a whiff of smoke. I think they're cooking deer. That or my wishful stomach is making up things."

I chuckled and turned. Bracing myself on the branch, I took a moment to orient myself. The country spread out like a map. Fire Falcon's briar patch lay at the confluence of three brush-choked streams, the channel they formed draining off to the southwest. Most of the uplands consisted of cleared farmland with patches of brush and nut-bearing trees around scattered farmsteads. These were obviously abandoned and looked forlorn. Many had been pulled down, possibly for building materials to use in the city.

And there, a couple of hands' run to the northwest, lay Anhaica. The surrounding fields had been burned off, leaving the approaches cleared of cover. Behind the char, Anhaica's bastioned palisade appeared like a rickety stick fence. Over the distance I could make out the tiny shapes of guards atop the bastions. Their helmets winked silver in the afternoon light.

"Where are the woodpiles?" Pearl Hand said. "Wait, I see."

She pointed and I followed her finger to what looked like a little dimple across the distance. Then I located another, and another. Four of them, equidistant, perhaps a bow-shot from the palisade. "Some kind of shelter?"

She shook her head. "What kind of shelter would you make with a single standing pole? Even a lean-to needs two uprights and a crosspiece."

Sharp Nose added, "Not a shelter. And the wood's all mixed up, including crooked pieces, broken and half-burned poles. It's just junk if you ask me. I've sneaked close at night to see."

"That takes us back to a signal fire," I muttered, half to myself.

"Then they are signaling in all directions," Sharp Nose said. "There are two more that you can't see on the other side of Anhaica."

Pearl Hand looked thoughtful. "Maybe they're to provide defensive light in case of night attacks. Archers and thunder-stick men have to see their targets. The woodpiles are just in range of the palisades."

"Then who's going to light them?" Sharp Nose asked. "They don't leave guards on them at night. And yes, there's kindling there, so they wouldn't be that hard to light. But when we make a night attack, we don't exactly shout out that we're coming beforehand. The whole idea is to catch them by surprise."

Pearl Hand frowned. "So they'd have to be manned from sunset to sunrise every night."

"And if they were," Sharp Nose replied, "one of us would sneak up close in the dark. A lone Kristiano is a dead one. It's just a matter of time."

"Wait, what's this?" I pointed.

Ten cabayos, walking side by side, emerged from Anhaica's eastern gate. Behind them marched parallel ranks of soldados: some spear-ax men, a couple of thunder-stick shooters, and a single captive. This poor individual was bound at the wrists, a chain running from the collar on his neck to one of the cabayos. If the cabayero put spurs to his beast, the collar would snap the man's neck when he hit the end.

For a hand's time we watched as they wound their way in our general direction. For a time they would disappear behind trees or into a swale, only to reappear that much closer. No effort was made to hide their travel, nor did they venture anywhere close to cover, but seemed to pick their path along the high ground.

Finally, atop one of the hills—completely visible from all directions—they stopped. The clear sound of a horn could be heard, the sweet note rising and falling on the cool winter air.

The sound of a Kristiano horn couldn't be mistaken. No conch horn could approach that tone. But why blow it? Obviously it was a signal; but to whom? Scanning the country, I could see no formation of Kristianos waiting to spring a trap as they had at Napetuca. Nor was a single Apalachee warrior visible anywhere.

The soldados formed a hollow box, facing out. The captive remained inside. Two of the cabayeros dismounted; one removed an ax from his saddle, and I stiffened. Even across the distance I knew that thin build, the way he moved in that oversized armor. I could imagine his hatchet face, the straggles of beard around his pursed lips, the anger buried behind his eyes.

"Blood and pus!" I growled.

"Antonio," Pearl Hand said in agreement. "Even from this distance you can't mistake him."

"Makes you wish we were closer, doesn't it?"

"You'd never get past the cabayos before they skewered you and sliced your hide into thongs."

"Maybe he'll do something stupid again."

Sharp Nose sounded skeptical. "You know that Kristiano?"

"Captured him once down in the peninsula," Pearl Hand replied. "He's not much to look at, but he has a particularly brutal approach to life."

"We killed his father in an ambush just south of Uzachile town last fall. Antonio turned tail and ran, but Pearl Hand managed to send him off with an arrow protruding from his belly."

"We were hoping it had gone deep enough to pink his

gut and kill him when his juice turned rotten. Apparently it didn't."

"No matter how noble the cause, a bit of hail falls on us all," I said sourly. "What's he doing?"

As the eight mounted cabayeros rode sweeps around the box of watchful soldados, Antonio and his companion approached the captive. Across the distance, it was hard to tell, but it seemed like Antonio struck the man, knocking him down. Again the horn sounded, a portent of something terrible.

One of the soldados stepped forward and, at a signal from Antonio, tied something around the man's right leg, then the left. He did something similar with both arms above the elbows.

Puzzled, I watched as Antonio lifted the ax, swinging it in an arc that intersected the captive's leg. Then he cocked his head, as if studying his handiwork.

A bloodcurdling scream carried faintly to us.

"What are they doing?" Sharp Nose asked, rising warily on his perch.

In the distance, Antonio's ax rose and fell again. A breath later, a second scream came. And then again, and again, each eliciting a gut-twisting shriek of agony.

Antonio gestured to the soldado. The man wrenched the captive's arms over his head, pinning the bound wrists to the ground. The ax flashed once, twice, and then Antonio stepped back, the ax crosswise before him. It was hard to tell, given the distance, but he seemed to look right at us.

A faintly barked command carried to our high perch, and we watched as Antonio and his partner mounted. The lilting call of the horn came again. Tugging on the control straps, Antonio and his companion circled their cabayos around the square of soldados and rejoined the other riders.

The soldados re-formed their ranks, tramping off in pursuit, not a one of them looking back at the remains of the man lying on his back.

Yes, it was far away. And it could have been a trick of the slanting pale winter light, but even so, I could see the legs and arms. They'd been severed at the knees and elbows.

All that remained were the wrenching screams, wavering in the afternoon air.

Just after dusk we were cooking our evening meal and discussing what we'd seen. No one had any idea about the odd woodpiles that concerned Fire Falcon. Nor did the mutilation of the captive make sense. Surely he would have immediately bled out—dead before Antonio could re-form his ranks.

"Why march him all the way out to a lonely hilltop?" Blood Thorn mused. "When I was captive and anyone did anything, they assembled us to watch the person's execution. It's not like the Kristianos to waste a death. Especially if there's no one to see it."

"But we did see it," Pearl Hand replied. "After they blew that horn, every set of eyes in the country was fixed on that hilltop."

"What do they want to teach us?" Bear Paw asked. "We're already dedicated to killing every last one of them."

"Is it a warning?" Blood Thorn wondered. "'This will happen to you if we catch you'?"

"They certainly won't get me alive." Wide Antler's

gleaming dark eyes fixed on the glowing walls of the fire pit.

"I hadn't planned on being taken alive either," Blood Thorn said dryly. "Sometimes it doesn't work out the way you planned."

"For me either," I added, shooting a grateful glance at Pearl Hand. "It's a risk we take."

Blood Thorn nodded, absently rubbing his hands together. "I've been thinking of obtaining a small gourd of water hemlock. Something to be hung around the neck so that if capture seemed certain I could pull the plug out and gulp it down."

"Not a good way to die." Pearl Hand's expression went grim. "I've seen it. And what if you don't get enough of a dose?"

"They'd kill me anyway." Blood Thorn's calloused and dry hands made a soft shushing as he rubbed them. "As soon as the convulsions began, they'd chop my head off."

"You sure?" I asked.

He continued rubbing his hands. "Twice while I was with them I saw women go into fits. Both times the Kristianos panicked. They started calling out '*diablo*' and '*bruja.*' You should have seen the fear in their eyes. I'll tell you, they didn't waste any time killing those poor women. They had other slaves carry their corpses out of camp. And I mean right now. Then their priests came and splashed water around. They carried those long-stemmed crosses and muttered some chant under their breath as they did."

"So, water hemlock might be a good idea," Wide Antler mused. "We'll have to find the right kind of healer, that or a medicine elder." He looked at me. "Peliqua? Do you ever carry it in your trade?"

"No!" I told him flatly. "I won't take chances with the stuff. If even a little spilled in the packs . . ." I sighed, giving it up. "What you do is up to you. But if you make that decision, be very careful about the container you put it in."

"A gourd?" Blood Thorn asked.

"Better than any kind of ceramic jar," I said in agreement. "And even then I'd seal the insides with a thick coating of wax first."

"And glue the stopper fast with pine pitch," Pearl Hand added. "Lots of it. Just so there are no accidents."

At that moment a low call—"Mikko! We're here"—sounded from the brush. Apalachee warriors rose from their fires, glancing toward the western trail.

Fire Falcon rose from where he sat in conversation with Back-from-the-Dead and a couple of nicoquadca. He made his way to the trail head and greeted men as they emerged from the brush.

In the gloom I could make out something heavy and long swaying from poles they carried between them. Their burden might have been a deer carcass suspended in netting.

Fire Falcon directed the men toward his fire, and I gestured for the Orphans to stay as I followed the crowd of warriors in their wake.

With utmost care the burden was lowered before Fire Falcon's hearth. As it touched the ground, a pain-filled whimpering could be heard.

As the netting parted my stomach cramped, a sick sensation at the back of my throat. To ward it off, I gritted my teeth in frustration.

In the faint light I could see the thick ropes, sunk deep

in the flesh, that had been tied above the elbows and bit deeply into the thighs just above the knees. The limbs ended in bloody stumps.

So, you didn't die. They'd tied off his arms and legs so tightly he couldn't bleed out.

The image of Antonio and the swinging ax replayed in the eye of my souls. If only it were possible to go back in time. I'd had Antonio but a pace away as I stared down my drawn arrow. My beloved dog Fetch lay dying beside me. And I'd allowed Pearl Hand to stay my release.

If I'd known then, Antonio, you'd be long gone to your accursed paraíso. And so many others would have avoided the misery you inflicted upon them.

"Tastanaki?" the maimed man rasped.

"I'm here." Fire Falcon knelt on the spread netting. "Do not strain yourself. The great hilishaya himself is here and will heal you."

"No, Tastanaki. With respect, I ask that you simply carry me out and leave me somewhere, perhaps for a bear to find, or float me into an alligator's pool."

"Make no such choices when newly wounded."

"I will not live like this. I am Fine Shell, of the Wind Clan, White Moiety. A tascaia. My Power is obviously broken. Otherwise they would not have captured me. They would not have placed a metal collar about my neck and worked me like a common slave. I would not have been chosen to be ruined and bear you this one last message."

"What message is that, Tascaia?"

Fine Shell swallowed hard. "I was told to tell you: Stop the attacks. You have been warned before. The attacks did not stop. Now the *Adelantado* says that you have forced him to do something. He says it is your fault, the fault of all those who continue to resist."

"What is?"

"At high sun tomorrow"—Fine Shell took a deep breath—"he will do something terrible."

"What?"

"I couldn't understand what those filthy beasts were saying. A man can make more sense out of the cooing of pigeons. But they are laughing about it. I know they are hoping that you will be so outraged that you will attack."

"Did they tell you that? That they wanted us to attack?"

"No. They talk through a line of translators. One of the Kristianos speaks to one called Ortiz, who speaks to a Timucua, who speaks to an Uzachile, who speaks to me in the Apalachee tongue. The Timucua, a man from far down south, he told the Uzachile to tell me."

"He had a wooden cross upon his chest?" I asked from the side. "A tall man, with starburst tattoos on his chest?"

"Yes."

All eyes turned my direction. "But Ortiz didn't tell him to say we should attack?"

"No." Fine Shell's eyes flickered, as if his focus was growing fuzzy. "It's as though the Timucua wanted me to get mad. He told the Uzachile to tell me that all Apalachee are weak as children and that tomorrow we would watch, and then we would run cowering. To tell my chief that."

"But Ortiz didn't," I mused.

"What does that mean?" Fire Falcon asked. "You know this Ortiz?"

"He's de Soto's translator. The Southern Timucua we know as 'Ears' because he used to have a trophy necklace made of them. When he was given to de Soto by his chief, he adopted the Kristiano religion and became their servant."

"Then why is he trying to goad us into an attack?" Fire Falcon asked.

"Because he's a fool," Pearl Hand said from behind me. "Understand this: Whatever de Soto is planning for tomorrow, he's hoping that you will attack and that he can unleash his forces to achieve a decisive victory and replenish his slaves."

"How do you know this?" Fire Falcon demanded.

I replied, "Because Ears is so desperate to make it happen that he dared to bait Fine Shell in defiance of Ortiz. Ears thinks that by insulting the Apalachee you will lose all sense and do something stupid."

"He is mistaken." Fire Falcon sank back on his haunches. "Fine Shell, what is going to happen tomorrow?"

The ruined warrior swallowed hard, the stubs of his severed limbs twitching. "I don't know, Tastanaki. Something bad. Before I was chosen to give you the message, they were separating the slaves, taking the sickest and the troublemakers and chaining them together. I was to tell you that if you do not leave in peace, what you see tomorrow will be repeated over and over." His expression twisted in pain. "And as they did to me, they shall continue to do to any warrior they capture. They say it is your decision."

Fire Falcon pursed his lips, thinking. I could see Back-from-the-Dead standing just under the ramada, listening carefully. Now he stepped out, saying, "You need not worry, Tishu Mikko. After tomorrow the Kristianos will no longer be a threat."

I was taking a breath to object when my wife laid a hand on my shoulder, whispering, "Forget it, husband. You will be wasting air in a useless dispute. Come, let's go eat and consider."

I let her lead me away, my thoughts on Singing Tail, Fine Shell, and all the others who would follow. Hernando de Soto had no concept of how Apalachee thought, how their sense of honor worked. He assumed that by maiming captives, he would frighten anyone from making an attack. Instead, all he did was encourage warriors to test their Power, to see if they were the blessed ones who could carry the battle to the enemy.

Like Back-from-the-Dead, who sincerely believed that he was going to marshal Power into his hands and use it to blast the very soul right out of each Kristiano's breast.

And what are you going to do about it, Black Shell? Just let the arrogant fool march out and be killed? And if you let their hilishaya die, the Apalachee will erode away like sand in a hard rain.

TWELVE

"BLACK SHELL?" THE SOFT VOICE BARELY PENETRATED.

"Black Shell? Wake up."

I blinked, aware of darkness, the chirping of crickets, and the distant hoot of an owl.

"Try not to wake Pearl Hand. Nothing's wrong. I just need to see you."

Somehow my sleep-fogged mind managed to place Tishu Mikko Fire Falcon's voice. I carefully slithered away from Pearl Hand's warm body and crawled out from the blanket. Chill caressed my skin, and I reached around to locate my hunting shirt and cloak.

"Tishu Mikko? What do you want?"

"Come with me."

I stared at where his dark shape hunched against the faint glow of false dawn. "Come where?"

"That's an order, Trader." He stood, pointing off to the

south. "Take your weapons with you. One of my people will explain to your wife and the rest if you are not back by the time they awake."

I muttered to myself, pulling on my shirt and draping my cloak around my shoulders. Grabbing up my quiver and Caddo bow, I carefully followed in his footsteps as we picked our way across his camp and then down the trail that led to the creek.

Trying to thread our way through that mess in near pitch-black was no fun.

I barely ducked as a branch flipped back after his passage. "What are we doing, Tishu Mikko?"

"Perhaps saving the world."

"Of course."

"Careful of this fallen log. It's slick with dew."

"Why are we out here?"

"The hilishaya wishes to see you."

"The answer is no."

"You haven't heard the question yet."

"I have. He just hasn't heard the answer."

Fire Falcon sighed. "Myself, Trader, I don't know what to believe. My heart tells me that the hilishaya will conjure Power. He will gather it about him and unleash it against the invaders. Afterward, once they are weakened by Spirit Power, we will finally crush them once and for all."

He hesitated, ducking a thorny vine. "We know these things in our hearts because we know the stories of the Beginning Times; we've seen the hilishaya conjure, heal, and bless. These things are our truths, and if they do not work for us now, what is left?"

"Ourselves, Tishu Mikko. Our strength and faith in our

ability to finally beat the Kristianos through intelligence, skill, and courage."

"Then . . . what? Spirit Power is meaningless? Is their wooden cross more potent than white and red Power? Is that what you're saying?"

"Blood and muck, no! I've *been* to the Spirit World, seen Horned Serpent. He's *real*. It's all real. Here's what I think is happening: The Spirits the Kristianos believe in, this *dios-jesucristo* of theirs, and this *paraíso,* along with their wooden cross and gold cup, these things balance our Power. Like the red balances the white, neither dominant, but each different. One cannot destroy the other any more than light can destroy dark or earth can destroy water."

"Then you think the Kristiano Spirits are part of the Spirit World?"

"Part of a *different* Spirit World," I replied. "One that exists in another place, separate from ours."

"But they have brought it here?"

I shrugged, tripping over a tangle of honeysuckle. "Perhaps. I don't know. Were we to travel to their world, would red and white Power accompany us? Infect their Power? Who knows? These aren't things traders are taught to understand."

"Unfortunately, they are not the province of mikkos, either." He stepped out onto a sloping bank beneath overarching trees. I could make out the black lace of branches against the brightening sky. The stars were fading.

A fire burned just to the left, wood popping and sending up sparks. Fire Falcon stopped just shy of an upright stick. Twisted into the soil, it stood, a falcon feather hung by a thong from its top. I could see the shaft had been painted, but the light was too poor to tell the color.

Down by the water I could just make out another and realized what I was seeing: Sacred ground had been marked off. These were boundary sticks marking the eastern extent of the holy enclosure. Off to the west, beyond the fire and what I now discerned as a sweat lodge, would be two more sticks, forming a square.

Seated around the sweat lodge were the hilishaya's assistants and the litter carriers. I could hear the soft cadence of voices as they prayed.

Even as Fire Falcon and I watched, the flap was thrown back on the sweat lodge and Back-from-the-Dead emerged, his naked body wet and shining in the firelight. Without a glance our way, he lifted his arms high, walking, head tilted back, his voice raised in song.

The sepaya on my chest began to throb.

In unison, Fire Falcon and I dropped to our knees, heads bowed, hands offered palm up. Belief is as much a part of us as the heart, liver, or lungs. It flows through us as does our blood. We are Mos'kogee right down to the bone, and Powerful medicine was being made before us. I could feel it, thick in the air, an almost electrical prickling of the skin. I'd felt the same just before the Sky Beings pitched lightning at a high peak.

The sepaya on my chest began to vibrate.

Water splashed as Back-from-the-Dead bathed in the stream. Hilishayas never let sweat dry on their skin. Rather, they let water wash it away, leaving them even more pure.

In the increasing light, I watched as Back-from-the-Dead emerged from the creek, water sluicing down his lean body. Just within the boundary of the sacred ground, a large shell bowl had been set on a square of fabric. I could just make out the slender piece of cane resting on the cloth beside the bowl.

Here Back-from-the-Dead stopped and knelt. He began to sing, lifting the painted cane tube. Then, placing it to his lips, he inserted one end into the liquid-filled bowl and began to blow. A hilishaya used his specially blessed medicine stick thus to insert Power words into medicine brews.

I cleared my thoughts, seeking peace and purity out of respect for the solemnity of what Back-from-the-Dead was doing. The sepaya's heat began to warm my breast.

Finished, Back-from-the-Dead began cupping up water and rubbing it over his face, head, neck, and chest. He proceeded to slick down his arms, then his belly. The bowl was lifted and poured over his back. Setting it down, he scrubbed his genitals and then worked down the legs, ending at the feet.

"Red root," I murmured. The Spirit root was carefully collected, prayed to, then chewed to loosen the fibers. Finally it was boiled according to ritual, in water from a special spring.

Back-from-the-Dead retrieved his medicine stick and walked up to the fire, where his carriers and assistants sat in two rows. As he passed between them, each man raised his arms, calling out a Power blessing.

At the edge of the fire I could make out a large whelk-shell cup. The smooth white exterior had been engraved but I was too far away to determine the design.

Back-from-the-Dead lifted the cup high, firelight bronzing his muscular body, illuminating the tattoos that wound up and down his limbs and across his belly.

"Giver of Breath and Life," he called to the heavens,

"hear my plea. In the name of the three worlds, I call on you. In the name of light and darkness, in the name of the Sky World and Underworld, I call on you. In the name of the plants and animals, I call on you. In the name of the ancestors and those unborn, I call on you. In the name of the white and red Powers, and all things, I call on you."

He placed the shell cup's rim to his mouth, drinking, his eyes still on the graying heavens.

Only when the cup of black drink was empty did he lower it, crying, "Give me Power. Help me to destroy the abomination!"

Then he turned, bent, and began to vomit. After the last of the black drink had spewed onto the ground between the lines of his assistants, he turned. I saw him toss a bundle of something into the fire. As a great billowing puff of red smoke arose he stepped straight into the center of the flames.

And vanished.

For long moments we waited, all eyes locked on the fire as the smoke began to dissipate. Even as I watched, it was apparent that no man stood among the burning embers—not that anyone could have withstood that kind of heat.

The rows of assistants remained where they were, singing prayers, their hands extended toward the sky.

I shot a look at Fire Falcon, seeing the awe and confusion in his face. The sepaya jerked back and forth on its thong.

"Why did you bring me here, Tishu Mikko?"

Fire Falcon blinked, confused, and swallowed hard. "Because . . . Because . . ."

"Because I asked him to," Back-from-the-Dead said behind me.

I whirled, struggling to my feet. Where he had been naked, now a brilliant red breechcloth sporting a spotless white apron graced his hips. A cloak of cardinal feathers hung from his shoulders past his knees. His face was painted red and black, while a tall copper headpiece in the shape of a falcon pinned his tight hair bun. White swan's feathers— like a sunburst—protruded from behind the headpiece.

Then my eyes fixed on the long copper mace clutched in his hands. The design was what we call a turkey tail, and the thing was polished to a shine. The length of my arm, it was obviously heavy.

He smiled tiredly, noting my fascination with the macc. "It is old, Black Shell, dating to the foundation of the Apalachee Nation. Some say it was carried by our ancestors from Cahokia itself, a gift from the god emperor to the first of our hilishaya."

"Why am I here?" I felt confused, my souls loose and adrift.

"I *need* your sepaya. I cannot win today unless I bear its Power. Do you understand? Horned Serpent's Power, mixed with all the rest, will enable me to prevail. By tonight, the invader's magic will be broken."

Reflexively I reached up and gripped the leather pouch, which seemed to burn like an ember. Numb, I could only repeat, "I took this from Horned Serpent when he was killing me."

"That makes it the most important concentration of Horned Serpent's Power known. Others have obtained bits of horn, usually through trickery or payment. Your courage, what Horned Serpent did to you, that he passed you and the sepaya back to this world, makes that piece incredibly potent."

I might have been stone, unable to move as his glowing black eyes seemed to search my souls. I could feel the Power radiating from his body, as if fit to explode it.

My hand seemed to move of its own volition, rising to lift the thong from my neck. I couldn't breathe, my heart still in my chest, my flesh nothing more than inert clay. The sepaya's Power pulsed between my fingers.

I was in the process of extending the thong, pouch swaying below, when a scream tore through my souls. "No," I gasped. "Wait."

The swirling depths behind his black eyes seemed to enlarge.

"I . . ." I swallowed hard. "I'll go with you. Bear it, if you will. Like your carriers move your sacred articles from place to place."

"And if I must have it?"

"Then I'll give it to you."

"You're unprepared. Uncleansed and polluted. I can smell a woman's odor all over you. Your souls are a mixture of red passion smudged with the black of death."

"I am exactly who I need to be to fight this war." I don't know why I said it. "I am part of the sepaya's Power. We work together, like the balance between the red and the white. Without me, the Power is dissipated."

His eyes seemed to enlarge, swelling in his head. The effect was downright eerie. Then he said, "I understand. Come."

I gave Fire Falcon a pleading look. "Tell the Orphans where I've gone. What I've done."

Still on his knees, his hands in the supplicant's position, he nodded, speechless.

The sepaya drawing me forward, I followed Back-from-the-Dead, the carriers and assistants lining out behind us. They lifted flutes, playing a sacred melody as we started along the creekside trail leading toward Anhaica.

I walked in a daze through most of the morning, the sepaya's Power radiating in waves. The events just before sunrise kept replaying in the eye of my souls. Had I actually seen what I thought I had? Back-from-the-Dead stepping naked into a pillar of smoke, only to reappear behind me, painted, dressed, and bearing an ancient copper mace?

Was I dreaming? No. That cold hike from Fire Falcon's camp to the river had been too arduous, and I had the scrapes from thorns, as painful now as when I'd received them.

And no, Black Shell, you didn't have anything to eat or drink that might have been laced with spirit plants to give you visions.

That left the final conclusion: Back-from-the-Dead had stepped into the fire, vanished into the smoke, only to be deposited—fully dressed—somewhere outside the sacred square, behind us.

But . . . how?

I glanced up at the morning sun, now almost two hands above the tree-lined and hilly horizon to the southeast. I exhaled, and cold breath hung before me. When would the sun actually warm my unnaturally cold skin? Or was this just Power—perhaps the illusion Back-from-the-Dead spun around us?

Through narrowed eyes I studied the back of his head. The canted copper headpiece looked as ancient as the mace. In the days of the great empires, the high minkos had valued such pieces. The copper had been traded down from the far north, though some continued to be found in the mountains east of Coosa. Once the coppersmiths had beaten the pieces into thin sheets, they'd placed them upon wooden molds. Using delicate hardwood, antler, and bone dowels they had carefully pressed the copper into the mold, creating falcons, images of Eagle Man, Seeing Eyes, and other sacred designs.

More than one hundred years before, a series of droughts, wars, and migrations had destroyed the mighty empires, leaving the peoples now bearing their names but a shadow of their ancestors and our current cities but pathetic reminders of the great urban centers that had dominated entire river systems.

And now I followed a renowned hilishaya bedecked with the copper of long-dead high minkos to do spiritual battle with the invader.

Old-Woman-Who-Never-Dies told me flat out: This will be won or lost by men.

So, why am I here?

Because deep in my heart, despite all that I've experienced in the Spirit World, I still believe.

I glanced down at the thong I'd wrapped around my hand. The pouch swung with each step I took. Somehow I'd been unable to replace the cord around my neck. As if the sepaya hung halfway between the hilishaya and me.

We were climbing up from the concealment of the creek bottom now. Back-from-the-Dead led the way, me behind, the two ranks of assistants followed by the carriers. The sound of the flute music echoed weirdly in the morning. As if the playing priests and I were walking inside a large clear bowl.

When I listened, the normal sounds of morning—

birdsong, insects, the sigh of wind through trees—was missing. I shook my head. None of it seemed real. Even less so than when my souls had ventured to the Spirit World.

I should have felt hungry, or perhaps thirsty since I hadn't drank since the night before. But the way I felt I might have just stood from a full meal, a lightness to my step.

I'm driven by Power.

Not just driven, but born on the euphoria of it.

Why, in the name of bloody pus, am I walking headlong toward disaster?

Because, fool, for reasons of its own, the sepaya wants you here.

And as we crested the next rise, I could see Anhaica in the distance. Back-from-the-Dead was taking us on a direct line, headed for the eastern gate.

I could see distant cabayeros and soldados. Morning light was gleaming on their silver armor. Clusters of what looked like slaves were being guarded in the vicinity of the curious wooden piles.

Come on, Hilishaya, we're betting everything on you.

Reliance

The cold leeches into her ancient flesh as she watches the ceremony, and with it comes threads of memory. She sits back against the tchkofa, butt on a bench, wrapped in a blanket. The hopaye leads a procession into the great plaza. The man is dressed in a feathered cape crafted so that when he extends his arms, eagle feathers spread like wings. The effect is so real she half expects him to leap, flap, and rise into the clear winter sky.

She winces at the pain in her burned hand, now wrapped in cloth and treated with ointments. She needs but close her eyes and the fires of Mabila will burn brightly again.

Instead she watches the hopaye approach the tchkofa where she sits. He dances, his steps imitating those made by Eagle Man back in the Beginning Times.

The sound of flute music, accompanied by the deep thumps of the pot drum, are mirrored by hundreds of voices as the spectators lining the square begin to sing. The rhythm and harmony carry her back . . . back to memories.

Trouble and holy men, a mix that can turn volatile.

Priests, they are all the same. The unkind thought comes unbidden. She makes a face that rearranges her wrinkles and exposes her toothless gums.

Those around her misread it as joy—such is the ruin that time has made of her once-smooth skin.

Then she is falling back into the memories. Images of priests firming and fading. The one that finally rises to dominance is of a cold morning. Yes, she knows that place: a forest camp filled with Apalachee warriors. And in the rear towers a mighty beech tree.

She'd been cold—like today—as she awoke and threw the blanket back. Rubbing her tired face, she'd glanced around, searching for Black Shell. The rest of the Orphans lay in their blankets on the flattened grass. Faint tendrils of smoke rose from white ash in the deep-set hearth. Packs had been placed alongside fallen logs draped with half-crushed vines. The dogs were there, some catching the last of their dreams, others watching her. She remembered Skipper with his odd eyes, one brown, one blue, staring at her, and then looking plaintively across the Apalachee camp toward the trail that led down to the creek.

But nowhere had she seen Black Shell.

Driven by a prickle of unease, she'd stood, straightened her sleep-wrinkled dress, and drawn her cloak over her shoulders. Picking her way among the sleeping Orphans, she stepped over the log and made her way to where Fire Falcon's camp lay.

She looked up from his empty blankets just as the tastanaki appeared from the creek trail, his face troubled, eyes haggard from no sleep.

"Greetings, Tastanaki. Have you seen my husband?"

He'd met her worried stare with one of his own. "I just left him. He's accompanying the hilishaya. They have gone to destroy the Kristianos with Spirit Power."

She'd stared, dumbfounded. "Let me get this straight: Black Shell has gone to help the hilishaya destroy the Kristianos?"

Fire Falcon had nodded, his face blanching. "I saw it myself . . . the hilishaya, draped in Power, shimmering like a morning sun. He wanted the sepaya Black Shell carries, would have had it. But at the last moment, Black Shell agreed to accompany him. To augment the Power."

She relived the growing disbelief, the sensation of confusion. Only when Fire Falcon stared anxiously back at the trail had the fear burst loose in her souls.

She'd turned, sprinting back across the crowded camp, leaping logs and fire pits, bolting past rising warriors.

"Get up!" she'd shouted at the Orphans. "Grab your weapons!"

"What's wrong?" Blood Thorn demanded as he clawed the sleep from his eyes. The others were scrambling out of their blankets, reaching instinctively for weapons.

"I'm not sure yet," she'd answered in a fear-cold voice. "But whatever Black Shell's doing, he's not in his right mind."

She was already plucking her crossbow from the ground, strapping the quiver of short metal-tipped arrows around her shoulders.

"And bring the dogs! We may need them."

The fear was pounding through her now, and she turned . . .

"Elder?" a voice asks, and she flinches, staring around her. Eyes blinking, she realizes that the high minko, the tishu minko, and the clan elders are all watching her. She knows that worshipful look in their eyes.

Fire Falcon's camp is gone, and she stares out at a hopaye dressed as Eagle Man as he pirouettes in the city plaza, scores of people watching, clapping, and singing.

"Dreaming," she whispers self-consciously. "I was back . . . So long ago . . ."

"Yes, elder," the high minko says solicitously. "It is a day of Power."

They are so accommodating about her visions, her slips into the past.

"Yes." She brushes the images of that long-gone day from her souls as though they were cobwebs. This is a day of life, of celebration.

But that was a day of death.

"Black Shell," she whispers inaudibly. "What made you do it?"

For a moment, she relives the fear she felt as she and the Orphans went tearing down the trail, seeking the tracks of Black Shell and the crazy hili-shaya . . .

THIRTEEN

FOLLOWING BACK-FROM-THE-DEAD—HIS ASSISTANTS and carriers still stumbling along behind—I tried to make sense of why I was doing this. We'd walked down into a swale, paralleling a thick patch of berry bushes, plum trees, and rosebushes in the creek bed to our left. From its midst rose chinquapins and persimmons. Since all the plants were fruit producing, it was no doubt one of Cafakke's groves.

As we climbed up out of the swale, I realized that we'd strayed, our path taking us toward the southeastern corner of the palisade. And directly before us, illuminated in the midday sun, stood a party of Kristianos. Through the knot of them I could make out one of the ragged piles of wood with its upright post.

In that instant, the post's purpose became horrifyingly clear. Two soldados were tying three women to the post, their feet perched awkwardly on the pile of wood. I caught just a glimpse of a long-haired woman who faced our direction. She might have passed twenty summers, her hair filthy and matted, her bare breasts full. Once she might have been attractive, but a dark bruise mottled her left cheek; a badly cut lip was swollen. Her haunted eyes echoed with hopeless defeat.

And as quickly a Kristiano stepped in the way, blocking my view. Unconsciously I began to count, coming up with nearly thirty Kristianos. An assortment of soldados—most with spear-axes—crowded in a ring around the woodpile with its bound women. Other slaves sat on the ground to the side, their necks chained, heads bowed in either exhaustion or defeat. Perhaps five shooters had their thunder sticks grounded by the butt. And there, in the middle, stood one of their priests, wearing long robes belted at the hip. He supported a slim pole that ended in a Kristiano cross that he raised high, his voice carrying as he addressed the women.

Over the distance the words "*jesucristo,*" "*díos,*" and "*paraíso*" could be heard. At this, the soldados dropped to their knees, touching their foreheads and stomachs and crisscrossing their breasts.

As they did, I watched a man advance and thrust a burning branch into the kindling at the base of the woodpile.

They remained so engrossed with the process they never looked our way. I could hear the women weeping, one of them making a piteous mewing sound.

At that moment the sepaya began to bounce on its thong. I snapped to my senses. "Hilishaya, whatever you're going to do, do it now. The one in the middle wearing the robes is one of their priests. He's calling on their god right now."

Back-from-the-Dead stopped, raising his hands, head tilted back. From where I stood, I could see his face, blissful, almost shining in the midday sun. He immediately raised his voice, singing in beautiful tones.

I felt the Power rising around me and, despite the circumstance, looked up at the cloud-speckled winter sky. What did I expect to see? Eagle Man? Horned Serpent? Perhaps one of the thunderers? I didn't know, but the sun's warmth bathed my face.

Something made me look back. The Kristianos had turned, staring in surprise. As one they began scrambling to their feet, accompanied by the clatter of armor and shouted amazement.

Is it working? I watched, desperate for Back-from-the-Dead's dreaded Power to be unleashed. The sepaya had grown still in its leather pouch.

"*¡Alto!*" The Kristiano priest's voice thundered.

I watched him step forward through the ranks, his golden cross held high.

Perhaps two bow-shots of distance separated us. In that instant the air went still, an unearthly quiet surrounding us. Back-from-the-Dead's melodic voice continued to call to the heavens. Then the invader priest's voice rose in competition, chanting vigorously in his sonorous language.

Time seemed to cease, though I felt the anxious beat of my heart.

I could see sweat beading on the faces of Back-from-the-Dead's bearers, their feet shifting nervously. Among the Kristianos, the soldados were doing the same, glancing at the priest as they fingered their weapons.

One of the thunder-stick men opened a little metal pot hanging from his belt. I could see him insert the ropy cord that fixed to his thunder stick. He blew and withdrew the smoldering cord. I watched as he raised the long tube, could see his anxious eyes as he leveled the thing, aiming at Back-from-the-Dead.

In my hand, the thong began to vibrate, and I could feel the heat as the sepaya shivered in its pouch.

Back-from-the-Dead and the Kristiano priest continued to throw their Power at each other. I swear the air began to shimmer. We waited, each side expecting lightning, thunder, something.

The tension—the Power—had my skin prickling. Even the listless slaves had looked up, hope shining in their eyes as they discovered us. Behind the Kristianos, flames were climbing through the wood. The stalemate continued to hold. Then the bound women screamed in abject terror.

The priest shot a look over his shoulder. Back-from-the-Dead hesitated in his song, startled. The shooter touched his burning cord to the thunder stick.

"Duck!"

The weapon's boom rang out, gray smoke belching. Though the shooter aimed at Back-from-the-Dead, it was his assistant, standing just to my left, who spasmed in time to a loud popping sound. His knees gave, and he flopped backward onto the grass, eyes wide, mouth in a disbelieving O.

The women's screams grew louder.

"Run!" I bellowed, reaching around for my bow, pulling an arrow from the quiver in one smooth motion. Even as I drew, the other thunder-stick men were scrambling for the pots at their belts. Orders were being shouted, the soldados readying their spear-axes.

I set my feet, drew, and—taking aim at the robed priest—released. Given the distance, they had plenty of time. One of the soldados violently shoved the Kristiano priest to the side, my arrow slicing air where he'd stood but a moment before. The priest staggered, snared a foot in his long robe, and tumbled to the ground, his gold cross flying.

Back-from-the-Dead just stood there, gaping like an idiot, his copper mace in his hand.

I grabbed him by the shoulder, spinning him around, bellowing into his stunned face. "Run! The cabayos will be here any moment!" Then I gave him a mighty shove.

Another of the thunder sticks popped. I knew that meaty snap, and the head of one of Back-from-the-Dead's assistants exploded with a pop, bits of skull, brain, and blood spattering us.

I yanked another arrow, turning and drawing. I watched it arc through the sky, Kristianos leaping from its path. Others, entranced, were watching as yellow flames rose around the screaming women's legs.

"Run!" I yelled like a wild man. "Blood and guts, man, don't you understand? They're going to kill us!"

I gave the uncomprehending Back-from-the-Dead another angry shove, literally propelling him back toward the hollow. Finally, he and the others seemed to catch on. They started slowly, like men in a dream, only to pick up their feet as another thunder stick boomed and something cut the air beside us with an angry hiss.

Then we were running full out, tearing back the way we'd come.

"Stay next to the brush!" I ordered. "If they follow, it's the only way to escape."

"Can't we outrun them?" one of the carriers asked.

"The soldados, yes. But not if they come on cabayos." I shot a last look over my shoulder, and the image was seared into my souls. Half the soldados were charging after us. The others had bent, attending to the priest.

But behind them? The women were jerking like fish on a stringer, writhing in the heat. The screams had stopped, the expression on the one woman's face terrifying as she burned alive. The last I saw her disheveled hair was bursting into flames.

Then I was over the crest of the rise, my heels hammering the grass. The sound of a horn could be heard behind us. Summoning cabayeros, I was sure of it.

I thundered, "Hilishaya, whatever happens, don't you dare stop! If they capture you, it will destroy the Apalachee. *Do you understand?*"

Back-from-the-Dead shot me a quick glimpse, his eyes like those of a scared rabbit's. "What?"

"When we get there, you dive into that brush along the creek. Wiggle through it like a fish if you have to, but keep going. No matter what you hear, you go. Understand?"

"Why?" he almost cried. "Why are you doing this?"

"To save your sacred hide," I puffed. "The rest of you, if we're caught, you stay with me."

Terror filled their eyes. Would they give themselves up to save Back-from-the-Dead?

I'd have had better odds betting the sun would rise black in the west.

On we ran, my orders keeping them on a line to the

thicket when they would have cut straight across the open fields in a more direct route.

The assistants were lagging, falling behind one by one, and I could see that Back-from-the-Dead was fading, his lungs sucking, sweat gleaming on his skin.

Ahead of us, just past a looted farmstead, lay the brushy creek bottom. If we could only make that, the cover might allow us to catch our breath, then sneak along the creek bed, slowly, but invisible.

Invisible. That's what Back-from-the-Dead's Power was supposed to keep us. I made a face. Actually, could I say that it hadn't? Until he began to sing, no Kristiano spotted us. Had it kept us safe? How long had we stood facing each other as the two holy men called upon their Power? Only when the woman screamed, and Back-from-the-Dead hesitated in his song, did a Kristiano dare take a shot.

We were pelting past the jumble of the destroyed farmstead, the fastest of us already hammering his way beyond into the dimpled corn and bean field. Here footing became tenuous due to not only the irregular surface but the occasional squash vines that ensnared our feet.

I kept my pace even with Back-from-the-Dead's, reading the hilishaya's growing exhaustion. He was stumbling now, his mouth open, arms flying. Somewhere he'd lost both the ancient copper mace and the headpiece. I felt a twinge of sorrow at that.

I shot a glance over my shoulder, horrified as the first cabayeros came flying over the crest behind us. Slender lances were extended, the riders bent low over the animals' necks.

Most of Back-from-the-Dead's assistants and one of the carriers were behind us, strung out in a long line. They were soft and used to loafing around the temple, not running for their lives. Many were older, with flabby muscles.

Shifting my bow, I grabbed Back-from-the-Dead's hand, pulling him staggering and stumbling behind me.

One by one, the more fit carriers threw themselves into the brushy bottom. I didn't dare spare even a moment to see how close the cabayeros were, but a ragged cry told me they'd caught the last straggler.

At the brush line, I literally threw Back-from-the-Dead into the vegetation before whirling, clawing for an arrow.

"Follow the stream bottom!" I ordered through ragged panting. "To the right! Downstream."

Then I turned, nocking my arrow. No more than ten paces away, the closest assistant shot a look over his shoulder just as a cabayo ran him down. The great beast hit the man with an armored shoulder, knocking him head over heels.

I drew as the cabayero turned his attention to me. He was grinning down his long lance, turning his horse. Behind him, others circled the Apalachee they'd run down, shouting in glee.

Careful, Black Shell.

I held my draw, let the cabayero get close. It had to be just right. Too soon, and he'd recover and skewer me. Too late, and I'd have no time to dodge.

Now! The order seemed to come of empty air.

I released, my shaft a streak in the sunlight. At the last minute, he seemed to comprehend. His eyes had begun to widen, but the jerk of his head came too late. He screamed as my arrow impacted just right of his nose, the lance point slipping off to the side. I threw myself right, ducking. Even as I scuttled away, the cabayo plunged straight into the brush, lost its footing where the bank dropped off, and somersaulted onto its back amid a crackle of stems and branches.

I had time to shoot a quick look at the remaining cabayeros. The smiles died on their bearded faces. And to my horror, I realized one was Antonio.

No sooner did our eyes meet than I saw recognition.

Then I was diving through the broken branches, literally scrambling over a sumac to avoid the upside-down cabayo's lashing hooves. I landed hard on my shoulder, rolled, and came up in the creek bottom. The cabayo was wedged on its back in splintered brush, legs pumping, the broken rider crushed beneath.

Downstream! It took a moment to get my bearings, then I started off, ducking willow and bending branches. Gaudy red feathers marked Back-from the Dead's route where they'd been torn from his cape.

"Black Shell?" Back-from-the-Dead called from ahead.

"Quiet. They'll hear," I hissed.

Pushing past an overhanging plum, I found him crouching, still gasping for breath. I grabbed his hand, dragged him after me down the ankle-deep stream.

"What . . . ?" He seemed in a daze.

"Shh!"

Behind me I could hear the blowing of cabayos, and voices called in *español*. Brush snapped and someone cursed. I heard the trapped cabayo scream its fear and pain. An angry voice bellowed, "*¡Mierda!*"

"*¿Concho Negro?*" Antonio's voice demanded from beyond the screen of brush. "*¿Dónde estás?*"

I could translate: "Black Shell, where are you?"

I bit my lips, quietly leading Back-from-the-Dead through the mucky water. Only when I looked down did I jump. The current was red with blood. And it just kept coming.

Back-from-the-Dead, too, stared down in fascinated horror. At his questioning glance, I whispered, "The cabayo was badly hurt. They probably cut its throat."

Confusion grew in his dark brown eyes.

My lips to his ear, I whispered, "They'll show mercy to a cabayo. But never to us."

Working as stealthily as we could, we eased down the creek bottom. Behind us I could hear Kristianos arguing. Antonio's shrill voice was demanding. I kept hearing the words "*Indio sucio*" over and over and "*Él matado mi padre.*" "Filthy indio." He must have meant me. And the other? Oh, yes. "He killed my father."

It was all I could do to keep from throwing caution to the winds, stomping out, and doing my best to drive an arrow through his skull. Memories of him wielding an ax on the warrior he'd maimed were too close to my souls.

Somewhere ahead of us I could hear brush crackling as a heavy body pushed through it. One of the carriers? I could see their tracks in the mud along the bank.

I realized that I still carried the sepaya in its bag, the thong wrapped around my left hand where it grasped the bow. I paused long enough to slip it over my head, then, leading the way, crept forward. Using my bow, I held the branches back, but in places Back-from-the-Dead and I had to literally drop to our bellies and wriggle through the bloody water to pass low-hanging branches.

In one such place, I heard someone force his way through the brush where he'd tried to bypass it by going around. A Kristiano called, one of the crossbow arrows hissed, and a man screamed in pain. More brush snapped as he fell and thrashed. The gurgling sound could have come only from pierced lungs as they filled with blood.

Back-from-the-Dead's eyes were wide with fright, his face smudged and filthy, his red and black face paint smeared into a travesty. I yanked on his crimson-feathered cape, breaking the ties, and left it behind.

I eased onward, knowing that within moments Antonio's men would be searching to see who they'd killed.

Pus and blood, Black Shell, how'd you get yourself trapped like this?

I shot a mean-spirited glance at the hilishaya. I could have blamed him, but deep down it was my own bull-headed fault. I'd allowed myself to be seduced by his Power and that stubbornly deep-seated belief that no matter what Old-Woman-Who-Never-Dies had told me, our Spirit Power would win.

We crabbed around a gum tree bole and hurried as fast as we could without splashing too loudly. The thick brush was as threatening as it was reassuring. As well as it hid us, it could hide a Kristiano with a crossbow.

If anything was working for us, it was that cabayeros hated to get off their beasts for any purpose. I prayed fervently that not even Antonio's desperation could induce them into the brush on foot.

Time wore on, endless moments of terror spiked by occasional calls as our hunters rode along the brush, searching for us.

Back-from-the-Dead was trembling, partially from fear but mostly from exhaustion. He'd been up for more than a day, praying, fasting, sweating, and making himself ready for his great Spirit battle. Now, looking at him, I could see that the toll was mounting. The man was at the end of his reserves, and being a priest, while fit, he wasn't going to make it for any great distance.

Behind us, a horn sounded, and I winced, wondering what new allies were being called.

"Come on," I growled curtly when he tripped and fell, splashing loudly. "Call on Power. It will keep you going."

The look he gave me was that of a lost man. "Leave me. Let me die. I failed."

I squatted down in the mud, face-to-face with him. "Had you failed, they would have seen us the moment we emerged from the swale. Or their priest would have killed you with his own Power. Instead, you were matched—one for one—until the women screamed. Their priest turned away. You hesitated. Both of your Powers wavered. That doesn't mean you failed."

My gaze bored into his. Breath and thorns, I had to convince him. Otherwise, he'd go back a broken man. And then what? The Apalachee would believe Power had deserted them.

He read my burning insistence, nodded, and clambered up. Pace by pace we continued on our way.

"Where are the others?" he asked, panting.

"Ahead . . . somewhere." I gestured past a screen of willows. "They'll be waiting, looking to you for direction."

He swallowed hard, easing through the willows. But I could see terror just under the tenuous hold he struggled to maintain.

The creak of leather followed by a stomping as a cabayo stood impatiently could be heard just above us. I straightened, slowly raising my head until I could see that a cabayero waited no more than ten paces upslope. A tall hickory had created an open space that ran down to the stream.

I signaled for silence, reached back, and pulled an arrow. I motioned for Back-from-the-Dead to go first. He'd frozen, fear burning bright in his eyes. I gave him a shove, refusing to mask my anger.

Back-from-the-Dead began to shiver, took a breath, and with trembling hands, parted the willows. I followed, easing my bow through the stems, concentrating so the arrow didn't snag.

Then we ran out of cover.

Back-from-the-Dead stopped short. I peered over his shoulder. A trail crossing left an open space no more than two paces across. And there, blocking the stream and making a little dam, lay one of the carriers, facedown in the water, dead.

I gestured for Back-from-the-Dead to wait; he nodded too quickly, more than willing.

Like a snake, I wiggled through the willows, doing everything to keep the tops from swaying and giving away my position. To my disgust, I realized that this grove had been a major source of cuttings where people had come to collect staves for matting and baskets. My cover thinned into nothingness and the cabayero was sitting just eight paces away. Worse, his cabayo was staring right at my hiding place; the Kristiano, no fool, was following the animal's alert gaze, a crossbow at his shoulder.

Wait, Black Shell. One wrong move and you're a dead man.

He'd drive an arrow through my guts before I could manage to even rise and nock my own.

We waited: He—ready to shoot—was unsure of his target; I, knowing just where to shoot, couldn't get in position.

I'm a trader, used to patience. Neither Back-from-the-Dead nor the Kristiano shared that virtue. Terror proved too much for the hilishaya. He broke, rising to his feet, charging across the open space.

The Kristiano and his cabayo, surprised, turned their attention to the crossing. I pulled up a knee, rising and nocking my bow.

At my movement, the Kristiano hesitated. It was just enough time for me to draw. He was swinging his crossbow back my way as I released. Then I was on my feet, crashing through the willows.

I leaped the dead carrier, pounded across the trail crossing, and crashed into the brush, hard on Back-from-the-Dead's heels. Behind me I could hear angry cursing. But no Kristiano arrow had pierced my hide. Shouts drew pursuit our way.

I could hear Back-from-the-Dead bumbling through the brush ahead of me. Nor did it take long to catch him. When I clamped a hand on his shoulder the man almost jumped out of his skin.

I dragged him down, both of us squatting under a raspberry bush, heedless of the thorns.

"You've got to be quiet."

"I thought you'd left me back there." He was frantically searching my face. "Did you kill him?"

"I'm *not* leaving you. And no, I'm sure his armor stopped the shot. I didn't have time for a good aim. If we gained anything, it was to keep them mindful that we're still dangerous."

As if to prove my point, additional shouting could be heard behind us. Then we heard the thundering of cabayo hooves as several riders passed just beyond the brush screening our little creek. The clank of armor, glimpses of cabayos, and the creak of leather sent shivers through me.

"Come on." I took the lead, resuming the careful and slow progress through the nearly impenetrable brush.

"We're not going to get out of this, are we?"

I gave him a smile I didn't feel. "All we have to do is avoid them until dark. Then we go home."

He almost smiled in return. "Is there anything I can do to repay you?"

"You owe me a copper piece," I growled. "Now be quiet."

Brush began crashing ahead of us, and I knew someone was forcing a cabayo through the thicket.

Similar sounds came from behind. Shouts came from all sides. My heart began to pound.

FOURTEEN

"WE'VE GOT TO FIND A PLACE TO HIDE." I STUDIED the brush around us, what I could see anyway, given the thicket of branches. "There. Up in that maze of plums."

I led the way, showing Back-from-the-Dead where to step so we didn't leave tracks. With my bow, I eased us past branches and dropped to my belly at the edge of the plums. Like snakes we crawled into the gray stems.

"Try not to disturb the leaves more than you have to."

My bow and quiver made the task maddeningly difficult. And convincing myself to move slowly took all of my will. Nevertheless, within a finger's time we had found a spot in the plums where the wrist-thick trunks and higher branches created a haven of sorts.

Motioning for Back-from-the-Dead to stay flat, I rearranged myself and found that with contortions I could stand with my head screened by branches.

You couldn't call my spot a vantage point by any means, but through the screening brush, I watched something flip through the air and land in a nearby myrtle. Whips of smoke rose.

They're trying to burn us out.

Fingers of smoke lifted where the torch had disappeared in the brush. With my foot I tested the leaf mat, feeling it spring under my weight. We'd had rain not so long ago. But was it enough?

The Kristianos kept calling back and forth. I caught sight of another of the burning brands as it arced through the air a bow-shot to the south.

More calling.

Anxiously I watched the smoke as it thinned and finally vanished. I sighed from relief.

"What's happening?" Back-from-the-Dead whispered.

"Quiet," I hissed back.

Movement.

I picked out a helmeted head as it passed a gap in the brush. Figuring the distance, I placed the Kristiano at twenty paces to the south. Twigs were snapping, snags rasping on his clothing. The man looked like a soldado, and he was anything but happy to be there.

I tried to swallow, realizing how thirsty I'd become. A branch snapped behind me. I slowly turned my head, unable to see through the gray thicket.

A mockingbird exploded from the brush a stone's toss to the south. As the panicked bird flapped away, I eased my head around. Two soldados—each with a crossbow—stepped into view, then vanished. I heard the clink of metal, the distinct scratching of thorns on cloth.

Wedged as I was in the plum branches, I could figure

no way to use my bow. Nor did I have an open shot in any direction. Short of a miracle, an arrow would be deflected by the maze of branches.

My leg began to cramp; I carefully worked myself into as comfortable a position as I could. Back-from-the-Dead gave me a questioning look. I shook my head, signing, "Many. All around us. Quiet."

He signed back: "What do we do?"

"Wait."

He nodded, looking very unhappy.

Moments later, a Kristiano called out, "*Hay un indio aquí. Él esta escondido en una zarza.*"

The announcement was followed by the breaking of stems, excited shouts, and, sometime later, a man's screams. From where we hid, the sounds of his capture were agonizing. You'd have thought they tore up half the thicket dragging him out. We could hear the man shouting, "No! No! Please!" as if it ever did any good with Kristianos.

"*¿Donde está Concho Negro?*" Antonio's voice could be heard as they dragged the captive up the slope. He repeated it over and over, as if the poor carrier would know who Concho Negro was.

Then quiet descended, broken only by the occasional shout of a Kristiano or the crackling of their passage through the brush.

Back-from-the-Dead quivered with each sound. Finally he looked up at me, signing: "I have traveled the Spirit Worlds. Why, then, am I so scared?"

I signed back. "Because you are smart." Blessed ghosts, I was plenty scared myself.

Looking up, I could see from the shadows that we were

well into the afternoon. How long until dark? And then what? Could Antonio—as a *capitán*—insist the soldados stay out after dark? Generally that was a death sentence.

Except that Antonio hates me with all his heart.

So we waited, hearing a new sound. It took a while to figure out what it was: a rhythmic thumping accompanied by occasional snapping. It started upstream and grew ever closer.

So odd was it that I shifted, getting my feet under me. Then I rose ever so slowly, muscles trembling as I worked up through the branches. Careful to keep my head screened, I chanced a glance, seeing soldados. Each had a long stick and was beating at the brush.

When I'd lowered myself, I signed: "They are poking the brush with long sticks. When they get here, make no sound even if they poke you." I willed my resolve into his eyes. "Do you understand?"

As if his nerve had failed completely, he dropped his forehead onto the leaf mat and nodded.

They came, all right. They hammered at our plum thicket. Twigs and last fall's leaves rained onto us. I spent the time developing an empathy for every rabbit I'd ever flushed from cover using exactly this same tactic.

Then I stifled a grunt as one of the weasels jammed a stick across my back. I must have felt like the mud I was covered with, because the pole was withdrawn and jabbed in again, just missing my head where it pressed on the musty leaves.

Thinking back, the ordeal couldn't have lasted that long. It just seemed half a lifetime.

And then they were gone.

I shuddered, exhaled in relief, and lifted my head. Back-from-the-Dead gave me a hollow stare. He slowly shook his head in despair.

We waited as they moved on. More Kristianos crisscrossed the brush-choked drainage, shouting as if to nerve themselves for the pursuit. Who was more afraid of whom?

Shadows were lengthening, the light fading when I finally nudged Back-from-the-Dead with my foot and wiggled my way through the stems. How long had it been since we'd heard anyone? A hand of time? Two?

I emerged from the plum thicket like some oversized water moccasin, lifted my bow, and fit an arrow. Gesturing for Back-from-the-Dead to follow, I worked down to the creek and began sneaking downstream. We moved with the stealth of hunters, taking a step at a time as we searched the shadows.

When, I wondered, had I spent such an incredibly long day? Maybe in the water at Napetuca, but Blood Thorn had been there sharing the ordeal with witty comments and grim humor. I glanced at Back-from-the-Dead. The man just reeked of desperation.

We'd traveled little more than a bow-shot's distance when the brush began to thin. I used a stand of tall grass as cover as I inspected the drainage ahead. Another of the trail crossings loomed in the dusk.

This would have been Antonio's choke point. The place stank of cabayo, and several piles of their droppings could be seen in the track-stippled dirt.

I rose higher, looking around, seeing no one. On the other side, three junipers stood like dark sentinels. Did we wait or make a run across the open space? Easing out, I craned my neck, searching where the trail climbed the slopes on either side. No one waited in ambush.

"I think they're gone," I told Back-from-the-Dead. "As much as they want us, they want even more to be back at Anhaica by dark."

He gave me a puzzled look. "Chicaza, why are you doing this? You don't even like me."

"Because your people need you. Come on. Head straight for that brush beyond the junipers. If anything happens and we get separated, keep going. The important thing is that you get back and help Fire Falcon lead the fight."

He reached out, taking my arm in a firm grip. "Thank you, Black Shell."

"You can thank me later."

He nodded. "I've been seeing it all over in my head. They burned those women. And they had so many piles of wood."

"Let the memory continue to burn inside you." I gave him a grim smile. "You know now why we fight."

At that I turned, arrow nocked, and hurried forward in a half crouch. He sloshed out of the water, following my tracks along the bank.

The distance wasn't far, maybe ten paces, and we were most of the way across when a soft voice called, "*¡Alto!*"

I stopped short, staring in disbelief as two men detached themselves from the junipers. Both had crossbows leveled, ready to release.

My bow wasn't drawn, the arrow clamped by my left forefinger. Could I pull and make a snap shot before they killed me?

"*No, amigo,*" the one to the left said, as if he could read my mind. "*¿Quieres morir?*"

Did I want to die?

"Black Shell?" Back-from-the-Dead whispered.

I lowered the bow, straightening. Desperate images went whirling through my mind: Ortiz, the metal collars, snapping war dogs, and a lingering death at Antonio's hands. My decision was made.

"When I shout, Hilishaya, you run," I said reasonably, knowing the Kristianos couldn't understand. They were easing forward, never lowering their crossbows. "I'll make sure they put both arrows into me. Just promise me you'll escape. No heroics, Hilishaya. Promise?"

"Yes," he said weakly.

My heart battering my ribs like a hammer, I smiled, holding my bow out to the side, and stepped toward the Kristianos. "*Yo rendirse,*" I said with a shrug, remembering Napetuca and the words that granted survivors a short-lived clemency.

They both laughed at that, as if I'd said something funny. Then one asked, "*¿Eres el Concho Negro?*"

"*Sí,*" I replied.

The one on the right began chattering happily, the excited words more than I could comprehend. I did catch mention of "Don Antonio" a couple of times.

I was closer now, almost within spitting distance. For the first time, the man on the left changed his aim, wisely considering me to be the greater threat.

Within a few heartbeats, I am going to die.

A sensation of peace settled over me. I pushed images of Pearl Hand out of my souls, focusing on what I had to do next.

"Ready, Hilishaya?" I asked. "On the count of three. One. Two . . ."

A voice from the brush shouted, "Now!"

The *hiss-thunk* of an arrow broke the evening stillness. One of the Kristianos jumped at the impact.

More arrows whistled in the gloom, thudding into the Kristianos. I threw myself to the side as the Kristiano before me triggered his weapon. The wicked little arrow tore the air beside my head.

I landed on one knee, my bow up, and clawed the arrow back. I imagined more than saw my opponent's face over my stone-pointed arrow. Then I let fly, my shot driving home.

As he fell, dark shapes were charging out of the forest. The Kristiano on the left turned to face them. He jerked with the impact as arrow after arrow thudded into his padded armor.

Setting his feet, he took aim, and I heard the peculiar twang as his crossbow released. One of the charging figures stumbled, dropped to his knees. Hands clutched at his breast, he pitched forward.

Blood Thorn flew out of the gloom and bodily knocked the Kristiano to the ground. Straddling him, Blood Thorn hammered the screaming man's head with his war club.

Pearl Hand strode out of the brush behind the junipers and stopped long enough to prod the man I'd killed with a toe. She shot me an evaluative glance, saying, "Nice shot. Right through the left eye."

I blew the tension out with a hearty exhale and took her hand as she hauled me to my feet. "Nice to see you."

"What were you doing back there?" she demanded hotly. "I waited as long as I dared. I thought you were going to die."

"Peliqua?" Corn Thrower called.

I turned to where he crouched over the warrior who'd been shot.

"Bear Paw is dead, Peliqua. The Kristiano's arrow went through his heart."

I winced. "May the ancestors welcome his souls."

Blood Thorn and Wide Antler rushed over to see.

"Hilishaya?" I called. He stood as if rooted to the ground, staring in the dim light.

The single blaring note of a Kristiano horn startled us. Three cabayeros stood at the top of the trail, silhouetted against the darkening sky.

"Let's run!" I shouted, taking only long enough to step back and shove Back-from-the-Dead before me. Corn Thrower tossed Bear Paw's body over his shoulder and trotted for the safety of the creek bottom.

We'd barely made the brush before hooves could be heard. I was all for running headlong, but Pearl Hand's order brought me to a halt.

"Let them come," she called from up the slope. "In this twilight, maybe we can get another one. Vengeance for Bear Paw."

I pushed Back-from-the-Dead behind a haw bush, saying, "Stay put. Don't move."

Then I reached for another arrow, clambering up to find a shooting position.

I could have saved myself the effort. Pearl Hand whistled, pointing. Bark and Squirm in the lead, my dogs burst from the brush, howling, barking, and sounding like fury unleashed. The riders pulled up, mounts bucking and squealing.

Amid the cabayeros' shouts of rage, the first arrows slammed into their armor. Driving heels into the cabayos' sides, they ducked low, raced up the hill, and disappeared into the gloom. Pearl Hand shouted, slapping her thighs, chasing after them. The dogs slowly returned, one by one, tongues lolling, tails slapping, delighted with themselves.

I released the tension on my bow, watching as the Orphans collected around Bear Paw's body.

"How did you find me?" I asked Pearl Hand.

Her teeth flashed. "We looked for the largest concentration of Kristianos, figuring you'd be in the middle of them." She tilted her head toward the dead Kristianos. "Did you understand all that? What they said?"

"All what?"

"Antonio will pay the man who catches the Concho Negro. Those two thought they were going to be rich. Even if they had to stay out after dark to do it."

I rubbed my neck, stiff with tension. "He came close a couple of times today. Come on. We've got to get the hilishaya back before I fall over."

And we had a body to prepare; another Orphan was dead.

My body was drained, my feet as heavy and clumsy as lumps of stone. It took incredible effort just to keep my eyes open, and I fought yawn after yawn. The trail back to camp might have stretched across an eternity. I kept stumbling over roots and sticks, Pearl Hand catching me on occasion.

Why am I so tired?

I might have been up for days instead of since just before dawn. But then, I'd never felt the abject euphoria of the morning coupled with the violent terror of the afternoon. I shot a glance back at the hilishaya. He was stumbling along like a man in a dream, partially supported by Blood Thorn. A slack expression dominated his face, his eyes glassy and hollow, mouth hanging open like a fool's.

I staggered along for an eternity only to have Pearl Hand pull me aside as we approached Fire Falcon's pickets. She muttered something I couldn't hear to Blood Thorn and gestured for the rest to precede us.

I blinked stupidly, my souls focused solely on the bedding that awaited my exhausted and depleted body. Sleeping, maybe for days, filled my desires.

As the last of the Orphans passed, followed by the dogs, I forced one of my stone feet forward—only to have a hard hand clap my shoulder and spin me around.

I found myself eye to eye with Pearl Hand. Even in the dark I could see the pinch in her lips, the swell of her knotted jaws. Her shoulders were hunched; fists clenched tightly. Oh, and I knew that hot look in her eyes.

In acid tones she demanded, "By the Piasa's balls, Black Shell, *what possessed you?*"

I'd been the target of her rage a couple of times. Given a choice between a tongue-lashing from Pearl Hand or a Kristiano slave collar? . . . Well, you get the idea.

"Possessed me?" I answered weakly.

"Are you *so* tired of life?" She barely controlled her voice. Her face jutted closer to mine, her eyes flashing. "Because if you are, *I* will gladly *bash your silly brains out* if you ever do this to me *again!*"

"Do what?"

"*Blood and pus!*" She was literally shaking, pointing back toward Anhaica. "What did he do to you? Cast some spell, knock you in the head so hard that any good sense you had leaked out? What?"

"Huh?"

"Black Shell, I wake up alone, to hear that you've gone off with Back-from-the-Dead to conjure Power to destroy the Kristianos? With that priest? He hates you! Did you take leave of all your senses? Or did he drug your tea?"

"I don't . . . I didn't drink anything. The Power . . . it was everywhere . . ."

"But for me, you'd be dead!" she said, fuming. "Or worse, captured! Then what? I just spend the rest of my life knowing that the man I love more than life is suffering his way to an early death? You didn't even tell me what you were doing. You *left* me there, asleep."

I ground my jaws as her hot glare burned into mine. Her mouth worked and she swallowed hard. In the moonlight, I could see the gleam as a tear leaked from the corner of her eye.

"How do you think that makes me feel, Black Shell?"

My gut sank, a sick feeling sucking at my souls. "I'm sorry. Fire Falcon asked me to go see the hilishaya."

"Fire Falcon! Oh, that makes me feel so much better." She slapped her thighs, turning away, head down.

"I'm sorry."

For long moments, she stared off into the night, refusing to meet my imploring gaze.

"What if I hadn't come?"

"I don't know."

"Yes, you do," she whispered, not even bothering to look at me as she pushed past. "Don't you ever do this to me again."

And she headed off down the trail, anger projected by the swing of her hips and her pounding steps.

I sighed, staring at the dogs. They were glancing back

and forth between me and Pearl Hand's retreating form, wondering who to follow.

"Should have just let those Kristianos shoot me," I muttered.

For a solid week we endured a cold and soaking rain. Pearl Hand and I, along with the Orphans, moved our camp back into the forest close to the creek where we could build crude shelters. The conditions were miserable, the wood wet, and despite the good intentions of the Apalachee, the food was even worse.

If anyone had any doubts about the Timucua, they'd been erased by the rescue of the hilishaya and the sacrifice of Bear Paw's life.

In a stunning gesture of respect, Fire Falcon delegated eight warriors to escort Bear Paw's corpse back to Uza-chile under the White Arrow so that his body could be prepared by kin. Bear Paw, at least, was assured that his souls would make the journey to his ancestors.

In the aftermath, by ones and twos, tascaia and nico-quadca came by, offering gifts of war arrows, bows, captured Kristiano artifacts, and ornaments.

The difference in the Apalachee was apparent. The monster had burned thirty captives that day. From all over the forest, warriors had watched in horror as their people were tied to the posts and the woodpiles lit.

One of the carriers who'd been captured was mutilated and left on the hilltop as Tascaia Fine Shell had been before him. He, too, was carried back to deliver his message: If the attacks didn't stop, more would be burned alive, and the mutilations would continue.

In the beginning, de Soto might have been the invader;

the Apalachee had considered him a challenge to be over-come—more of a nuisance or pest to be rid of. After the burnings, the fighting took on a brutal and merciless quality. You could see it in the warriors' eyes, a hard glittering hatred that burned within them like sacred fire.

I thought about it, wondering. I'd seen men driven to that kind of encompassing madness. My Orphans were that way. Life, beyond the killing of de Soto, had no meaning, had even become inconceivable. But to see an entire Nation so gripped?

I tried to make sense of it one day as I poked our smoking fire with a stick. Unlike so many, we had a *hierro* ax. The sharp edge allowed us to split wood down to the dry center.

Pearl Hand and the others were out scouting, keeping an eye on the Kristianos. Me, I needed time to put things into perspective. I looked down at the pouch where the sepaya now rested in silence. It would have been nice if it had started to glow, jumped around, or done something to come to my rescue the night Pearl Hand had vented her anger on me.

You wanted me to save the hilishaya. Why? What role is he to play in the future?

We had delivered Back-from-the-Dead—exhausted to the point of staggering—to Fire Falcon. But the next morning he turned up missing.

So, did he run out on you? In the end was he so broken by the experience that he's gone into hiding?

The thought left me grinding my teeth. Now, more than ever, his people needed him. Each day his warriors were being killed in ones and twos, battling to their last breath to wear down the monster. Where was their hilishaya?

With a bitter anger, I jabbed the fire, seeking to vent my frustration on something.

"Black Shell?" a soft voice asked.

I looked up from the shelter of our lean-to, and there he stood. Rain pattered off a bark hat and dripped from an elk-hide cloak around his shoulders. His tattooed face was drawn, a gleam in those once fearsome eyes. A long hunting shirt was belted at his waist, and beneath it an apron hung down past his knees. I noted the badger-hide bundle he held before him, something long wrapped within.

"So, you're back?"

He nodded, his expression curiously humble. "I've been away. Out in the forest. I had to make sacred ground, pray, fast, and speak with the Spirits. In the end, the Little People came. I listened to their wisdom and was given a task."

I relented enough to gesture that he should come in out of the rain. The Little People had been around since the Creation. Mostly they avoided the world of men, hiding among the forest shadows, in hollows under fallen trees and in the ferns that grew along the banks of streams.

They appeared only to the greatest of hopaye, healers, or sometimes to the dying. It was said that they were tremendously wise, thoughtful, and often malicious if given the chance.

He settled himself beside me, careful to keep from dripping on our bedding. Not that it would have mattered, as everything was damp. For a long time he stared at the fire, watching it sizzle as stray raindrops penetrated past the overhang. The badger-hide bundle rested under his smooth brown hands, cradled as though precious.

"I'd begun to think you might have deserted us."

He nodded, water dripping from the edge of his rain hat. "How do you think Breath Giver views us? We are, after all, his Creation, imbued with so many gifts. And at the same time we stumble over our own pride, our arrogance, and our stubbornness."

"Nothing in Creation is perfect." I shrugged. "Not even the Spirit Beasts. That's all part of will, I guess. Our ability to think and act for ourselves."

"We learn, but at the cost of so much pain. I have prayed for Bear Paw. Asked that his souls be blessed on their journey to the Uzachile's afterlife."

"Thank you." I gave him a hard stare. "Hilishaya, have you figured out what you're going to do?"

An amused smile curled his lips. "I'm going to do what I should have done long ago."

"And that is?"

"Anything I can to help destroy the monster." He smoothed the badger fur. "Our warriors need me. They need to see me praying, making medicine, brewing black drink, and blessing them as they sacrifice themselves to save the world."

I closed my eyes, sighing in relief.

"Black Shell?"

"Yes?"

"You saved my life when I should have paid the ultimate price for my pride. I watched you—a foreign Chicaza trader—step forward and offer your life for mine. You and Bear Paw have laid an unbearable debt upon my shoulders, one I will never be worthy of."

I waved it away. "Just do your best for your people."

"I had to save myself before I could save them." His

gaze went back to the fire. "And I owed you a piece of copper."

He handed me the heavy badger-hide bundle. Shooting him a skeptical glance, I unwrapped the soft fur, finding the ancient turkey-tail mace he'd carried to battle the Kristianos. As I touched it, I felt a tingle: The thing pulsed with Power.

He continued. "It took all of my courage to go back and find it. I hid during the day, searching the route we took as we fled. The second night, almost at dawn, it finally considered me worthy. I heard it call to me." He paused. "And I found myself."

"This is worth much more than the piece we played for, and your people might need it." I tried to hand it back. He declined.

"Not even that sacred mace is fair exchange for what you have done for me and my people. As I said earlier, no matter what I do for the rest of my life, no matter how hard I try, I shall never be completely worthy of the faith you place in me."

"Don't underestimate yourself."

"Follow your own advice for once, Black Shell. Out of all the Nations, Horned Serpent chose the worthiest man he could find. I have been honored to know him."

And with that, he stood. It shocked me to my toes when he touched his forehead in the ultimate sign of respect and walked off into the rain.

FIFTEEN

THE BITTER FIGHTING ESCALATED. DE SOTO CONTIN-
ued to burn screaming human beings in his bonfires and
to maim the occasional unfortunate warrior. And by doing
so, he fed the rage burning red in Apalachee hearts.

The stories of courage and resourcefulness are many
and compelling. I was born Chicaza, taught to believe that
no people on earth share our bravery or commitment to
war. Of that, I am no longer sure. I watched individual
Apalachee take the fight to the Kristianos at every level.
Warriors beyond hope used whatever they had at hand,
even broken arrows, to attack the monster.

We helped in any way we could, offering labor to con-
struct elaborate traps for cabayos, digging pitfalls along
trails, planting sharpened posts in deep grass, and then
taking turns inciting cabayeros to chase us into the ambushes. In each case we might kill one or two, and perhaps

maim a cabayo. Then, when the Kristiano horns called for reinforcements, like mist after a rain, we would filter away through the brush.

Fire Falcon used every trick he knew and then created more. He learned, changed his tactics, adapted.

But so did the Kristianos; rarely did they fall for the same trap twice. Pearl Hand once had warned me that eventually their arrogance would be replaced by caution. That day had come.

I remember the morning—three weeks before the spring equinox—when de Soto finally had enough.

Pearl Hand and I were cooking breakfast as dawn grayed the east. Someone had given us a pot full of dried corn. We'd let the kernels soak overnight and had them boiling. Blood Thorn crouched opposite us, inspecting a batch of the stubby little crossbow arrows he'd taken from a wounded Kristiano.

Wide Antler sat down at the creek, head back, palms up to the sky as he offered his prayers to Power. Corn Thrower returned from his morning bath. Walking Thunder still lay in his blankets.

The dogs—looking lean—were wondering the same thing I was: How much of the corn were they going to get? Rations were scarce all the way around. With the forested sections infested with warriors, the game had fled. Every small lake in the area had been fished to exhaustion with nets. Nor did hunting migratory waterfowl provide much in the way of meat. It took time and exposed warriors to Kristiano patrols. Most food came from the surrounding areas, borne in on human backs and distributed by Fire Falcon. Not that there was much of that, either. Most people had lost their winter food stores to Kristiano raiding parties and been forced into the woods to hunt, dig roots, and collect nuts.

I was contemplating this state of affairs when Fire Falcon's youthful runner appeared. The dogs were immediately on their feet, barking to greet the newcomer.

The youth touched his forehead, saying, "Greetings, Peliqua. The tastanaki asks that you and Pearl Hand join him at the lookout tree. Something is happening in Anhaica."

I stood, asking, "Blood Thorn? Can you keep an eye on breakfast?"

"What little there is is way too precious to let scorch," he said, waving us off.

The youth was already headed up the trail as I took Pearl Hand's hand in mine and started after him. "What do you think?"

She gave me a sidelong glance. "Wouldn't it be nice if de Soto is packing up to take his accursed army to the coast and sail away on the floating palaces?"

We'd seen a large party take off for the coast days before. Scouts reported that they were headed to the ships waiting there and that cargo was being carried by boat and loaded. To the watching Apalachee, it appeared that the Kristianos were making preparations to leave.

We knew they were up to something. The number of patrols had dropped. Woodcutting parties had ceased foraging. Scouts sneaking in close at night noticed that packs and boxes were being prepared.

At the base of the beech tree, I climbed the ladder—a much more substantial thing than the wobbly pole that had preceded it. Throughout the winter, endless climbers had worn the bark off the old tree's branches, and every Y had a platform tied to it for observers to rest on.

We made our way as close to the top as the number of people would allow. The great tree had to have half of the tastanaki's warriors in it, as if they were a weird fruit.

I helped Pearl Hand up next to me, feeling the branch sway with our weight. Then we turned our eyes toward Anhaica. The sight was reassuring. Instead of armored riders, the cabayos were being loaded with packs. Even the cabayeros were carrying burdens on their backs. The line of remaining slaves were chained, packs on their backs, and already moving. We could see the soldados, too, bent under heavy burdens.

"They're leaving!" someone above us called.

"Which way?" a nicoquadca called up from the ground below. "South? Please, let it be south!"

I shook my head. "It's north, maybe northeast."

We watched, speculation running rampant, as the long line formed up, seeming to march at a snail's pace down the trail that led toward Many Oaks town. But why they went that way was anyone's guess since they'd looted Many Oaks long ago.

Fire Falcon called down from his high perch. "Black Shell? What do you think? Is it a trap?"

"Tastanaki, if it's a trap, it's a poor one. They're leaving Anhaica and its fortifications. The cabayos are being used as pack animals, led by their riders. I'd say they're leaving for good."

"But northeast?" Pearl Hand mused.

"And his boats are leaving, too," I said thoughtfully, trying to make sense of it.

For a hand's time we clung to our perch until the long

column wound out of sight. Then, one by one, we climbed down.

A knot of us gathered at the bottom of the tree as Fire Falcon made his way down. His feet touched the ground and he stopped, his face a mask of indecision.

"What," he asked, "is in the northeast?"

As we all thought about it, silence stretched.

I felt Horned Serpent's brow tine warm, and then a thought came to me. "Remember how the monster captured a trader, White Mat? With him was a boy, Periko, who told de Soto that gold could be found in Cofitachequi."

Fire Falcon gave me an incredulous look. "And de Soto believed him?"

I shrugged. "If you told a Kristiano that gold could be found on the moon, they'd start building a ladder to reach it."

"What are your orders, Tastanaki?" one of the nicoquadca asked.

Fire Falcon arched an eyebrow. "Detail scouts. The rest of us will follow . . . shall we say, urging them along? What we don't want to do is scare them into returning to Anhaica. Meanwhile, as soon as the capital is clearly abandoned, I want it burned, flattened. Not a structure or wall standing that they could return to."

"Yes, Tastanaki." Warriors immediately ran for their weapons.

I sighed, looking at Pearl Hand. "Let's go eat and pack. We're going to have a long march, and the dogs aren't up to covering long distances."

She gave me a smile, saying, "I know that country up there. I think de Soto is in for a tough time."

"As long as the Hichiti Nations aren't more interested in trying to kill each other, de Soto will find them a formidable foe."

When we left our camp later that morning, I looked at our small group. Apalachee had cost us a lot. De Soto, however, was heading into the interior. After all the death and fighting, what had we actually cost him?

As we walked out into the open—feeling oddly vulnerable—the first columns of smoke were rising over Anhaica. Throughout the day the plume would mark its location, a somber reminder of what the monster left in his wake.

De Soto didn't get out of Apalachee unscathed. He lost six men—a seventh was badly wounded—when the soldados wandered out to see the sights. Otherwise his column received the occasional long-distance arrow, just enough to keep them awake.

For our part, we barely traveled as fast, spending most of our time hunting, searching for food, anything to keep five humans and four dogs fed. We ate a lot of roots: cattail, thorny walking stick, arrow-leaf root, and so on. They take time to clean, peel, pound, and boil. Farmsteads had been picked clean, mostly by their owners, who were hiding in the forest. We picked up a lot of last year's nuts, but most had gone bad or were wormy. Spring shoots, however, especially goosefoot, were coming up, so that helped.

Even Wide Antler remarked that a stint in Cane Place town didn't seem so bad now.

Rain came with a passion, and we lost a day searching up and down the Bald Duck River, until we stumbled upon a local who dug out his hidden canoe. He'd been watching from the trees the day before as the Kristianos crossed the same flood-swollen waters. He delighted us with the knowledge that one of the armored Kristianos had fallen in and drowned.

There are advantages to being a trader: I knew the trails. De Soto, following his guides—most of whom were captives, prodded on at the point of a sword—headed straight into the swamps.

The people who lived there—called the Capacheeki—were an offshoot of the Apalachee. Years past they had broken away after a nasty little civil war to find security in the mosquito-infested swamps. There they fished, hunted alligators, and grew a little corn. While the Capacheeki occasionally traded with the Apalachee, they certainly weren't interested in establishing relations with anyone. Even the traders avoided them. And of course they'd undoubtedly heard the stories of what was happening around Anhaica, so I welcomed the thought of de Soto's men being used for Capacheeki target practice.

Rather than wade through the muck, I led the way around, sticking to the highland trails. As we proceeded, I kept noticing Walking Thunder. The man kept casting longing glances to the south, unease in his manner. Nor was he the only one. Corn Thrower, too, had lost his usual easygoing ways. And anxiety had come to rest in Wide Antler's normally crazed eyes. In camp at night, the three Orphans tended to isolate themselves, praying, making offerings to the ancestors.

One night I asked Blood Thorn about it.

"They worry, Peliqua. Until the arrival of de Soto, they had never even considered going as far away as Apalachee, let alone to a land this distant."

"I fear we are going farther."

Blood Thorn gave me a reassuring smile. "They will be fine. It's just an adjustment."

After six days' travel we entered the thicket-like no-man's-land that marked the northern border of the Hichiti Nation called Toa.

The Toa were Mos'kogeans speaking the Hichiti dialect. When not battling with other Hichiti—the Ochisi and Ocute, who occupied contiguous river valleys—they periodically raided the Apalachee, the Timucuan peoples to the south, and the mighty Coosa to the north.

The Hichiti Nations were strung in parallel strands along the major river drainages running down from the mountains, each having a capital city where a high mikko held sway. Smaller towns were ruled in the high mikko's name by a relative who served as the local mikko. Villages and farmsteads filled out the valleys. Matrilineal clans owned different farm plots and hunting, collecting, and fishing grounds. From the lowliest forest farmer, tribute flowed up, eventually ending in the high mikko's elevated granaries. In return, the high mikko and his councilors redistributed the stores in times of famine, provided military protection against raids, and ensured that the people were on good terms with the supernatural.

When a high mikko died, his palace was burned, the locals summoned, and a new layer of earth added atop the ashes. Then the people pitched in, building a new palace, furnishing it with benches, boxes, and carvings. Each leader wanted a more imposing palace than his predecessors, so the new building had to be taller, with more rooms and increasingly opulent furnishings.

I removed my trader's staff from its quiver, carrying it

before me. Walking in the presence of three Timucua, I wanted no mistakes as to our identity or purpose, and we had no idea of de Soto's whereabouts. Hopefully he was dreadfully lost in the swamps or the hilly forest that separated Toa from the reclusive Capacheeki.

Then—of course—we took a wrong trail, finally stumbling out three days later at a farmstead. The people were reserved, wary of the Orphans, and happy to provide us with directions to the nearest town in exchange for a couple of pieces of shell.

"Do these people practice witchery, Peliqua?" Walking Thunder asked.

"No more than any other," I answered. "They're Mos'kogean, believing much the same as the Apalachee."

Heading south on the trail, we began encountering locals. They in turn sent us to a mikko who held sway at Black Stone town, the northern Toa outpost.

The word for "town" is *talwa* and to the Mos'kogean peoples, it means more than just a collection of buildings. The talwa is a social entity—another of the fibers woven through the fabric of society. First comes the individual, then his family. The family belongs to a clan, and the clan to a moiety. Those are the vertical, or warp, threads. The weft—or horizontal connections—can be thought of as linkages across kin lines, such as village affiliation, membership in the talwa, and finally membership in the Nation itself. Even people in villages and dispersed farmsteads thought of their first political affiliation as belonging to the talwa. A small talwa might have an *oreta,* or village elder. A larger talwa had a mikko in charge.

We walked through farmsteads where people worked to prepare their fields for spring planting. And as we emerged from the last band of timber, there lay Black Stone town. We entered the outskirts just in time to see people loading baskets of corn into canoes down at the landing.

The town itself sat just back from the river, dominated by a low mound with the mikko's palace. The building rose above a cluster of daub-walled houses roofed with split cane. Granaries poked up here and there on tall posts.

The arrival of unexpected visitors slowed but didn't entirely stop the proceedings. As we made our way to the plaza, people flocked around; I held my trader's staff high, ordering the dogs to behave as the local mutts came swarming to see.

The mikko descended wooden stairs from his steep-roofed palace, its ridgepole adorned with sculptures of ivory-billed woodpeckers. He was a middle-aged man with some gray in his roached hair. The falcon motif of the ruling moiety was tattooed on his face. A well-rounded belly demonstrated that he'd taken to a lifestyle filled with food and leisure.

Wearing a black apron, his shoulders covered with a raven-feather cloak, he walked stately forward, an old chipped stone mace in his hands. I could see the question in his eyes. Foreign traders were rare enough in this day and age, those arriving at a lesser town even more so.

"Greetings, Mikko," I called, raising the trader's staff high. "I am Black Shell, of the Chicaza. With me are my wife, Pearl Hand; Blood Thorn, iniha of the Uzachile; and Walking Thunder, Wide Antler, and Corn Thrower— known as the Orphans. We come under the Power of trade and bind ourselves by its laws."

He looked us over one by one, nodding. I could see a barely disguised disappointment in his expression, something about the set of his lips. "You are welcome, Black Shell, by the Power of trade. I am Egret, of the Chief Clan, of the White Arrow Moiety, and mikko of Black Stone town."

He went on, listing his various ancestors, war honors, and finally his relationship to the high mikko in Toa, the capital a half day's travel downriver.

Then his eyes narrowed as he asked, "What is your purpose here?"

I gestured with my trader's staff, wary as more and more Toa came to surround us. Some were muttering uncomfortably behind their hands. I didn't like the curious hostility in their eyes. The fact that we'd interrupted their emptying of the granaries meant de Soto was close.

I announced for all to hear, "We come under the Power of trade and would engage in that, assuming it pleases Mikko Egret. We are also interested in news of the Kristianos." I gestured again with the staff, pointing at the baskets being loaded with food. "It would appear that you are wisely removing your valuables prior to their raiding parties arriving here."

Egret's thick lips curled into a pouting smile. "Then it would appear that you are wrong, Trader." He saw my surprise and continued. "The Kristianos arrived at Toa yesterday. While the elders had wisely evacuated the town, several remained and had conversations with the Kristianos."

"Are they already in chains?" Pearl Hand asked.

"No, lady, they are not. The Kristiano mikko, this de Soto, has treated them equitably, offering metal goods and glass beads in exchange for food and labor to transport his baggage and equipment. High Mikko Toa—after ensuring the Kristianos' peaceful intentions—is happy to accommodate them."

My heart sank. "I have followed the monster all the way from Uzita, a country far down in the peninsula. His path has been marked by rotting corpses and ruination. Tell me that your high mikko doesn't trust him."

Egret had that superior smirk on his lips. "Things are different here, Trader. Unlike the Timucua"—he glanced at the Orphans—"we are not savages. In contrast to the Apalachee, we are not wedded to the red Power of war. When dealing with strangers, we cling to the white Power and seek to understand those not familiar with our ways."

"I have yet to see the monster give a rotten acorn for anyone's ways." But that old trader's sense was tickling me, the warning to back off. "But perhaps you are right. We come only under the Power of trade."

He fingered his chipped stone mace, suspicion in his eyes. He gave the Timucua another narrow-eyed stare, then sighed, as if in resignation. "If that is truly the case, let me make you welcome"—he stressed the following—"under the Power of trade."

I inclined my head. "We thank you."

Pointing with the mace, he said, "You may store your belongings there, under the ramada. Please, take your ease and feed your dogs. Then, tonight, you shall be my guest. I will hear your story and inspect your trade." He hesitated. "I have questions."

"Thank you for your kindness. Your questions shall be answered."

"You are welcome, Trader, under the Power of trade.

Now if you will excuse me, I must see to the packing of our tribute."

With that he stalked away, issuing orders that we were to be left alone.

I glanced at Pearl Hand, who had been translating for the others. I'm sure they got most of it, even though the Hichiti dialect posed problems after living with Apalachee.

"What's happening here?" Blood Thorn asked as we walked to the ramada and began unloading the dogs.

"I'm not sure." I unlaced Gnaw's pack and placed it beside Skipper's. The dogs were shaking, scratching, and sniffing the town smells. They insisted on trying to stare down the local dogs who circled just out of range. Several children had been appointed to keep the local mutts off.

Walking Thunder was visibly nervous, his eyes darting this way and that. He seated himself close to Wide Antler, whispering into the man's ear. I noticed that all the Orphans kept their weapons close at hand.

"He kept emphasizing the Power of trade," Corn Thrower noted. "As if it were somehow foremost."

"We're here to kill Kristianos," Wide Antler muttered, but he, too, looked ready to bolt.

I gave him a warning stare. "We're here under the Power of trade. Even when we arrived in Apalachee, we received Cafakke's permission before killing Kristianos."

"I don't understand, Peliqua."

"Wide Antler, be patient. We are guests in Toa territory. Wait, mind your manners, and do nothing without my prior agreement. Do I have your word?"

He nodded, the crazy gleam in his eyes oddly unsettled. "Yes, Peliqua."

"Good. The same goes for the rest of you. And, by the Piasa's teeth, put your weapons away. Out of sight. Now, let's go through the trade, see what we've got left. After months of war, I can't even remember the inventory."

As we laid out the packs, we watched the local Toa finish emptying their high granaries. These are elevated cane-sided structures, perched atop smooth poles. Up in the air like that, the contents stay ventilated; the support poles are usually greased to keep raccoons and mice from climbing them. Wide roofs made of overlapping halves of split cane keep the rain off, and access is by ladders.

"They are just giving their corn away?" Blood Thorn mused. "Just like that . . . and without a fight?"

"Doesn't make sense, does it?" I said, going through my skeins of buffalo wool.

"Be sure there's a sense to it," Pearl Hand murmured. "We just have to figure out how it affects us."

The locals continued to swing basket loads onto their shoulders; we watched them disappear through the houses as they tramped down to fill waiting canoes.

I struggled to figure out the Toa's angle. And what was that hesitation on Mikko Egret's part? I couldn't help but get the feeling that he wasn't at all happy to see us. There was something more to it, as if only the Power of trade stood between peace and a darker reception.

With nothing better to do, I flopped back on the packs and rubbed Squirm's ears while I tried to figure out de Soto's evil intentions and why the Toa were being so complicitous. The sepaya had turned stone-cold on my chest.

SIXTEEN

A HAND OF TIME BEFORE SUNSET, THE MIKKO HIMSELF came to get us. "Two of my oretas are overseeing the transportation of tribute to the capital," he informed us as he led us to his palace.

Off to the right, a roasting deer carcass hung suspended over the fire, its sides sizzling and popping as juices dripped to flame in the fire.

Several women tended a huge pot of bubbling hominy, while baked squash was piled on a long wooden trencher. Another pot held steaming black drink.

Two guardian posts in the shape of huge, white-painted arrows stood on either side of the palace stairway. We climbed the split-log steps to a wide veranda guarded by two man-high cougar sculptures.

Inside, huge wooden reliefs—carved to depict Morning

Star's victory over his father and Morning Star as he took Eagle Man's guise—dominated the back wall.

Benches lined the room while the floor was covered in cattail matting. Textiles had been intricately woven to depict Mother Spider bringing the first fire down from the sun, her little clay pot on her back. Here, too, I saw images of Piasa, Horned Serpent, Snapping Turtle, Falcon, and other Spirit creatures. Carved wooden statuary in the form of Raccoon, Bobcat, Deer, and Ivory-Billed Woodpecker were placed every couple of paces along the wall benches. Beneath the benches were sacks of dried corn, intricately carved and inlaid wooden boxes, and large storage pots. Blankets were rolled and stacked, along with tanned hides and ceremonial pottery.

A large cross-shaped fire crackled in the center of the room and was attended by two boys who occasionally fed it from a stack of firewood near the door. High overhead, the pole roofing was soot coated; net bags filled with dried-and-smoked meats hung from the rafters.

Egret's elevated chair behind the fire was covered with the traditional panther hides, and a line of women were seated to his left, five old men to his right. They watched us enter with a curious intensity.

Egret took his seat, calling, "Under the Power of trade and in the name of High Mikko Toa we bid you welcome, Trader. Under the Power of trade and the White Arrow, we also bid the Orphans welcome. In a gesture of our goodwill, we ask you to smoke, worship, and partake of food and sacred black drink."

I stepped forward, extending a packet I'd brought. "In return for your offer of kind hospitality, we would offer this Taino tobacco, obtained in the far south. It is grown on islands far out in the gulf and rarely traded this far north."

One of the boys stepped forward, taking the pouch and touching his chin. The other trotted back for a box carved in geometric patterns, its top bearing the likeness of Old-Woman-Who-Never-Dies. This he presented to the mikko. Egret reverently opened the box and removed a sculpted stone bowl in the shape of a frog, and separately, a long stem carved in the likeness of a tie snake. These he carefully fitted together and carried to the fire.

The second boy opened my sack of tobacco, shaking some of the finely cut leaf into the bowl. Then he used a well-worn and stained stick to tamp the leaf. Finally he offered the pipe to the mikko and, taking a lit brand from the fire, held it while Egret sucked the pipe to life.

Tilting his head back, Egret blew smoke toward the roof, praying, "Breath Giver, grant us life and health. See us as we honor the Power of trade, and bring us the blessing of good crops, success against our enemies, and gentle rains."

I took the pipe when it was offered, inhaling the sweet tobacco, then blowing it upward. "Grant us humility and peace. Bless our kind hosts with serenity and knowledge. Keep them from disaster."

Pearl Hand followed, puffed, and mimicked my prayer. Then one by one, my fidgety Timucua took their turns, each calling for peace in badly pronounced Mos'kogee.

A shell cup was produced and black drink ladled from a brownware pot behind the fire. Again we drank and offered prayers.

When all was done, Egret invited us to sit while the

boys produced wooden plates. Mine was carved into a likeness of a raccoon, head on one end, the ringed tail on the other.

To my complete surprise, Pearl Hand took hers—a badger effigy bowl—and once it had been filled with steaming deer, squash, corn bread, and hominy, she excused herself and went to sit with the wives.

Blood Thorn shot me a curious look as his plate was filled, but I gave a slight shrug.

"Tell us your story, Trader," Egret declared as he received his own plate and went to perch on his chair.

I offered a bit of meat to the fire first, calling upon the deer's spirit, thanking him for the gift of his body so that I might be fed.

Then I launched into the tale. Egret and the rest listened, rapt, clearly annoyed when I stopped to enjoy a taste of the meal. I tried to be concise, anxious not to have the food turn cold.

At the end, Egret was nodding. "It is much as we have heard. It is true about Napetuca?"

Blood Thorn, most of his meal destroyed, said, "Yes, Mikko. I was iniha, received at Uzachile's council. I lost everything at Napetuca."

The Orphans were nodding, expressions grim. Egret could see the truth of it in their eyes.

"And you wore a metal collar, Trader?" Egret turned his thoughtful gaze my direction. I lifted the shell necklaces I wore so he could see the scars. So did Blood Thorn.

"Why didn't you tell them you came under the Power of trade?" one of the elder oretas asked, looking mystified.

"I did," I replied through a mouthful of hominy. "Ortiz gave me a blank stare. A human life is of no more value than a strand of old rope, the Power of trade but a mad-man's delusion."

"Which brings us back to the Power of trade," Egret said, his half-lidded stare fixed on us. "You are in Toa under the Power of trade. You are bound by its laws."

"We are."

"Then you must understand that while you are here, under that Power, you are bound to commit no hostilities against the Kristianos."

So that was it! I made a calming gesture before any of the Orphans could protest, my warning glare fixed on Wide Antler. "We are bound, Mikko. While we are in your country, none of us will do anything to incite trouble with the Kristianos. You have our word, under the Power."

Blood Thorn's mouth had become a thinly pressed line, his eyes hard. "The Orphans honor the Power of trade." Then he asked, "What happens, Mikko, if the Kristianos do not?"

Egret dipped up hominy with his corn bread. "That will be a problem for the high mikko. My concern is here, in my town."

"And we honor your hospitality," I replied.

Egret seemed to be weighing something down deep in his souls, then he smiled. "You have a reputation as a man of your word, Black Shell. I am pleased to discover you are."

I glanced over at Pearl Hand; she was nodding, smiling, talking with the wives as if they were old friends. But why on earth was she missing the chance to be in the middle of things? Generally she insisted on being part of the men's council.

"Tell me"—Egret interrupted my thoughts—"why do you think de Soto has come to our land?"

"He's in search of gold."

Egret gave me a blank look. "Does it serve a purpose among them? Perhaps it is part of their Spirit Power?"

"Their priests do have a golden cup. Other than that they wear it for decoration. I guess you would say it is their version of copper."

"Ah." Egret nodded. "So, like copper, they think it filled with Power from the Underworld?"

"They don't believe in the Underworld or its Power."

"That doesn't make any sense."

"Tell that to the Kristianos."

He frowned, confused. "What Power do they call on to make them so great in war?"

I explained as much as I could of the Kristiano god.

He really looked confused. "But, if their god is good— white, if you will—how can they call on it for war?"

I shrugged.

"How can you mix the two?" The notion seemed impossible to him. "War is death and chaos, the spilling of blood and the passion of souls. It would taint any quality of a good god."

"Myself, Mikko, I wonder if you haven't just found the problem: They have mixed their god with warfare until he's tainted, similar to the way mold infests a corn crop. It creeps in, corrupting the kernels, rotting it from the inside of the husks out."

He shook his head. "How lucky we are that Breath Giver was wise enough to create separate worlds, each with its own Power. And the red and white to run through it all, balanced so that when one expands, the other retreats, only to advance again."

I smiled at that. "And while the Sky World and the

Underworld may be at war, neither side can conquer the other. Our world is a masterpiece. But can you imagine what life is like in theirs?"

Egret made a face. "No wonder they came here."

"Enough of such depressing talk." I slapped my knees, full to bursting. I tossed the last scrap of meat I'd saved into the fire and offered one final blessing to the deer who had fed me. "What of Toa? Tell us the news. Is Fast Deer still high mikko? Was the crop good? What do you hear about the Ochisi and Ocute? Have you had any trouble with the Coosa, up north?"

He shrugged. "For the last couple of years the Coosa have stayed on their side of the boundary. One of their towns, Napochies, has been making trouble. But their biggest concern is Tuskaloosa over in the west. Beyond that, we prefer to keep to ourselves." He smiled self-indulgently. "We have enough problems here."

I nodded. He was no doubt referring to the perennial bickering and politics that consumed any Nation: individuals vying for authority, scheming, and intrigue.

"The confederacy is still stable?" I asked, wondering if Ochisi and Ocute were still amicable.

Egret made a calming gesture. "There are always snags along the trail, but for the most part, yes. We seem blessed by mikkos who would rather talk than fight for the time being, and the white Power reigns."

It hadn't always been so.

"What of the Apalachee?" he asked. "We heard the vaguest of stories, tales of incredible fighting."

I nodded. "The first thing the Kristianos did was raid the Apalachee for slaves to carry their baggage. The Apalachee, however, were wise enough to avoid a frontal assault, choosing instead to wear the invader down, picking off ones and twos."

Egret was silent for a moment, thinking. "But there was no doubt the Kristianos started it?"

"No doubt." I frowned. "What I do not understand is why they entered Toa peacefully."

"Perhaps they heard of the valor of our warriors?" Egret, like so many, considered his warriors the best in the world. "I saw them just after they arrived. Dirty, filthy, and carrying most of their belongings on their backs, they looked exhausted. Why on earth did they cross the Capacheeki lands? Those people are little better than animals."

"No matter how they looked after wading through the swamps, never underestimate them. I've seen the Kristianos fight."

He studied me thoughtfully. "Black Shell, you have a reputation. Like the traders in the old times, you've been many places, seen many peoples. You were raised Chicaza, people renowned for their prowess in war. Are Kristianos that good?"

I lowered my head, feigning humility. "Even my Chicaza would be slaughtered in an open fight."

I heard the trap in his question as he said, "Then they could vanquish the Coosa?"

"If you are thinking of an alliance, don't. They serve only their own ends."

At that moment, a weary-looking young man appeared at the door. He was dressed in one of the fine Hichiti myrtle-fiber blankets and carried a painted stick. He stopped just inside the threshold and dropped to one knee, head bowed, the stick raised before him.

"Enter," Egret called.

The youth stepped forward, circled us, and presented Egret with the stick. "I have news from the high mikko."

"What word does my cousin send?" Egret took the stick, inspected it, and nodded, apparently at its authenticity.

"He thanks you for the provisions you sent and offers his blessings. The majority of the Kristianos will stay for a while, but their mikko, forty of his nobles, and many of the great beasts have ridden on to Ochisi."

"Do you know what the Kristiano mikko is planning?" Egret asked, a slightly confused look on his face.

"Only that he is riding across the divide to Ochisi. If he is pleased, he will call the remainder of his men to follow."

"Are there any instructions for me?"

"No, Mikko. Only that you await additional orders from the high mikko."

"Thank you." Egret paused. "But you're sure they are just passing through?"

"Yes. The high mikko has ordered as many people as are needed to carry their possessions to Ochisi if the Kristianos are ordered to leave."

I shot a look at Blood Thorn. He nodded. If de Soto was leaving, so were we.

Egret noticed. "Yes, Black Shell?"

"He has heard that there is gold at Cofitachequi. Now that he has determined there is none in Toa, he will go on."

Egret's lips made a wry curl. "And is there gold in Cofitachequi?"

"No, Mikko. De Soto hears what he wishes to hear."

"And if he leaves, you will be after him." It was a statement rather than a question. "Well, if we are to trade, we'd better have the best of your goods before you are gone. Meanwhile, let us share more black drink. Then I shall call musicians, and we shall all dance."

Under a midnight sky, I walked back to our ramada, Blood Thorn and the other Timucua still skipping along, dancing in time to one of the traditional tunes. Somehow, after the Toa dancers, they had been induced to exhibit their own style of fancy footwork. The Toa had been amazed. The only other Timucua they'd seen had been captives brought back from raiding parties sent down south.

At Egret's request, Pearl Hand had peeled herself away from the women. She had begun to dance and left the room enraptured as her sinuous body swayed and stepped to an old Mus'kogee rhyme. I'd stared like an idiot, having had no idea she could move like that.

"Silly," she told me, "how do you think a bound woman beguiles a man? I learned as a girl, and believe me, my ability to dance like that made the man who owned me the envy of many a mikko."

I could believe it. I was still smiling as I checked on the dogs and took them for a walk beyond the edge of town. Pearl Hand walked with me, a cloak tight around her shoulders against the night chill.

As the dogs found their spot, I asked, "Have fun among the women?"

She shot a glance over her shoulder to ensure we were alone. "Oh, yes. And once I got them to chatting, their tongues were wagging all night. There's a deeply ingrained need to show up a foreign bitch like me. I just let them tell me everything . . . like the curious fact that Antonio told the Toa all about us."

"What?" I forgot the dogs, gaping at Pearl Hand.

She looked so smug, standing there in the darkness, her cloak tight around her shoulders. "He sought out the high mikko after de Soto was finished with him. Using Ears to translate to an Apalachee, he informed them that he would exchange a wealth of metal, cloth, glass beads, and other things for you and me."

A cold shiver—born of more than the night—ran down my spine. How vividly I remembered the look Egret had given us, the way he'd emphasized the Power of trade when we'd arrived. Knowing he had us—and could have so much more—but for an ancient code must have been eating him alive.

"That complicates matters for us."

She responded, "There's more."

I hated it when she used that tone of voice.

Her eyebrow arched. "De Soto has evidently changed his ways. Perhaps it was advice from a captive Apalachee, or maybe it was just the circumstance of his arrival here. However he did it, he's come to the conclusion that following the established rules of protocol between mikkos is more fruitful than walking in and sticking them with swords."

"And what did they say about this council meeting de Soto held?"

"The women were almost hysterical. In between bouts of laughter, they said that not even a back-swamp Capacheeki hunter could be so rude. The Kristianos interrupted High Mikko Toa and his nobles time after time, demanding things as if they were untrained children. But the fact that they came in peace, are so unique, and gave away such extravagant gifts almost made up for it."

"But what does it mean for us?"

I could feel her gaze through the darkness. "If Mikko Egret didn't honor the old ways, we'd be surrounded, under guard, tied up like turkeys, and headed to Antonio as we speak."

I called the dogs and started back to our little camp under the ramada. To my surprise, I noticed a young man perched on the palace steps. And promptly figured it out: We were being watched.

Indicating the dark figure, I said, "Well, there goes any chance of slipping away in the night."

Head tilted, she shot me a questioning look. "So, what do we do?"

"Hope that Mikko Egret isn't having second thoughts. Make sure he's pleased with the trade tomorrow. And act very humble and devout."

Having Wide Antler in the party, and as skittish as the other Timucua were, I hoped desperately that we could pull it off.

SEVENTEEN

IF WE'D BEEN IN TOA—A CITY OF SEVERAL THOU-
sand—we'd never have had a chance. Someone would have
figured out a way to betray us to Antonio. Too much political scheming went on at the seat of government, and
too many untouchable relatives would have been looking
for one-upmanship—no matter how sacred the Power of
trade might have been.

Black Stone town, however, was small, and too far
from the Kristianos. If we'd been nabbed, Egret would
have noticed immediately and taken steps to ensure his
authority.

Nor was this my first tight scrape. I was practiced at
getting out of town fast. The first thing I did was offer a
shell bracelet to one of the locals at the canoe landing. He
and his brother would canoe us across the river when we
decided to leave, and yes, he'd gladly wait. He assured me

of that as I left him fingering his new bracelet. The enticement was that he'd get a piece of Kristiano metal when we were safely on the other side.

As we laid out trade after breakfast, I quizzed other locals on the trails across the river. Which ones led to major villages versus those that meandered off to isolated farms or hunting grounds in the forest?

Mikko Egret showed up about the time the sun was a hand's distance above the eastern hills. He inspected our goods and was immediately entranced by the Kristiano items we had. Let me guess: He was thinking what Antonio would give him for our warm bodies.

To Egret's delight I traded him one of our Kristiano swords, a couple of their fabric shirts, and a handful of their little round metal pieces. The latter, I explained, were prized by Kristianos. They carried them in leather pouches on their belts. Many had pictures, crosses, and curious characters embossed on them. Once drilled and hung from a thong they would make wonderful little pendants.

Of all our trade, the Kristiano goods were the easiest to replace. We just needed to kill more Kristianos. In return I managed to obtain a couple of nicely engraved shell cups, five of the remarkably fine blankets the Toa made, and small but exquisite wood sculptures of Eagle Man, cougars, and falcons.

Egret lugged his booty up to the palace, then proceeded to tour the town, one of the too-tight Kristiano shirts pulled over his expanding belly, the Kristiano sword swinging before him like a flail. I wondered how many townsfolk, small children, and local dogs would be accidently sliced open before sunset.

At high sun, I gave the signal. We were packed, the dogs were loaded, and our weapons were slung posthaste. Egret was in a clan elder's house, no doubt swinging his sword, because I heard a panicked cry followed by the sound of breaking crockery.

It was a good time to board the canoes, wave farewell, and look back at Black Stone town across the roiling waters of the Toa River. On the far shore, I flipped the piece of Kristiano *hierro* to the brothers, bid them good health, and we were on our way. We didn't exactly run, but we made swift progress across the farmland, waving to locals as we passed, my trader's staff held high.

Once across the floodplain farmlands, we took the trails into the forest, mindful to hide our tracks—such as we could with four loaded dogs. The information I'd weaseled out of the townsfolk proved good and by midafternoon, we were deep in the timber, climbing one of the ridges that would take us northeast. But, with the exception of Blood Thorn, the rest of the Timucua looked like they were ready to jump out of their skins.

No one complained when I pushed them to keep going after dark. Even in the poor light, I could see Skipper was lagging and kept having to call him onward. I even stopped long enough to check his paws and make sure he didn't have a thorn. A better inspection would have to be made in daylight.

The ridge we climbed was mostly open under the majestic old growth; the ancient leaf mat helped to hide signs of our passage. Partly cloudy skies, coupled with a quarter moon, kept us from stumbling too much, but had we been a couple of weeks later in the season, the leaves would have cast a nearly impenetrable blackness. Just like our future—

assuming we couldn't figure out a way to overcome de Soto's newfound obsession with peace.

"Will Egret follow?" Blood Thorn asked as we made camp under a sandstone outcrop just across the divide. Daylight was breaking in the east, false dawn visible through the bud-heavy branches. Around us the forest was waking, birds beginning to sing, insects whirring.

Pearl Hand yawned as she kicked the leaf mat into shape and spread our blankets. The dogs were chewing on slabs of jerked venison I'd traded for. When finished they'd go down to drink where Corn Thrower was digging out a mossy seep in the drainage below.

Wide Antler attacked the branches around us, breaking up small sections for a fire.

"I'm thinking not." I met Blood Thorn's haggard stare. "Egret seemed much too delighted with his new toys. But word will make it to Toa that we were there. Someone will carry it to Ears, and he to Antonio."

"And that means?" Wide Antler asked as he rolled out his blankets and laid his weapons to hand. He kept glancing uneasily at the surrounding trees, jumping at every forest sound.

"Antonio knows we're following."

Blood Thorn tossed out his own blankets. "How important is that? We've been following since Napetuca, you and Pearl Hand for even longer than that."

Pearl Hand straightened from her work, arching her back and making a face. Her hair was a mess, clotted with forest debris and bits of spiderweb. You'd think we'd stumbled through a forest all night long.

She said, "The problem isn't just Antonio. We ambushed Antonio and his father south of Uzachile town and killed seven. The *Adelantado* knows we were ambushing his men around Apalachee and were giving advice to Cafakke and Fire Falcon. And we killed more the day they almost trapped Black Shell and the hilishaya."

"Good. They know to fear us and our Power," Wide Antler said insistently, as if he were desperate to convince himself. He pulled off his breechcloth and slipped under his covers, a grim expression on his face.

"Since when does de Soto fear anything?" Blood Thorn asked. "Let alone our Power."

"He doesn't." Pearl Hand looked thoughtful. "But we've stung him too many times. I fear we've really managed to get his attention. Understand this: We got lucky among the Toa."

"And had enough trade to entice Egret into thinking that honoring the Power of trade was worth it. The next mikko we run into might go ahead and trade, then double his wealth by taking us captive and turning us over to the Kristianos." I glanced around, taking their measure. "Anyone curious as to how we'll be treated? Burning? Dismemberment? The old-fashioned quick execution? Or just slapped in the collar and worked to death?"

"Better not to find out," Blood Thorn growled as he rolled up in his bedding.

"Akasam. May it be so," Pearl Hand said as she pulled off her travel-splotched dress and slipped under the covers.

I made a final check of the packs, undressed, and crawled in beside her. "Blood and muck, I'm tired."

"Me too." She laced an arm around me. "Why do we always do this, travel so hard we ache for days afterward?"

"Because we would hurt so much more if the Kristianos captured us."

"If they are traveling under the White Arrow, how do we take the fight to them?"

I reached up and pulled a twig from her hair, tossing it away. "I don't know. The Kristianos have always been their own worst enemies, killing, raping, enslaving, and pillaging. Made it downright easy to enlist local help in killing them."

"We'll think of something," she murmured, snuggling against me, hanging on the edge of sleep.

"Sure we will." *But what?*

The dream is so real. In it, I sit on the edge of our bedding, Pearl Hand sleeping under the rumpled covers. Her tumbled hair, still matted with bits of debris, spills out of the blankets, and I can just see her face. I smile down fondly, studying the lines, marveling at the look of innocence. Sleep does that, loosens the stress and lets the souls' true form emerge.

I never grow tired of admiring her delicate bone structure, those high cheeks and that straight nose. The light plays on her smooth brown skin and touches her lips. Closed eyelids cannot mask the jerking movements of her eyes as she dreams. I hope that I am in her dreams, smiling, sharing better days than the ones we live in this world.

I love her more now than ever. Memories of the sacrifices she has made for me intermingle with images from our past. I see her again in the Uzachile council, relive those moments as we accompanied Rattlesnake, Uriutina, and the others to face de Soto that fateful day before Napetuca. Scared to her bones, she was filled with courage, marching into the heart of the enemy's camp.

I remember how she carried me out of slavery and away from certain death at Uzita, a dead man's blood soaking her dress. Then I relive the mangrove-hidden camp where she nursed me back to health and the day I asked her to be my wife.

As if it were yesterday, I see her rise from the palmettos where she was cutting fronds that very first day I saw her. A jolt goes through me as our eyes meet—mine stunned at her physical beauty, hers curious and filled with challenge.

Moments, like flashes, of intimate times together filter through me. My loins tingle as I recall the way we first made love and how she still surprises me with her tricks and skill. Then there are the quiet moments, the shared looks, the touching of our souls in a bond beyond communication. When I am with Pearl Hand, we are like one, as if out of the entire world, no two people could so easily become each other.

With a physical pain, I am left to wonder how many days we have remaining. Somewhere, up the trail ahead, a soldado will take aim, or a cabayero will charge down, and her beautiful body will be pierced, slashed, or shot.

I drop my head into my hands, appalled even to imagine it. Yet it is inevitable. This is the path we have been chosen for. Horned Serpent led me to her in his own intricate way, knowing I needed her skill, bravery, and talent with the Kristiano language. Her hatred for them runs as deeply as my own. In all the world, only the two of us understand the depth of the threat.

Only the two of us.

I endure a sensation of loss and deprivation, realizing the impossibility of success.

A sneering voice intrudes. "What a pitiful wretch you are."

I raise my head, staring around. The Orphans sleep soundly in their blankets, undisturbed. The dogs are sprawled this way and that, exhausted from the long trek from Black Stone town. I see sunlight filtering through the oaks, maples, and gums that surround us and smell the first flowers blooming on the breeze. Above me the ancient gray sandstone is weathered and patched with lichens and moss. The leaf mat contrasts in faded yellows and browns.

"Down here," the voice calls, and I turn my gaze to the small seep. Out of the pool Corn Thrower dug emerges a sleek serpent's head, followed by a long and sinuous body. I meet the creature's slit-eyed stare, see its forked tongue scenting the air. A tie snake, one of the guardians of springs and waterways. Since the Beginning Times, they have lurked just across the threshold from our world. Creatures of the Underworld, they rarely mix with the lives of men, preferring their watery underground lairs.

I had met a tie snake before in one of my Spirit Dreams. That time I managed to prove myself, fought the urge to flee, and approached. The awesome sensation of stepping over his cold, scaly hide is fresh in my very bones.

"What do you want from me?" I ask hesitantly, afraid that once again I will be tested. Nothing about that foreknowledge is reassuring.

"Want from you?" The hiss emanating from the creature might be laughter. "How presumptuous to think that I might want anything from a pathetic human such as yourself." A pause. "Well . . . you'd always make a quick meal, but then any benefit you might have beyond becoming large and smelly feces would seem out of the question, wouldn't it?"

"Let me rephrase: What are you doing here?"

"Checking."

"What?"

"Perhaps I should say that I have come to investigate your progress." The head turns, sunlight shining on the serpent's sleek sides and reflecting in rainbow colors. I can see the bands and chevrons—red, white, blue, and yellow. The inky spots along the creature's sides have an empty blackness, as if they are passages into another world. "Looks like you're hot on the invader's trail, hiding up here on a distant ridge. Excellent plan, decidedly threatening."

"He has changed tactics, using our ways against us."

"I know." Once again the tie snake fixes his slit-eyed gaze on mine. Power, almost hypnotic, seems to emanate from it.

In defense I turn my attention to the top of his flat head, seeing how sunlight sparkles in crystalline patterns from the scales. "If you know, why are you bothering my dreams?"

Maybe tie snakes are incapable of appreciating human sarcasm? He continues to stare at me as if I were some sort of vermin. "The invader is in Ochisi, calling his army onward. The last of them crossed the Toa River this morning. One of the cabayos drowned. Have you tried eating one yet? Very tasty . . . if hard to swallow. My jaws still hurt from the stretching."

Knowing the size of a cabayo, and measuring the girth of the tie snake's head, I find that hard to believe. But who am I to call myself an expert on Spirit Beasts?

"He is heading for Ocute," the tie snake states matter-of-factly.

"Tell me something I don't know." I pause. "In fact, tell me what to do about it. The monster has placed a price on us. A wealth of trade to whomever turns us in."

"Clever." The serpent coils, and for the first time I see its tail, the large rattles pearlescent. "Let me tell you a little history: Traders have played a long and valued role in your world. For ages we've watched them. By the thousands they worked up and down the rivers, most operating out of Cahokia. As Cahokia's Power waned, and the lords took to fighting among themselves, the traders moved out, carrying copper, shells, fine furs, medicine plants, sculptures, and delicacies from one end of our world to the other. Great cities rose, their farmlands spreading along the rivers, choking them with silt and other garbage. The mussels and clams liked it, but they are delighted by the simplest of things."

"I know the history." I cross my arms.

"But do you know why the great minkos and their empires were brought down?"

"All empires fall."

"They came to think of themselves as gods. Such delusions were amusing at first, until they placed themselves above us. You know what serpent beings such as myself do for your world?"

"You call the rains," I state blithely; any child knows that.

"Yes. And about one hundred and fifty of your years ago, we stopped calling them. Not enough to kill the forests, but enough to parch the peoples' corn. We waited, curious to see if these self-proclaimed gods could call rain on their own." He yawns, stretching his wide jaws to expose the pinkish-white tissue and the long fangs barely hidden in the folds. *"Surprise! They just couldn't manage it."*

I think about that. Stories are told of the warfare that broke out, how Nations splintered, how famine drove the people to raid their neighbors. The great minkos had been toppled, rival clans seizing control in bloody civil wars. Peoples merged, split, migrated, and invaded, until our world was broken into the smaller Nations of today, each careful to maintain a boundary between itself and its neighbors.

"Played havoc with the trade," the tie snake says somewhat wistfully. *"We liked the old days. Periodically a canoe would capsize. Not only did we enjoy the meal, but the trinkets came filtering down. Copper and shell, as you know, have Power in our world."*

He enjoyed the meal? I shiver as I realize he is talking about the hapless trader.

"Does this have a point?"

"Look to the trade, Black Shell. Therein lies your solution. Are you clever enough to figure it out? Horned Serpent seems to think so; the Piasa and I have bet against him."

"Why doesn't that surprise me?"

"Oh, and Horned Serpent asked me to tell you something else. He said to turn your Timucua loose and trust to the world around you, but you already have the answer. Don't you?"

I blink, startled. Then, in a flash of light-silvered scales, he lunges into the air and dives headfirst into the little pool. I watch the length of him vanish into the earth, ending with the parallel lines of rattles. Rings lap the pool, the only sign of his passing.

. . .

The birds woke me. A flight of geese were winging overhead in long vees; their honking, mixed with the rasping of several hundred wings, brought me out of my dream.

I blinked in the late afternoon light, aware of the stiffness in my muscles.

Turn the Timucua loose? Trust the world? What kind of clues are those?

I eased the blanket back, my legs and shoulders stiff from yesterday's exertions, then walked down to the little seep. I stopped short, seeing water droplets beading on the dry leaves and places where the dirt had been washed by the tie snake's passage.

I squinted, rubbed the sleep from my eyes, and peered into the depths. The bottom of the pool consisted of gravels from which the water welled. I reached in, prodding the bottom. To the touch, the gravel was hard, resisting.

Feeling slightly queasy, I bent and drank. The last time I'd done this in the presence of a tie snake, I'd fallen into the Underworld. That hadn't ended well. I'd ended up owing Piasa my life. He would have had it if only he'd been able to think up something to trade for it.

This time, to my delight, I just ended up with a bellyful of cool water.

Another flock of geese went winging over, heading north. We were well into the migration.

North? I frowned, head bent, looking up at the sky. *Trust to the world.*

I nodded slowly, understanding. Okay, but why that history lesson about the traders? My kind was a vanishing breed. After the droughts and wars, the Nations had literally shrunk into themselves, creating large boundary areas between them and their neighbors. These empty zones served several purposes: First, they provided a sanctuary for game and wild plants. During periods when the harvest was poor, hunters and collectors would find a supply of deer and game, nuts, fruits, and edible roots: emergency forage during the lean times.

The second purpose was to keep warring peoples from bumping into each other and getting killed. The notion was: "This is ours, that is yours. You stay on your side, we'll stay on ours." And for the most part it worked. Except during those times of famine. Hungry people tended to forage farther afield. Chance encounters with the enemy ended in blood. Which—to balance the red Power such violence unleashed—called for retaliation. Which called for more retaliation. Each raid escalated until entire Nations were battling, killing each other, stealing each other's women and children, and burning what was left of the already dry cornfields.

No wonder the Spirit Beasts think we're rather silly creatures. Though to be fair, the winds, thunderers, tie snakes, and piasas engaged in their own warfare. They just never invaded each other's territory.

That was the original purpose of the empty buffer zones between Nations.

I sighed, oddly wistful for the past. What would it have been like to have lived back then, when the Power of trade was vibrant? A solid string of goods was carried from the far north to the gulf and back again. All borne on the backs of honored and revered traders.

And why did the tie snake make such a point of telling me that?

EIGHTEEN

I LET THE ORPHANS REST. MAYBE THAT WAS THE source of the odd discomfort and nervousness they'd been showing. They slept through most of the day anyway, and another night's sleep wouldn't hurt, given the plan that was forming in my head.

Besides, I noticed that Skipper had spent most of the day licking his wrists, and he seemed stiff when he got up to drink or wander off to relieve himself. I told myself it was probably nothing, then went about redistributing the load in his pack, replacing heavy items with light ones.

That night, as the fire crackled and sent its prayer of sparks toward the night sky, I outlined what I had in mind. Blood Thorn and the rest of the Orphans sat in a ring about the fire, the light reflecting from their tattooed faces. They listened, intent. Pearl Hand sat beside me, busying herself with sharpening her *hierro* knife. The blade made a ringing as she stroked it over flat sandstone.

"The way I see it, we have to get ahead of de Soto." I rubbed my hands thoughtfully. "As long as we are following we are at a disadvantage. Any Nation de Soto enters, Antonio will eventually get around to asking about us. Then he's going to offer his reward for our heads."

Wide Antler pulled at his big toe, avoiding my eyes. "If we're going to keep out-trading him, we're going to have to kill a lot more Kristianos."

I waved it away. "We all know that's tough to do while he's moving. His men don't stray during a march. And if they do, and we happen to be in the right place to jump them, a single yell will bring the whole column down on us, especially the cabayeros."

"And we don't know this country." Walking Thunder shot a glance at the dark trees around us. "If we flee into the brush, it might take days to get back together. We'd be . . . lost."

Wide Antler's mouth pursed, his attention still on his toes.

Pearl Hand's knife ground across the stone. "So, husband, what do you have in mind?"

"Getting ahead of them." I shifted to ease my cramping leg. "Way ahead of them."

"Cofitachequi," Blood Thorn said softly.

Pearl Hand stiffened, her expression suddenly pinched, mouth hardening into a line.

"That's right." I paused to prod the fire and glanced at Pearl Hand; her gaze was locked on some unpleasant memory deep in her souls. "Meanwhile, de Soto is going through the Ochisi and Ocute Nations. In both places he must stop, negotiate for porters and food, give gifts, and entertain. He has to wait while food is brought from the subordinate talwas up and down the rivers. Assuming he's smart enough to play the peace role, he must accept some of the offered hospitality and attend receptions for the rank and file."

"These Hichiti will insist on that?" Walking Thunder asked.

"They are old Nations," I answered, "steeped in ritual. The corn harvest has been good for the last couple of years, so they have a surplus. The people are fat and lazy, and they haven't had a real war for some time. For them, life is currently good. They'll insist on lavish entertainment for guests. Most recently, Ochisi have been hosting Ocute, and Ocute have been hosting Toa. You might say they're in the mood."

"Until the monster sticks his finger into someone's eye." Wide Antler sounded bitter.

"I'm not sure he will," I responded. "The Apalachee taught him a bitter lesson. He's smart, and the peace strategy is working for him . . . at least until he arrives someplace where he wants to stay."

Pearl Hand fingered the edge of her blade, still lost somewhere inside herself.

Blood Thorn shifted. "He's learning. In the peninsula, he spent all of his time running down slaves and stealing food. In Uzachile, he ended up killing his captives, and those ahead of his march were warned and fled into the forests. The Apalachee made his life miserable, and slave catching didn't replace the ones he let die. His army had to wage constant war and carry most of its own supplies when it left."

"And he didn't have a guide," Corn Thrower added. "He wandered right into the Capacheeki swamps."

"Right," I said. "By luck he managed to charm the Toa, deciding to play their game. It worked. He can dispense his trade, and as long as he doesn't crap on the tombs of the ancestors, or steal anything from the temple, or slap a high mikko, they will feed him and carry his supplies."

"And women?" Corn Thrower asked. "The ones his men rape?"

Pearl Hand returned to honing her blade, tight lines around her mouth. Her attention might have been focused halfway across the world.

"These are Hichiti," I replied. "They don't have the same rules for female behavior you Uzachile do. Most women will be compliant in return for a piece of trade."

At Blood Thorn's look of disgust, I added, "The matrilineages here are old and have great authority, owning the farmland, buildings, and households. When men marry, they go to their wives' homes. Decisions about who does what generally falls to the grandmother—with the consent of her daughters. Considering the novelty of Kristiano trade goods, what's a man going to do if his wife decides to lay with a Kristiano? He's more concerned about what his sister might be contemplating, but he's going to have to convince his mother to insist that sis doesn't spread her legs."

Wide Antler growled. "And by the time that happens, de Soto is loading his baggage on someone's back and heading for the next town."

"I liked it better when the monster just incited an immediate, loathing anger," Walking Thunder said, despondent.

"Unfortunately," I said, "he's changed the rules. So we, dear Orphans, must change ours, as well. If we can arrive at Cofitachequi first, maybe we can work this to our advantage."

"It's so far away." Wide Antler's face was lined. "Home is back to the south."

"Having second thoughts?" Blood Thorn asked.

Wide Antler shrugged. "The Apalachee I knew about. I'd at least heard of the Hichiti. But this Cofitachequi?" His gaze turned distant. "If I die up there, will my souls ever find the way home? Will we return to our ancestors? What kind of witches, monsters, and threats lie in these unfamiliar forests?"

"The same as in any forest," Pearl Hand replied too harshly as she studied her knife in the firelight. "Snakes, spiders, cougars, and poison ivy. That hasn't bothered you before."

"And the Spirits? The ghosts?" Corn Thrower asked.

"Is your medicine failing?" Blood Thorn asked, his voice like flint.

To my surprise none of the Orphans said anything, and they looked positively unhappy.

Turn your Timucua loose.

I cleared my throat to get everyone's attention. "I want you all to think about this: Just back across the divide is the Toa River. If you keep to the high divide until you are past Toa, then follow it south, it will take you to Uzachile. You know it as the Red Water River, the boundary between your country and the Apalachee. Keep to the east bank, and you end up home."

Walking Thunder shot a glance at the divide, a wistful expression on his face. The others followed suit.

I pointed downhill. "On this side of the divide lies the Ochisi River, which will take you southeast. Follow it, and you end up at the great eastern ocean. Every river we cross, from here on, takes you east. Each one farther and farther from home.

"Look at me." One by one, I met their eyes. "Starting tomorrow, we're headed straight for Cofitachequi. It's a long hard march. And once you get there, you will be in a mighty Nation that dwarfs even the Apalachee. Their customs will seem strange to you and incomprehensible. To them you will be exotic barbarians, a curious and amusing novelty. With the possible exception of some of the rulers, they have never even heard of the Uzachile. And if something happens"—I let it sink in—"I have no idea what happens to your souls."

Blood Thorn chuckled bitterly. "I'm with you. I gave my word."

"So did the rest of you." I fixed on Corn Thrower, Wide Antler, and Walking Thunder in turn. "But you are released. Go if you want. Each of you is a hero to me, to your people, and to the poor ghosts of Napetuca. If you go back, it will be to serve a greater purpose. Tell your people what you have done, how you have avenged the dead. The Uzachile will need your leadership in the coming days. If you would do anything for me, do this: Make yourselves a good life. Help heal the pain left by the monster."

From under lowered brows, Pearl Hand was cataloging each worried expression, her knife singing as it slid angrily across the stone.

I knew that look and shot her a warning glance before saying, "That is all that will be said about the matter."

Breakfast the following morning was uncomfortably silent. The Orphans moved as if their limbs were wooden, and I had to bark a sharp order when a heated argument broke out between Corn Thrower and Walking Thunder. Blood Thorn had a wistful expression as he cast knowing glances at the Orphans. And Pearl Hand? She remained locked in her head, jaws clamped, worry in her eyes.

"What are you thinking?" I asked her as I tied Skipper's pack to his back. Then I reached down, feeling the joints in his front legs. Even with his first steps I could tell he was hurting.

"I'm thinking that as long as we were in the south, the Orphans always had the knowledge that they could go home."

I turned to slip Gnaw's pack on.

She studied Walking Thunder where he was checking his quiver and bow. "Dying didn't scare them. Not in the beginning. But traveling to a land they'd never even heard of has shaken them to the bones." She very carefully asked, "You're dead set on Cofitachequi?"

"I am."

Her dark eyes hardened. "They're wondering what will happen to their souls if they're killed. Dying here, they know the way home. Even if they never make it to their ancestors, their ghosts can find their way back to friendly forests, familiar haunts."

I sighed, pulling Gnaw's pack laces tight. "But in Cofitachequi, dying means wandering lost forever."

"Just be ready to deal with it when the time comes." She stood, expression pinched. Then she reached for her crossbow and arrows.

"What's bothering you?"

She smiled, wistful. "Nothing I can't handle."

"But I—"

"Drop it, husband. There is nothing to discuss."

At the look she was giving me, I took my bow, slung my quiver, and led the way back up to the ridge top. Cofitachequi lay far off to the east-northeast. We had two possible routes, one through the hilly country skirting the northern boundaries of Ochisi and Ocute, the other south, beyond the fall line—flatter, but filled with swamps and backwaters.

"Which way?" Blood Thorn asked.

I turned to Walking Thunder, seeing a desperate indecision in his drawn expression. Neither Corn Thrower nor Wide Antler looked any better. I walked to each, clasping him by the shoulders, smiling. Then I pointed toward the south. "Go home. You are free. I ask only that you live honorable lives. The past is filled with horror; the future can be anything you make it."

"Peliqua?" Wide Antler asked. "If I leave, what will I have left? I swore myself to Power. To Horned Serpent."

I pointed toward our abandoned camp. "Tie Snake came in a dream. He told me that you could go if you wished. Power has freed you from your obligations. You are all blessed."

They looked at each other, hope and longing vying with shame and unease.

"Go," I said insistently. "I can see it in your eyes. You have served Power with honor and courage."

Walking Thunder was the first to nod, then Corn Thrower. Wide Antler looked as if his souls were being torn apart. I stepped up to him. "Don't do this to yourself. You're not abandoning us or your honor. Occasionally in a person's life, Power asks him to change direction. And that, too, my friend, is faith. The scars on your soul will never go away, but the anger that you feel toward the Kristianos must now be changed. Power wishes you to use that energy to heal. If you will continue to fight the monster, you must ensure that the survivors have food and are taught. You must instill the will to live, to hope, and to smile. Do that, and in the end, the Kristianos are defeated."

I could see his roiling souls, the battle he fought within.

I added, "Your struggle is now for your people. And it will be more difficult, more challenging than killing Kristianos."

"I understand, Peliqua." And he dropped to one knee, his palms up in obeisance.

One by one, the others knelt, heads bowed, palms up.

I took a deep breath, a tightness in my chest, an ache in my heart. Then I pulled them up, clasping them close, struggling to keep from mimicking Corn Thrower, whose tears streaked down his face.

Blood Thorn, too, clasped them, offered words of encouragement and advice. Then Pearl Hand said her farewells. The Orphans each hugged the dogs, and I turned away. A Chicaza never lets another human being see anything drip from his eyes unless it's blood from a wound received in battle.

And then, to avoid any further shameful excesses of emotion, I called to the dogs and started forth, never looking back.

I chose the northern route through the hills. The terrain was an endless up and down, forested with old growth, which meant easy traveling in the dappled shadows beneath ancient giants. Had we gone south, dropped below the fall line, the route would have been flat, with large rivers, endless swamps, and bugs. Either way, it was going to be a race.

No one spoke as we marched along under the spreading oaks, hickories, gums, and maples.

Why did they leave? I had a hollow feeling under my heart, a sense of loss mixed with guilt. *What should I have said or done that would have alleviated their growing discomfort?*

"It was only a matter of time," Pearl Hand said, reading the subtle clues of my posture and expression. "When they first came to us, the passion and hate were consuming. Enough so that they willingly followed you into Apalachee territory. They were welcomed there, and we had Kristianos aplenty to kill."

"I know."

Blood Thorn added, "The march around Capacheeki was a trial for them. By the ancestors, I understand how they felt. We were stumbling into the unknown. The events at Toa affected them like knocking posts out from under a granary. The idea that the people we were there to help had granted sanctuary to the enemy . . . It's worrisome, Peliqua."

"Yes, it is."

I was keeping an eye on Skipper. Once he'd loosened up, he was back to his normal sideways gait. The lightened pack seemed to help. I continued to lie to myself, thinking that he'd be all right.

"Part of the problem is that the world is so . . . *big*," Blood Thorn added. "Even I, who have heard of such places as Toa, never thought I'd actually see it. For the Orphans? Well, put yourself in their place. Imagine never traveling farther than the closest town and then finding out that not only is the world huge, but you're not even in the center of it like you had always believed."

"I remember." But as a Chicaza, being trained for the high minko's chair, I'd had to learn about the Nations and where they lay. "And you, Blood Thorn?"

"I have promised my souls to Power for the opportunity to drive an arrow into the monster's heart. That I'll never see my lands again, that my souls will be forever lost, is a price I'm willing to pay." He paused. "I can never go back. The memories would murder my souls."

I shot him a sidelong glance. "You have become a person of the world instead of an Uzachile."

"How so?"

"Think of Apalachee. You have friends there. Were you ever to return, you know the language, the customs. You are one of the famous Orphans. Cafakke would welcome you as an old friend. Fire Falcon would feast you, entertain you, and listen, again, to the stories of warfare with the Kristianos."

Blood Thorn nodded. "I begin to see."

Pearl Hand clambered over a twisted knot of roots, bracing herself on the tree's mighty trunk as she said, "I have no desire to return to the places I fled."

Something remained unsaid, her expression unusually grim.

"Even Apalachee?"

"I was referring to my life before you came into it, husband. Or do you have a burning itch to return to Irriparacoxi's lands?"

"You've made your point." I half skidded down a leafy slope, watching Squirm take the opportunity to try to scrape his pack off on an exposed rock.

Blood Thorn asked, "What do you know about Cofitachequi?"

Pearl Hand replied, "Cofitachequi controls a vast territory ranging from the ocean, up the rivers, and into the mountains. Even my Chicora paid tribute to the great lord. He is called Cofitachequi Mico, and his people believe him to be a god. His capital is at a place called Telemico, just below the Fall Line. He controls fifty or sixty subordinate micos and their peoples. You want to know why there's no main trail between Ocute and Cofitachequi? It's because the Ocute want to keep as much wilderness as they can between themselves and Cofitachequi's deadly armies."

She gave me a grim smile. "How long since you've been there?"

"Five years. Most of my trade was in the mountain towns. I made it as far as the capital, just to see it, and was told in no uncertain terms that Cofitachequi Mico would be unavailable to a lowly trader such as myself."

"Arrogant, aren't they?" she added bitterly.

"How was trade?" Blood Thorn asked.

"Not good." I pushed a vine out of the way as I stepped over a maze of roots. "I was low on exotics, things like whelk shell, large plates of copper, buffalo wool and horn, things the elite there don't normally have access to. If you're going to go trade with the rich and exalted, you'd better have outstanding merchandise."

"Do we?" Blood Thorn asked.

"Not as much as we did before we ran into Mikko Egret, but yes. We've got a few Kristiano pieces left, Taino tobacco, spoonbill feathers, buffalo wool, large pieces of shell, and those whelk-shell cups Egret traded us." I tapped my sword hilt. "And, if things turn complicated, our Kristiano weapons."

Pearl Hand snorted her derision, eyes slitting. Whatever was bothering her had put her into a downright foul mood.

I asked, "What's wrong?"

Her hard eyes met mine, and I saw that she was about to speak. Then she glanced away, shaking her head. "It's nothing."

Blood Thorn, in an attempt at levity, cried, "I'm surprised you didn't trade for all their gold!"

"I thought I'd leave it for the Kristianos."

"How far is Cofitachequi, really?" Blood Thorn stepped up beside us as we crossed an open section under a grove of magnificent black oaks.

"If we don't have trouble, we can make it in twenty days of hard travel."

"De Soto will be slowed by his soldados and those accursed *puercos*."

"But he's on far better trails." I looked up, judging the angle of the sun. "At least until he reaches the other side of Ocute. The buffer zone is a forested mess, filled with swamps, the trails running every which way, only to vanish into a maze of brush. Power willing, he'll get lost, and we won't."

"The Ocute won't guide him?" Blood Thorn asked.

"It depends on how de Soto treats them."

"Pearl Hand said that the Cofitachequi military is even better than the Apalachee's."

"And the Cofitachequi know about Kristianos," Pearl Hand said. "They're just upriver from where my father's Kristianos tried to build their town. Who knows what stories they've heard?"

"Then perhaps they won't be fooled by de Soto's peaceful arrival," Blood Thorn suggested hopefully. "But what about us? We're three warriors short. Ambushes will be that much harder to pull off."

I shot another glance at the slanting sun. "Somehow, Iniha, I think that if de Soto goes back to his old ways, we'll find recruits enough to fill our ranks."

Under her breath, I heard Pearl Hand ominously whisper, "Twenty days . . . to Telemico . . ."

Sacrifice

"Elder?" the voice asks, intruding into her dreams. "Elder? Is something wrong with your meal?"

She starts, aware of the incomprehensible babble filling the tchkofa. In an instant, she is back in the present. The bones in her neck grind as she turns to the high minko. Blinking, she takes in his copper headpiece, the eagle feathers spreading in a starburst behind it. The man's tattooed face is painted in white with red circles on his cheeks, a yellow line down his chin. He wears wrapped strands of shell necklace, a white apron, and a beautiful shell gorget on his chest.

He looks at her with sympathetic eyes, the question lingering in the set of his lips.

"I drifted . . . ," she whispers.

"Where?"

"Back," she hears herself answer, as if from a great distance. "Back to the fear."

"Fear?" he asks, suddenly unsure.

"Isn't that always the price?"

"The price for what, venerable elder?"

But the high minko, the feast, the tchkofa, all have faded, blending with the images of the past. She sees the resolution in Black Shell's eyes, knows in her soul that he is right.

The choice, of course, is hers. Even setting foot in Cofitachequi will place her life, and possibly Black Shell's, in peril.

Will anyone even remember me after all these years?

Hah! As if they could ever forget her and what she cost them!

She makes a face, squinting as if something bitter lay upon her tongue. What made me even think we'd get an audience with the Cofitachequi Mico in the first place? Let alone that I'd be recognized.

But then, she, of all people, knew the way to manipulate the oretas, micos, and yatikas of Cofitachequi. Yes, she could make it happen.

The price Power has placed on ultimate victory now comes terribly clear. Paying it will cost her everything she loves, her happiness, even her life.

Where did I ever find the courage?

NINETEEN

I HAD ONLY TRAVELED THIS WAY ONCE. TO THE SOUTH of the foothills lies a huge forest of pines, the soil poor. But the country we were fighting our way through was rougher than I remembered. In the end we kept descending ridges, struggling through trees, clambering over roots, weaving through vines, until we skirted just north of the frontier farmsteads in the Ocute valley. From there I set my bearings and followed the fall line, where foothills with sluggish and brush-choked drainages vanished into the pine barrens.

Each day we rose just before dawn, ate, packed, and started walking, seeking our way through the maze of game trails that led east-northeast. Old fires and tornados left patches of deadfall covered with brush, vines, and saplings that had to be crossed or skirted. Streams had to be waded, the packs carried across before the dogs could swim them, and swamps avoided. When nightfall came, we cooked whatever we'd shot, collected, or harvested and fell into our blankets, dead to the world.

We said little, our effort spent on ducking branches, wiggling around grape and greenbrier, or stepping over roots. When I stopped once for a breath, it was to look around at the endless forest, wondering if people really did exist, or if they'd become an imaginative image spun of the forest itself.

Flowers were everywhere, the trees budding with vibrant green life. The smells of nectar, new leaves, leaf mat, and damp soil filled the world. At times we almost cringed from the noise; bees, wasps, dragonflies, cicadas, crickets, and humming insect wings vied with squirrels, chickadees, robins, mockingbirds, crows, jays, waxwings, siskins, cardinals, and so many others. Turkeys and passenger pigeons were plentiful, and we shot opossums, beavers, raccoons, and even a spring bear.

Then we came to the river. In the mountains to the west, its headwaters were dominated by the Tugalo Nation. Where we emerged on the floodplain below the fall line, the leaf mat beneath the trees had the telltale signs of abandoned farmsteads long surrendered to the wild. No structures remained; people had left there at least a couple of generations past. Nevertheless, faint trails took us to a curving oxbow. A long-abandoned city covered with second-growth forest lay across spring-swollen waters.

"Pearl Hand, do you know that place?" I pointed to the tree-studded ruins of the town opposite us.

"When I was traded south, it was along the coast. I heard talk. Several Nations once flourished up here. They were said to be a ruthless people. One of their priests supposedly became evil, and the last inhabitants weighted his body with stones and tossed him into the river. Even as his body sank, he turned into a giant snake and dived into the depths, the ropes and rocks slipping from his body. The people left, but where they went, no one knows."

Blood Thorn continued to scowl at the water. "Either we find a canoe or grow wings. Upstream, or down?"

I looked up and down the water course, only to have my bit of Horned Serpent's brow tine pull to the right. "Down."

Moving back from the willows, water oaks, and bald cypresses that lined the bank, we discovered an old trail worn into the ground.

Not that following it was easy; more than once meanders of the river had washed away whole sections, and in other places the vegetation had grown so thick as to leave the trail impassable. But by evening, we emerged on yet another abandoned town.

From the growth of the trees, I estimated it had been at least one hundred years since the place had been inhabited. Two mounds—one cone shaped, the other a chief's platform mound—rose to either side of a small plaza.

We walked across grass and spring flowers, feeling the irregularity of old house floors. Occasional burned timbers poked up from the vegetation.

Climbing the chief's mound, I saw where a good-sized palace had once stood; burned timbers, like faded ghosts, haunted the heights. Perhaps the palace had been overrun and torched by enemy warriors. Maybe the chief died, his people in poor circumstances because of an early frost, corn blight, or a raid that had burned their granaries. They would have set his palace afire, spiritually cleansing it along with its dead master.

Blood Thorn kicked a large ceramic pot from a slump in the side of the mound. Human bones spilled from within the stamp-decorated urn.

"Forgive me," Blood Thorn told the burial, touching his forehead in respect. Then he knelt, carefully replacing the bones and doing his best to re-cover them.

Where rainwater had run, charcoal, stamped pot sherds, and bits of burned bone could be seen. I led the way down to the river as the dogs sniffed around.

What had obviously been a canoe landing was overgrown, the river slowly eating away at it. I took a deep breath, smelling water, mud, and spring-green vegetation. Off to the west, black and ominous clouds were packed against the mountains. From the looks of it, it was raining by canoe-loads up there.

"Water's going to be a lot higher come morning."

That's when Pearl Hand parted the brush to my left. "Black Shell? Look."

I waded in after her, to where a canoe lay inverted on a support of rotting logs. Pulling back the haw bushes, I could see the rounded bottom was weather checked and gray, with a long crack in the middle. "It's been here awhile."

With Blood Thorn's help, we muscled the thing out of its resting place. The workmanship was excellent, and while mushrooms and mold had found places to lodge, the inside looked serviceable. All but that crack in the bottom.

"We can seal that with pitch," Blood Thorn announced. "The problem is paddles. Are there any back in the brush?"

I pushed my way back into the thicket, looking under the rotting logs. "Nothing we can use."

"We can make something to serve," Pearl Hand called as Blood Thorn trotted off in search of pine pitch.

By the time I'd retrieved the Kristiano ax from Gnaw's pack, Pearl Hand had returned with two charred timbers. We had them split and formed into paddles long before Blood Thorn was back with a clutch of resin balls.

"It's a long way back to the pine," Blood Thorn panted.

I glanced to the west, where the setting sun silhouetted the tops of the angry clouds. "Even if we have to set up camp in the dark, I'd like to be across."

"You know"—Blood Thorn dropped his hardened sap into Pearl Hand's pot—"it's going to be days before anything we cook in this pot doesn't taste like pine sap."

"Pine isn't a bad taste," Pearl Hand answered shortly. "It's the film it leaves on your teeth that drives you crazy."

She proceeded to stir the mix into a gummy mess. Then came the laborious job of dabbing it into the crack.

"It won't last long in the water." Blood Thorn stared skeptically at the patch job.

"All we have to do is get to the other side." I started unlacing the packs from the dogs. If this went wrong I didn't want them to drown under the weight.

In the deepening dusk, Pearl Hand declared the job done. Wading out into the river, we floated the craft, seeing only a little seepage. Just as quickly, the dogs were loaded, the packs stowed, and we shoved off. I grimaced at the water lapping barely a hand's width below the gunnels of the overloaded dugout.

The current immediately grabbed us; we paddled and prayed, driven by the fear of swamping and drowning. The dogs, oblivious, happily wagged their tails, ears pricked, eyes agleam.

"Downstream," I said reasonably. "But stay toward the north bank. If we sink, we can toss the packs over the brush and pull ourselves up by the branches."

I kept glancing at the sloshing water growing ever deeper around my feet. The river seemed to be climbing the sides of the hull.

"There," Pearl Hand called from the bow. "The bank's lower."

As we drove in, she stepped out to battle the brush and hold the craft in place. Bark bailed out, the others after him. It turned into a churning mess, dogs wading, shaking, clawing at the cattails, and finally wiggling through. One by one I handed the packs to Blood Thorn, who handed them to Pearl Hand.

The canoe was filling fast. With the last quiver of arrows handed over, I let the vessel go and stood there, watching it spin slowly away in the current, a dark and lonely silhouette against the silvered water.

"Thank you," I whispered. "And to the long-gone craftsman who made you, may his ghost smile in return for our gratitude."

Then I struggled through the maze of cattails to find Pearl Hand and Blood Thorn.

"We're not done yet, people," I said reluctantly as I looked around the marshy surroundings. "This whole area could be underwater by morning. Our best bet is to make it to that city."

Silly me. It was almost dawn by the time we'd stumbled

our way to the ruins. But with first light, I was proven correct: The river was over the opposite bank.

"Who were these people?" Blood Thorn wondered. We sat on the lip of the tree-studded chief's mound, a light rain falling. Just climbing the steep sides left a person breathing hard when he finally reached the summit. Once there, the flat top was a long stone's throw in length and nearly as wide. Kicking around in the leaf mat and dead saplings turned up charred timbers.

A total of six mounds could be seen, and the view of the river from this high perch must have been stunning before the trees reclaimed it. Anyone arriving by canoe would have been left in awe, not only of the high mound but of the great palace that dominated it.

A large defensive moat had been excavated below river level around the town—an impassable barrier before the few rotting bits of palisade. Back in the forest, hidden by trees, was the barrow pit from which dirt to build the mounds had been removed. After all these years, the one-time excavation now formed a sizable lake.

Given the number of mounds, the amount of land contained within the town, and the extent of the abandoned cornfields around it, many thousands of people must have lived in the vicinity, the total augmented by those in Canoe Town, as we called the ruins we'd found across the river.

Behind us, beneath a ramada we'd thrown up, Pearl Hand busied herself over a fire. I could smell turkey cooking, and the dogs had feasted on a couple of raccoons I'd found back in the forest.

Looking out at the flooded river below us, I said, "Nations rise and fall. Like people, each has a life of its own. Maybe this is the town Pearl Hand spoke of, the one where the priest turned evil. Or maybe the soils lost their fertility after years of cultivation."

Turning my attention to the chunkey court—it was barely visible in the grass—I imagined feathered and decorated players rolling their stones, casting lances. All the while a crowd yelled with delight or dismay as a priest called out the score and the game master twisted a stick into the earth.

Were their bones resting in this very mound? Perhaps just below where I sat? From the way the river was eroding the bank, even the great mound upon which we sat would eventually be consumed. When the last bit of earth surrendered to the river, who, then, would recall the greatness of this place?

"Maybe the town just wore out," Blood Thorn mused. "It's hard to imagine. I've never seen a city this large." He slapped a hand to the high earth where we perched. "Nor can I imagine the amount of work it took to build this."

"I've seen bigger," I told him. "And soon so will you, in Cofitachequi. But there have been even greater cities. The ruins of Cahokia are said to overwhelm anything now in our world."

"How did they do it?" Blood Thorn gazed around at the surrounding mounds and the wide ditch just off to our east. "Even in Uzachile, with all of our people, it's all we can do to keep the palisades up, the buildings repaired. I'm not sure my people could build the likes of this."

"Blood Thorn, what men build, they inevitably destroy."

"Makes you sad, doesn't it? That we carry the plantings of greatness and ultimate rot down in our souls?"

"Nothing is forever," I replied.

"Except the sun and the Spirit Beasts." He had such simple faith in his eyes.

But I remembered Piasa's fear when it came to de Soto and his god. Not even Spirit Beasts could count on forever. At the heart of things, they depended upon people. Living human beings, just like the ones who had once raised, then abandoned this city to the wilderness.

For four days we followed the ghost of an old trail that led from the river north across the swampy bottoms and finally to the divide. Along the way we found the remains of old towns, villages, and farmsteads, now little more than revitalized forest.

Once we crossed the low divide, I kept us heading east-northeast; we found no trails beneath the endless spreading trees. Skipper hobbled along in obvious pain. I kept lightening his pack. Pearl Hand—growing ever more introspective—watched him with worried eyes.

"What is it?" she asked one night.

"His joints are failing," I answered glumly. "Pack dogs have a good life, all things considered. But everything comes at a price. Trade dogs wear out faster than their town-bred cousins. I'm afraid Skipper's time is coming."

"What will we do when it does?"

"Find a young dog to take his pack."

She gave me a penetrating look. "He's not that old."

"Maybe it's that sideways gait of his. Maybe it's because his bones aren't as strong."

She considered that and petted Skipper on the head.

He looked up at her with adoring eyes, tail thumping. "Come, Cofitachequi," she told the dog, "we'll find someone else to bear your load."

I nodded, remembering Napetuca—and Skipper wading into the fight with the Kristiano war dogs. Yes, he'd be taken care of, even if it meant our own bellies would be empty.

Then I studied Pearl Hand's grim expression. "That takes care of Skipper. What's wrong with you? The farther north we go, the more worried you get."

With a grim smile she waved me off. "It's nothing."

Sure, nothing. *Maybe it's just this endless forest.* Walking in the perpetual shadows was even getting to me.

The sepaya brought me awake, almost vibrating on my chest. I blinked, staring around. A whip-poor-will called in the night, the breeze stirring high branches. The perfumed odor of forest, leaves, flowers, and damp earth filled my nostrils.

Pearl Hand wasn't in bed. She sat staring at the gleaming red embers in the fire through large dark eyes. The glow illuminated her sadness, accented by the set of her full lips, the hollows of her smooth cheeks, and the tumbling veils of thick black hair that framed her face and high brow. I could see her slim fingers absently twirling a thick twist of her long hair.

Blood Thorn snored lightly—a dark shape wrapped in his blanket. The dogs were shadowy blotches where they slept among the packs.

"What's wrong?" I asked softly. "It's the middle of the night."

She turned. "Husband?"

"Yes?"

"I need to speak to you."

I sat up, pulling the blanket back. "Whatever it is, we can deal with it."

She surprised me when she said, "Life is but a series of cycles: Beginnings lead to endings. Endless circles that carry a person back to face who they once were. The past clings fast to a person as if it were a cloak woven of a spider's web."

"Uh . . . excuse me?"

"When we reach Cofitachequi, I need you to trust me."

I rolled my shoulders and yawned, still sleep-addled. "What are you talking about?"

"When I left Cofitachequi, it wasn't under the best of circumstances. Things happened there. Things that I . . ." The words died in her throat.

"Pearl Hand, I don't—"

"The young are cursed with terrible passions. I . . . I've been dreading this. Going back there."

"Then we won't go."

Her dark eyes sought mine, appearing as black holes in her pale face. "We have to. We'll never have a better chance to destroy the monster. I know that. You know that." She smiled in a futile attempt to mask the bitter irony. "But I must ask something of you."

"Anything," I told her in a kind voice.

She hesitated and I knew her well enough to realize she was trying to find the right words, to predict my reaction. She finally took a breath, saying: "Can you trust me?"

"Of course. Why do you ask?"

"If you play your part, follow my orders without question, I may be able to get you into the very heart of Cofitachequi."

"Why are you talking like this?"

Her smile grew sad. "Because the destruction of de Soto's life may very well come at the cost of my own."

"But you can't—"

"Shh!" She placed her fingers on my lips. "We made our bargain with Power long ago. Our lives, hopes, desires, and dreams were surrendered to fate. Just tell me that you trust me, that you will let me do this my way. Promise me that you will not interfere or argue."

"I still don't understand."

"Cofitachequi's rulers take themselves very seriously. As traders it might take us a full moon to be granted an audience. If you let me do this my way, I can have you face-to-face with the Cofitachequi mico himself within a day of our arrival. I know them. How they think. How to use their arrogance to manipulate them."

"You can do that?"

"Oh, yes."

"Pearl Hand, you're not telling me everything."

"I asked you to trust me."

"But I—"

"Then please do so."

I nodded reluctantly.

My first warning of trouble was when Squirm scented the air, stopped short, and began growling, his hackles rising. The other dogs immediately responded in kind, sniffing, barking, and informing me in no uncertain terms that something dangerous was lurking in the brush to either side of the stream crossing we approached.

I gave the sign to stop and pulled my trader's staff from its quiver. Raising it, I called, "Greetings! I am Black Shell, a trader."

I hadn't even gotten the words out when Pearl Hand pushed by me, speaking fluently in Cofitachequi dialect: "In the service of the Cofitachequi mico, you are ordered to come out—bound by the white Power of peace—and show yourselves."

A young man rose from the brush, an arrow drawn. Pearl Hand stepped forward, a haughty set to her head. Or at least as haughty as she could pull off given the spiderwebs in her hair and her travel-stained clothing.

Blood Thorn was behind me, stock-still, waiting to see what unfolded. The dogs had their ears pricked, fixed on the hunters, their muscles quivering with the desire to spring on the newcomers. I ordered them down.

One by one, the three remaining hunters rose, until an older man—bow at the ready—stepped out onto the trail. Head cocked, he inspected first Pearl Hand, then me, and finally Blood Thorn. A faint smile crossed his lips as he took in Blood Thorn's Timucua hair pom and his unusual tattoos.

Pearl Hand continued. "I travel in service to the Cofitachequi mico. The traders who accompany me come under the white Power. In the name of the Sun Ruler, I command you to lower your weapons." She paused. "Or aren't the four of you bright enough to figure out that two men, a woman, and four dogs are a poor excuse for a Hichiti raiding party?"

"Forgive me, Oreta," the older man said, bowing his head out of respect and lowering his bow. "I am called Turkey Track, son of Clay Woman, of the House Clan, of the Tight Cloth Moiety. These others are my male kin: Red Cat to my right, Fox Tail, and the young one is known as Rabbit."

Oreta? Invoking nobility was risky business.

Pearl Hand arrogantly said, "With me is Black Shell, of the Chicaza. This man is Blood Thorn, of the Uzachile. They come under the Power of trade and bind themselves by its rules."

Turkey Track inclined his head to Pearl Hand. "How can we be of assistance to the oreta?"

I shot a curious glance at Pearl Hand. Blood Thorn and I might have been no more than ornaments.

"We come from the south," she snapped, "with important word for the Cofitachequi mico. I must be taken to him immediately."

Turkey Track and his cousins reacted visibly, touching their foreheads. With great care, Turkey Track wet his lips. "Perhaps the oreta has not heard. He who was above all of us has sent his souls to live among the ancestors. His sister has taken the chair and is now Cofitachequi mico."

"We had not heard." Pearl Hand's expression narrowed. "Our hearts are both saddened and happy. While we grieve for the loss of so great a man, we rejoice that his souls are now returned to the company of his ancestors. What was the manner of his passing?"

"A terrible illness, great Oreta." Turkey Track now appeared uneasy. "It came upon us a year ago fall, perhaps from the coast, since such dark afflictions seem to breed there. Our healers and priests tried everything, but the pestilence remained unchecked until recently."

He gestured to his companions. "Like so many, we fled to the forest. Entire towns are abandoned, the fields fallow. To ensure survival, many have taken to full-time hunting. Only recently have the survivors begun returning to their homes, cutting weeds, preparing fields. It is our hope that whatever the evil, it has sated itself, or been vanquished by the sacrifices made by our holy people."

I studied them. The Cofitachequi dress in finely tanned buckskin pants and wear decorated hunting shirts of either buckskin or myrtle fabric. They prefer soft-topped moccasins and favor long capes during cold weather. The hunters we'd encountered had obviously been out for a while; their clothing sported dried blood splotches on the sleeves and greasy spots on the fronts.

Their bows, however, looked first-rate, the staves varnished, their quivers full of turkey-feather-fletched arrows. Each man had a butchering kit hanging from a belt pouch.

Pearl Hand turned to me. "Did you understand that?"

"You'll be surprised, Oreta, to learn that even with my limited comprehension of Mos'kogee, I managed." I tried to keep the sarcasm out of my voice.

Pearl Hand turned her dark eyes my way, saying in Timucua, "You promised."

I stiffened, feeling dumb. *Yes, wife. Do it your way.* But as a Cofitachequi oreta? She'd be found out the moment we set foot in Telemico.

Turkey Track shifted uneasily. He might have seen thirty winters and was of average height, with bad teeth. Red Cat looked younger, his flat face weather browned. A crow feather was stuck sideways in his hair. Fox Tail was easy to spot; he was the one with the scar on his cheek. Young Rabbit had an awed look and couldn't seem to meet anyone's eyes.

"Any news of de Soto?" I asked.

Pearl Hand formally asked, "What have you heard about the Kristianos coming through the forest from the south? From the Ocute."

Turkey Track's eyes widened. "We have heard nothing. Our apologies, Oreta. Outside of other hunters from our clan, you are the first strangers we've seen in over a year."

I nodded, smiling at Turkey Track and his friends. "Oreta, please ask them if they would camp with us tonight. In return for a piece of trade, we'll share our meal and get directions to the capital."

Pearl Hand dismissed me with a look, her crossbow hanging from her back. To the hunters, she said, "You will accompany us for the rest of the day and guide us on the quickest route toward Telemico. We will share our food and reward you for your service."

"Yes, Oreta!" Turkey Track touched his forehead respectfully. Moments later we were following them back along the trail.

"What's going on?" Blood Thorn asked. "I only caught a couple of words. As different as Toa is from Apalachee, their speech is almost incomprehensible. And what's with Pearl Hand? Is she trying to insult them, or what?"

"Beat me with a stick if I know, but I promised her that I'd let her do this her way."

I slipped past Gnaw so I could lean close to Pearl Hand as we splashed across the creek.

I asked as casually as I could, "Why are you acting like a snotty, spoiled bitch? And posing as an oreta will get us only as far as the first local mico before someone exposes you as a fraud."

She shot me an irritated look. "We're in Cofitachequi now. Can you act like one of their nobles, Black Shell?"

"What about just saying: 'We're here under the Power of trade and want to tell you about a monster coming up from the south'?"

"Tell me. Last time you were here, did you enjoy the Cofitachequi mico's fine hospitality?"

"I was barely let in the gates."

"Then shut up . . . and let me do this my way."

"Want to at least tell me the plan so I can play along?"

"Just be yourself."

I dropped back, frowning, aware of the tension in her shoulders and the way her feet pounded the trail. What, by Piasa's balls, had come over her? Then I realized. *She's scared half out of her skin!*

I let Gnaw crash through the grass and resume his place, then glanced back at Blood Thorn. "Just follow Pearl Hand's lead."

"Oh?"

"She's got a plan."

"Which is . . . what?"

"If I knew what, it wouldn't just be her plan, would it?"

"So you're as baffled as I am. That's reassuring."

We camped that night in a mulberry grove. Before I could get her off to one side for a talk, Pearl Hand rummaged through Bark's pack. She pulled out a trade dress, shell, and jewelry, and left us under the lengthening shadows beneath the beech and gum trees. I watched her disappear behind the rushes that bordered the creek.

Blood Thorn began plucking our fowl while Turkey Track's hunters produced a chipped and battered brownware pot. After filling it with water they added mulberries, knotweed seed, and wild onions. Red Cat produced a rabbit they cut into quarters and chucked in with the stew.

"You have traveled far with the oreta?" Turkey Track asked casually.

I turned my attention to sorting through our packs, seeking a proper bit of trade in return for their service—assuming Pearl Hand didn't drive them off first with her sham superiority. "From down in the peninsula. We've been keeping an eye on de Soto."

"He's the new Kristiano?" Turkey Track gave me a wary, sidelong glance.

"He is."

"Ah." He nodded to himself. "That makes sense. She serves her lady well. No one would expect a woman spy."

Now I understood exactly . . . well, nothing. "She serves her lady?"

He shrugged, a calm acceptance in his sober brown eyes. "The Cofitachequi mico. She has been the Sun Ruler since her brother's death. Having lost her son, she has only herself to rely on. There are her two nieces, of course, but neither is old enough for the responsibilities." Even as he said it, I could see him wince. "Please do not repeat that." He indicated the rushes where Pearl Hand had disappeared.

"Absolutely not."

Now it began to fit together. Turkey Track and the others thought Pearl Hand had been sent on a spy mission by the Cofitachequi mico. I wondered what else was lurking under the surface and how it played into Pearl Hand's game.

"Pearl Hand is not who we always thought she was," Blood Thorn mused in Timucua.

"I think the oreta farce is going to fall flat the moment we're out of the forest."

Blood Thorn laughed out loud. "And here I always thought you were so smart." Then he gave my shoulder a pat. "Come on, wily trader. She's your wife. Are you really that dense?"

Was I? Pearl Hand spoke the language of the nobles. And just where—idiot trader—had she learned that? Her mother had originally sold her, and to whom would that have been, the Chicora being a subservient people to the Cofitachequi Nation?

Somewhere here, she's afraid she's going to run into her old owner. Probably some influential mico in the court at Telemico. She's scared to death that he's going to recognize her . . . and the gods know what circumstances under which she left his household!

I was considering that when Pearl Hand emerged from the rushes. She'd wiggled into a striking white trade dress. The thing clung to her like a second skin, emphasizing every curve of her perfect body. Her hair, combed glossy, hung in raven waves over a white swan-feather cloak. Her lips were reddened with ocher, a black mascara darkened her eyes, and she wore a wealth of shell necklaces from the trade pack. On her chest rested a whelk-shell gorget carved in the rattlesnake design.

I'd always thought her a great beauty, but decked out like this? She was stunning.

All eyes turned her direction as she came striding up, back straight, head high. In the silence around the crackling fire, she ordered, "Black Shell, find me something to sit upon that won't stain the fabric."

She was using that formal stilted speech. I shot a glance at Squirm, who was lying at her side. Naw, he'd never obey a command to bite her.

Instead, I rose and walked off in search of an appropriate log to make a chair out of.

"Just wait until we get under the covers tonight, wife,"

I promised in Timucua as I placed her "chair" before the fire.

She gave me her most ravishing smile, the one that melted my bones. In Timucua, she replied, "Sorry, husband. A high-ranking Cofitachequi oreta would never share her bed with a lowly foreign trader. You've become the hired help."

"But, I . . ." *Hired help?*

"Doesn't mean you can't dream about me tonight." Her eyes flashed; she was teasing me for all she was worth.

"I could have just left you with Irriparacoxi way back when."

"You'd have been so bored."

TWENTY

PEARL HAND WAS UP BEFORE THE REST OF US; SHE dressed in her travel clothes again.

The hunters had scrambled at her every whim, cooking, filling her bowl, refilling it, offering her first servings of everything. They had taken the dishes, washed them, kept the fire, built her a small shelter, and one even offered his little cooking pot for a night jar. The fact that the bowl was empty and obviously unused in the morning erased a curious anxiety that had plagued my sleep.

Blood Thorn bore all this with a detached amusement. Nor could I tell who entertained him the most: me or Pearl Hand.

She didn't let us linger but had us packed and on the trail by sunrise. As we worked out of the backcountry, we began encountering people. Each time we did Turkey

Track called out, "Make way for the lady! She goes in service of the Cofitachequi mico! Make way!"

And they did, scurrying off the trail, dropping to their knees, palms uplifted, heads down, as we passed.

"So much for the chance to learn anything about what's happening locally," I growled to Blood Thorn. Traders thrive on the local gossip: Who's squabbling with whom? What items are in demand? The personal habits of the leaders? Little fascinating facts and insights? These can make a big difference in a trader's ability to profit.

Blood Thorn's barely hidden smile proved more irritating than a blister beetle in my breechcloth. He smugly said, "Now you know how the rest of us felt in Toa and Apalachee."

"At least I told you what we were up against."

"Yes. And you always ended it with 'trust me,' even though it seemed incomprehensible at the time."

"Worked out, didn't it?"

He arched an eyebrow. "That's why I've surrendered my souls to you . . . and Pearl Hand."

Mollified, I continued to hurry along and kept an eye on Skipper. His pack was half-empty now. The poor old man was pushing himself just to keep the pace.

We began passing inhabited farmsteads. But when we crossed through a small village, the houses were empty, weeds growing in the gardens, grass thick around the barricaded doors. The ramadas had a ratty look, with strips of roofing hanging loose; water pooled in the mortars while grass grew at their bases.

A hand of time later we wound through a small town that was empty, forlorn, and weed-choked. Only the charnel house off the plaza showed any sign of maintenance, the weeds pulled, the paths leading to it heavily traveled. The stench revealed why: The place had to be full to the rafters with victims of the pestilence.

"I'm getting a bad feeling about Cofitachequi," Blood Thorn said in Timucua.

"Whatever happened here, it's bad." I wondered what that meant for de Soto's arrival. I'd been expecting the vibrant and thriving Cofitachequi I'd seen five years ago. Now I was wondering if even Telemico would be inhabited.

By late afternoon—after passing through two more abandoned villages—we broke out of the forest into a heavily farmed bottom on the south side of the Cofitachequi River: a winding brown barrier that curled and twisted, its banks clotted with cottonwood, bald cypress, water oak, and stands of cane.

Across the water I could see a prominent talwa and was told it was Tagaya town. I'd been there, but what I saw looked forlorn and run-down. The sepaya felt like dead weight in its pouch.

"We will find canoes," Turkey Track announced, head bobbing respectfully. "We apologize for the lady's inconvenience." Then he touched his forehead and, his companions at heel, vanished into the rushes.

Pearl Hand waited, standing stiffly to one side. I took the opportunity to stroll over, placing a hand on my hip as I followed her distant gaze to Tagaya.

"Okay," I said. "What's our next play?"

She gave me a dull look, her expression pinched. "I'm thinking."

"About what?"

"What do you think?" she snapped.

"It's not too late. We could try something different."

She inclined her head at Tagaya. "The last time I was there the streets were crowded, people waving, bowing, offerings held before them. Those who looked up had a shining incredulousness in their eyes. They all thought I lived in a glorious world, the fools."

I squinted across the river. "You know, a lot of people have died in this plague. Maybe half, if I can gauge from the empty farms we've passed. Their fields are choked with weeds. Even Tagaya over there looks like it's in need of a major refurnishing. Chances are good that the man who owned you is dead."

She fixed her worried eyes on mine and was about to say something when Turkey Track burst from the rushes, crying, "Oreta! We have canoes coming. I have sent Red Cat across the river. He will inform the mico at Tagaya of your arrival."

And with those words, I saw Pearl Hand's resolve tighten like a fist.

I pulled my trader's staff from my quiver, uncertain whether to reach out with a reassuring hand. "Don't worry, my love. I'll take care of you." *One way or another.*

"Promise"—her voice almost broke—"that you'll follow my lead . . . do as I say. Remember: The important thing is stopping de Soto."

"I—"

"Promise, Black Shell."

"I promise."

To my surprise, no less than six canoes arrived, all propelled by local men. The vessel they brought for Pearl Hand had been crafted by a master—thin hulled, with decorative carving below the gunnels. I admired the wide beam and the way the interior had been sanded and waxed. Canoes like this weren't paddled but towed by a rope—a sign of the occupants' status and authority. Two young boys rode in it, each holding a colorful feather sunshade.

I saw to the loading of the dogs and packs in the other craft and managed to get a seat—along with Blood Thorn—in Pearl Hand's boat. I sighed, centering myself. I thought I could get used to this kind of treatment.

Pearl Hand might have been carved of granite. She sat facing forward, smack in the middle; the boys held the shade over her head. I didn't see as much as a flicker of emotion on her face.

We'd no more than left the bank, the rowers stroking in unison, when a delegation emerged from Tagaya. Several men walked in advance of a litter upon which rested what I assumed to be the local mico.

They were waiting when our canoes landed. The rowers sprang out and lifted our thin-walled craft out of the water before gently lowering it on high ground. This, of course, was so that Pearl Hand wouldn't get her feet wet.

Pearl Hand made a gesture, and the boys tilted the sunshade back. While Blood Thorn and I clambered out, Pearl Hand seemed to rise like smoke, elegantly stepping over the side.

I called the dogs over, asking, "Blood Thorn, could you see to the packs? That little wooden fish carving is for Turkey Track in return for his service."

"And miss this?" he said, chiding me. "Sure."

I raised my staff high, stepping up behind Pearl Hand. The mico's chair was placed on the ground, his carriers fading back. The four elders—advisers and councilmen called *ynahaes*—stood behind. Ynahaes are a step below oretas in the Cofitachequi pecking order. Their expressions turned curious as they studied Pearl Hand. Obviously they didn't know her, nor did the mico from his arching eyebrow.

We'd caught them by surprise; the usual finery wasn't in evidence. Poor fellows, they were just in their normal everyday clothes.

But then, we weren't looking any too impressive ourselves. And Blood Thorn was having his own trouble with the dogs. They weren't used to taking his orders.

Pearl Hand bowed deeply, touching her forehead. "Mico Tagaya, I am Pearl Hand, once of the Chicora. I arrive with these traders bearing important news for the Cofitachequi mico. An army of Kristianos approaches from Ocute. Their leader goes by *Adelantado* Hernando de Soto. His army numbers around six hundred warriors, many of them riding cabayos—perhaps two hundred of the beasts. Unlike Ayllón, they come not to build a town or simply raid for slaves. They come in the name of their high mico, *el rey Carlos de España,* to claim Cofitachequi as their own."

At the news, the mico turned thoughtful, then asked, "You speak like a noble, but I do not know you. Nor do you introduce yourself with your lineage, clan, or moiety." He shot a meaningful glance my way. "And you arrive in the presence of strangers."

I stepped forward. "I am Black Shell, of the Chief Clan, of the Chicaza's Hickory Moiety. The man who accompanies us is Blood Thorn, iniha of the Uzachile. We come under the Power of trade and bind ourselves by it. It is our request that we be granted passage to speak with the

Cofitachequi mico and inform her about the arrival of the Kristianos and their army."

He studied me a long moment, then studied Blood Thorn's foreign tattoos and pom hairstyle. "Interesting." His gaze went back to Pearl Hand. "But you still do not answer my questions."

Pearl Hand gave him a cold look. "I am bound by service to the Cofitachequi mico herself. With respect, Mico Tagaya, that is enough."

Bound by service! I kept my expression in check; my heart, however, was leaping around like a panicked frog. Pearl Hand had just made a bold move. Perhaps the only one she could . . . but to claim *service* to the high chair itself? How in the name of a blind piasa were we going to get out of that when they figured out it was a lie?

In Timucua, I whispered, "Careful."

She ignored me. "Mico Tagaya, we *require* passage now! The Kristianos may arrive at any instant. Every moment we hesitate could have dire consequences." Her voice turned cold. "*Do you understand?*"

I swallowed hard, fighting the urge to wince as the ynahaes' eyes widened in shock.

Mico Tagaya narrowed an eye but nodded. "Ynahaes, see to packing my things." Two of them touched their chins and left at a run for the town gates. Mico Tagaya looked at the paddlers who'd been standing by the side, heads down, and no doubt shocked to their bones. "You will bear the *lady* to Telemico with greatest haste. Yatika?"

The yatika—a man skilled in languages and oratory—stepped forward. "Yes, Mico."

The mico glanced up at the sun, estimating the time. "You will leave now, taking a fast canoe and as many paddlers as you deem necessary. Bear the news of our arrival to the Cofitachequi mico."

"Yes, Tagaya Mico." The man touched his forehead again, turned, and began shouting orders. Within moments a slim canoe was removed from its rack and the yatika seated himself inside. I watched the muscular paddlers pick the thing up and carry it to the river, and with a push, they were gone, their long pointed paddles driving them away.

"Blood Thorn?" I turned, seeing where he was about to lace a pack onto Squirm. "Forget it. We're back in the boats."

He nodded, and not a finger's time passed before we were on the river. This time, however, Tagaya Mico rode in the towed canoe. We were jumbled into the others. I'd managed to squeeze in with Pearl Hand. Bark—just ahead of me—perched on his pack, enjoying the ride.

Dogs can be so naïve.

"So," I asked in Timucua, "we're in service to the old lady herself now?"

Pearl Hand gave me a humorless smile. "You're not, Black Shell."

"I'm having trouble with all of this. Why are you taking such risks? What if good old Tagaya back there had decided to order us confined until he figured out who we really were?"

"He wouldn't have dared."

"You're sure about that?"

"As sure as rain falls." She stared out at the bank, hardly seeing the trees. "We know the stakes: De Soto is coming." She shook her head. "What I didn't count on was that half the Cofitachequi would be dead."

"I don't understand."

She gave me a miserable look. "Think about the forest we just crossed. Then think about the Kristianos. We ate well every day, hunting, picking fruits and roots. But the Kristianos? How do you think they're faring out there in the trees and swamps?"

"They'll be hungry," I muttered. "They'll have eaten everything, maybe even their scurrilous *puercos*."

She nodded. "And what kind of shape will they be in when they stumble out of the wilderness with their half-starved cabayos? What kind of formations can their soldados keep, wobbling on their feet?" She smiled wistfully. "If there has ever been a chance to beat them, it is now."

"A cleverly planned ambush could smash them." I took a breath. "But why didn't you tell me how far you were planning to go with this?"

"I wasn't sure. I mean, I wasn't sure I wanted to give up everything I had . . . just to destroy de Soto."

"What do you mean, give up everything?"

I was about to repeat the question when she said, "If de Soto's destruction must come at the cost of my life and happiness, I'll pay it."

"The people you knew may not have survived the sickness."

She looked sadly at the passing bank. "Some didn't, no. But whatever happens, I will do what I must." She met my eyes, her desperation building. "And you, my beloved husband, can you trust me? No questions?"

I was about to object, only to remember how she'd come out of the night at Uzita and the sacrifice she'd made there to save my life. And at Napetuca? Everything had depended on her, her knowledge of Kristianos and her insistence on bringing the dogs. "Of course."

"Do you swear on that bit of sacred horn you carry?"

I grasped it, saying, "I do."

She vented a defeated sigh. "Then we might have a chance after all."

She turned her worry-hollowed eyes to the bank, watching the endless trees pass in the slanting late afternoon light.

"I just wish you'd tell me why you're taking such risks." I paused. "I thought we were past secrets."

She sniffed, "So did I. Until we came here . . . until I realized what the stakes were. But for the moment, I need to do this my way. And you must bind yourself to your promise."

"Pearl Hand—"

"It's necessary, Black Shell." The corners of her mouth quivered. "In this case, my love, what you do not know protects you."

"How's that?"

"In time, my love . . . In time."

By Piasa's teeth, she doesn't think she's going to get out of this alive.

TWENTY-ONE

OUR FLOTILLA OF CANOES ROUNDED A BEND, AND there atop a bluff stood Telemico, resplendent in the golden light of sunset.

Looking across, I could see Blood Thorn's face, a mask of wonderment as he stared at the city. High gabled cane roofs rose above large houses, masking the approach to both the Cofitachequi mico's elevated palace and the still higher mound beyond it. Upon that high eminence stood the temple. The structure jutted up above the houses; its shell-clad walls added to the illusion of height before the steeply pitched roof pierced the purple sky. Sculptures of Falcon and Rattlesnake adorned the ends of the soaring ridgepole, as if to threaten the Sky World itself. The mosaic of shells on the walls and roof burned pearlescent and fiery in the sunset.

"I'd forgotten how grand this place is," I whispered.

Further thoughts on the matter were abandoned as the canoes put in at the landing. While the Tagaya mico's boat was carried ashore, Pearl Hand and I scrambled out and helped Blood Thorn with the dogs and packs.

"Someone carry those," the mico ordered, seeing that we were about to lace the packs onto the dogs. Apparently he was more inclined to order his subjects to do a dog's work rather than endure the wait.

I got my belongings in order, slinging my alligator-hide quiver and carrying my trader's staff before me; the white feathers danced in the breeze. Pearl Hand insisted on walking before me and Blood Thorn. I ordered the dogs to heel.

The mico's chair was unloaded from a canoe, and he took his seat, burly paddlers hefting his weight onto their shoulders.

With the ynahaes in the lead, we began the march up from the landing, treading on charcoal-stained soil. The usual bits of pot sherds, stone flakes, and cooking stones winked underfoot as they caught the slanting light.

At the crest of the rise, we passed the first houses— large things with split-cane roofs, many of them decorated by clan totem sculptures. Guardian posts were set to either side of sealed doorways. Once-brightly-painted clay walls were cracking and faded. The tattered latrines behind lacked the simplest of repairs.

The great city was mostly abandoned. Weeds grew where they shouldn't. The yards were unkempt, mud having washed into fire pits, the ramadas worse for wear. Even the upright log mortars were weather-grayed, with dirt blown into their hollow bowls.

"Mico? How long since the people left?" I called, remembering the last time I'd walked up from the landing.

Then it was into a bustling community of several thousand. I remembered the colors, the diverse peoples speaking Mos'kogee, Catawba, Cherokee, and the incomprehensible tongues of the coast.

"Since the beginning of the Death," one of the ynahaes replied. "It was worse here. Those few who didn't become ill found their comfort among distant relatives. Most were gone by last spring."

I nodded, thoughts stuck in the past: Local traders had lined the route, their wares displayed on blankets; hunters had game hung from racks; weavers hawked their latest fabrics; and potters sat before rows of freshly fired, stamped bowls, jars, and pots.

Their places now grew grass and goosefoot, the lonesome soil hardened and rain-cracked.

Blood Thorn asked, "How many houses, Black Shell? I mean, just here, in the city itself?"

"Six, seven hundred," I replied as we followed the main road into the center. "And just beyond, in every direction, are smaller towns, and beyond them, villages. This is just the capital. My guess is that had the pestilence not struck, Cofitachequi could have fielded ten thousand warriors against de Soto without even straining."

"And now?" He gave me a dark look.

"I have no idea." And I began to understand the crushing sense of defeat Pearl Hand was feeling.

As we passed beneath the first of the granaries perched atop its high posts, I could see the door hanging open. As was the case at the second, third, and fourth. In the distance, between gaps in the houses, I could see more of the raised storehouses. Some, however, were still tightly sealed. That gave me a bit of hope.

We passed one of the elaborate clan houses, this one festooned with magnificent raccoon carvings; one was seated atop the ridgepole over the doorway, his forepaws dangling. The weathering beast, his paint now faded, stared down at me as if in question.

From behind the clan house came the cloying reek of the associated charnel house. I could imagine what it looked like on the inside: every bench piled with the dead.

A flock of finches fluttered past. Before the Death, they would have made a living from dropped corn, knot-weed, and maygrass seeds; now they had to be thriving on goosefoot and other invaders.

Passing the Raccoon Clan house, we entered the central plaza. The stickball field should have been a rectangle of well-trodden grass instead of a meadow crisscrossed by trails. Weeds spotted the closest chunkey court, to my dismay.

I glanced up at the high temple with its towering roof and imagined priests atop the long wooden stairs as they watched the games, wagering on the outcomes depending upon their particular Power. How long had it been since figures other than ghosts had perched there?

Blood Thorn gasped as he looked up. "I didn't think men could build such things."

The great building, with its inlaid shell walls, continued to reflect the reddish sunlight, as though possessed of a fire all its own. I could feel the ancestral souls inside, the weight of generations, all unaware of the scourge approaching from the south.

Across from the temple, the palace stood atop its own square—if not as high—mound. Unlike the rest of the town, the palace had suffered no neglect but radiated life and Power. The Cofitachequi mico's edifice had been built with consummate skill, each timber perfectly fitted; the walls—first plastered with white and red clays—had been inlaid with crushed shell, the surfaces burnished with smooth round stones until they shone in the light.

Shells, too, had been laced to the split-cane roof to impart a brilliant luminescence. The high roof left us feeling dwarfed as we approached the steep stairway to the imposing veranda.

Two guardian posts—giant rattlesnakes rising from the earth—rose on either side of the stairs. I could almost believe the serpents were alive with their copper-inset eyes, forked tongues, and rainbow-scaled sides.

The wooden staircase leading up to the veranda was polished, oil stained, and perfectly set. At the base, the mico gave an order, and we waited.

Pearl Hand, however, strode up, demanding, "Do you expect us to enter the Cofitachequi mico's presence dressed like this? We're fresh out of the forest, hardly fit to appear before the Sun Ruler."

He glanced at her, taking in her worn travel dress. Perhaps to prove his superiority, he took his time about it, then gave a wave of the hand. "You may use the house just behind there. Its occupants are long gone. Ynahae, take some men with you and show them where I mean. But have them ready to come at a moment's notice."

The man touched his chin, shot a disdainful look at Pearl Hand, and said, "This way."

At Pearl Hand's signal, Blood Thorn and I gestured to the porters carrying our packs. Then, slapping a hand to my thigh, I called the dogs to follow.

The ynahae led us around the side of the mound to a

well-fit house. Its wooden door hung on dried-leather hinges. A dusting of leaves had blown up against the walls. Muttering a prayer to the Spirits who inhabited the house, he opened the wooden door and gestured to us.

Stepping in, we found a spacious main room with pole benches built into the walls. Dust lay over everything, and motes of it could be seen in the shafts of light penetrating around the eaves. Hangings covered two doorways in the back wall—storerooms, no doubt, or segregated sleeping quarters.

"Will this do?" the ynahae asked.

"It will." Pearl Hand took her pack from one of the porters and retreated to the left-side doorway. Pulling back the hanging, she stepped inside.

"What do we do?" Blood Thorn asked in Timucua as he stared around the house. In his country, only a great holata would have such a place.

"We're about to meet one of the most important women in the world. Perhaps we should look like more than just scruffy traders?"

He agreed. "Of course."

So we took our packs, slipped off our travel clothing, and began making ourselves pretty. By the time Pearl Hand stepped out, decked as she'd been in the forest, I had my hair pinned with my copper turkey-tail pin, strands of shell around my neck, and a large copper breastplate hanging over my chest. I opted for one of the Toa blankets—this one dyed in a vivid scarlet—and placed it around my shoulders. Blood Thorn, his hair seen to, took a yellow one.

I retrieved what was left of our paints and used grease to mix it. Then Blood Thorn and I took turns dabbing it on according to our individual whims. He opted for a traditional Timucua design. I had him paint me to look like a Chicaza minko. The only thing lacking was a Kristiano mirror to see just how good we looked.

When we'd donned half the trade, we could have been minkos ourselves. With each step, our shell necklaces tinkled musically, and bracelets were stacked on our wrists. Finally, I lifted out the copper mace Back-from-the-Dead had presented to me. The mace in one hand, my trader's staff in the other, I felt ready.

Pearl Hand, despite her other concerns, stopped short, seeing the red breechcloth I'd adopted and the iridescent spoonbill feathers we'd laced into our hair.

"You cut a dashing figure," she said, a wistful smile on her lips. "Onc to keep forever in my memory."

"As do you. But if I dare say, it's not the same as that night at the fire."

"At least this time you won't have to find me a chair."

Her attempt at humor did more to reassure me than anything else.

The ynahae stuck his head in the door, eyes widening at the sight of us. "The Cofitachequi mico requests your presence."

Calling the dogs, we walked out into the dusk, rounded the palace mound, and joined Tagaya Mico. He didn't get the whole effect, given the poor light, but I saw his eyes widen.

Oh yes, you overstuffed fool, we're just as rich as you are.

The yatika was waiting at the head of the stairs, and now he called out, "Come forth from the world below. It is the order of the Cofitachequi mico that you ascend to her world, leaving behind any pretension of guile, misdirection, and animosity. Come, and be pure of heart, gracious, and forthright in the presence of Cofitachequi."

I translated the gist of it to Blood Thorn as we followed behind the mico's litter bearers. They did an admirable job, keeping his chair level as they climbed. At the veranda, appropriately, they lowered the chair in a fluid motion. He rose and walked past two ranks of six warriors armed with copper-headed war clubs. They inspected us with interest as we proceded through great double doors carved in relief with clawing cougars.

A roaring fire filled the great room with yellow light. The usual pole benches lined plastered walls decorated with brightly dyed textiles, weapons, trophy skulls, and wooden reliefs of Rattlesnake, sun symbols, Piasa, and Falcon.

No piece of wood in the room had been spared the carver's blade. Each was a masterpiece—right down to the supports for the pole benches.

The back wall was made of tawny cane woven into geometric patterns that defied the eye with their intricacy. What appeared to be a single mat covered the entire floor, for I could find no break in the weave. Below the benches, large wooden boxes of masterful construction depicted mythical creatures, heroes from the Beginning Times, images of Mother Spider, serpents, and stunningly rendered geometric designs.

Then I turned my attention to the people. Ten ynahaes stood in a solid rank to one side. I assumed the older men and women, maybe thirty in all, behind them to be various oretas and clan leaders. This was reinforced by their clothing, much of it bearing raccoons, cougars, falcons, and deer.

On the Cofitachequi mico's right stood a couple of warriors, a well-dressed and obviously high-ranking young man, and two young women. The females wore fine white dresses, but they were nowhere as revealing as Pearl Hand's form-fitting garment. Their long black hair was combed and fell over their shoulders. Each had a virgin's belt knotted at her waist, and a wealth of pearls hung in heavy strands from their necks and wrists.

As we approached, the older one—perhaps seventeen summers—bent and whispered something to the younger, who might have been thirteen. The young nobleman—wearing a colorfully painted fawn-skin shirt, leggings, and supple moccasins—gave her a disapproving scowl.

She gave Pearl Hand a scathing look, as if she really didn't care to have any woman more beautiful than herself in the room. And yes, she was gorgeous.

The Cofitachequi mico, however, dominated the room. She sat on a magnificent raised chair, its sides draped with cougar hides. From the back rose a large, carved eagle's head, as if the fierce bird were staring out over the mico's head at the room's occupants. With polished-pearl eyes, a gleaming yellow beak, and a white-feathered head, the thing might have been alive.

The Cofitachequi mico herself had once been an attractive woman; haggard lines ran from the corners of her nose down to the sides of her mouth. Sunken cheeks mimicked her mascara-darkened eyes. Her hair remained black and was gathered in a matronly bun at the back of her head; a polished copper pin, done in turkey-tail style, held it in place. She wore a beautiful purple-fabric dress, its front adorned with pearls and bits of mica that glistened in the light. Given the weight of the pearls around her neck, it was no wonder her back looked stooped.

She watched us through tired eyes, as if the fire had been long burned out of them. Both elbows rested on the chair arms and added to the image of someone pushed too hard, for too long. I guessed she'd seen close to forty winters and probably didn't wish to see many more.

Tagaya Mico stopped just this side of the fire and lowered himself to one knee, head bowed, palms up. Blood Thorn and I followed suit along with everyone in our party.

And there we waited. Except that I had my trader's staff in one hand, the ancient mace in the other, so I propped their butts on the matting to give the appearance of reverence.

Staring at the matting, I wished I could have seen what transpired, but I heard whispering. Finally the yatika called, "Arise, Tagaya Mico, and tell us why you have come."

From under lowered brows, I watched the man reclaim his feet and listened as he related our arrival at his town.

"And who is this mysterious woman who claims to be in the Cofitachequi mico's service?" the yatika called in a voice we were all supposed to hear.

Just ahead of me, Pearl Hand stood, stepping forward. *Enough of this.* I raised my head.

Pearl Hand stopped beside Tagaya Mico, drawing herself to her full height. "I am known as Pearl Hand of the Chicora, and I come from the south with news about the arrival of a new army of Kristianos under the leadership of a man calling himself *Adelantado* Hernando de Soto."

"Wait!"

The room went silent, and I could see the old mico stiffen in her chair. She said, "I know you."

Pearl Hand might have been a meadow vole, paralyzed as a hawk shot down from the sky. Her whole body tensed, her fists knotted.

The old woman rose from the chair, walking slowly forward until she stopped an arm's length from Pearl Hand. For long moments the two stared at each other.

Then the old mico said, "To see you here, alive and before me, is to know that Power has really deserted me."

Pearl Hand seemed to quiver.

"Who is she, Aunt?" The gorgeous young woman stepped forward, her virgin's skirt swaying. A gleam of anticipation filled her eyes. "You know this woman?"

"Evening Breeze," the old mico rasped, as if even the saying of it cost her.

A gasp sounded around the room, looks of horror on every face. The girl's eyes went wide, and she walked up whispering, "It is! *It's her!*"

The old mico continued, her voice almost a hiss. "You don't know how much I offered, sacrificed, fasted, and prayed. With all my heart I pleaded that you would die a miserable and lingering death."

That brought a cold chill to my spine, and I stared at Pearl Hand like a gaping idiot. *Evening Breeze?* That was her real name? And, by Piasa's teeth, what had she done to earn such hatred?

Pearl Hand's voice wavered. "Not all of your prayers were in vain, great Mico. I have lived my share of misery."

"But obviously not enough." She paused, firelight sparkling off the pearls in her dress. "After what you did to me, what prompts you to come before me now, at this of all times?"

Pearl Hand took a deep breath. "Great Sun Ruler, you

can deal with me as you see fit. But first, hear my words: I come in the company of these traders to warn you that an army of Kristianos is approaching your southern borders."

The girl—who'd been staring at Pearl Hand with rapt attention—blurted, "We've heard of no Kristianos. What was left of them fled years ago. The rest are long dead."

"White Rose, be quiet," the old mico growled.

Pearl Hand kept her eyes on the mico's. "The Kristianos landed far to the south, in the peninsula, more than a year ago. Over a thousand of them, their war cabayos and dogs. Since then they have been working their way north, through the Uzachile, the Apalachee, and the Hichiti Nations. Now they are coming here."

"Doing what?" White Rose demanded. Her aunt seemed to be overwhelmed for the moment.

I'd had my fill of kneeling. I rose, taking my place at Pearl Hand's side, bracing my trader's staff on the floor, mace in my right hand. "Killing, stealing, raping, and destroying," I said with the arrogance that was my blood right. "They've marked their path by spirals of vultures wheeling over their victims."

"And who are you?" the girl asked, turning her attention to me. I saw the pupils widen in her dark brown eyes as she took in my fine dress and Chicaza paint. Then they fixed on the copper mace, her interest growing. When her eyes met mine, they were dancing with invitation, matching the smile that now bent her full lips.

"I am Black Shell, of the Chief Clan, of the Hickory Moiety, of the Chicaza Nation. I come under the Power of trade and bind myself—and my companions, including Blood Thorn, iniha of the Uzachile Nation—under its Power."

"A Chicaza?" The girl almost sighed. "A warrior from the other side of the world? Here?"

"You have my name; I do not have yours," I replied as a high minko would to an equal.

I could see shifting around the room; the warriors behind the younger girl and the young noble were fingering their clubs.

"I am known as Blooming White Rose, niece of the Cofitachequi mico, of the Sun Clan." That she left off her moiety and people amused me. She obviously didn't think it necessary.

"Black Shell," Pearl Hand said stiffly, "you do not need to meddle in this."

"But I do." I turned my attention to the mico. "Great Sun Ruler, we came with all haste. The monster de Soto is currently making his way through the forest, probably with Ocute guides. He will arrive at any moment."

She pried her gaze from Pearl Hand, giving me a sober inspection from the top of my head all the way down to my feet. Her eyes, too, hesitated at the sight of the copper mace, long a symbol of rulers.

She shot a glance filled with loathing at Pearl Hand. "You come in surprising company, Chicaza. The sort to make your words suspect."

I met her wary gaze. "Great Sun Ruler, I am tasked by Power with the destruction of the monster. For more than a year, I have fought him, killed his soldados and cabayeros, and watched thousands weep in the wake of his passage. So too has this woman, whom you know as Evening Breeze. Had she wished, she could have introduced herself as Evening Breeze Mankiller, or Nicoquadca, though I do not believe the term is used here."

"What did she do," the mico asked bitterly, "squeeze them to death, one by one, with her renowned sheath?"

"Actually," I said coolly, "she prefers the Kristiano crossbow, though more than one died by her sword."

That made an impact among the listeners.

"You have proof?" the old woman asked.

"Of her kills? No, great Mico. The ihola'ka were presented as tribute to Mikko Cafakke of the Apalachee. And trophy heads, you must agree, are a bit cumbersome on the trail."

She gave me an irritated look. "I meant about the coming of these Kristianos."

"We still carry some of their weapons."

"You could have come by them anywhere," White Rose added, her thoughtful eyes on mine. She kept glancing at Pearl Hand, then me, obviously trying to suss out our relationship.

The mico waved the brat down, still struggling to keep from glaring at Pearl Hand. "Why would they come here? Twice they have landed on our shores, and twice they left in ruin."

She sounded so sure of herself. I felt that building frustration in my breast. "Among the Uzachile they captured a trader, White Mat by name. With him was a boy he was teaching the trade: Periko. When the Kristianos quizzed him about gold, Periko told them there was plenty of it here, in Cofitachequi."

"What is this gold?" White Rose asked.

The mico gave her an irritated look, saying, "A worthless metal. Kristianos, however, are endlessly enamored of it." Then she turned back to me. "Why would they believe some boy?"

Pearl Hand said, "Because they want to, great Sun Ruler."

The old woman snorted. "And just what did you expect me to do, Evening Breeze? Thank you for coming with such information? Forgive you? Restore your status, perhaps offer you some other poor soul to ruin?"

Pearl Hand flinched. "The Kristianos will be in dire straits after crossing the forest. By means of a carefully laid ambush, you will be able to hit them while their cabayos are weak, their formations scattered. But if they manage to take a town, raid its granaries and resupply, nothing you can do will stop them."

The old woman drew a deep breath, her eyes closed. "All right, I believe you. As far as that goes."

Mico Tagaya asked, "Then what do we do?"

"What can we?" she demanded bitterly. "Half of our warriors lie dead in the charnel houses. The rest, but for a handful, are scattered throughout the forests, hunting, struggling to keep their families fed. My micos are on the verge of revolt, hoping to exploit our weakness for their own ends." She shot another venomous look at Pearl Hand. "Oh yes, you picked a *fine* time to return."

Pearl Hand wavered on her feet, eyes closed, and I almost reached out to steady her. She said, "There is another way, though what it will cost you, I can't say."

"Really?" the old woman asked. "What it will *cost* us? The last of my hope? What remains of my heart? This time, I'm fresh out of sons, you foul piece of filth."

I shot a nervous glance at Pearl Hand, seeing her take a deep breath.

Pus and blood, wife! What did you do?

TWENTY-TWO

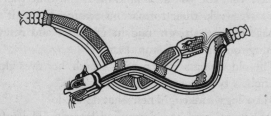

PEARL HAND GATHERED HER COURAGE, SAYING, "DE Soto fought his way up the peninsula, then through Uzachile, and finally realized his folly when the Apalachee battled him to a draw. After the swamps of Capacheeki, he realized that if he professes peace, Nations will feed his army, carry his supplies, and their women will service his men in return for trinkets."

"Which means?" the old woman asked skeptically.

"If you convince him there is no gold here, feed his army, supply porters to carry his goods, and offer suitable high-ranking hostages to ensure his army will not be attacked, you can probably persuade him to pass through."

I shot Pearl Hand a sidelong glance. I thought the plan was to *trap* de Soto and make him *bleed* his way through Cofitachequi.

"And which hostages did you have in mind?" The mico shot her jaw out. "Hmm? Me, perhaps?"

I said, "De Soto would prefer you. In the past he's been satisfied with different holatas . . . uh, chiefs, if you will. He even had Mikko Cafakke in his grasp for a while."

I could feel the growing anger in the room and added, "But placing yourself in his grasp would be a terrible mistake. He's not known for his kindness."

White Rose had been studying, listening, thoughts racing behind her flashing young eyes. But why the cunning look? There was no advantage to be had here. And why did she keep shooting me those inviting smiles, as if I'd be dumb enough to dally with a mico's niece? One apparently in line for the high chair itself.

Again the Tagaya mico said, "We should dispatch scouts, great Sun Ruler. Our people are all over the forest, hunting and fishing. If these Kristianos are really coming, we'll have word of it long before they find their way here."

"See to it." The old mico ran bony knuckles under her jaw, glaring hatred at Pearl Hand all the while. "Coordinate with the war chiefs and other micos. Send warnings to the southern talwas; tell them to remain alert. Rot it all, half of them are empty anyway."

White Rose narrowed her eyes. "Aunt, the people might panic. After the Death, they might run like rabbits before a hawk, spreading even more panic before them. They need a symbol, someone to indicate that we are aware of the situation and have it under control."

The old woman turned suspicious eyes on the girl. "And you think the local micos can't?"

"The micos are part of the problem." White Rose crossed her arms, emphasizing her full breasts. "One of us must go, demonstrating that the Sun Clan is not impotent in this crisis. We've been holed up here for too long. People think the Death has weakened our authority, that our Power is diluted."

I watched the interplay between them, the sort of subtle signals that only long and rocky history entailed.

"Are you so quick to put your life on the line?" the old woman asked. "If some Kristiano takes you, you'll never ascend the high chair." She made a tsking sound. "And I thought you were so desperate to outlive me."

White Rose bristled, pointing at the young noble. "So send Fire Otter. He's your favorite. Let him represent you."

"He's not Sun Clan, and everybody knows it."

"They know that you trust him more than me or any of the micos." White Rose tightened her crossed arms, snugging the fabric of her dress around her breasts. She was doing it for my benefit, but I could tell Blood Thorn was more fascinated.

"Then go, niece." The old woman relented, a mocking smile trying to escape her tight lips. She turned. "Fire Otter?"

"Yes, great Mico?" The young noble stepped forward. He had a round face, honest eyes, and a muscular body. Chunkey player, I decided.

She gave him a genuine smile, reached up and affectionately patted his shoulder. "Go with White Rose. Make sure she doesn't do anything stupid . . . like getting herself killed. You will keep me informed of everything, even the smallest details. Take sufficient runners."

"Wonderful," White Rose muttered, "my own personal spy."

"Listen to him, niece. For once, use your head. You

wanted a chance? This is it. If the Kristianos *are* coming, find out. Then get back here as quickly as you can."

"And what are you going to do?" White Rose demanded.

"Try to think of a way to either destroy the Kristiano army or broker the best deal I can." The old mico was fingering her chin, eyes distant.

"And what about her?" White Rose indicated Pearl Hand with a lift of her shoulder.

The mico turned her slitted eyes on Pearl Hand. "I'm still thinking."

"Hang her in a square, Aunt."

I stiffened, thumping my trader's staff on the matting. "We are here under the Power of trade."

"You are, Chicaza. She isn't. She remains property of the Sun Clan." Her thin lips curled. "No matter how long she's been gone."

I was on the verge of taking a step toward her, raising the heavy copper mace—and of course, dooming us all—when Pearl Hand said to me, "I have your word, High Minko. *Stand down.*"

That she'd called me "high minko" stopped me cold. Doing so wasn't lost on anyone in the room. All eyes focused on me. Almost trembling, I took a deep breath. "As I promised."

"Interesting," the old woman mused. "So, she's got you right where she wants you, eh? Poor fool." She turned to one of the ynahaes. "Find the high minko and iniha quarters and food suitable for their rank."

"And," I asked, "Pearl— Evening Breeze? Her welfare is important to us. She has great value when fighting Kristianos."

"Along with her other talents, no doubt. She stays with me." The old woman smiled like a ghoul.

Pearl Hand looked as if she were about to faint.

"Great Sun Ruler, before you do anything, you should know she speaks the Kristiano language." I was desperately grasping for anything.

"And that means . . . what?" She was giving me the same look she'd give a useful dog.

"Among the Uzachile, it kept their great holata from ending up with a chain around his neck." Then I gave her a thin smile of my own. "You should also know that, upon my honor as a Chicaza, she falls under my protection."

"Is that right?" She was giving me a predatory stare.

"Our goodwill could either be of help to you in the coming crisis, or not." I managed a grim smile. "Your decision."

"I'll be all right," Pearl Hand said insistently. "Go, High Minko, and thank you for everything."

As the warriors came to escort us out, I caught that last desperate flash of love in her eyes.

I braced my legs, the copper mace clutched, ready to strike. I was filling my lungs to protest when Pearl Hand turned pleading eyes on mine, saying, "You gave your word."

And then, as I suffered a desperation unlike anything I'd ever known, we were whisked out of the palace and into the night.

Very nice houses were in abundant supply in Telemico, which, simply translated, means "Chief's Town." The Death had seen to that. Based on the honorific Pearl Hand had bestowed upon me, and the opulence of our dress, we were escorted to a fine four-room house just behind the palace and next to the dusty one where we'd changed.

In the light of pine torches I inspected the place, looked at our warrior guard, and summarily ordered: "We need servants, a fire, food for my dogs, and clean bedding."

The warriors bowed, touching their chins. Only the chin? Not the forehead? Well, I was a foreign lord, not one of their own.

While one remained behind with his torch, the others hurried away. I shot a half-panicked look at Blood Thorn. "Pus and blood! What are we going to do? Pearl Hand—"

"Is more than capable of taking care of herself," he said, stepping close, placing a hand on my shoulder. "Trust her, Black Shell. She's had a plan the whole time. She *knows* these people in ways you do not. Never underestimate her."

I slumped, wondering how it had all gone so wrong. "I pray you're right." A pause. "Did you follow any of that?"

"Not really." He was watching me with cautious eyes. "But I can see why Pearl Hand really didn't want to come here."

"By Piasa's balls, why didn't she tell us the whole story?"

"Because she believes in Power. She believes in your dreams, in the sepaya you wear, and in the destruction of the monster."

I sucked a cool breath into my hot lungs. "That woman in there hates her. Blood and serpents, Pearl Hand did something to her son. Maybe killed him for all I know."

"Who's the girl with breasts, the obnoxious one with the virgin's belt?"

"The high mico's niece . . . and probably her successor." I pointed a finger. "Don't even think it."

He grinned. "She's a real beauty—and knows it. Did you see the way she was looking at you? Not to mention the way she posed so as to leave no doubt about the merchandise?"

"And did you, Iniha, notice that she's a cunning little lizard with acid in her heart?" I paced the floor, smacking the heavy mace into my left palm.

Pearl Hand, what are they doing to you?

I tried not to glare at the poor warrior holding the torch. It wasn't his fault. And we'd been speaking Timucua, which was apparently babble to him.

"She'll be all right," Blood Thorn said softly. "Did you see how she manipulated that mico up at Tagaya town? Making us dress the part when we got here, then calling you a high minko? She's taken us beyond the Power of trade, Black Shell."

"That old woman . . ." I took a swipe at empty air, the mace whistling. "I swear, if the old bitch has cut her throat, I'm caving her skull in."

"She hasn't." Blood Thorn crossed his arms. "Believe me, that one hasn't lived this long without having her wits about her."

"You know this, do you?"

"Rulers who stand the test of time are the ones who place their emotions second to the necessity of the day. And for the moment, Pearl Hand is too valuable to kill."

"I wish I could believe that."

"De Soto is just down south, perhaps stumbling out of the forest as we speak. The moment the old woman hears he's on the way, she's going to want to know everything we do. Keeping Pearl Hand alive is part of maintaining our goodwill."

I nodded as a line of servants bearing our packs, firewood, food, and every other necessity entered. I considered the looks they were giving me.

So, by dripping pus, Pearl Hand had made me a high minko? Uncle, Mother, and the rest of my teachers had trained me for the part. Pointing with my mace, I gave orders with the expectation that they'd be obeyed. Within moments the house was lit, food was provided, my dogs were eating on the porch, and I'd even been given two litter chairs for Blood Thorn and myself.

That didn't mean I wasn't constantly shooting worried glances at the back of the palace, positive that Pearl Hand wasn't spending a pleasant evening. The knowledge left a sick sensation in my stomach.

We were demolishing the last of a plate of baked fish, honey-sweetened hominy, and spiced squash when the yatika appeared.

The man carried his ceremonial staff of office as he stepped inside, announcing, "High Minko Black Shell, this person respectfully requests that you accompany him on the Cofitachequi mico's business."

"That was quick," Blood Thorn mused.

"See to the dogs?"

"Of course." He gave me a reassuring look. "I know she's your wife, but keep your wits, old friend . . . and be smart."

I'd had time to recover my self-control. As I followed the yatika out into the night, I was already coming to grips with the new rules. This was now a game of statecraft, not that much different from trade, actually. The stakes were just a little higher, the players more sophisticated—and Pearl Hand's fate depended upon it.

I wasn't surprised when we rounded the mound and climbed the steps to the palace. Fortunately, I was still dressed for the part, and the heavy copper mace—as its crafters intended—could serve more than just ceremonial functions.

Warriors opened one of the doors for us, and we walked past the fire, now burning low. The old mico was still seated, the eagle-back chair looking just as fierce. Pearl Hand was nowhere to be seen.

The yatika raised his staff of office. "I present the high minko of the Chicaza, great Sun Ruler."

She lifted a hand in thanks, eyes on me. "So, I'm to believe you are the high minko of the Chicaza?"

I gave her a wry smile. "For the moment, my younger brother sits on the panther stool. Power saw fit to change the course of my life."

"Power? Really? It just told you, 'Leave your palace and authority, turn your back on your people, and go wander the world'?"

"Mico, what you believe is no concern of mine. For reasons of its own, Power presented me with a terrible choice, and knowing the stakes, I have accepted. But do not delude yourself that such a decision comes without cost."

"And what cost did you pay?"

"My birthright; everything I had striven for, dreamed of; and my people. Even if I defeat the monster, I shall die alone. My bones will not rest among those of my ancestors." I turned, gazing around the room, unconcerned—an equal engaged in a conversation.

She nodded slightly, the look of weariness settling into her aged expression. "How did you come to be here?"

"This de Soto, he's different from the ones who came before. He threatens everything we hold dear. No matter what, Mico, he cannot be allowed to win. Defeat him, and we buy time for everyone."

She worked her lips, as though something tasted sour. "The Death originated among the Kristianos. It began among the coastal peoples after Ayllón's invaders left, afflicting those who had served the Kristianos, taking out one community and then moving to another. And finally it came here."

I nodded, sympathetic. "I suffered from one of their sicknesses down in the peninsula. I understand."

"What you and Evening Breeze claim . . . It's true, isn't it?"

"Great Mico, we expected to find you strong and ready to destroy the monster as he staggers out of the forest, half-starved. Evening Breeze bet her life on it."

She fingered the panther hide on her chair. "Assuming, that is, that you could have talked us into it. Following Evening Breeze here wasn't the smartest thing. My brother, were he still alive, wouldn't have cared why you came. He'd have hung her in a square and sat before her, cutting pieces off her body, burning the wounds to stanch her blood."

"She knew that. Expected it actually."

She glared at me. "Then why did she come here?"

"Because she believed the sacrifice of her life to be worth the monster's destruction."

"She told you that?"

"I had no clue until tonight."

She paused. "What is she to you?"

I considered, then opted for most of the truth. "I won her from a petty little chief in the peninsula. The fool thought he could outshoot a Chicaza lord. After the Kristianos captured me she infiltrated their camp and carried my fevered and dying body to safety. She accepted the call of Power and followed in the wake of the Kristianos. Accompanying the Uzachile chiefs, she marched into the Kristiano camp and listened as the monsters conferred, telling us exactly what they planned.

"Forewarned by Evening Breeze, the Uzachile tried to kill de Soto. But through treachery, the Kristianos were warned and butchered the Uzachile army. Since then, she's fought them, trapped them, and saved my life again when the Apalachee hilishaya and I sought to battle them outside Anhaica."

"Yet she came here?"

"The stakes for which we fight are greater than the value of a single life." I swallowed. "Even hers."

The old woman studied me, silence stretching. "And you, High Minko? Is it worth yours?"

"If you could promise me that you would mass your forces and kill de Soto's army to the last man, I would open a vein here, tonight."

"Curse me for a fool, but I believe you." She stared absently into the distance. "Very well, let's get to the facts. Given the Death, I doubt I can gather even five hundred men."

Her admission staggered me. "What about the Catawba and Cherokee? Could you recruit them in time? Or has the Death been there, too?"

"It hasn't. If the Kristianos are as close as you say, it's

too late. Not that I'd want them down here to see just how badly we've suffered. That might bode worse for us than the Kristianos." She squinted. "But if we were to withdraw, leave them only vacant towns and empty granaries, perhaps we could keep them weak while we gather some kind of resistance."

"That's how the Apalachee did it. Picking them off by ones and twos, killing their cabayos. But it will come at a cost."

She gave me a cunning look. "If we bleed them, somehow entice them to go fight the Nations upriver, I might buy time for my people to recover."

"Perhaps. Can you figure out a way to keep Cofitachequi bellies full at the same time de Soto's are left empty?"

She made a dismissive gesture. "Stored food isn't a problem. My people were dying faster than they could eat it. And most were out in the forests, hunting and gathering." Then she shook her head. "The biggest obstacle is coordinating any kind of resistance. So many of the nobles are dead that my command structure is in shambles. The talwas are chafing, the micos unsure. The Death has shaken confidence in the Sun Clan. *I* was supposed to *protect* them."

And how does a government without officials coordinate anything?

She sighed again, looking beaten.

I shifted the mace. "However this works out, great Mico, abandon Telemico. Strip it of food. Once de Soto's out of the forest, this is the first place he will come."

"Only if he can find it. My people will not betray me."

"They will," I said softly. "The common people, farmers and craftsmen, might be willing to die rather than betray you. But when de Soto starts burning their families alive, and cutting their sons and daughters apart before their eyes, they will talk."

She gave me a look that seared the souls. "They would do that?"

"Didn't Ayllón?"

Her expression was one of misery. "Thank you for your advice, High Minko. Go and have a pleasant evening. I have much to think about."

"Yes, you do." I paused. "Oh, one last thing. Blooming White Rose is right about the people's need to see their leaders in this time of invasion, but whatever happens, don't let her fall into de Soto's hands. The monster wouldn't hesitate to use her against you."

She nodded, lost in thought. "Have a good night, High Minko."

I considered saying something about Pearl Hand but thought better of it. Showing too much interest would give the old vulture even more leverage than she already had. Far better that she simply believe Pearl Hand was my bound woman.

The yatika indicated that I should follow him.

At the door I took one last look, seeing the old mico, slumped in her chair, bowed under the entire weight of her world.

We had descended the long stairs—an escorting warrior carrying a torch to guide our way—when a young man approached, touched his chin, and whispered to the yatika. The yatika in turn gave me a quizzical glance and shrugged, leading us not back to my house, but to an imposing dwelling on a slight rise overlooking the plaza and adjacent to the palace.

I frowned, gripping the heavy mace, as the yatika stepped onto the porch and spoke to a warrior standing by the door.

"What is happening?" I called.

The yatika gave me a slight bow, saying, "The lady Blooming White Rose requests an audience with you, High Minko."

I almost said no, then sighed. One doesn't turn down the opportunity to learn all he can of a people or their politics.

"Of course. I am honored."

The door opened and I was admitted to an opulently furnished room, replete with carvings, the finest textiles, and burnished, stamp-patterned ceramics. Beautifully dyed hides were draped over the pole beds. The place was huge, perhaps twenty-five paces in each direction. I walked across tawny matting and looked up to see the high roof, clouded with smoke.

I was ushered to a raised seat before the low fire, given a ceramic mug of what tasted like raspberry juice mixed with mint. Then the yatika headed for the door.

So I am to be alone with White Rose? What kind of trap could this be? Should I order him to stay? Before I could decide, he was out the door. I was on my feet, ready to follow, when White Rose stepped out from behind one of the door curtains in the rear.

"High Minko," she said in greeting, almost floating across the room; the thin white dress she was wearing conformed to her ripe young body as if molded. That was no accident. Yes, yes, I was male enough to appreciate the promise in those high breasts, her narrow waist, and what lay hidden deep inside her delightfully shaped hips.

I nodded, cradling my drink with one hand, the mace in the other. "Lady," I answered cautiously. "Do you always receive strange men without an escort?"

She gave me a beguiling smile. "It is said that Chicaza men are most particular about their behavior in the company of women."

"You know a lot about a people on the other side of the world."

She smiled at that, seating herself across from me, knees together as was proper. I wondered about that virgin's belt she wore.

"How was my aunt?"

"We discussed the coming of the Kristianos. I'm sure she will give you the details."

I watched her cover disappointment with a disarming smile. "We share everything."

Of course they did. I gave her a great big smile in return. "Why am I here?"

"To talk." She gestured her innocence with a willowy motion.

I set the drink down. "About what?"

"Well . . . about Chicaza. I have heard only stories. Your people are supposed to be terribly fierce. And they are said to take honor most seriously. Is it true that they field the finest military in the world, that they rarely lose a battle?"

"With the exception of the Kristianos, you have heard correctly. I will also assume that you've heard we get right to the point. What is yours?"

She dropped the mask, giving me that cunning look. "I am thinking about taking you with me tomorrow."

"You make an assumption that I would go."

She considered her words, rubbing her delicate hands together. "My aunt is old, and Cofitachequi has been shaken by the Death. The people have become disheartened, feeling somehow that Power has abandoned us. They need a symbol, something that can give them new hope."

"And what would that be?"

She stared straight into my eyes. "Perhaps an outsider, a great lord who was sent to us in our time of need. A man who could be equated with the heroes back in the Beginning Times. Someone strong, capable. A mighty warrior who could reform our military and knows other Nations. I think we need someone who would cow the rebellious talwas and lesser micos, cause them to think twice about challenging an order."

"That might be a moot point when the Kristianos arrive."

"Have you commanded armies?"

I couldn't help but think about how Uncle had made me direct imaginary formations into battle. And then I remembered the day I gave orders to the remnants of the shattered Uzachile warriors.

I chuckled. "And what would induce me to do this?"

Her gaze didn't waver as she said, "The day is coming when the Cofitachequi mico will be forced to relinquish her authority to her heir." She paused. "But tell me, High Minko, who governs in your place while you roam about the world?"

"My younger brother."

"And why are you here and not there?"

The girl was no one's fool. "That is between me and my Spirit Being."

She was expecting any answer but that. Two little frown lines incised her forehead. She pressed her hands together, leaning forward. "So you are a reverent man? The people would respond to that."

"I take Power very seriously."

"What you said about the Kristianos . . . Are they that dangerous?"

"Lady, I watched them destroy the best the Uzachile could muster—and no matter what you've heard, Uzachile fight well. Hundreds were left dead, and to my knowledge, not a single Kristiano died. My Chicaza are the best in our world, but the Kristianos would cut them to ribbons."

"Yet you came here? Looking to us to defeat them?"

"What Kristianos cannot do is feed themselves." I grinned at the thought. "After weeks in the forest, they'll be starving, disorganized, their cabayos down to bone racks. Had the Death not come, Cofitachequi would have been able to crush them to the last man."

She frowned at that. "What do you mean they can't feed themselves?"

"They don't know how to live off the country." I tapped my mace. "By the time they stumble out of the wilderness, they'll probably be prepared to trade their souls to their *diablo* for a solid meal."

She thought about that for a long time. "Why did you think we would be willing to attack them?"

"Untold wealth in *hierro*, beads, armor, and fabric, along with the prestige of having destroyed them. Not a bad bargain."

"But the Death changed all that."

"Unfortunately." I fixed her with a hard stare. "I understand why you think you have to go out there. Yes, your people need to see their leaders, to know they are not abandoned. But if the Kristianos get out of the forest, reorganize, your best hope lies in evacuating the country ahead of them. Burn the towns—the granaries, too, if you can't relocate the food. If you try to face them in the open, they'll inflict terrible defeats. The way to take them is to ambush a few at a time, lure them into traps."

She studied my face. "You certainly act like a high minko."

"Uncle would be so proud."

She smiled at that. "I think I could come to like you. You don't treat me as a child. But attacking them by ones and twos? Ambushes, traps? You're talking about a long and drawn-out conflict. My people need to attend to their farms, rebuild. We can't invest in an endless raiding war."

"Once Kristianos realize there's no gold here, they'll be headed somewhere else. You just need to encourage them to leave sooner rather than later."

"Can they be dealt with? Perhaps with a delegation?"

"No," I answered coldly. "Pearl— Evening Breeze and I attended one such meeting before Napetuca. She understands their language and heard every bit of treachery they discussed."

"What did the Uzachile have to offer them? I mean, surely there must be some common ground between—"

"There isn't. Stay as far from their clutches as possible."

She gave me a crooked smile. "Afraid you'll lose me to this de Soto?"

"We haven't established that I'm the man you're looking for. And de Soto is a monster without souls. He's going to be interested only in food for his men, people to carry his supplies, and gold. Nothing more."

"So, food is everything . . . his weakness, if you will."
She was calculating just how to use that. "But once fed,
you tell me his military is invincible." She gave me a crafty
glance. "Currently, Cofitachequi is vulnerable to all of our
neighbors. Is there a way to turn the Kristianos against
the Coosa, or perhaps the Algonquian Nations up north?"

I arched an eyebrow. "When Holata Uzachile tried
that, they murdered hundreds, took his town, and enslaved his people. Did the Chicora benefit under an alliance with Ayllón?"

"But if they were handled correctly? Manipulated to
our will?"

I spread my arms. "Didn't you hear a word I said?
White Rose, they're only interested in gold, food, and
what they can take. You can't manipulate them, intimidate
them, or bend them to your will."

Her frown lines deepened. "Everyone can be manipulated."

"Not Kristianos."

She smiled at me then. "It seems you have a great deal
to teach me. All the more reason you should come with
me tomorrow."

"What about Fire Otter?"

"He's harmless. Aunt's darling little boy. In her dreams
she sees us married."

"Apparently you don't?"

"The candidates I was considering didn't survive the
Death. And things have changed. You intrigue me, High
Minko. Everything you said tonight has value. Imagine
what fruit future conversations would bear. My Nation is
in need of new blood, and I am in need of a confident and
capable man. I *will* see Cofitachequi return to her former

glory. Are you the man who can help me accomplish that goal?"

I arched a skeptical eyebrow. "So, we can be married tomorrow?"

"Perhaps we should see how well we can work together." She gave me a provocative smile. "Once away from prying eyes, we can . . . shall we say, explore the possibilities of our relationship?" Her lips parted, excitement in her large dark eyes as she leaned close.

I arched a conspiratorial eyebrow of my own as I considered the implications. "Exploration always has possibilities. Unfortunately, the Cofitachequi mico has already requested that I be available for consultation as word from the scouts comes in. Meanwhile, go and fulfill your duty to your people. I'll be here when you return." I smiled. "With a much richer understanding of Cofitachequi's needs."

She rose, tightening the virgin's belt at her slim waist, as if making a point. The action pulled the gauzy fabric against her breasts and emphasized the curve of her hips.

She stepped close, and I could smell the magnolia petals she'd rubbed in her hair. "I'll even let you keep Evening Breeze. She did me a favor once, though I didn't know it at the time."

"Indeed? What sort of favor?"

She gave me a saucy wink for an answer. "Thank you for a delightful evening, High Minko."

I inclined my head respectfully. "When we know more about the Kristianos and the condition they are in, we can all plan with greater effectiveness."

Her eyes searched mine, as if to ensure that I heard the full intent of her words. "I will do *whatever it takes* to return

Cofitachequi to greatness. Pay any price." Her smile turned seductive. "Assuming the right man will help me."

Her desperation was palpable; I needed only to step forward, pull her to me, and everything she had was mine. A prickle ran down my spine. Forcing a conspiratorial smile, I said, "I look forward to your return."

I stepped out into the night, the mace clutched in my hand, and wondered if the old mico knew just how dangerous her niece was. Or the lengths to which White Rose would go to feed her ambitions.

The yatika was waiting, and as I emerged, he nodded and dutifully led the way to the house I shared with Blood Thorn.

When I entered, the dogs mobbed me, looking behind as if wondering where Pearl Hand might be. *Gods, Black Shell, don't even think about it.*

I walked over to our bedding on the wall benches. In the dim light of the fire I began stripping off all of my finery.

"Interesting evening?" Blood Thorn asked from his blankets.

"You might say that. The mico has a broken empire. Kristianos are about to appear at any moment, and there's no way to stop them. Lady White Rose is busy maneuvering to become the next mico and plotting how to return the Nation to prosperity—with a Chicaza-style army to increase its holdings. Oh, and I can marry her and do the heavy lifting."

"Silly me. I thought you were out accomplishing something important."

After a moment, he asked, "And Pearl Hand?"

"I think she's safe for the moment. If I marry White Rose, I can keep Pearl Hand, too."

"Charming little household."

"Definitely."

Blood and pus, I remembered what I hated about politics.

That left me with a long night ahead, worrying each instant about what was happening to Pearl Hand. And wondering why White Rose had unleased a rattling hail of worry deep down in my gut.

TWENTY-THREE

THE FOLLOWING MORNING AFTER SERVANTS HAD fixed our breakfast, the yatika arrived to inform us that our presence was required by the Cofitachequi mico.

After a troubling night—filled with dreams of Pearl Hand suffering every indignity—I was desperate to see some evidence of my wife.

Blood Thorn and I dressed and used the last of our paints to re-create our lordly personas. Exploring the options available to a captive high minko, I ordered the servant to obtain more paint in all the colors. The man nodded and left.

It's interesting. People just do things for the nobility. I had watched my family act like this for years. Only when you become a trader do you realize that everything has to come from somewhere—and that someone without choice has to surrender it.

Stepping out into the morning, I looked at the two litter chairs resting on the porch. The bevy of servants was lingering, not having much to do. So I gestured to Blood Thorn and went to sit in the closest one.

The servants immediately began to scurry, and Blood Thorn and I were borne forthwith to the crowded plaza before the palace.

White Rose, looking imperious, sat in an ornate litter on the hard-packed plaza just below the palace stairs. Her younger sister, wearing a white dress, rested in a second litter behind her. Both had servants holding feathered sunshades to keep them cool. Fire Otter and an assemblage of ynahaes, oretas, and attendants were lined up behind the litters and carriers. In the rear, servants and porters had formed three lines. The entire entourage before me consisted of over a hundred people.

White Rose gave me a smile, as if to say, "See? You could be here at my side."

Crowded as the Cofitachequi mico's veranda was, we weren't getting a ride up the long stairs. The yatika indicated that we were to climb, so Blood Thorn and I stepped out of our lowered chairs and ascended the steps, a multitude of eyes upon us. I could only imagine the rumors passing from lip to lip.

At the top, the Cofitachequi mico waited in all her finery; swan-feather splays at each shoulder accented a striking white fabric dress adorned with pearls and bits of mica that glittered in the light. Her hair was pulled up with an eagle-feather spray, like rays behind her tightly coiled hair. She held a ground-stone mace; her face was painted in alternating bars of red and white.

The yatika indicated a place for us on the left, and I

looked at the other ynahaes and oretas that crowded the veranda. They were all dressed in their best, looking suitably dignified, and stared down at White Rose's party in the plaza when they weren't giving me sidelong glances.

Two priests approached, attendants following with eagle-feather sunshades. These they skillfully held so their masters were spared the blinding sun.

Beyond the procession, the plaza still looked unkempt, and I came to the conclusion that but for a handful of onlookers and servants, only this collection of nobles and priests remained in the city.

The straits into which Cofitachequi had fallen couldn't have been more apparent. Before the Death, this would have been an occasion for a thousand spectators or more.

Silence fell as the priests began singing, calling upon Power and the Spirit Beasts to bless the mission with success. Then the ancestors were invoked to ensure the safety of the travelers. Finally, the ten accompanying warriors—resplendent with shields, war clubs, bows, and arrows—knelt, palms up, to be blessed and instilled with courage and prowess.

The yatika blew a conch-shell horn; carriers lifted White Rose and her sister's litters to their shoulders.

"May Power go with you," the old mico called. Accompanied by the hollow boom of a pot drum and lilting flute music, White Rose's little procession started for the avenue that would take her to the canoe landing.

We all stood in witness, the ynahaes and oretas mumbling prayers until the procession passed behind the Raccoon Clan house and out of sight.

I watched the old mico sigh, relaxing her shoulders so

the feather splays slumped. She turned, making a gesture, and a chair was placed in the shade. Into this she settled and rearranged her dress with a fragile hand. The other still clasped her stone mace.

"Let us get to business," she said, eyes on the priests as they started across the plaza, following one of the trails across the stickball field. They paused only long enough to lay reverent fingers on the World Tree pole with its faded red-and-white spirals.

Blood Thorn and I stood near the rear, me translating, as the old woman went through the morning business. Periodically the yatika called up a messenger from the knot of people at the bottom of the stairs. These were runners sent by subordinate micos from the surrounding talwas. We heard reports of the number of people returning to their homes after the Death, how many plots of land were being put back into cultivation, requests for seed corn, and the like.

And to think I could have been home, back in Chicaza, listening to many of the same reports—without the Death, I hoped.

And if White Rose has her way, someday you can listen to them here. But when I looked out at the great abandoned city, I wasn't so sure.

How many people can a Nation lose before everything falls apart? Who coordinates the dispensation of tribute? Who cuts the wood? Who sees to the maintenance of all these houses? For the first time, I realized there is a point of depopulation beyond which a people cannot sustain itself. The more sophisticated a civilization, with its military, economics, artisans, and administrators, the greater its vulnerability.

Musing on these things, I was surprised when the yatika called, "High Minko of the Chicaza. Approach."

I stepped forward, mindful of the circumstances, and dropped to one knee, palms up. But I stared straight into the old mico's eyes, a symbol that I recognized her status and authority but remained cognizant of my own.

"Arise," she said softly. "You others may leave us now. The high minko and I have things to discuss."

The oretas shot irritated glances at each other, touched their foreheads, and slowly descended the stairs to plaza level. The knot of spectators immediately mobbed them, eager for gossip.

I motioned for Blood Thorn to come over.

"How can we be of service?" I asked, aware that the yatika remained standing to the side.

"Did you have an interesting talk with my niece?" The old woman watched me with hawkish eyes.

"I did," I answered evenly. "We talked about the Kristianos and about Cofitachequi mostly." How did I couch this? "She thinks there are opportunities here for a man like myself."

The old woman's eyes narrowed. "And what do you think, High Minko?"

"Your niece has the potential to accomplish great things in Cofitachequi. Assuming she has the opportunity to mature, learn, and avoid a crippling blow by the Kristianos." I glanced down at the empty plaza. "And I pray that you have a long life, which will allow her the time to accumulate such wisdom."

A thin smile came to her lips. "You're not jumping at the chance to stand by her side?"

I thumped my copper mace onto my left palm. "My future is dedicated to one purpose only."

"You didn't at least consider it?"

"I did not. Nor did I tell your niece anything that would dash her hopes in that regard."

"Why not?" she snapped.

"In the coming days de Soto is going to find his way to one of your border towns. The monster about to be unleashed on Cofitachequi is beyond White Rose's comprehension. The girl's half-convinced that Power has sent her some magical Chicaza high minko who can turn the tables on the invader. She has hope. Do you want to dash that?"

"And your gain in all this? Perhaps her bed, a nice empire to rule for your own?"

"If I wanted an empire, I'd be in Chicaza. Meanwhile I will do everything in my ability to harm the invader and protect your Nation. When we've bloodied him enough, or when he determines his accursed gold isn't here, I will be racing him for the next Nation, then the one after that. That is my promise."

Her smoldering eyes dimmed. "You always sound so convincing. Can you truly be so simple?"

"No, Mico. And you know it. My service here comes at a price."

"And that is?"

"Evening Breeze. Just so there is no misunderstanding."

"Out of the question."

"De Soto comes." I pointed my mace at the forlorn plaza. "But you already know the danger. Ayllón occupied the coast for only a short time. Yet you live with his legacy: the Death. Defeating such evil comes at a price, Mico."

"Sorry, I've promised to repay the pain she caused me."

I shot a glance at Blood Thorn, who'd been struggling to keep up with the unfamiliar dialect. To the mico I said, "I don't know what she did to your son or who she was back then. I know only the woman I found in the peninsula and the things she has done since. The iniha and I will continue to fight the Kristianos, but whether we help you depends on if you return Evening Breeze to us alive and unharmed."

She laughed bitterly. "You think you can come here, demand things of *me?*"

"Respectfully, Mico, I do not demand. We are in negotiations for an exchange. The future is an uncertain place. You may take Kristiano captives, or the *Adelantado* may send a delegation to speak with you. In any case, who do you have who speaks their language? Or can interpret their treachery?"

"I could keep her for these things."

"You could. The iniha and I shall cease to be of service."

"And what is to keep me from ordering you confined as well?"

"The Power of trade."

"Bah! Look around you. Cofitachequi is already in shambles. Who'd know?"

I gave her a delighted smile. "You are a worthy and great ruler, Mico. And it's an artful bluff. I fear, however, that I've taken your measure, as you have taken mine. Having come in peace, as allies, you will not order us detained. We both descend from the ruling class. Traditions, protocols, and honor are part of our very blood and bone. You will—"

"Do not count on my honor. For the moment it shouts

at me to hang your lovely Evening Breeze in a square just so I can listen to her screams."

"I understand. But you did not rise to the high chair by surrendering to your emotions."

"Actually I got the chair because I was the only surviving heir after my brother was taken by the Death. Me . . . and those two girls who just left."

"You are plenty formidable, great lady. As much as I would enjoy the bluffs and feints, the offers and counter-offers, we don't have time to make a game of this." I pointed south. "The real threat lies out there, somewhere. And that leaves you facing your choice: You can take your vengeance on Evening Breeze or have our dedicated counsel in dealing with the Kristianos."

"I need only to raise my voice to have you detained."

I stepped to the head of the stairs. "And by the time the yatika could summon enough warriors to capture us, I could be at the canoe landing, telling White Rose that I think her offer is worth exploring."

"Why do I put up with you?"

"Perhaps because a long time has passed since you had the opportunity to pit your wits against an equal, great Mico."

She chuckled. Then her expression saddened. "Evening Breeze belonged to my brother. He got her as tribute from the Chicora. At first she was a frightened thing, as beautiful then as she is now. Pus and blood, he fawned over her. Made his wives half-silly with fury as he showered her with wealth, dressed her up, took her everywhere. Wasn't long before she was putting on airs. And haughty. She enjoyed being the Cofitachequi mico's woman. Gods, even the thought of it is enough to make a slug puke."

She reminisced for a moment, lips twisted. "And then she turned her greedy little eyes on my son."

We waited, Blood Thorn shooting me an uneasy glance.

"My son," she whispered. "Tall, straight, muscular, with bright eyes and a quick mind. He'd been born for this chair, and what a way he had with the ynahaes. When the micos would come bearing their tribute he had them in the palm of his hand. Knew just how to compliment them, could play to their vanities as though he knew the most intimate quirks of their souls."

We waited again.

"I don't know when it happened, but I could see it. The looks they gave each other, the hidden little smiles. Then they'd catch themselves, see if anyone had observed."

She wiped at her lips. "Don't think I didn't give the boy a lecture, for all the good it did. And he gave me that wide-eyed look, assuring me that he'd never think of touching the Cofitachequi mico's woman. That even he knew better."

"They were both young," I said softly.

"Young," she snorted. "Why is that always the excuse? Plotting little swamp witch, she got him into her bed, then led him by the penis wherever she wished."

Her jaw worked, lips puckered. "My brother knew . . . saw it on my boy's face. I thought he was going to thrash the lad to within an inch of his life, but I called him off. Barely kept the scandal from bringing down the whole clan."

"So how did it go bad?"

She knotted her fist, staring down at the tendons under

thin skin. "My brother had her locked in a room. Let some of his trusted warriors have at her for a while. Then he was going to hang her in a square"—she pointed—"right down there where everyone who passed by could spit on her, cut her, burn her."

I arched an eyebrow.

"But my son . . ." She shook her head. "He couldn't think beyond his aching loins. Late one night he let her out. And the cunning little sheath begged him to go with her." She waved around. "Give up everything, all this . . . for her."

Blood Thorn shot me a knowing look, as if waiting for a command. I shrugged, fascinated by the story.

"And your son?" I asked. "What became of him?"

"Dead," she whispered. "Down among the Guale somewhere. Afraid to come home for fear of his uncle's rage. Secretly I had his bones brought back." A pause. "But for her, my son would be Cofitachequi mico today."

I watched her gaze slide to where White Rose had vanished.

"She did me a favor once, though I didn't know it at the time." Yes, she did. Ran off with your cousin and left you the sole heir to Cofitachequi.

I bowed, touching my forehead respectfully. "Great Sun Ruler, your choice is more difficult than I would have thought. I offer you my most sincere respect."

She squinted an eye at me, reading my honesty, knowing it changed nothing. "Go on. Get out of here."

I nodded to Blood Thorn. "Iniha, we are excused."

I walked slowly down the stairs, head high, acting every inch a high minko. The old woman was watching me the way a falcon does a sparrow.

Reaching the plaza I asked, "Play chunkey? We'll have to pull some of the weeds first."

"Have you lost your souls to the winds? I caught the gist of what she was saying about Pearl Hand . . . about her son. We've got to do something!"

"Men who were as upset about it as we are would run straight to their house and begin plotting how to break Pearl Hand out of that palace and run for it."

"But we're going to play chunkey instead?"

"Proving that we are exactly who we say we are, that emotion is not a factor in the gamble we're making."

"Why is that important?"

"Because we're lords, you and I. Remember? A lord doesn't lose his head over a woman."

"And neither should the current Cofitachequi mico," he said, catching on. "Chunkey is not a Timucua game."

"Then it's high time you learn it."

"You'll win."

"Don't I always?"

The waiting began. For five days Blood Thorn and I were denied further contact with the Cofitachequi mico. To keep from doing anything stupid, we worked on the chunkey court, pulling weeds and practicing. As a Timucua iniha, Blood Thorn had been trained on the lance, and he was an athletic sort anyway. Within a day, he had the basics down, could run, roll the stone, shift his lance, and cast before overrunning the mark.

A week doesn't make up for a lifetime of training, but he was good enough for a village competition. And it did keep our minds off the more pressing matters.

Knowing that our household servants were spies reporting everything we did, we attended to the rituals. I was observed praying to my sepaya, holding the pouch before me. We never forgot to offer bits of food to the fire.

And we practiced with our bows, having the servants collect old pieces of matting and lash them between two sticks as a backstop for our arrows. During these sessions we freely gave advice to the almost constant stream of spectators. Many of these included warriors who were becoming ever more evident. Apparently the word was out that the Kristianos were coming. What began as a trickle had turned into an intermittent flow as individuals gravitated to the capital. The warriors were most interested in where Kristianos were vulnerable and where their armor was impervious—which was just about anywhere there was armor.

Blood Thorn and I were playing a couple of the younger ynahaes at chunkey when the first runner arrived. The young man came pounding up from the canoe landing, rounding the Raccoon Clan house and panting his way to the palace. Within moments, the yatika had him up the stairs and on his knees before the mico.

"News?" Blood Thorn mused.

"Evidently."

When nothing immediately happened, I turned back and watched the Eagle Clan man cast. The arrival of the runner had broken his concentration, and although we were up by two—my work, not Blood Thorn's—he had been the most consistent competition. They'd bet a beautiful basket filled with silky blue mulberry cloth against a couple of our shell bracelets.

Throughout the week, our trade had increased substantially, compliments of chunkey and the occasional archery match.

Blood Thorn was taking his turn, balancing his lance, staring down the court, when the hollow blare of a shell horn caused us to turn.

"If you will excuse us?" the Eagle man said, his eyes going to the basket they'd wagered. "By the rules, because we must withdraw, the cloth is yours."

"No, take it." I offered it, hoping to gain goodwill. "We can play for it later, same stakes."

The man's partner smiled at that. "We thank you for your kindness, but it was wagered under Power. Perhaps later we can win it back?"

"We honor your offer." I nodded humbly.

But they were already hurrying headlong for the palace. Ynahaes were coming from all over, climbing the stairs, taking their places on the large veranda.

"What do you think?" Blood Thorn asked.

I collected our marking sticks from the ground, hefting my stone. "I think the monster has arrived."

And may Power help the Cofitachequi.

TWENTY-FOUR

To my surprise we weren't called until that evening, perhaps because the old mico was good at playing her own game. We were eating supper, discussing plans in Timucua—much to the continuing irritation of our servant spies. I wondered what they were reporting back to the ynahaes. Surrounded by sad-eyed, drooling dogs, I was chewing the meat off a turkey leg when the yatika announced himself and requested our presence.

Blood Thorn and I donned our fancy dress and took our own sweet time getting ready as the yatika shifted nervously from foot to foot. I knew better than to try to weasel any information from the man. If I had to have a yatika, I would have wanted him.

When we were ready, we dispensed with the chairs, told the dogs to stay, and trotted the short distance to the palace.

The yatika announced us with fanfare, and we entered the main room, only to find it filled with thirty-some warriors. These weren't the ones we'd been talking to in the plaza but hard men, kneeling in rows. They carried shields, bows, and quivers full of arrows. A single sniff of the normally perfumed air told me they'd been on the river; its scents mingled with long-stale sweat. From the looks of them, they'd come hard and fast to get here.

They looked up, eyes widening at the sight of our fancy dress. Well disciplined, their murmurs of curiosity were muted.

The yatika led us around them, past the fire to where several ynahaes—including our chunkey partners—stood to the right of the mico's chair. On the left I found a burly man, midtwenties, tattooed, with a stunning cloak made of overlapping falcon wings hanging down his back. His hair was roached, a warrior's beaded forelock hanging down almost to his nose. The war club dangling from his belt was old and well used.

At the man's feet lay a map drawn with charcoal on tanned buckskin. The quick glance I stole showed rivers, Xs, and black dots.

"Greetings, High Minko." The old mico gave me a sour look. "Your Kristianos have arrived."

I dropped to one knee, palms up. "Bad news, great Sun Ruler. For once in my life, I would have delighted in being wrong."

The burly warrior was giving Blood Thorn and me a thorough inspection—nothing friendly in his eyes. I didn't blame him. We must have made quite a sight, dressed as we were.

"High Minko, rise." As Blood Thorn and I got to our

feet she added, "The man before you is my tastanecci. He will direct our defenses and has just arrived from the northern towns, where he has been watching the trails out of the Catawba provinces."

"Tastanecci, I am honored. I am Black Shell, of the Chief Clan, of the Hickory Moiety, of the Chicaza Nation."

Blood Thorn, his language improved, introduced himself, elevating his chin as if he were an Uzachile great holata.

"I am Wind Cat, of the Falcon Clan, tastanecci of the Cofitachequi Nation." He took another look at our expensive dress, skepticism in his eyes. "The Cofitachequi mico tells me you have fought the Kristianos. And won."

"At times, Tastanecci. And at other times we have suffered grievously." I paused. "With hundreds of dead to show for it."

"You don't inspire confidence."

I met his hard eyes. "Against this enemy confidence can be had, but only with the greatest of cunning, discretion, and superior tactics. What is their condition?"

It was the mico who said, "As you anticipated. They are in poor shape, their cabayos weak." She was watching me with worried eyes. "A hunter came from Aboyaca, a village paying tribute to Guiomae—our southernmost talwa. All he saw was an advance party, but he knew more Kristianos were strung out in the woods. Watching from a tree, the man claims the Kristianos burned some captives alive, demanding to know the direction here."

"And this information is how old?" I asked.

"Several days, at least," Wind Cat said. "The hunter ran to Guiomae, where he told his story to Guiomae Mico, who told the Cofitachequi mico's runner. The runner then had to make his way here."

I took a deep breath. "Is there any way to get your warriors south? Harass his line of march, slow them down?"

Wind Cat shot a glance at his men. "We have come as quickly as we could; my men are weary. We were unaware of the seriousness of the situation. My warriors need at least a day of rest and food. Once refreshed, we require another long day's travel to reach there."

I said, "There are additional warriors in Telemico, perhaps fifty. Meanwhile you need to order the Guiomae mico to evacuate his people, remove—or burn—the food stored there."

"There's not much," the old mico growled. "Fortunately, those granaries are about empty."

"Assuming de Soto's still at Aboyaca, how long would it take him to reach Guiomae?"

Wind Cat bent down, pointing at the map. "Guiomae is on the north side of the river, at least two days' march from the village. Once the invader arrives, he must cross the river. It's up to the banks with spring runoff. To cross hundreds of soldados, cabayos, and his supplies? Four days, perhaps, as he builds rafts or seeks to find canoes."

"That or he'll have to build a bridge," I replied. "Figure six days, and we've already lost two while the message was brought here. Meanwhile, you have time enough to get your people out of Guiomae, burn the food you can't carry with you, and pick the best places to ambush his march on Telemico. But hear my words, Tastanecci: Any direct assault across open ground, in traditional formations, will be a disaster. Do you understand?"

The look he gave me would have frozen water. "We are warriors of Cofitachequi."

I glared back. "And I am Chicaza. But as good as my Chicaza are I would never throw them against a massed formation of Kristianos. Even half-starved, their cabayeros will break your formations and butcher your warriors to the last man."

At the fury building behind his eyes, I gestured my sincerity. "Tastanecci, your courage, your valor, and the skill of your warriors are not at question here. The fact is that the Kristianos have a better army, superior weapons, and those accursed cabayos. Once they are organized, fed, and in battle order, they can't be broken by direct assault. They can, however, be defeated. It's just that, as a wise paracusi once said, you don't eat a buffalo in one gulp. Just a bite at a time."

For the first time, Wind Cat smiled. "I think I understand, Chicaza."

"All right, what's at Guiomae that de Soto could use?"

"The town is only partially occupied," the old mico replied. "White Rose should be there by now. She can give us a report."

I shot her an incredulous look. "Call her back, Mico. Immediately."

The old woman gave me a sour glare. "I've already ordered her to evacuate the town, burn anything left in the granaries. As to the temple there, well, surely he has no use for the dead?"

"We can't move the ancestors anyway," Wind Cat said. "And if he desecrates the graves, it will certainly bring the wrath of the Spirit World down on his head."

"Any other source of food for him?" I asked.

"Ylasi," she said. "I've been keeping emergency stores there. But it's a hard two-day march overland, and way off to the north. From what you've said, the Kristianos would have no reason to go there."

"No, my guess is that having built his bridge and found Guiomae empty, the granaries burned, the monster's going to come here. In every instance, he's marched on the capital first thing—and always found food. He'll have no reason to think this time is different. Meanwhile, traveling on empty bellies, his men are going to have to scavenge, pick mulberries, roots, anything else they can find. That means they're going to be straying into the brush by ones and twos. His columns will be disordered, perfect for hit-and-run raids."

"And Telemico?" Wind Cat asked.

"Evacuate. Remove all the food you can; burn the rest. Do the same anywhere in advance of his route."

"Do you know what you're asking?" Wind Cat looked incredulous. "*Burn our capital?*"

"I do, Tastanecci. The food is lost. One way, you burn it. The other, de Soto's army eats it. And if the monster finds food, he will stop right here to devour every last kernel. He'll use the time to sweep the surrounding country for slaves. Better that your people experience empty bellies, rebuild a burned house or two, than suffer being worked to death under a Kristiano lash."

Wind Cat was silent for a moment. "What gain comes of our suffering?"

"A weaker monster. When he heads north, it will be with hungry and very dissatisfied soldados. Discipline will crumble, his formations collapsing. Then the Tuscarora, the Coosa, or whoever can finally finish the job." I straightened. "It hinges on you, Tastanecci. If you can keep him hungry, moving, harassed, Cofitachequi might be able to do what even the Apalachee couldn't."

Wind Cat was about to object with great vehemence when the mico said, "Power indeed works in strange ways." She snorted in wry amusement. "Their own Death—by killing so many of our people—might just have created the very circumstances to destroy them. Isn't that a bitter irony?"

"We have a chance, Mico," I told her.

"And where will you be during all this, Chicaza?" Wind Cat asked.

"The iniha and I will be with you, Tastanecci, killing Kristianos as we have been since the beginning." I looked at the old woman. "Provided we have our translator, Evening Breeze Mankiller."

"And if you don't have her?" the mico asked mildly.

"We will leave and hope for better cooperation in the next Nation."

She grunted to herself, the corners of her lips twitching. "My choice is not made yet, High Minko. Instead I will wait, see how long it takes the monster to reach Guiomae. Who knows? Finding it burned and abandoned, he might simply turn downriver, return to the coast. Follow that accursed Ayllón's people back to wherever they came from."

"They might. But they won't."

"Why not?" Wind Cat asked, perplexed by the layers of hidden meaning between his mico and me.

"Because he still thinks you have gold."

TWENTY-FIVE

AT NOON THE NEXT DAY, WIND CAT'S WARRIORS WERE preparing to leave. Oretas and ynahaes had been scrambling in and out of the palace; another ten canoes had been procured for the additional warriors Wind Cat was using to swell his depleted ranks.

"Hard to think," Blood Thorn said, looking around. "Here we are, in the capital of one of the greatest of Nations. Within a half day's walk there are another six large towns, and then the outlying talwas with all their associated villages."

"Huh?" I asked, my attention on the palace. It's hard to concentrate when the person you love is suffering. Coupled with years of experience, I have a very good imagination. Here Blood Thorn and I were, playing chunkey, socializing, eating like high minkos, and Pearl Hand had to be in excruciating pain.

My deepest hope was that my warnings, coupled with the growing uncertainties facing Cofitachequi, were sufficient to keep the old woman from really hurting Pearl Hand. I was betting everything that the old mico was smart enough to balance her best interests and survival against the desire for vengeance. Was she smart enough to—

"Black Shell!" Blood Thorn interrupted my thoughts.

"What?" I blinked, staring at him.

"Did you hear a single word I said? I was talking about how big Telemico is and what a lost opportunity we face."

"And your point is?"

"Before the Death, Cofitachequi could have fielded ten thousand warriors." He gestured. "Wind Cat is scrambling just to take eighty south."

I shot a last glance at the palace, sending brave thoughts Pearl Hand's way. "The good news is that they won't be tempted to try to wage a pitched battle."

"He did listen about the tactics we used at Apalachee." Blood Thorn hesitated. "What do you think, Black Shell? Will they do it? Burn the granaries and towns? Leave nothing for the monster? Or at the last minute will they hesitate?"

"The Cofitachequi mico has ordered it burned." I shrugged. "But what the local micos will do? Who knows? Prior to the Death, they'd have swallowed hard and lit the torches. Now, with the central authority so weakened? I'm not so sure."

The runner came staggering in from the east, appearing at the corner of the plaza. That the man had traveled some distance was readily apparent; he was stumbling, body glistening with sweat, lungs sucking for air.

Wind Cat straightened from where he and a warrior were working on a pack.

All eyes were on the man as he crossed the plaza and collapsed on the palace steps.

Blood Thorn and I ran, grabbed him up, and bore his limp and panting body up the stairs. On the palace veranda, the yatika was just stepping out when I ordered, "Get the mico. This must be important."

The yatika was gone in a flash of his pretty blue shirt, feet thumping against the matting inside.

"Water?" the runner whispered. Blood Thorn looked around, finding none, then bolted down the stairs to return with a warrior's bottle gourd. The runner lifted it in shaking hands, gulping it down.

"Enough," I told him, pulling the gourd back. "Too much, as hot as you are, and you'll launch it back up the moment the Cofitachequi mico arrives. And what a great impression that would make, yes?"

The man gave me a weak smile. "Long run. All night."

"What's happening?" the mico herself demanded as she stepped out, a day dress wrapped around her thin frame. Her hair was up, though not formally pinned.

"Great Sun Ruler," the man gasped. "I have come from Guiomae talwa at my master's bidding."

"You're Fire Otter's man, aren't you?" she asked. "The one who wins him all that wealth in the races?"

"Yes, great Sun Ruler."

"What news?"

"Fire Otter wishes you to know that White Rose has met with the Kristiano high mico, the man they call *Adelantado*. She sent her younger sister, the lady Garden, with an escort of ynahaes to ascertain the Kristiano's intent. And when they returned with a favorable report, she had herself carried across the river. The lady White Rose met with them for most of yesterday afternoon and returned—accompanied by the Kristiano leaders—to Guiomae last night."

I shot a look at Blood Thorn, hoping he was following the man's exhaustion-slurred speech, uttered as it was between gasping pants.

"What?" the old mico cried, a stricken expression on her face. "She *met* with them? In *violation* of my orders?"

Wind Cat had climbed up in time to hear the report. He looked dumbfounded, stunned.

The runner took a breath and added, "Fire Otter wants you to know that he warned her against this, explicitly stating your orders. But White Rose disregarded his counsel, telling him that she was there, on the spot, while you were away in Telemico. And being there, she was much better suited to determine the Kristiano's intent."

I actually had to reach out and stabilize the old woman. She was wavering on her feet, as though about to collapse. Her expression was shocked—as if someone had just reached in through her navel and squeezed her heart.

"And the burning of the town?" she whispered.

"White Rose canceled it. I was there as she ordered half of the local people to move out, offering the vacated houses to those Kristianos whom she had already carried across the river."

"She is *carrying* them across?" I asked, reeling at the implications.

The man swallowed hard, nodding. "She ordered Guiomae Mico to obtain every craft he could. They will rope the canoes together, and in so doing have the entire army in Guiomae town by high sun tomorrow."

"So," I said, stunned, "de Soto has a town . . . and full granaries."

"He has informed White Rose that he will eat only what his men need, leaving some for the people. White Rose has his promise."

"What other bad news do you bear?" Wind Cat asked bitterly. "Has she officially surrendered our warriors?"

"No, Tastanecci, but she has given the Kristianos her word—as a lady of the Sun Clan—that they will not be attacked in our country."

My head was swimming. Did I get mad, stomp around, and smash things . . . or just break down and weep my despair?

"My master, Fire Otter, is in a panic," the runner said insistently. "White Rose has done all of these things in the name of the Cofitachequi mico. He told me not to rest until I had informed you."

"You have done well," she said, looking physically ill.

"My master will be sending more runners, great Sun Ruler. He will dispatch them secretly when the opportunity arises." The man was still panting. "And there is one more thing: Last night, just before I was sent, White Rose assured the Kristianos that she was your agent. And her word was binding."

"My *agent*? She is no more my agent than she's a buzzard's guts. Which will make hanging her in a square that much more pleasurable," the old woman rasped.

The runner wasn't finished. "You need to know something else: The great chief of the Kristianos wants to meet with you. He is sending ynahaes to request your presence in Guiomae. They are to escort you to de Soto immediately."

Wind Cat was cursing, striking emptily at the air around him. Down in the plaza, his warriors were all on their feet, watching with awed gazes.

I took a deep breath, struggling to keep from lashing out myself. "Tastanecci, you and your warriors need to escort the Cofitachequi mico to safety. Someplace—anyplace—beyond the reach of the Kristianos."

His expression like repressed thunder, he said, "This advance party that's coming here? I have a mind to kill them all as traitors."

"It's not the ynahaes' fault. The monster will take it out on the people he now has hostage. Perhaps on White Rose herself since she agreed to the mission. Or even poor Garden."

He nodded, thunder blackening behind his eyes.

"Forget it," the mico muttered as she stared absently into the distance. "White Rose has given them her word . . . *my* word of safe passage." Still looking stunned, she turned her attention to Wind Cat. "Send runners to intercept the ynahaes. Tell them I will not meet with the Kristianos. They are to return bearing that message."

"Meanwhile, great Mico, you must get away," I told her gently. "Someplace where they won't think to search for you." To Wind Cat I said, "When you intercept the ynahaes, tell them the Cofitachequi mico has left Telemico, that she is on the road. It may buy us some time."

Wind Cat glanced at his mico. She nodded, broken and disbelieving.

I looked at Blood Thorn. "And you and I, old friend, had better be about packing the dogs. If the *Adelantado* finds us here, we'll suddenly have very short and incredibly miserable lives."

"White Rose?" Blood Thorn asked, shaking his head. "Went over to *them*?"

I took Wind Cat's arm. "We won't be leaving until just before they arrive. If you need advice, help, anything, do not hesitate to ask."

"Thank you, High Minko." He seemed genuinely grateful. "It's just . . . figuring out where we go from here."

"Keep the Cofitachequi mico safe. Get as many people as you can out of de Soto's way."

"Why?" the old woman cried out as she sank to the matting beside the runner. "Why would she do this?"

It was the yatika who spoke, a curious sympathy in his eyes. "She has effectively made herself the Cofitachequi mico, great lady. Knowing there is nothing you can do about it."

Blood Thorn and I had loaded the packs, seen to feeding the dogs, and gathered our things. I left my cadre of servants—expressions of unease on their faces—squatting in the shade by the dogs. Our personal possessions in order, I led the way back to the palace, leaving the dogs in the shade of our house veranda.

"You ready for this?" I asked. "One way or another, we're not leaving without Pearl Hand."

He gave me a curt nod, eyes narrowing.

The plaza was filling, Wind Cat having organized the local people, telling them to fill burden baskets with all the available corn, beans, and squash from the remaining granaries. They were to remove all that they could carry. Where once Telemico and the surrounding towns would have produced ten thousand willing souls, now only six or seven hundred had assembled.

Blood Thorn and I climbed the palace stairs, past boxes, burden baskets, and ceramic jars. Obviously more than could be carried away.

"What's the plan?" Blood Thorn asked. "Just so I know in advance if I have to kill someone."

"We do whatever it takes to gain Pearl Hand's freedom." I resettled my quiver, a Kristiano sword at my side.

He gave me a humorless grin. "And to think that I've told you so many times that I was dead already. Silly me."

No yatika stopped us at the great double doors. We walked into the main room, now dark with the fires burned low.

As our eyes adjusted, we could see that most of the opulent furnishings had been removed.

So, this is how a Nation dies. Betrayed by a foolish young woman in the pursuit of her own ambition.

The Cofitachequi mico sat in her eagle-backed chair, Wind Cat, the yatika, and several of the oretas clustered around her. We walked up as if we were old friends come for the eulogy.

The discussion was heated: raised voices, lots of arm waving, that sort of thing. For the moment, White Rose's treachery wasn't my problem—though it remained a seething burn that had come to live under my heart.

"High Minko Black Shell," the old woman called, seeing us approach. The room went suddenly silent, her people glaring at each other and then at us.

I walked up, an opening forming as the crowd stepped back. Ritually I dropped to my knee, palms up, then regained my feet. She was still the great mico, after all.

"These brave souls"—she waved absently at the nobles—"have all the sense of a flock of hen turkeys. I'm being told to do everything from welcoming the conqueror—and my idiot niece—on bended knee to attacking Guiomae. You, however, have real experience with this pus-sucking Kristiano. What is your advice . . . just to stir it into the stew, so to speak."

I looked around, seeing frightened old men, and a few young ones. Only Wind Cat didn't seem afraid, just incredibly angry.

"There is no need to mince words, great Sun Ruler. Your chance to defeat the monster is lost. With White Rose as an accomplice he will take what he needs and go where he will. From our experience, anyone's best hope is to avoid capture. That means you foremost, great Mico. And you"—I pointed at the ynahaes and oretas—"second most. He *will* use you as hostages to ensure compliance from the local people."

"And then?" one of the elders asked. "When he takes the capital? Demands tribute? What do we do? Keep hiding in the forests?"

"He won't stay long," I told them. "Expect him to rest his army, eat your food, and look around. When he finds no gold he will move on. Perhaps in a couple of weeks, perhaps in a month or two."

I watched the interplay of expressions. Then they all started talking at once.

"Silence!" the old woman shouted, and the room again went quiet. She looked up at me, taking in my clothing, the quiver on my back. "You look as if you are ready to leave."

"For the moment, great Sun Ruler, we would like to accompany you to whatever place you and Wind Cat have decided. Our presence gives you three more warriors, and while our counsel has not been of much service up to now, perhaps it might in the coming days."

She narrowed her eyes. "Three more warriors? Do you and the iniha have another hidden somewhere?"

"The iniha, myself . . . and Evening Breeze. The time for your decision has come."

She kept staring at me, her fingers playing along the arm of her chair. Finally she asked, "Why would she serve me . . . and not try to cut my throat?"

I heard gasps, the shuffling of feet.

"Because she came here to destroy Kristianos." I lowered my voice, stepping close. "And after your niece's treachery, you may be short on reliable allies."

For a long moment, we held each other's gaze, neither willing to waver. Then she glanced at the sword hanging by my side, noted that Blood Thorn's quiver was easily in reach and that he'd strung his bow. Her glance at Wind Cat, who was now whispering to an elder, told me all I needed to know. I dropped a casual hand on the sword's hilt and saw the desperation of defeat when it finally flickered behind her eyes.

"Yatika," she ordered bitterly, "bring the woman called Evening Breeze."

He gave me a hooded look, turned on his heel, and strode to one of the rear doors.

"Thank you, great Sun Ruler. We remain your allies in peace. And on our honor, we will serve you to the best of our ability until such time as the Kristianos leave Cofitachequi."

But she was staring off into space. Her clenched jaws reflected the turmoil in her souls as what was left of her world crumbled around her.

I turned anxious eyes on the door through which the yatika had gone. My heart had begun to pound. The worry I'd sustained over the long days came back like a terrible storm. Had I played this correctly? Was I right that the old woman wouldn't have harmed her, cut her tendons, tortured the woman I loved?

Every moment that Pearl Hand didn't materialize added to my building terror.

Pus and blood, what's taking so long? If she's maimed or dying, so help me, not a single one of these worms is leaving this room alive.

In my souls, I measured the distance to Wind Cat. I'd have to kill him first. Then the old woman. If Blood Thorn could get to the door, we'd have the rest trapped.

And then the yatika pulled the hanging back, leading Pearl Hand behind him. I felt the first rush of relief. She was walking, her head up. That she was unkempt and wore a simple servant's dress came as no surprise. Then I noticed that she seemed stiff, pained. Each step was planted as though by will alone, as if she didn't trust her feet.

Rage—mixed with worry—tied my souls into a knot.

When her eyes met mine, the effect was electric, and it took all of my restraint to keep from rushing to her and crushing her in my arms.

Easy, Black Shell, act the part. I waited, forcing myself to stand like a Chicaza lord instead of the enraged and impetuous love-struck boy I wished to be at that moment.

Pearl Hand's wrists were bound before her, a rope leading to the yatika's hands. She kept her eyes locked with mine, defiant, angry.

In Timucua, I said, "Should I just kill them?"

"Not yet," she answered tightly. "What's happening here?"

I felt a rush of relief. She was thinking with her usual clarity. "Play the game with me, wife. We're not out of this yet."

She gave a slight nod, eyes narrowing. Then she shot the old woman a look of venomous hatred.

I asked the yatika, "Would you please release her?"

His questioning look went to the mico, who nodded absently, her gaze still fixed on a far and unseen horizon.

The yatika handed me the rope. With care, I slid the Kristiano sword from its sheath, aware that the surrounding ynahaes stepped back, Wind Cat tensing.

As I severed the tight leather laces binding Pearl Hand's wrists, I said wryly, "Please, my love, no matter what they've done, don't precipitate anything rash."

"Took you long enough," she muttered darkly, plucking the last of the bindings from her bruised and scabbed wrists. Then she gave me a dark and haunted look that shook me down to the bones.

In Timucua, I replied, "Things have been complicated since I became a high minko, but I thought your release would be accomplished better by being smart rather than dumb."

"Of course," she answered, and, head lowered in a feral manner, gave the oblivious old woman another menacing look.

Slipping the sword back into its scabbard, I turned my attention to Wind Cat, saying, "No matter what the others say, you must get the Cofitachequi mico out of Telemico. The Kristianos will have made her capture a priority."

Wind Cat exhaled his tension. "I agree."

Seeing that the old woman was lost to misery, her expression vacant, he took charge, saying, "These are the tastanecci's orders: Be ready to leave within a hand's time for Yca talwa." He pointed. "Yatika, a deception is called for. I want the following message to be delivered to Fire Otter. Tell him that because the Kristianos are headed to Telemico we are taking the Cofitachequi mico downriver. Tell him we are bypassing Guiomae at night, using the Pasque trail. Tell the runner that after he has delivered his message to Otter, he is to seek out White Rose, tell her the same thing, and that he now accepts her as the great Sun Ruler. Can you find a man to do this?"

The yatika nodded. "I have such a man. It will be as you order, Tastanecci."

Wind Cat looked at the rest of us. "No one in this room is to mention that we are really headed north to Yca town. We leave Telemico within a hand's time. Any who do not accompany us are on their own. May Power help you."

I stepped close to Pearl Hand. "Come on. We've a hand's time. Let's get you out of here."

She shot one last look at the broken woman slumped in her chair. "The sooner, the better."

"Can you walk?" I asked in Timucua.

"It hurts . . . but no matter what it costs, they'll never see it." She took the lead, heading for the door, head up, looking proud. But I could see she was in agony with each stiff-legged step.

It wasn't until we were outside that she folded. Blood Thorn and I caught her as her legs gave out. In the sunlight I got a good look at the bruises, my gut twisting. Then, together, we carried her down the stairs.

I hoped no one noticed the tears of frustrated rage that beaded at the corners of my eyes.

TWENTY-SIX

Back in our house, Blood Thorn and I lowered Pearl Hand onto one of the benches. The dogs clambered all over her, licking, barking their joy, tails lashing. I ordered water and food. The servants took off like frightened chipmunks.

"Dogs! Down!" I said, terrified that they might hurt Pearl Hand even more.

"No! Please. I've prayed for this." And—tears streaking down her cheeks—she tried to wrap all four of them into her arms at once. Her smile was a thing of beauty.

I let it go on until it was apparent the dogs were getting out of hand, their excitement becoming reckless. I ordered them back, made them lie down, and dropped to my knees, taking her hands in mine. The sight of her bruised arms and legs, cut lip, and swollen cheekbones, the filth-matted hair and bloody wrists, stabbed like a thorn through my heart.

"I love you so much," I said softly, staring into her eyes. "I was worried sick."

She whispered hoarsely, "Worried? You have no idea. Blood and muck, that woman hates me."

Blood Thorn stood behind us, arms crossed. "As much as she hates you, she's smart enough to know that keeping you alive outweighed any delight she'd have felt killing you."

"What did they do to you?" I asked, afraid to hear it.

"When they took me, I thought I was headed straight to a square, or perhaps a beheading. But she kept me in her quarters, on my knees, my wrists tied to my ankles behind me. Until you've experienced it, you can't imagine the pain. And then the beatings." She shook her head. "I cried . . . I begged her to just kill me. She told me she'd have enjoyed that, but she had other uses planned for me."

I interrupted to say, "Blood Thorn and I made it plain to her that your death would ill serve her chances of surviving the Kristianos."

"Next time, just let me die. Someday I might actually get around to thanking you." Her attempt to smile failed. "Maybe."

"We were worried she'd mutilated you," Blood Thorn added. "It would have complicated our chances for survival after we bashed her head in."

"So," Pearl Hand asked as pots of water and food were borne in by the servants, "when do we get out of here? Where are we headed? Where is de Soto?"

"We'll leave with the old woman and Wind Cat," I said. "And, no matter what, Blood Thorn and I need your help."

She gave me a cold glare.

"You expect *me* to travel with *her*? After what she's done?"

I took a deep breath. "Here's the situation . . ." I outlined the plans we'd originally made, finishing with White Rose's treachery.

Pearl Hand closed her eyes and swallowed hard. "White Rose . . . always the calculating little swamp witch. So that's what happened . . . the reason the beatings stopped."

"Come on. Water's here. Let's get you cleaned up and into some decent clothes."

I helped her undress and winced at the discovery of additional welts and bruises. Using a damp cloth, I carefully sponged the days-old sweat from her body while Blood Thorn sat to one side, a beautifully carved trencher in his lap, spooning food to her by the bite.

Pearl Hand winced when I hit sore spots and told me between bites of roasted turkey, "She never hit me hard enough to break anything, just enough to add to the agony."

"Dear wife, you have to make a decision: Do we stay, continue to advise Wind Cat on how to hurt de Soto? Or do we consider Cofitachequi a lost cause, take to the forest, and see if we can beat him to the next place?"

The tension around her eyes increased. Who did she hate more? The Kristianos, or the mico?

She fingered her stringy and matted hair, wincing at the pain of raising her arm. "I'll think better when my hair's clean. And, Black Shell, for the moment, I'm not going far in any direction. You should have heard me whimper when the yatika pulled me to my feet. As it was, he had to support me until my legs would hold. And the agony of having my limbs straightened? I thought I'd faint."

"You'll ride in a noble's chair," I added. "Borne by porters."

She arched her eyebrow, hinting at the old Pearl Hand. "Hey, you made me a high minko. Remember?"

A flicker of a smile died. "And the sick-souled old bitch would see me riding along behind her, wouldn't she?"

Blood Thorn added, "You'd be referred to as Nicoquadca Evening Breeze."

"Nicoquadca?"

"They rotted well know what it means." Blood Thorn scraped the horn spoon full again. "And that broken old mico would hear it over and over."

I couldn't help but add, "Provided you don't bow to your richly deserved vengeance and smack her in the skull."

"Which would, of course, get us all killed," Blood Thorn said solicitously.

"It would require a certain restraint on your part."

She should have given me a look that would have roasted smilax bread. Instead her eyes appeared oddly blank.

Blood Thorn and I helped her wash her hair, then we fawned over the combing of her long locks, got her dressed in her trail clothes, and fed her the last of the turkey.

A horn sounded, the signal that time was up. "We going or staying?" I asked.

She stared dully at the floor. "All those years ago when I was here? I never got to ride in a litter. Will I have a sunshade as well?"

"Would you like one?"

"I would."

"Blood Thorn," I cried. "Call the servants; find a sun-shade. The nicoquadca is ready to travel."

And I was dancing down in my souls. Pearl Hand was back. Subdued, sore, and nursing the Piasa's own rage, but back nevertheless.

Pearl Hand—riding in the litter and bedecked with jew-elry—looked majestic. Two servants walking behind held her sunshade on long poles that were braced just so against the back of her chair. The dogs, their packs carried by porters, were delighted to be on the trail again. I had the rest of my household lined up in the rear as we took our place behind the mico in her litter. I could see Pearl Hand's squinted appraisal of her former captor.

"What do you think?" Blood Thorn asked, standing beside me in the sun. "Will Pearl Hand snap and break the old lady's head or not?"

"I'm betting not. You?"

"Not. She's going to enjoy 'putting on airs' too much."

I laughed softly, hiding my worry at the darkness be-hind my wife's eyes.

Wind Cat's warriors did an exemplary job of getting the whole procession started, and in a long line we snaked our way around dwellings, winced at the overpowering stench from the charnel houses, and headed out on the northern trail that would lead us to Yca talwa, a day's march to the north-northwest.

Yca was a good choice, allowing communications with Guiomae to the southeast and Telemico to the south, and it had a network of well-traveled trails leading off in whatever direction would ensure safe evacuation should the Kristianos come prowling.

At the forest edge, I stepped out, taking one last look back at Telemico, its shell-covered temple rising above the abandoned capital.

Here, a great Nation had once ruled from the mountains clear down to the ocean. Only two years past, Cofitachequi had been the equal of any Nation, including the Coosa, the Tuskaloosa, and the Natchez. How could such a mighty people collapse so quickly?

Looking back from where I stood, I saw the corpse of a city—one that would never see her glory returned. What the Death had begun, de Soto would complete.

White Rose, so desperate to rebuild Cofitachequi's strength and authority, had made her bargain with its ultimate destruction. Poor deluded fool; I wondered if she'd live long enough to appreciate the enormity of her mistake.

Or what her blind ambition would ultimately cost not only Cofitachequi, but all the other thousands who would suffer for it in other Nations.

"Thinking of something?" Blood Thorn asked as I rejoined the march.

"White Rose. And why I didn't reach out and strangle her to death that night."

He made a throwing-away gesture. "People insist on sowing the seeds of their own destruction. Makes you wonder, though: What are our real chances of finally winning this thing?"

"I don't follow you."

"White Rose won't be the last." His expression was somber. "You and I, we know the stakes. How do we save

our world when someone like White Rose—seeing a
vantage by allying with the Kristianos—will throw it aw
for selfish gain?"

I grunted, remembering the promise in her eyes that
night. Had I accepted, offered to marry her, help her rebuild Cofitachequi, and accompanied her south, could I
have changed the outcome? Would Wind Cat's warriors
even now be harrying de Soto's starving soldados through
the burned ruins of Guiomae?

So who had been the real blind fool here? White Rose,
or me?

At Yca talwa, a town of about five hundred souls, we were
given a house; the Cofitachequi mico had the occupancy
of the mico's palace. We settled in while the servants saw
to the task of preparing the meal.

"How are you feeling?" I asked Pearl Hand. She had
begun to limp around unassisted, slow and sore.

"I'll be myself in a couple of days," she said insistently
while she fussed over her crossbow. But her fingers were
shaking and she avoided my eyes when she asked, "So, how
does it feel to be a high minko?"

"Making me a high minko probably saved your life. But
could we have a little more warning next time we come to
a place where you've worn out your welcome?"

She ran her trembling fingers down the polished wood
of her weapon. "I didn't think I'd be recognized." She
blinked, as if against tears. "I was so young back then . . . a
girl when I was given to the great mico."

"I've heard the old woman's side of the story. What's
yours?"

She swallowed hard. "I went to his bed a virgin. After

first time he told me in no uncertain terms that as ...g as I pleased him, I would benefit. He would teach me ...e things I needed to know."

She paused. "I . . . I dedicated myself to the task. Experimenting, trying this or that. He'd lost interest in his wives, and I was new and exciting, unhampered by the restraints of a 'woman of virtue.' Every time I left him gasping and begging for more, I was appropriately rewarded, got to travel with him, was showered with gifts."

"And the old woman's son?"

She shrugged, the crossbow forgotten in her hands. "The mico was an older man; I had to use every trick to keep his interest, make his body perform. Then, here was this vigorous youth, a little older than me. I could talk to him, laugh with him. He looked at me as if he saw something more than just a talented sheath." She gave me a plaintive look. "Just to be recognized as another human being can have the most profound consequences . . . and fire foolish hopes."

"And the boy had desires of his own," I guessed.

"I was exotic, forbidden. That kindles its own passion. I was already a master. I played his body for everything it had." Her eyebrow arched higher. "After that first tryst we couldn't keep our hands off each other."

"Until the mico found out."

She made a face. "Any illusions I might have had about life . . . they died the night he locked me into that room with his warriors. What was left of me was to be hung on a square the next day. And when the end came, my sweet young lover was to have the responsibility of cutting my heart out."

"I heard he wasn't quite up to the honor."

"He came for me in the middle of the night. We ran. But nothing was quite right after that." Her expression turned sad. "What did I know? Any time I'd been with a ... it had been about pleasure. What the warriors did to ... seeing ... world for what it really is. I was ... ... And at night ... But I ... I with the price he'd paid to save me. We ended up among the Guale."

"I heard he died there."

She stared absently into the past. "Not until after he paid me back for the unhappiness in his life. After extolling my abilities, he gave me to the Guale chief. Payment for protection."

"So you killed him?"

A wistful smile bent her cut lip. "I never saw him again. I was locked up, my life depending on how well I pleased the chief. And believe me, after having a knife put to my neck, I found untold motivation. But the Death had broken out among the people who had survived Ayllón. So many died: my lover, the Guale chief . . . I just walked out of the palace one day."

"Your version makes more sense than the mico's."

She shrugged uncomfortably.

"There has never been another woman like you," I told her. "That's why Power placed us together."

"Makes you terribly skeptical of Power, doesn't it?"

"Never."

"Then I sincerely hope you're not planning on making a living as a trader. You obviously don't have a knack for it."

At her acid tone, I leaned close, asking, "Are you all right?"

With pained eyes, she shot me a look, whispering, "I don't know, husband. What she did to me . . ."

"Pearl Hand, talk to me."

She shook her head bitterly. "When I'm ready. Maybe. For now, leave me alone."

"But I—"

"Pleas—"

That's when the yatika stuck his head in. "The tachequi mico requests the high minko's presence."

I stood. "Formal? Or war council?"

"We are no longer in Telemico, but a certain level of respect would be appropriate."

"Thank you, Yatika. We will be there as soon as we can dress."

After he left, I glanced meaningfully at Blood Thorn, then said to Pearl Hand, "You rest, we'll give you a complete—"

"I'm going." She ground her jaws, her gaze dropping as she tightened her grip on the crossbow. "Do you understand? I *have* to."

"Can you walk, or do you need the chair?"

She made a face as she pulled herself to her feet. "If I'm a nicoquadca, I'll walk. Anything left in the packs for me to wear?"

"We're overstocked in jewelry. Cofitachequi ynahaes, it turns out, really can't play chunkey."

"So," she murmured. "I'm tied up like a sacrificial turkey . . . and you're gambling on chunkey?"

When we arrived, the palace was packed; we fit ourselves in at the edges, happy to be out of the center of attention. I kept shooting glances at Pearl Hand, prickling with unease. Whatever the old woman had done to her,

Pearl Hand wouldn't say. I was faced with the odd new fact that I had no idea what my wife was about to do or if she would get us killed in the process.

To make matters worse, Wind Cat had us dragged up front and center. Pearl Hand stood so erect she might have been made of wood. Face-to-face with her captor again, I flinched at the strain in her brittle expression.

In the name of Power, wife, don't do anything foolish.

Why didn't I insist she stay with the dogs?

The old woman gave Pearl Hand a disdainful look, then said, "All right. Here's what we know: White Rose has told the Kristianos about the seven big granaries at Ylasi talwa off to our north. She's *given* them to the invader. Even as we speak a large part of his army is headed there."

Groans filled the room.

The Yca mico—a young man obviously elevated to the position because of the Death—cried, "We should march on Ylasi, great Sun Ruler, fortify it, and deprive the invader."

"We cannot," the old mico told him, acid in her voice. "My niece has granted them safe passage in my name. You know the protocol. I cannot revoke their safe passage without a loss of honor. I could overrule her, of course, but doing so means dividing our people right down the middle, asking them to declare an allegiance to her or me."

"We serve you," the young mico declared vehemently. "She has betrayed all of Cofitachequi."

"You will remain quiet." The way she said it, I thought the young man was going to swallow his tongue.

The Raccoon Clan oreta asked, "Hasn't she already declared herself to be the Sun Ruler?"

"Not that I've heard. And until she does so, I'm assuming she's smart enough not to create such a division. It would mean civil war, my supporters against hers. And while I believe she sees my tenure in the mico's chair as limited, ineffective, and irrelevant, she won't push the issue."

Wind Cat asked, "What if we just provided a demonstration? Massed warriors before the town?"

Blood Thorn answered, "The Kristianos would take it as an invitation for combat. They've seen exactly such displays at Tapolaholata, Ahocalaquen, Napetuca, Anhaica, and too many other places. Each ended in a massacre with hundreds dead."

Wind Cat didn't like it, but he nodded acceptance.

The old mico—glaring venom at Pearl Hand—said, "And the moment fighting starts, both of my nieces, Fire Otter, the ynahaes, and the micos will be made captive."

"White Rose made her choice," one of the ynahaes called from the rear.

"My nieces are *Sun Clan*. Provided we can find a way to survive this without a bloodbath, one of them will eventually ascend the elevated chair. Do you understand?"

At her tone, the man swallowed dryly, nodding. He dropped to one knee, his palms up, head down. The old mico left him that way.

I smiled grimly.

She sighed, rubbed her nose, and said, "Not all is against us. We have heard that Otter is heading south with a *capitán,* Añasco, and his soldados to capture me. White Rose has either fallen for the ruse, or—coming to realize that she has made an alliance with a black sorcerer—is complicit. This means, for the moment, we are safe in Yca."

"No movement toward Telemico?" I asked.

"Not yet." She gave me a cold glance. "Advice, High Minko?"

I gave her a nod. "Racing the Kristianos for Ylasi with warriors is out of the question. But ordering the immediate evacuation of its people is another thing."

"And that gains us?" she asked warily.

Pearl Hand, fists knotted, hesitantly said, "White Rose gave them the food stores . . . but she didn't give them the means of carrying it away. After gold and food, the monster wants slave porters. If the people are gone, the only food de Soto's men can carry is what's packed on their backs or cabayos."

"Finally," the old woman whispered, "we begin to understand why the high minko *values* Evening Breeze. She has an imprecise ability to state the obvious."

Her response was cruel. Pearl Hand had answered her question. I stiffened, about to object, when Blood Thorn laid a restraining hand on my arm.

Pearl Hand's expression turned brittle, and her eyes slitted, as if to mask any expression. The old mico, however, looked as if she could chew Kristiano *hierro*.

The old woman ground her jaws and asked, "So he's got the food? Why do we care if he carries it away?"

Pearl Hand swallowed hard, a shiver running down her back. Anger? Or fear? "Because it leaves his forces split, without unified command. And the longer the invader is separated from half of his army, the more uncomfortable he will get. The trick to beating Kristianos is to keep them off balance, fragmented, with the possibility of dissent in the ranks."

The old woman snorted with disdain. Pearl Hand

went stiff. Nevertheless, the old mico said, "Tastanecci, send a runner immediately. My order is that Ylasi be evacuated. Send just enough warriors to ensure that I'm obeyed and that the people are scattered throughout the forest. And then have the warriors out of there before the invader arrives."

"Yes, Cofitachequi Mico."

It was a small victory—barely an inconvenience for the Kristianos—but a major one for Pearl Hand. She took a deep breath, the corners of her mouth quivering from the strain.

Wife? Are you going to be all right?

Later, as we stepped out of the palace, I reached over to take Pearl Hand's arm, only to have her shake it off with the warning, "I don't want to talk about it."

"But I was only—"

"Don't, Black Shell. Just . . . just leave me alone."

I stopped short, stung to the heart, and watched as she hobbled painfully across the dark plaza toward our house.

"Give her time." Blood Thorn paused beside me. "She's fighting a battle inside herself."

"And if she loses?"

He gave a slight shrug of the shoulders. "Nothing is forever, Black Shell. None of us are ever as strong as we lead ourselves to believe."

When I finally entered the house, it was to find that Pearl Hand had moved her bedding to a bench across the room. She was already in the blankets, her head covered. From the way the blanket was quivering, I knew she was sobbing.

That night I was awakened by odd mewing sounds. I sat up in the darkness to see Bark, too, was awake. He stood by Pearl Hand's bed, his head cocked, ears pricked.

I was about to yell at him when I realized he wasn't the source of the suffering sounds. Like me he was fixed on Pearl Hand's sleeping form and I realized the muted screams and whimperings had their origins in her dreams.

Before I could call Bark back, he reached up and pawed at her. His touch was enough that she shifted, turned onto her side, and dropped back to a peaceful sleep.

TWENTY-SEVEN

FOR TWO DAYS, BLOOD THORN AND I LIVED AS IF WE were walking among coiled rattlesnakes when we were in Pearl Hand's presence. She said nothing, eyes locked on something only her souls could see. She barely ate and spent most of her time sitting away from us. On occasion she would call Bark to her and walk off into the forest, disappearing for hands of time.

Each time I tried to initiate a conversation, tried to joke, Blood Thorn would shoot me a warning look and give a slight shake of his head. My souls cried.

On the second day we were in council with the Cofitachequi mico when a runner arrived, dropped to his knee, and gave the following report: The Kristiano force in Guiomae—including the *Adelantado*, White Rose, young Garden, and the other ynahaes—was en route to Telemico. The impetus, apparently, was that de Soto had raided the tombs in the Guiomae temple, found pearls, and was told by White Rose that many more could be had for the taking from tombs in the great Telemico temple.

The messenger looked up, face slightly ashen. "Great Sun Ruler, the lady White Rose asks me to inform you that if you were to ambush the Kristianos on their march north, she might escape during the fighting."

Blood Thorn and I exchanged glances. Pearl Hand just smiled knowingly, as if the information somehow amused her.

Evidently roosting with vermin had somehow changed the lady White Rose's mind. Or perhaps it was the desecration of the temple? The one at Guiomae didn't hold the bones of Sun Clan ancestors, but the Telemico temple did. And the very mention of sending the Kristianos there to loot the graves of her ancestors must have sent a chill down White Rose's back as she made the offer.

The old mico, face grim, glanced at Wind Cat. "Can that be accomplished?"

Wind Cat, of course, looked to us.

I shook my head. "She doesn't understand Kristiano warfare. White Rose will be surrounded by de Soto's cabayeros as well as ranked soldados. While the soldados would be tough enough, the cabayeros will ride wide, breaking up any formations you throw at the main column. It will be a slaughter, and de Soto will tighten his guard around his prisoners."

"How then?" Wind Cat asked.

"Unless the monster does something uniquely stupid"—Pearl Hand bit off the words—"your best chance is to wait de Soto out. As long as White Rose remains compliant, he'll keep her safe. The moment she crosses him, she'll be placed under guard . . . or worse."

"So, she and Garden are lost for good?" A weary defeat had settled in the old woman's eyes.

"Probably not," Pearl Hand told her coldly. "He'll have no use for her once he finishes looting you clean and leaves your borders."

As the old mico's anger flared and she took a breath to respond, the messenger—his expression even more pained—said, "And there is one more thing, great Sun Ruler. You are aware that Fire Otter took a group south in search of you?"

"Yes." She looked down at him expectantly.

"I am to inform you that Fire Otter—in the fulfillment of his duty to you—decided to take his own life rather than either betray the lady White Rose's confidence in him or divulge your actual whereabouts. He is dead."

I watched the old woman swallow hard, her eyes narrowing in grief. "I raised him, you know. He . . . He became the son I lost."

You could feel it in the room, an almost unbearable disbelief.

I gave Wind Cat a knowing look, saying, "Perhaps we can reconvene later today?"

He nodded, gesturing for the room to be cleared.

I looked back as we exited the palace, seeing the old woman, sunk in her chair, her eyes staring at something in the distance only she could see.

Even more disturbing, Pearl Hand could barely conceal a grim smile.

The next day we were called to the mico's veranda as another runner arrived. Breathlessly, he told us, "The Kristianos marched into Telemico in force. Even as they occupied the palace, others rushed up the steps of the temple. I watched as they shouldered the great doors open." He looked up at the yatika and surrounding nobles. "They immediately began looting the burial boxes. They are like vermin . . . without respect. I saw them turning the burial boxes over and dumping the bones of our ancestors on the floor."

Tears beaded in the man's eyes. "I am Sun Clan. The bones of *my* ancestors are scattered about the floor like litter. The Kristianos kicked them out of the way, crushed the fragile skulls under their heavy feet. I can hear the souls of the ancestors screaming in anguish!"

"Why?" the horrified yatika cried, a look of consternation on his face. "Have they no respect?"

"Pearls," the runner whispered. "They take only the pearls, stripping them from statues, rifling through the sacred bones. Respect? They could not be more vile if they were pissing on our very souls!"

I watched the yatika stomp off, head down, fists clenched so hard the muscles in his arms looked like twisted wood.

"What can we do?" he cried. "How do we kill them all?"

I walked over, placing a hand on his bunched shoulder. "You can't, my friend. Even if you massed the few warriors you have, no matter how enraged, they would kill you all. Cofitachequi would consist of an empire of corpses when they finally left."

Nor did it stop there. Reports came filtering in of slave sweeps: The soldados apparently believed that any woman they found—no matter how she tried to fool them by acting otherwise—would be delighted to have them throw her to the ground, pry her legs apart, and gang-rape her.

Several men who had tried to interfere were either beaten senseless or simply killed on the spot.

As word of the atrocities spread, arrows had been loosed from the brush, the locals filtering away afterward. Then came word that some of the Cofitachequi porters had thrown down their burdens, adamantly refusing to carry them another step. When they demanded to speak to the Cofitachequi mico, they were surrounded, clapped into collars, and chained together.

Our understanding was that White Rose went to the *Adelantado* and insisted they be released. I wondered how she felt these days, climbing up the palace steps, asking for an audience with the unwashed Kristianos who now slept in the palace her ancestors had built.

Is this the Cofitachequi you were so anxious to re-create?

From the veranda of our loaned house, we watched the Yca palace. These days a guard of warriors stood before the door. For two days no one but the yatika and individual messengers was allowed inside to disturb the old woman's grief.

"I can almost feel sorry for her," Pearl Hand said, finally relenting, as she oiled her crossbow. "Even if she gets White Rose and Garden back alive, she's still lost everything."

I glanced down, saying, "These days it's better to be a dog than a high mico." The dogs were sleeping in the shade. About the only preoccupation a dog had was whether he'd get his next meal. Their only regret was that they'd not had more to eat at the last.

I'd been looking over the village dogs, finding nothing to my liking. A couple were large enough to take Skipper's place, but none seemed to have the inherent personality necessary.

I took a chance. "Want to talk?"

"No."

Wind Cat had been out of sight since the night we heard Fire Otter's fate. Now he came trotting in from the south, ten warriors following as they wound through the cane-roofed houses. His bow was in his hand, his body sweat-streaked.

Seeing us, he veered our way, his face grim.

"Greetings, Tastanecci," I called, and we all stood. The dogs raised their heads, took his measure, and fell back to their rest. Contemplating what was for dinner, probably.

"High Minko," he said tersely as he stopped before us.

"Someone bring the Tastanecci and his men water," I ordered, and my servants snapped to, procuring a pattern-stamped jar and handing it to the war chief.

As he drank, I studied Pearl Hand from the corner of my eye, then dared to say, "Come in out of the sun. It's a hot day, and it looks like you have come far and fast."

He and his grateful men did so, divesting themselves of weapons, passing the drinking pot back and forth as yet another was procured.

"What news?" Blood Thorn asked. "You heard about the looting of the temple?"

"I did." Wind Cat wiped sweat from his brow. "I was so enraged I was contemplating something foolish, biding my time. Then I finally saw the cabayeros in action. The Unharca mico took offense to the way his niece was abducted. The poor girl was plucked up, thrown across a cabayo, and hauled off to Telemico like a sack of squash. What they did to her . . ." Wind Cat's expression hardened. "Let us say that it was more than the Unharca mico's honor could withstand. I told him it was the Cofitachequi mico's order to desist, but he was enraged beyond any reason. Called me a coward when I would not allow my men to join his party. He gathered together what warriors he could and attacked a mounted Kristiano patrol."

"Power have mercy," Blood Thorn whispered.

"We followed at a distance. Thirty-some of them attacked four cabayeros. The fight—what there was of it—was sobering."

"How many did the mico lose?" Pearl Hand asked tonelessly.

"He made them swear to stand to the last. They were honorable men." Wind Cat looked off at the puffy white clouds visible over the house tops to the east. "The Kristianos were yipping and laughing as they rode through them. They might have been at play rather than war."

Wind Cat gave us a long-suffering look. "In the past, High Minko, I doubted you. After the atrocities committed on my dead ancestors, I boiled in rage. But I followed the Cofitachequi's orders. On this day, I thank you for your advice."

"Any other news?" I asked.

He hesitated, then spoke in a low voice. "I intercepted a messenger from White Rose. She wishes me to come in the night, kill her Kristiano guard, and sneak her away. She wishes to lead a war against the Kristianos."

Without a hint of emotion, Pearl Hand asked, "You thinking of trying it?"

"Should I?"

I quickly said, "It's not worth the lives—yours or your men's. The *Adelantado* is no fool, especially after Mikko Cafakke—who he thought was a cripple—got away from him."

"Then how do I free her?"

Pearl Hand softly said, "The same way I was freed: When the time is right."

He nodded, handing the empty jar back. "Thank you. The water was most welcome." Then he rose, the rest of his warriors picking up their weapons, all of them nodding, touching their foreheads in respect.

"I must go and report," he said. "Another hard day for the mico, I'm afraid."

We watched him go—a tired man with souls like stone.

"The *Adelantado* has only half of his men," Blood Thorn mused. "Do you think there is any way we could slip through? Perhaps sneak into the capital some night? Shoot some of them in their blankets?"

"We might," I said.

"But once the alarm is raised, how would you get out?" Pearl Hand went back to oiling her crossbow. "True, Telemico is full of houses to hide in and among, but you'd never avoid a systematic search. And the land surrounding the capital is wide open." She gave him a hard look. "Or have you figured out how to outrun a cabayo?"

Blood Thorn grunted uncomfortably.

"The lady White Rose chose her own trail," I said softly. "My suspicion is that she'll have to walk it until such time as the *Adelantado* finds another noble he'd rather have in her place."

One evening, a couple of days later, the yatika arrived as we were finishing supper. Again we dressed, seeing to our hair and clothes but skipping the paint and excessive jewelry.

I bent close to Pearl Hand. "Promise me you won't claw the old woman's eyes out."

"Maybe," she answered in clipped tones.

"This isn't like you," I said hesitantly.

"*You* try being her captive next time."

I flinched, biting my lips to keep from retorting.

When we were escorted to the Yca town palace, it was to find only the old woman and Wind Cat. The yatika shot a thoughtful glance at the two wooden boxes beside the old woman's chair and, after announcing us, excused himself.

We approached, dropping to our knees, palms up. Pearl Hand, however, remained standing, her arms crossed. The old woman just smiled, as if it were a response from a different lifetime. Then her lips thinned, her expression pinching at Pearl Hand's disrespect. I could see her anger flare; it fled as quickly as it had come. At her gesture, we stood, and I got a good look at her.

She'd always looked old, but now she seemed positively ancient. Her hair hung in unkempt tangles; the lines on her face sagged. Even her eyes seemed to have withdrawn into her skull. Where once she'd been vibrant, authoritative, she now came across as frail, easier to break than an old stick.

"Tell them," she said hoarsely, eyes on the smoldering fire pit before her.

Wind Cat turned to us. "We have heard from Telemico. The Kristianos began packing today, assembling the porters. When our people were told they'd be leaving in the morning, they refused. The *Adelantado* brought White Rose out to order them to carry the Kristiano packs, but she, too, refused."

"Let me guess," I said dryly. "De Soto dropped to his knees in apology?"

Wind Cat shook his head, apparently too far gone for humor. "Our spy saw her cross her arms and declare that since the Kristianos were leaving, they had no further use for her. That they had broken their word and that she, as Sun Clan and the future Cofitachequi mico, was under no further obligation to them."

Pearl Hand muttered to herself, shaking her head.

Wind Cat continued, proving me wrong about his capacity for humor. "This, of course, stunned the Kristianos right down to their roots. Distraught by her words, they just laughed . . . and had her guard physically drag her to the palace, where they locked her up."

"I'm sorry," I said, meaning it. "How did the captives take it?"

"The people, shocked as they were by the affront to their lady, began to shout. At which time dogs were loosed on some, whips used on others, and the flats of swords on still others. A few—mindless of the danger, or beyond caring—were killed on the spot, their heads cut off, and other captives were brought and chained in their place." He paused. "Order was inevitably restored."

Blood Thorn and I shot meaningful looks at each other.

Wind Cat took a deep breath. "The Kristianos are leaving Telemico in the morning, headed upriver for the Catawba country. I'm told by spies that they expect to find gold there. And if not, they will go to the mountain territory of the Cherokee at Joara, and if not there, on to the Coosa."

I nodded. "Then our service to you is ended."

At this juncture, the old woman spoke. "They are taking my nieces with them as hostages to ensure the behavior of my people. They have sent word that if they are attacked, White Rose and Garden will be killed." She looked up, eyes dull. "We will, of course, accede to their demands."

The old woman pointed at the two carved wooden boxes.

Wind Cat bent, lifting the lids off both. Each contained a wealth of trade: carved shells, strings of pearls, polished copper headpieces, the finest embroidered fabrics, valuable feather capes, and pouches that I took to be medicine herbs.

"That is yours," she said, "if you will find a way to free my nieces. Just bring them back to me. Safe."

I sighed. "Great Sun Ruler, the wealth of your offer is not lost on us, but we cannot accept. Not that we won't be willing to undertake the task if the opportunity presents itself, but our first duty is to the destruction of the monster. We cannot afford the time to escort her back to you."

She nodded, as if in anticipation of this. "That is why Wind Cat and some of his warriors will accompany you. Take whatever porters you need. Free my nieces, even if you must buy them back. The Tastanecci will see to their safe conduct back to our lands. No matter, the payment is yours."

I dropped to my knees before her, looking into her desperate eyes. "We will do what we can. That I promise. And if by some happy circumstance she is freed without our involvement or risk, the payment, in full, will be returned to you."

She studied me, the old mico momentarily shining in her eyes. "Why?"

"We came under the Power of trade," I answered. "As

we have told you from the beginning, we serve Power, not ourselves."

She seemed troubled by that, as if I'd said something beyond her comprehension. She glanced at Pearl Hand. "This is true?"

Pearl Hand kept her arms crossed, unrelenting.

The old woman wet her lips. "Then I have been a fool." She paused. "We've lost so much. Surrendered everything to satisfy our selfish desires. Perhaps it is well that we are destroyed." And I saw a tear leak past the corner of her eye and slip soundlessly down her leathery cheek.

The Test

She sits in the sunlight, her bony back supported by the plastered wall of the house they have given her. People pass, bent on their daily business, each nodding respectfully to her. Most, she notices, glance warily at her bandaged hand. The hopaye had smeared it with bear grease mixed with jimson weed to deaden the pain and invoke healing.

She grunts her amusement; the story is already going around. But another awe-inspiring tale to be added to the compendium of her life.

She fills her ancient lungs, taking in the burned-onion smell of crushed shell being fired. Like so many peoples, the Chicaza use it to temper strong pottery.

Across from her comes the thump-thump of a tall pestle as a woman mills corn in her log mortar. Children laugh, and dogs bark. Behind her house, out of sight, someone is humming.

They are so oblivious. She gapes toothlessly at the autumn sun. But isn't that the whole purpose?

Her vision turns silvery, images shifting and merging down between her souls. Cofitachequi remains sparklingly clear to her, as if but moments past she had walked out of the Yca town palace and away from the broken old woman.

"Now," she whispers, "all these years between us . . . what have we to say *for ourselves? Was what I forced you to endure worth the gutting of Cofi-tachequi?"*

She grins up at the sun, feeling a sliver of drool slip from the corner of her mouth. "You tested me, and I endured. But for what you did to me, I never could have faced the future."

TWENTY-EIGHT

WE LEFT BEFORE DAWN, THE DOGS PACKED WITH light loads, porters carrying burden baskets filled with a wealth of trade and additional supplies.

Wind Cat, with his ten chosen warriors, led the way, taking us out of Yca town. He chose a westbound trail that would skirt Tagaya and eventually intersect the Kristianos' route somewhere just this side of Guesa town. Guesa was one of Cofitachequi's western possessions.

We camped that night in a grove of mulberry and sassafras. An old farmstead—now fallen into disrepair—dominated a weed-filled terrace above a slow stream. The grove where we camped had probably provided additional fruits for the family.

After the fires were made and the camps laid out—

Pearl Hand's bed still separate—Wind Cat came to join us. I was massaging Skipper's sore joints—he happily groaned and licked my hands—while Blood Thorn saw to arranging the packs. The servants had already drawn water from the creek and were preparing supper.

The Tastanecci seated himself, staring silently at the fire before asking, "You have followed the Kristianos for a long time now. What is the best way to obtain White Rose and Garden's release?"

"The best plan would be to get ahead of them. Scout the route they will be taking and find a place where they will be working through rough country. Someplace the cabayos can't follow when we make our escape."

"What if she breaks from the column? Makes a run for it?"

"That would be a problem." I squinted up at the leaves overhead. "She'll be guarded, and most of the main trail is fairly flat and open until it enters the mountains. If she runs, they'll chase her down immediately. The second problem is that we'll be traveling in the open too, vulnerable to capture ourselves."

He considered that, thinking. "How long do you think he'll keep her?"

"That depends on Cofitachequi's influence with the western chiefs. The Cherokee chiefs will still respect her authority. So, too, will the Catawba towns in the foothills. As long as she's useful, he'll want her."

"Guasili," Wind Cat mused. "It's the last of our mountain talwas before the Cherokee territory. Above Guasili town, the trail goes over a pass."

"Tell me about it." I gave Skipper a final pat, and he thumped his tail.

The war chief jabbed a stick absently into the dirt. "She won't be much use to de Soto beyond Guasili. The Cherokee are independent, placed as they are between us and the Coosa. They control the mountains and survive on hunting, collecting, and some farming. For the most part they act as middlemen in the trade for copper, mica, and goods crossing the divide. They deal with us, the Tuscarora, the Coosa, and the Catawba."

"The valley narrows before Guasili, doesn't it?"

He nodded. "Lots of forest in there. Good cover from Yssa town up the valley to Guasili."

I gave Pearl Hand a questioning look where she sat at the edge of camp, overlooking the creek. Bark lay on his back, four feet in the air, tail thumping as she rubbed his belly. "Then our task is to race de Soto to Yssa. Get ahead of him."

Wind Cat shrugged. "It's worth a try. We're a smaller party, and as we consume supplies, we can send back the porters who start to lag."

I pointed a finger at Wind Cat. "Tastanecci, understand, we'll get only the one chance. Once de Soto is alerted to our presence, he'll do everything possible to ensure we don't succeed—even kill the two women."

"I understand." But the man didn't look happy. A moment later he indicated Pearl Hand. "I understand the reasons behind her ill will toward us, but will her anger compromise our chances for success?"

I sighed. "Tastanecci, as a good friend of mine once said, 'Only time will tell.'"

Even as I watched the woman I loved, my heart skipped. *Come back to me, wife. I miss you.*

And then the cold thought came to me. What if Pearl

Hand was the price I had to pay to finally destroy the Kristianos?

The next morning we were on the trail by sunrise, pacing ourselves for the long days ahead.

The path we followed, which had been used for generations, seemed to slither over the low ridges, across creeks, and along gentle slopes. We picked our way over roots, ducked around low-hanging vines, scampered across uneven rocks, and waded quick-flowing streams. The occasional rainstorm left us soaked to the skin, and the sapping heat had us parched and sweat-streaked by the time we stumbled down to water.

Occasionally we encountered locals who provided us with whatever supplies they had. The rest of the time we had the joy of bug bites and close scares with water moccasins and copperheads, and were even stalked by a cougar for a while. Skipper was limping each night as we made late camp. We ate quickly cooked food and fell into our blankets, exhausted.

As the supplies were consumed, we began releasing the porters, gifting them with small pieces of trade in return for their service.

But we emerged at Guesa talwa one morning to learn that de Soto's advance cabayeros were expected to arrive at any time. Wind Cat ordered everyone to flee, and we barely hesitated on our way west, following the river trail as it climbed into the foothills.

Though we had hoped the approaches to Yssa would work, the forests proved too open. Onward we went, the valley narrowing as it snaked into the mountains. For those who have never been there, long ridges lead up to the high mountains. The slopes are thickly forested, rising in humps, as if sloughed from the imposing peaks beyond. The creeks run clear and cold, their banks brush-choked, flowers everywhere.

Wind Cat conscripted new porters as ours wore out under their burdens. He also employed local guides who pointed out shortcuts and led us through thickets and marshy bottoms, enabling us to enlarge our lead on de Soto.

After the small town of Dudca, we found what we were looking for. Here the trail narrowed, following the bank of a rushing, rock-bottomed stream. Mountains rose close to either side, clouds hanging in their forested tops. To the west lay the divide that separated the actual lands of Cofitachequi from the Cherokee territory.

On a shoulder of the mountain, we found a hidden meadow watered by a seep, the trail leading to it steep, torturous, and, to our minds, impassable by cabayeros.

If de Soto spent the night in Dudca—which he probably would given his normal rate of march—the most likely prospect was that he would run out of daylight before reaching the summit. With the mountain encroaching on one side, the brush-filled stream on the other, his camp would be elongated—just like the narrow, grassy meadow in the valley bottom below us. If we were to have a chance to sneak White Rose and Garden away, this would be our best opportunity.

For a solid day we scouted the steep-walled valley, learning the trails and deciding on the best way to escape and avoid detection.

Then, in late afternoon, from a hidden vantage on the

mountainside, Wind Cat and I watched the first of de Soto's cabayeros emerge from the lower end of the flat. They rode slumped, the butts of their lances riding in stirrup holders. Sun shone off their armor, but without the brilliance we'd come to expect. The cabayos plodded onward, heads down as if they, too, were worn.

I glanced off to my left, knowing that Blood Thorn and Pearl Hand had a similar vantage point a bow-shot away.

The leader of the party pulled up, sending five of his cabayeros ahead while the rest stepped down, letting their animals graze.

I could feel the quickening of my heart.

"What are they doing?" Wind Cat asked where he lay beside me.

"It's a long climb," I told him. "My guess is the *capitán* sent his strongest mounts ahead to see what's above."

"Which is another long climb up a narrow trail." Wind Cat chewed his thumbnail with deliberate consideration.

"And as soon as the advance scouts figure that out, they'll be back, reporting that this is the last possible camp before the summit. The main party can travel only as fast as the porters and *puercos*. There's no way they can make it over the top before dark, and de Soto won't want his line of march strung out all over the mountain come nightfall." I grinned. "They'll camp here."

Wind Cat sighed. "Then it's simply a matter of figuring out just where White Rose will be. From there, we can sneak in."

As the sinking sun shot beams across the high peaks we watched de Soto's main force tramp its weary way into the flat, the *capitán* mounting, riding back to the approaching party.

I pointed. "There he is. The rider out front. That's the monster himself." Across the distance, I could see de Soto's familiar long face, the hook of his nose, and his pointed beard. He rode erect, purple cloth flapping beneath his saddle. He was glancing around the flat, issuing orders that we could barely hear over the distance.

"The ones around him are the nobles. Notice how brightly shined their armor is? How much better fed their cabayos, and how clean and colorful their clothing?"

"If you could have any wish right now, what would it be?" Wind Cat was watching them through slitted eyes.

"The ability to take my best arrow, nock it, and shoot it clear across the valley and into his left eye," I answered without hesitation.

"You and me," Wind Cat whispered passionately.

Another hand of time passed while the camping spots were apportioned, and we finally saw White Rose and Garden accompanied by their servants—all young women. They were placed in a camp just below that of de Soto himself. That made it more dangerous to approach, but a thick patch of berry bushes and willows beside the stream would provide excellent cover.

I barely heard Pearl Hand's arrival as she wiggled through the leaves to a place just behind us.

In those irritatingly clipped tones, she said, "What you can't see from this angle is that they've placed a guard on the lower end of our trail. If we all go, there's a good chance we'll be discovered and an alarm raised."

"So, what's your idea?" I asked.

"Let me go. Alone."

Wind Cat grunted. "That's crazy."

"Anything but," Pearl Hand replied. "If the guard sees me in the dark, he'll ask 'Who's there?' and I'll reply in his own language that I'm a slave who got lost. Either he'll just point out the right direction and tell me to get back to where I belong, or I'll plead loneliness, get close, and cut his throat."

"Too dangerous," Wind Cat retorted.

This is it, Black Shell, the moment you've been dreading. What are you going to do? Trust her? Or tell her no?

I made my choice, heart thumping. In one outcome, Pearl Hand would recover her old balance and confidence. In the other, I would lose her forever. "This is Pearl Hand—er, excuse me, Evening Breeze to you. When she speaks we listen." I bent my head around so I could see her. "And what next?"

She gave me a cool shrug. "I walk right into White Rose's camp, let her know we're out here, and see if I can walk out with her. Or, if she's too well guarded, she and I can discuss it, figure out when they pay the least amount of attention to her, and plan something for tomorrow on the march."

"No," Wind Cat said at the same time I told her, "All right."

The tastanecci and I stared at each other in surprise. Then he relented. I could see the worry and mistrust he tried to hide.

Filling my voice with confidence, I said, "If you walk White Rose out and you haven't killed that guard, he'll still be on the trail."

"Not if I come back and tell him I'm feeling lonely."

Then she added, "After what I went through in Cofi-tachequi, I'm ready to kill someone."

Ah, my Pearl Hand.

We spread out along the trail; each of Wind Cat's warriors found a place to hide that gave him a clear shot of the trail itself.

Blood Thorn took a position on top of a boulder that let him shoot down on anyone passing below.

As the gloom deepened Wind Cat and I accompanied Pearl Hand to the bottom of the slope. She had sorted through the packs, finding a hunting shirt that almost re-sembled a woman's dress. De Soto's servants wore just about anything they could get their hands on.

Pearl Hand would try to walk out with White Rose and Garden. If, however, they were discovered, Pearl Hand would lead them at a run up the trail. Anyone who followed would be ambushed by the warriors spread along the trail sides. In the darkness, they might not make a kill-ing shot, but any Kristianos would lose ardor for the pur-suit when arrows started thudding into them or hissing past their ears. All the warriors had to do was buy time for Pearl Hand to get the women away. Later we would ren-dezvous at a spring a half day's journey back toward Dudca town.

"Second thoughts?" I asked Pearl Hand as I felt her fidget beside me in the settling dark.

"I'm headed into a camp of Kristianos. What do you think?"

"We can come up with something else," Wind Cat said.

I could feel her shake her head. "No, this will work. They've been traveling unmolested for so long their guard will be down. They're getting careless. This is the best chance we've got. Once beyond the pass, the land opens up. They'll put her camp right in the middle of a town."

"All right. Just be careful." I took her hand, giving it a squeeze.

"Always," she whispered.

I felt her check the *hierro* knife in her belt, then stand. "Shoot straight if we come back at a run . . . just be sure you shoot whoever's following. Not me."

"We'll be careful," I told her. "Come back to me."

"I will." I had to imagine her smile.

Then she was gone.

After a while Wind Cat said, "I hope you know what you're doing."

"I think she needs to prove something to herself."

"As long as it doesn't get White Rose killed."

Or my beloved Pearl Hand.

So we settled down to wait. Just us, our weapons, a cloud-darkened night . . . and all the fear a human soul can imagine.

Over the burble of the stream, the whirring of insects, and the night calls of birds, we could hear the sounds of the Kristiano camp; clanking metal, chopping, and calls mixed with the mingled voices of several Kristianos who were singing, the melody eerie and foreign.

I tried to resettle myself, not to think of what Pearl Hand was doing or how many things could go wrong. Instead I watched the flickering of the few fires visible from where Wind Cat and I huddled in the night.

A cabayo made that stuttering snuffle, and someone laughed, the sound carrying in the night.

Time passed, dragging like a great stone. Without the stars for reference, I realized I was spending an eternity just from one beat of my heart to the next.

Patience, Black Shell.

Yes, right.

I fingered the wood of my strung bow. Nocked an arrow. Drew it, let it slide through my fingers. Then I did it again. Anything to burn the nervous energy, to speed the eternity.

How long had it been? My grandchildren were dying of old age, assuming I'd ever had any. Which I hadn't.

Even so, every moment that passed without shouts and chaos erupting from the Kristiano camps gave me a desperate sense of hope.

The faint "*pssst*" from the darkness almost made me jump out of my skin.

"It's Pearl Hand," she whispered. "Don't shoot."

Wind Cat and I emerged from the sumac where we'd been hiding, searching the darkness to see how many were coming. I could make out only Pearl Hand's form.

"What happened?" I asked as softly as my tense throat would allow.

"Saw her. Talked to her," Pearl Hand rasped, and I could tell she was angry.

"And?" Wind Cat was craning his neck, searching the darkness behind Pearl Hand for his two women.

"She *gave* me orders!" Pearl Hand almost spit the words.

"What orders?" I asked, a sinking feeling in my gut.

"She's not ready to leave because she couldn't bring a basket of pearls with her." Pearl Hand's annoyance could almost be felt. "I'm not kidding! The silly swamp bitch is willing to risk herself and her sister over a batch of pearls."

I could sense Wind Cat's wince at the derogatory term.

"Tell us from the beginning," I said with a sigh.

"I had no trouble," Pearl Hand told us as she started up the trail. "The guard wasn't even where he was supposed to be. So I waded down the creek to the brush patch beside White Rose's camp. It took me a while to ease through it, and I slipped up to one of her servant women. I whispered that I was a messenger and that if White Rose was alone, I needed to see her."

So far so good.

"The woman went and checked, then came back and led me to White Rose's shelter. They gave her one of the Kristiano fabric ones."

Pearl Hand growled, "She received me like I was some lowborn farmer instead of the woman who's trying to save her accursed life." The irritation was back in Pearl Hand's voice. "Wanted me to kneel and act as if she were the Cofitachequi mico herself!"

"Which of course you did, right?" I asked dryly.

"By Piasa's bloody balls, I did no such thing! And that's not all. She had a man with her, apparently one of the *capitán*'s servants. Not trusting him, I demanded to speak to White Rose alone. From the way they looked at each other and the condition of White Rose's bed, I'd say they are lovers."

"Lovers?" Wind Cat asked.

"How would I know? I stood there until he left. Then I told her flat-out that the tastanecci's warriors were in the forest, and if she wanted to go, now was the time. I explained that no one would know she was missing until morning, and by that time, we'd all be well away."

"And she didn't come?" Wind Cat sounded astonished.

"She said she'd choose a time that suited her but that your orders are to be beside the trail, just across the pass. She will pick a thicket to her liking and step aside as if to relieve herself. That way she'll have her porter with her to carry the pearls."

I groaned, closing my eyes. "A thicket to her liking? And we're just supposed to be there? Just like that?"

"Just like that," Pearl Hand said insistently. "I told her that it would be putting her warriors and tastanecci at risk, that the chances of being recaptured would rise to a certainty."

I made a face. "And how did she reply?"

"She said that surely the tastanecci would be able to defend her from any ragged band of Kristianos, and in fact she'd order her warriors to kill every last one of the vermin."

"Oh, sure," I grumbled.

"What of Garden?" Wind Cat asked, still sounding perplexed.

Pearl Hand's rage was evident. "White Rose said that she'd be responsible for her own escape."

"But Garden is her sister!" Wind Cat cried. "What do I tell the Cofitachequi mico? That I just let Garden go?"

Unkindly, I told him, "White Rose cares only for herself."

"But what am I going to do?" Wind Cat turned to Pearl Hand. "She didn't say where her sister was?"

The angry shake of Pearl Hand's head could be seen despite the darkness. "I asked. She said her sister has a Kristiano lover." A pause. "And you should be aware, Tastanecci, White Rose is bringing this man with her when she comes. She says she won't leave without him."

"So," Wind Cat said meekly, "we're just supposed to tag along? Wait? And hope that Garden gets away on her own? Has White Rose no honor?"

"Tastanecci, I'm sorry. We've done our best. Pearl Hand—at considerable risk to herself—just walked into the Kristiano camp, provided White Rose with the opportunity to escape, and she didn't take it."

"I understand." Wind Cat had stopped dead in the trail, his head hanging.

I couldn't help but add, "It grieves me to have to return the mico's boxes of trade, but we're finished."

I heard Wind Cat chuckle, then he said, "I think you should keep the Cofitachequi mico's trade."

"Why? We haven't earned it."

"You've done everything in your power to save us. The lady Evening Breeze was taken, tortured, and humiliated. White Rose—even after you warned her—betrayed her own people. Just now you would have brought her to safety in spite of all she's done. Take it all. I insist."

"But I—"

"Do it for the aggravation, if nothing else."

TWENTY-NINE

THE FOLLOWING MORNING WE WAITED WHILE THE Kristianos broke camp and started up the steep mountain pass. Meanwhile, one of Wind Cat's warriors had searched out a series of deer trails that would allow us to parallel the main trail. Our small party proceeded slowly; our route on the steep slopes proved rugged, winding, and often treacherous. Fortunately, we traveled under old forest, weaving among the boles of trees that spread a high canopy over our route.

As we made our way, Wind Cat detailed five of his warriors to shadow the Kristiano column. They'd race ahead, pick a point of vantage, and try to keep an eye on White Rose.

For most of the morning, Blood Thorn and I fumed. Pearl Hand stalked and cursed, slashing the air with her knife. Myself, I confess to an evil in my souls that sincerely wished de Soto would spot White Rose trying to leave, clap her in chains, and provide her the future she really deserved.

But White Rose didn't leave. From high in the trees we watched her and her lover enter the tent her women put up that night. And the following morning, we watched her step out, still in the company of the man.

White Rose didn't make her escape until we were well down from the pass. She chose one of the partially open valleys the Cherokee periodically burn to encourage fruit-bearing brush. To our surprise, almost a hand of time passed before the Kristianos realized she was gone. By the time they fanned out, searching for her, White Rose had actually managed to escape.

That evening she showed up with one of Wind Cat's warriors, her lover, and a servant woman bearing a heavy pack box on her shoulders.

White Rose might have been the high mico, all right. She began by issuing orders, telling Wind Cat to have his warriors build her and her man a shelter. I didn't see a great deal of enthusiasm on the part of the warriors as they fanned out into the darkening forest to find building materials.

We kept to our adjacent camp, having nothing to say but feeling incredibly sorry for Wind Cat and the future of Cofitachequi. Well, Blood Thorn and I felt sorry. Pearl Hand just smiled to herself, a wry twist of the lips having replaced the scowl I'd flinchingly become accustomed to.

The next morning, Wind Cat appeared out of the dawn, crouched by our fire, and stared woodenly at the dancing flames.

"I have been ordered to proceed to Joara. There, as

soon as the Kristianos pull out, White Rose wishes to meet with the Cherokee chief and his council. She considers this an opportunity to solidify relationships with them in anticipation of becoming the Cofitachequi mico."

We gave him a sympathetic look, but it was Blood Thorn who asked, "What are you going to do? Continue to serve her?"

Wind Cat returned his stare dully. "I will deliver her safely to Telemico. That is my duty as tastanecci. But after that, no. I will go home to my family. She can find another to serve her."

"What of Cofitachequi?" I asked.

He smiled sadly. "I think its greatness is past, Black Shell. First the Death killed the majority of our people. Then the Kristianos came, disrupting things even more. The subordinate micos will seek to break away. Perhaps there will be war. But I just want to find a farmstead, take my wife, and raise my family." He looked up. "And you?"

"We will race ahead, see if we can enlist the Chiaha mikko to fight the Kristianos."

His weary smile went flat. "I think you are too late. At the request of the Kristianos, White Rose has already dispatched runners to relay the Kristianos' message of peace to the Chiaha mikko and asked him to relay it to the high mikko of the Coosa Nation. De Soto informed the Chiaha that he wishes only to pass through their territory and on to Coosa itself. White Rose claims that the messenger returned, saying the Chiaha people will meet the great lord of the Kristianos in peace and, in return for trade, help them cross their territory."

I glanced around the fire, seeing Pearl Hand and Blood

Thorn's expressions. Our chances, once again, dashed by White Rose.

"Then we will go on," Pearl Hand said woodenly. "Perhaps the Tuskaloosa mikko will be more amenable."

I nodded.

Wind Cat asked, "Will you travel with us as far as Joara town?"

"No, Tastanecci. The way we feel . . . Well, White Rose has done enough as it is."

He stood then, offering his hands. "It has been an honor to know you. May Power bless your journey and keep you well."

"You, too, my friend." To the others I said, "Come. We must pack." Fact was, as wretched as the future looked, I'd have been tempted to strangle White Rose if she so much as looked crossways at me.

We were miserable in paradise. After saying our farewells to Wind Cat—and somehow managing to control our passions by not driving an arrow through White Rose— we took the lesser trails through the mountains.

The country is stunning, jutting slabs of mountain rising to the sky, the view itself a compensation for the steep climbs, the necessary fording of swift creeks, and the constant scramble over roots, rocks, and poor footing.

These mountains—what the Coosa call the "Backbone of the World"—stun the imagination. On the high trails we looked down at cloud-filled valleys below, sunlight washing the tree-matted heights. Though carpeted with forest, mighty stone outcrops gleam in the sunlight, and a blue haze shrouds thrusts of high country as the mountains fade into the distance.

In the Beginning Times, Vulture was said to have smoothed the newly formed earth. Here, he'd been beating his wings mightily, and the notion of just how great the bird had to be to pile such monuments of rock and earth defied my poor souls.

But stop to catch your breath and you can enjoy wooded slopes covered with oak, maple, and hickory, the bottoms resplendent in beech, basswood, and elm. The rivers here run clean and clear, the rocky bottoms with their fish and mussels cloaked by strands of green moss that waver with the current.

Afternoon rains—mostly gentle showers that cooled the already delightful weather—followed our path. I couldn't help but think back to last year in the peninsula and the sapping heat, muggy air, and sticky sweat. But here, walking in cool temperatures, enjoying a vista of towering outcrops of limestone, granite, and hard rock peering down over lumpy forest, it might have been but a fantasy.

For five days we worked our way down the valley, along the edge of the settlements, spending the night at lonely farmsteads. There we traded small items with the locals for an evening meal. Our remaining five porters found themselves treated as royalty, liberally fed, and housed in return for stories about Telemico and the splendor of Cofitachequi.

Through secondhand means and an occasional scout, we learned that the Guasili mico had given de Soto his town for a couple of days and that the Kristianos were planning on marching to Chiaha. There, it was said, they intended to rest and allow their half-starved cabayos to graze and recover.

Meanwhile small parties of soldados were scouting the countryside.

From a high point, we studied the Kristiano occupation of Guasili, and Blood Thorn asked, "What are you thinking? The porters are about to leave, and there's no way we can carry all the trade."

"Hate to leave it behind," Pearl Hand growled.

"I thought you'd become canny traders, full of tricks and crafty ploys," I told them, my eyes on the river that ran just below Guasili.

"I thought we were high minkos and a nicoquadca," Blood Thorn shot back. "Rich ones with no way to carry their goods unless we pay some Cherokee to carry it down to Chiaha. Which, if you will recall, is where the Kristianos are headed to receive a warm welcome."

I nodded and pointed downstream. "There's a town down there about three hands' travel distance. The porters will take us that far before we pay them off and send them home."

Pearl Hand gave me her questioning arch of the eyebrow. "It's a nice place for us to dump all of our trade? Lots of important people? The kind we can talk into killing Kristianos?"

"Probably not."

"Then why are we going there?" Blood Thorn asked.

"Because if you were real traders, you'd know they have something else," I replied.

"No doubt it's a delightfully relaxed atmosphere in which to trade for fish, corn, and mussel stew?" Pearl Hand muttered sarcastically.

"Something real traders cherish," I told them. "Canoes."

Translated from the Cherokee, the town was called "Clam Shoal Place." It was a collection of perhaps thirty houses on a terrace above the river. The local chief—currently off bowing to de Soto in Guasili town—was a subordinate of the Guasili mikko, who in turn was a bellicose subordinate to the Chiaha mikko, who paid homage to Coosa itself. But we weren't there for the politics. White Rose had already seen to ruining that.

After we'd made our entry, my trader's staff at the fore—and through signs and a Mos'kogee trade pidgin, managed to rent a house for the night—I ran down the local fishermen, who in turn were delighted to offer us their canoes for inspection.

The vessels I settled on were two large, thin-hulled, and shallow-draft dugouts. These were not the usual blunt-nosed half logs; they'd been expertly hollowed and thinned, the bottoms flat and wide of beam. We could probably have found better in Guasili, but, well, the Kristianos were there, and we doubted they'd take kindly to seeing us.

The next morning, we paid off our porters and warned them to keep away from the main trail and any chance of capture. After watching them head off for the forest, we stood on the landing, our two new canoes ready for loading.

The local Cherokee had gathered; they joked among themselves, offered gifts of food, and smiled as they chattered and pointed.

"How far do we go in canoes?" Blood Thorn asked as he saw to loading his share of the packs.

I studied the broad, rippling water. "This takes us past Chiaha, Coste, Tali, Satapo, and Chalahumi, then down to Hiawasee town, and finally to Napochies."

"What's at Napochies?" Pearl Hand and Blood Thorn asked in unison.

"Porters to carry our trade south over the divide to Coosa." I laid a pack in the bottom of the canoe I was going to share with Pearl Hand. This was the slightly larger vessel, and the craftsman who'd built it had carved the likeness of a raccoon out of the bow.

"Why the river?" Blood Thorn asked as he stowed the last pack.

"Because it's faster."

Pearl Hand grinned for the first time in days as she laid her crossbow and its attendant quiver atop the packs. "Meanwhile the Kristianos, burdened by their cabayos and *puercos,* have to take the trails."

"Exactly." And besides, even though the dogs had been carrying light packs, the rest would do them good. Especially poor old Skipper.

Together we dragged the canoe out, and I called for Bark and Squirm to jump in. I showed them their places and made them lie down. Bark was the only worry since he occasionally forgot that jumping up on the gunwales would roll a canoe upside-down in an instant. I hoped he remembered.

After dragging Blood Thorn's canoe out, I got Gnaw and Skipper settled.

We had just pushed Blood Thorn out and he'd taken a couple of strokes with his paddle when I heard a call. All it took was a glance to make my blood run cold.

A line of cabayeros was winding its way through the houses, the riders looking about with their usual arrogance. While their armor no longer reflected the burnished magnificence of the early days, it had taken on a hard-used look, more ominous in its own way.

The cabayos looked beat, as if they didn't have a good

run left in them. They were sweaty, plodding forward as if in misery. The tips of the lances the riders carried, however, sparkled in the sun—recently sharpened.

"Let's go," I called, almost toppling Pearl Hand into the bow as I pushed off.

Kristianos. Who'd have thought? Not that they'd have known who we were. But had they been a finger's time earlier, or seen the crossbow or the swords, that might have led to questions we didn't want to answer.

The river was more than a bow-shot across, the current moderate. I'd no more than managed to line us up when I heard a shout and saw the lead cabayero trot his animal down to the landing. People scattered this way and that. The rider pulled up at the edge of the bank, five of his fellows stopping just behind. Had they carried crossbows, or perhaps thunder sticks, their arrival might have caused us grief.

I took a second glance at that thin face with its stringy beard. At first he didn't recognize us, but as my eyes met his, I saw surprise, immediately followed by a consuming rage.

"*¡Alto!*" The cry carried across the water. "*¡Es el Concho Negro!*"

"Antonio!" I called, giving him a farewell wave. "Too late again, you skinny little slug!"

He actually forced his bone-racked cabayo out into the river, but the animal balked as the current reached its chest.

Pearl Hand shouted, "*¡Antonio! Tienes un pene como un gusano. ¡Adios, idiota!*"

By then we were in the main current, canoes lining up. The dogs perched to watch and growl at the cabayeros.

The fool actually tried to follow us, shouting orders, paralleling the bank for as far as he could. Then he tried to force his half-starved cabayo through a marshy area. I saw the animal buck and thrash, sinking in the rushes and goo. Rather than fight it, the tired cabayo just collapsed on its belly.

A bend in the river carried us safely out of his sight.

"That was close," Blood Thorn called.

Pearl Hand agreed. "Way too close." Then, to my delight, she threw her head back and whooped like a Chicaza lord.

"Do you think they'll get his cabayo unstuck?" I asked.

"Not without the lot of them wading through that black stinky mud." Pearl Hand flashed me a smile. "And even better, the story is going to be carried back. We've managed to humiliate him once again."

Just the sight of him stuck in the mud proved enough to lighten my mood. It was a little thing; sometimes the little things can mean so much.

Pearl Hand, it turned out, wasn't an accomplished hand at canoeing. She'd spent most of her life residing in palaces or walking. The previous times she'd paddled had been on still water, not a swift river. Still, she was young and muscular, and before long she managed to get the rhythm of working with the current.

We kept to the thread of the river, its current bearing us along at a steady clip. Blood Thorn chortled with delight.

"What's the matter? Don't they have rivers in Uzachile?" I called.

"Not that I've had the chance to ride like this," he answered. "And we're doing this for how long?"

"Maybe seven days. It will depend on the current, on the rapids. There are places we may have to get out and drag the canoes over shoals."

And that got me to thinking. I had two apparent novices when it came to rapids. How were they going to handle fast water? Would they know where to steer, how to avoid the rocks?

Oh, Black Shell, there's always something, isn't there?

We didn't even stop in Chiaha. The town and its mikko were already committed to the peaceful arrival of de Soto and his vermin. Instead, I held up my trader's staff as we passed the palisaded walls, seeing the palace where de Soto would soon be sleeping while feasting on their corn. People on the banks waved, as did the fishermen in canoes that we passed.

We camped at a small fishing village a couple of hands' travel below Chiaha and enjoyed roasted catfish, baked freshwater clams, and corn bread seasoned with sassafras root. I traded a bracelet for the use of a ramada since the night seemed warm.

Pearl Hand traded a couple of pieces of shell for a pot of unguent made from spruce needles, boiled pine needles, and red root. This served to keep the mosquitoes off.

We spent a pleasant evening talking with the locals, though most of it was through sign language. Traders were a novelty, and everyone wanted to know about the Kristianos and what their coming meant. We told them the truth, that their safest bet was to be far away.

When I finally left the fire and walked back to the shadows of our ramada, I realized that my bedding was enlarged. "Pearl Hand?"

"Come to bed, husband."

"Are you sure?"

"I think that nasty old woman knocked my souls loose. They may not be entirely returned, but I want to try something to coax them back. Are you willing?"

Oh, yes.

The following morning we were on the river by sunrise and made good progress most of the day. Pearl Hand and Blood Thorn survived their first encounter with rapids.

"What's the plan?" Blood Thorn asked that night. We'd pulled into a small fishing camp, having passed Coste talwa earlier that day.

I looked up from our fire to see the stars; it looked as if an endless frost were sprinkled upon the black. "From here on the game changes. We're in Coosa now, and not even Cofitachequi before the Death compares. When we reach Napochies, we'll hire porters to carry us to the capital."

"Do you think Coosa Mikko will even receive us?" Pearl Hand asked.

I squinted at the fire. Would he? "I think so, especially given the wealth of our trade. And I'll be carrying the copper mace. It's the symbol of noble blood going back to the Beginning Times."

Blood Thorn laughed. "Just don't take this high minko thing to extremes. You'll start to put on airs."

I grinned at that. "I'll save them for Coosa. You've got to understand. This is the biggest Nation in our world. Populous and vibrant, controlling more subordinate mikkos than Uzachile had villages. The Coosa mikko is considered by his people to be a living god, descended directly from the sun itself. And getting in to see him? That, my friends, might prove impossible were it not for the kind of trade we carry and who we pass ourselves off as."

"Which is?" Pearl Hand asked.

"Nobles." I looked around at them. "We've already had practice at Telemico. Pearl Hand, you've lived all your life among nobles. Blood Thorn, you're an iniha from a foreign people. You'll be given a little leeway, but try to learn from your mistakes."

He gave me a hooded look. "How do you see this working? Emissaries have already been sent. De Soto is entering Coosa lands as a potential friend. Remember when White Rose gave the Cofitachequi mico's word of safe passage?"

I nodded. "She was Sun Clan, heir to the Cofitachequi mico's chair. The mikko at Chiaha has no such authority. He's not even Wind Clan, from which Coosa rulers are descended. All the Chiaha mikko can do is advise—and from a very subordinate position at that."

Pearl Hand mused, "I liked it better in the old days. This new peace of theirs is a thorn in our butts." She paused before asking, "Then we have a chance to rally Coosa against the invader?"

"Maybe. Our best hope is that the Kristianos will prove to be their own worst enemies. All it will take is a couple of rapes, the desecration of the wrong temple, and too much abuse of the local people."

"And if they don't?" Blood Thorn asked.

"Can a fox become a rabbit?" I asked mildly.

THIRTY

THE RIVERS RUN TOWARD THE SOUTHEAST IN THAT
part of the country and parallel long, uplifted ridges forested with green. One channel leads into another before
joining the main course of the great Tenasee River, which
loops its way down a wide valley hemmed by imposing
ridgelines.

Those were delightful days for us, paddling along, letting the current do the work. We wound our way around
the oxbows, enjoying the tree-lined banks, camping each
night in a settlement. Back from the river stretched a
maze of fields tended by small farmsteads. Corn, beans,
and squash grew in abundance, their leaves spread to the
summer sun.

The river had slowed, turning lazy as it wound back
and forth. We hailed fishermen who plied nets over the
sides of their canoes or dove for clams and mussels. Tur-

tles sunned on logs, and huge canebrakes filled the back-waters. I almost cheered as we passed the first bald cypress, having missed them during our crossing of the mountains.

On the solstice we arrived at a crowded canoe landing at Hiawasee town. With barely enough room to pull our canoes from the water, we were able to inspect the local trade and stretch our legs. People were painted and dressed in their finest, the smells of cooking food heavy in the air while flutes, drums, and singing voices filtered down from the palisaded plaza.

Blood Thorn and Pearl Hand marveled at the huge mound-top palaces rising above the walls in the island town's center. The Hiawasee—a Yuchi Nation subservient to Coosa—divide themselves into the Chief and Warrior Moieties, which, while not quite coequal, had built their respective palaces beside each other. Each had its own ramped stairway. The Chief Moiety's palace—atop the higher eastern platform—obviously dominated, but so close were the ties between the moieties, all it took was a couple of steps up or down to enter the other's domain.

That night as we watched the solstice dancers enter the plaza by firelight, we saw cavorting figures, masked, painted, with a wealth of feathers bobbing as they danced to the sacred songs. Bodies shone in the light, the incense of countless fires burning red cedar filled the air, and thousands of hands clapped as my souls swayed in time to the gyrations of the dancers.

"This is a special night," Pearl Hand told me, her speculative gaze on the dancers.

"Why is that?"

"We may never see the solstice celebrated like this again. These people don't know it, but the monster is coming to ruin their world."

"Maybe. And maybe next year they will be celebrating the destruction of de Soto as well as the grace of Mother Sun."

She gave me a wistful smile. "Let us hope."

"I've missed you."

She sniffed slightly, as if in derision. "What makes you think I'm whole again?"

"Last night was a start."

I watched her face, soft and vulnerable in the glow. "I'm not sure I'm the same woman, Black Shell. She had me whimpering, pleading. I didn't know a body could hurt like that."

"Pain, like joy, will pass."

"Don't repeat old folk sayings. Pain feels like it lasts forever. Joy expires like a runner's breath." She closed her eyes. "You've got to understand. Somehow that old woman reached inside me and tore something away."

"What?"

"I don't know exactly. But I'm not the same anymore, Black Shell. Hard to explain, but it's as if there's less of me. And I can't figure out what's missing."

"I should have sneaked in in the middle of the night, brained the yatika, killed the guards, cut the old woman's throat, and taken you out of there."

She smiled at that, her large dark eyes glinting in the firelight. "Oh, sure. I went to Cofitachequi of my own free will. I knew I might be recognized. If I was, I thought it would be the price of de Soto's destruction. I could offer my life and future for his. The dead mico would have taken it. But not the old woman."

"I wish you'd told me."

"You'd have found an excuse to avoid Cofitachequi." She shook her head. "So I kept my bargain with Power to myself. Asked you, perhaps unfairly, to trust me."

"Pearl Hand, if you'd—"

She waved me down. "But the thing that really frightens me? It's that I kept my part of the bargain. I fully expected to die horribly when I was led away from you that night."

She turned, her eyes seeming to expand in the firelight. "Even with my sacrifice, why was Cofitachequi a disaster for us?"

"Because the Death was there before us."

She nodded. "You see, that's the worrisome thing. Not even Power can fulfill its obligations anymore."

A long day after leaving Hiawasee—on the evening of the new moon—we arrived at Napochies town. We put in at the canoe landing just up the Upahsee River from its confluence with the Tenasee.

The landing was full of canoes, many of them inverted on logs to keep rain from collecting within. Several ramadas stood around the peripheries, and we were lucky enough to find one but recently vacated. The locals, of course, came to greet us as we pulled in, helping with the packs and seeing to the storage of our craft.

I felt a sense of relief. We were deep in Coosa territory, where trade was still an old and honored profession. Here there were no uncertainties, just questions about conditions upriver, what we had seen, where we were going, and what sort of trade we were carrying.

In between answering, I had to fend off the local dogs with my trader's staff; a couple of the boys pitched in, chucking old pot sherds and the cracked remains of boiling stones at the curs.

Pearl Hand and Blood Thorn took this in, smiling, thanking people for their help, fending off offers of ducks, catfish, geese, turkeys, pots of corn, hominy, and boiled beans—all up for trade.

The men were dressed in breechcloths, some with light capes over their shoulders; bark rain hats dangled down their backs. Women wore textile skirts woven into becoming designs and dyed in bright colors. Their children scampered around naked, watching with large brown eyes.

We got our possessions settled under the ramada, and Pearl Hand managed to trade a small pearl for a load of firewood. Blood Thorn—with his pom hairstyle, his Uzachile-cut breechcloth, and his curious star tattoos—was a constant source of attention. He was pleasant but struggled in an attempt to understand the Mos'kogean trade pidgin.

I was seeing to the dogs' stomachs, having given away a little wooden carving of a great blue heron in return for a deer quarter. I had dropped the leg down for the pack to demolish and was watching them ripping and pulling when a booming voice called, "Black Shell!"

I turned to discover my old trader friend Two Packs and Red Tie, one of his sons. He was older than when I last saw him, his thick shoulders showing the irregular tan line of pack straps, but the bulging muscles of his arms and legs were still those of a strong man. His wide face was split in a smile that exposed gaps in his teeth. A dark twinkle filled his eyes. The gleaming black hair was greased and tied into a bun pinned through with copper that shone in the sunlight.

"Two Packs!" I embraced him before giving him a thorough inspection. "You look fit. Still peddling worthless rocks and broken shell to the gullible locals?"

"As many as they'll take in return for a mikko's ransom in copper. How about yourself? Still scavenging the forest for old bits of root that you can trade off as sacred medicine sticks? Or have you taken to a higher calling?"

"I'll go for the old root any day. Adds to the challenge of trade. Why, just the other day in Hiawasee, I managed to trade a half-rotten sassafras root for the mikko's chair. It took only a day of listening to the local oretas bicker before I took the root back and left the chair behind."

He laughed and slapped the young man beside him on the back. "You remember my son, Red Tie?"

I gave the young man a grin. "You weren't but fifteen. What's happened to you? You're a head taller and, if I'm not mistaken, grown into a man."

"It is good to see you again, Black Shell. And yes, I am a man now. Married. Complete with two children and another on the way. My wife's clan is appreciative." He smiled, displaying a full mouth of strong white teeth.

Ah, the joys of youth.

"Come," I said. "Meet my companions."

I led them to the ramada, where Pearl Hand and Blood Thorn watched curiously. "Two Packs, Red Tie, this is my wife, Pearl Hand of the Chicora. And this is Blood Thorn, an iniha of the Uzachile."

Nods and smiles were given all the way around, Blood Thorn having trouble with the language but signing his pleasure.

Two Packs tucked his thumbs into his waistband—a trait I remembered well—and continued with his gap-

toothed smile. His smile went even wider, a glaze of interest in his eyes, as he took in Pearl Hand's breasts, slim
waist, and long legs. I knew that look from old and ground
my teeth, happy to still have them.

"Black Shell and I," he announced, "have known each
other for years. Traveled together on occasion. Why, we've
hauled trade from the Caddo to the Apalachee and clear
up to the Kaskinampo."

"That we have," I said. "And now your son joins you?"

"Sons," he answered easily. "Their uncle grouses a bit about
them following me off to the ends of the world. But they
don't have many traders in my wife's clan. What they lose in
labor and hunting is more than made up for by the trade the
boys bring in." He was struggling to keep from losing his train
of thought as he ogled Pearl Hand. "And I'm not complaining
about having their stout bodies on the trail, let me tell you."
Then he frowned. "It's just that they eat so much. I swear I
lose half my profits to their growling stomachs."

Red Tie grinned, and to mock his father, he slammed a
fist into the hard ripples of his belly.

"So, Black Shell," Two Packs asked, his gaze still de-
vouring my wife. "It's been what? Two years since I've
seen you?"

"Three. We were down in Atahachi town, trying to
weasel Tuskaloosa out of any wealth he might have been
hiding."

"That long?" he mused, eyes unfocused as he fantasized
about Pearl Hand. "Well, old Tuskaloosa's been growing
richer with the passing of each moon. He's even pushed
the Chicaza back. Seems he's wrangled an alliance with
the Apafalaya on the Black Warrior River right on the
edge of their territory."

"That should be interesting. My relatives are not known for their sense of humor when it comes to interlopers."

"No, they're not. Now, where have you been?"

"It's a long story. Stop gaping at my wife. She's married, and I *don't* trade her out for the night."

"Too bad." He tore his gaze away and slapped me on the shoulders as he fixed on the trade we'd piled—including the Cofitachequi boxes. Then he noticed our weapons. Only the hilts of the swords could be seen, but Pearl Hand's crossbow was unmistakable.

Eyes filling with wonder, he asked, "Are those what I think they are?"

"You've heard about the Kristianos?"

"Rumors," he muttered, attention now as rapt on the weapons as it had been on Pearl Hand.

"They're coming here." I stared thoughtfully down at the sword hilts. "And after they do, nothing will ever be the same."

"They trading the likes of those?" Two Packs nodded, unable to take his eyes off the swords.

"Only at the cost of their lives. Kristianos don't like trading. They prefer to take."

He returned his attention to me, seeing the scars on my neck, the hardness in my body. "This is a story I must hear. Meanwhile, I don't think you want to just leave those things sitting around like that. Not even under the Power of trade."

"It wasn't my intention." I clapped my hands together. "Most of this is bound for Coosa. I need to trade these two canoes for porters to pack our goods over the divide."

He glanced at the dogs, knowing full well that four

weren't going to handle it. "Skipper looks old." Two Packs liked dogs—raised his own, in fact. Then he asked, "Where's Fetch?"

"Killed by a Kristiano down in the peninsula."

"I'm sorry to hear that. Fetch, well, he was more than just a pack dog."

"You have no idea," I answered reverently. "I'll trade my story for supper. We've been high mikkos lately and gotten used to having food cooked for us."

That brought a belly laugh out of him. He turned to Red Tie. "Why don't you go up and see what can be had? I think we can afford to feed this surly water moccasin and his two not-so-smart companions."

"Not so smart?" Pearl Hand asked, having endured the lascivious appraisal and watched the interplay between us.

Two Packs braced his thick legs, thumbs in his belt, and asked, "You really *married* him?"

"I did," she said coolly.

"My point is made." Then he gave her that winning—if tooth-challenged—grin and stepped forward, clasping her to his breast. I wasn't sure if it was motivated by affection or his penis.

When he turned her loose, he boomed, "Welcome to our world!"

Pearl Hand asked in Timucua, "And *he's* a friend of yours?"

"Among the best," I answered, and gave her a wink. "And if there's anything to be learned about Coosa, he will know it."

"You trust him?"

"With my life." I paused. "But as much as he honors the

433

Power of trade, he's never let *anyone's* marriage vows get in his way."

Red Tie returned just before sunset with his strapping younger brother, Black Rope. Behind them came several local women bearing large pots of food. We ate pit-baked venison seasoned with spices, smoked turkey, hominy, and walnut corn bread sweetened with bumblebee honey and berries, and drank large amounts of mint tea. When we ran low on firewood, Black Rope was sent for another bundle.

I told our tale from start to finish, leaving nothing out. Midway through, Blood Thorn surrendered to sleep. After the story of Napetuca, Two Packs asked to see my sepaya.

"And it's not from one of Horned Serpent's spawn"—he stared at it in the firelight—"but from the old guy himself . . . right up there in the sky?"

"It is. But since we've been away from the Kristianos, it's been silent. Perhaps, like me, it's trying to figure out what to do."

In the ensuing silence Blood Thorn snored softly.

Pearl Hand, whose eyes had been drooping, gave me a smile, adding in Timucua, "If I wake up and find Two Packs in my bed tonight, I'm cutting his throat. Friend of yours or not." With that she retired to our bed.

Two Packs watched her with obvious interest, his arms clasped about his knees. Then he gave me a clever look. "Sure you won't trade her for a night?"

"No," I said flatly. "And if you value your neck unsevered, you'd best not try anything."

He changed the subject. "So, you passed yourself off as a high mikko?"

"Her plan actually. Among the Cofitachequi, it saved our hides. But for that twice-accursed White Rose, we might have had a chance to break the Kristianos once and for all."

He grunted, rolling his thick shoulders. The man had come by the name Two Packs because of the load he used to carry. His thoughtful glance remained on Pearl Hand; the blankets conformed to her shapely body. "How about I trade you—"

"Forget it. What Pearl Hand and I have, it's more than just convenience. Do you understand?"

He nodded, thoughtful, then asked, "What if I just dream about her tonight?"

His sons chuckled at that.

"Dream what you will. Providing it doesn't involve lots of gasping and moaning, and you don't walk sheepishly down to the river in the morning to wash your bedding."

He made a throwing-away motion. "If that's my problem, there's a woman up in Napochies. She's missing her nose. Cut off a long time ago, either by her once-upon-a-time husband, or perhaps by her clan because of the dishonor she brought upon them. But I wouldn't be sleeping with her nose, just the rest of her."

I gave him a thoughtful inspection. Two Packs liked to eat boiled rabbit testicles, said it imbued a certain copulatory vigor.

He laughed. "She got the last laugh, I think. Given that she'll open her legs for any valuable bit of trade, she now lives in a house larger than any but the Napochies mikko's and covers her clan's wagers when they lose everything in a stickball match."

I'd missed Two Packs and his irreverent appetites.

He gave me a serious look. "You say the Kristianos have no respect for the Power of trade?"

"None. You remember White Mat?"

"He used to work over east and south, didn't he? Traded from Cofitachequi, through the Guale, Ocute, and down among the Timucua?"

"De Soto clapped a collar onto his neck and worked him to death."

"I'll keep that in mind."

"The Kristianos would like you. You can carry twice as much as their normal slave."

He grunted humorlessly. "Skipper's moving poorly."

"I need another pack dog. We've never managed to replace Fetch, and now Skipper's going. I've seen some dogs I liked, but none had the smarts."

"I've got two young dogs that would work for you at my place outside of Coosa."

I nerved myself. "What do you hear of the Chicaza?"

"They raid the Choctaw, sometimes the Shawnee. Mostly they war with the Natchez and Tunica. There have been skirmishes with Tuskaloosa. Nothing major, but with this new alliance, something will probably happen."

He glanced at the trade boxes and packs, thinking. "You take that home, Black Shell, and you could be a high minko in more than just name."

I shook my head. "Horned Serpent closed that door long ago."

"You wouldn't just be some akeohoosa coward on the run."

"I was a boy when Horned Serpent called to me." I shifted. "It's been so long ago . . ."

"And what if your nasty Kristianos go to Chicaza?"

"Hopefully we can persuade the Coosa High Sun to stop them first. And what he fails to mop up will fall to the Apalachee or the Tuskaloosa. It is my wish that they never make it as far as Chicaza."

"What do they want?" Two Packs seemed completely mystified. "Gold doesn't have Power, not like copper."

"In so many ways they remain incomprehensible."

He looked at me. "Coosa, huh? And you need porters? I'll pack your trade to the capital . . . for one of those Kristiano swords."

"To kill Kristianos, you need to use their own weapons against them. But if we can talk the Coosa High Sun into attacking the monsters in the right way, you'll have plenty of swords."

He studied me, the old crafty trader behind his eyes. "You've changed, Black Shell. Tougher, harder. And there's a look in your eyes that I'm uncomfortable even to contemplate. But assuming you can talk the High Sun into taking on the Kristianos, do you really think you'll have to do the fighting?"

"Yes. It's coming, old friend. I can feel it. The monster has discovered that he can gain more by claiming to be peaceful than by attacking outright. But a weasel still has its nature. And it's only a matter of time before he lets it show."

He nodded. "A weasel is the way he is. And the Coosa High Sun . . . do you really think you can sway him to your side?"

"If I can't, who's left?"

The following morning—appearing none the worse for his long night   Two Packs appeared at our ramada. Red

Tie and Black Rope followed behind him, along with six sturdy-looking porters. To these I offered the two canoes, and—being of the same clan and lineage—they took them to give to relatives who had fishing claims along the river.

By the time the sun was a finger's width over the horizon, we were on our way, following the Coosa road: a well-beaten path through Napochies's fields. We passed tidy farmsteads surrounded by tall corn, spreading beans, and squash vines. At midday we left the farmlands behind and began following the Upahsee River trail into the mountains that rose in the south.

We spent the first night in a fishing village consisting of ten small houses. In Coosa, the houses are constructed square, with rounded corners. A high roof supported by four poles rises to a clay-coated smoke hole. The interiors are partitioned into four cubicles separated by plastered dividing walls, sleeping benches to the rear. The doorways are small behind a tunnel-like entry.

In trade for lodging and supper, Blood Thorn—in all his regalia—told them stories about Uzachile and the great battle at Napetuca. Pearl Hand did the translations, adding to the exotic effect. Since they'd never heard of Uzachile, let alone seen a living Timucua, the locals left satisfied.

Pearl Hand had even come to a sort of understanding with Two Packs. She simply ignored the way he stared at her body. And for his part—being the trader he was, as well as an old friend—he made no advances. I thought, however, that by the time he made it back to his house outside of Coosa, he was going to be *very* glad to see his wife.

"How long have you known him?" Pearl Hand asked as we wound through pines, gums, and bald cypresses the next day. Around us the chickadees were singing, cardinals made their chipper songs, and squirrels chattered from the trees.

"I think we met the first year I began to trade. Coming from the Deer Clan of the Coosa, he had few prospects to become anything but a farmer or hunter. Now, after all these years, he's a renowned trader, wealthy enough, but consumed by the need to move."

She shot me a curious look. "And you? If we manage to finally defeat de Soto, are you going to be that desperate to go?"

"Will there be a world after de Soto? Will we even live to see it?"

"Nothing in your dreams these days? No hints?"

"I haven't had a Spirit Dream since the night before the Orphans left."

She walked silently, listening as the porters sang a local melody. Finally she said, "It's like we lost ourselves in the forest south of Cofitachequi. And we haven't been right since."

"So much changed at Cofitachequi. I can't even think about it without my stomach going sour."

She grunted softly to herself, the corners of her mouth tightening.

"Did you think I'd abandoned you there?"

She shook her head. "You did exactly as I told you. And, looking back, you handled it perfectly. You kept me alive, Black Shell." She straightened her arms, looking down at the smooth brown skin. "During the captivity, I wanted to die. Or I longed for you to storm into the old woman's room, split her head with a sword, and carry me away."

"I'm sorry."

"That's over. And perhaps—like when you were a Kristiano slave—I needed to undergo what I did. That night when the yatika came to get me? I hurt so badly I had to wipe away the tears. You'd come for me, Black Shell. Just as I came for you."

"I'm not sure it was the same. What you did . . . walking into the Kristiano camp, took incredible courage. Me, I just had to wait. And that was terrible enough."

She smiled. "On the other hand, you could have taken White Rose's offer." A pause. "Had you, even as a ruse, would it have worked out differently? Could you have stopped her?"

"Maybe. I don't know." How many times had I asked myself the same question? "She said I could keep you."

"I should have strangled the little swamp witch when she was a child."

"The world would have been a better place."

"And Coosa? What are our chances here?"

"Coosa's big, complicated, and full of layers and traps, but at least they're only political." I hesitated. "You didn't have dealings with the Coosa High Sun's nephew, did you?"

"Sorry. Never been here." Then she laughed wryly. "Which means I haven't given anyone reason to slip a knife into my back. Yet."

"Then we've a chance." I motioned to where Two Packs walked at the head of the trail, his trader's staff in hand. Even walking through the forest he made quite a sight. "Two Packs will help us. He's a notable character in these parts and knows how to pierce the layers of fawning nobles."

She gave the man's broad back an introspective look. "What are you thinking?"

"He's an interesting man. Nothing I can't handle."

I arched an eyebrow. "Handle . . . how?"

She just gave me a saucy smile in return.

THIRTY-ONE

THE COOSA VALLEY IS WIDE, FLAT, AND SURROUNDED by low hilly uplands. Situated at the confluence of several rivers, the floodplains contain fertile and productive soils. Coosa is an old Nation; the stories of its origins go all the way back to fabled Cahokia.

For generations, the original Mos'kogean settlers had expanded up and down the rivers, burning out forest, planting their fields, and building towns. Through conquest, marriage, or mutual agreement, Coosa had absorbed neighboring peoples into its fold until the core area was so interwoven with tribute, kin ties, and mutual reliance it had become a regional giant. Outlying and subordinate Nations like Napochies and Chiaha still retained their old identities, and had time allowed, perhaps they, too, would have eventually merged seamlessly into the whole.

As it was, the Coosa High Sun ruled his sprawling Nation with sense, compassion, and evenhandedness. His subordinate mikkos were treated with respect, and any who dared to defy the authority of the High Sun were faced with an overwhelming military threat.

For Blood Thorn, the journey down from the divide was an awesome experience. The first thing he noticed was the number of people traveling from Coosa to Napochies; we passed a constant stream of humanity: traders, emissaries, warriors, oretas borne on litters, messengers, and people bearing heavy burden baskets hung from straps over their shoulders.

Then as the route descended down into the broad Coosa River bottoms, we encountered hunting and collecting parties canvassing the forest for food, building materials, firewood, healing plants, and stone. As the trail widened into a road, we began passing individual farmsteads eking out a living on the lower slopes. Fishing camps were established on every stream.

Occasionally we would pass a shrine—generally consisting of a small structure filled with offerings of flowers, carved wooden effigies, and sacred sticks painted with colors and decorated with feathers.

When we finally walked out into the Coosa lowlands, Blood Thorn was amazed by the endless expanse of fields. At the Coosa River itself, a small town had grown up simply to serve the ferry traffic. In the town's center, locals offered fowl, meat, pottery, fabrics, corn, beans, squash, arrows, carvings, feathers, you name it.

Two Packs made arrangements for our crossing while Blood Thorn, Pearl Hand, and I walked through the bazaar, inspecting the local goods.

"And this is just a river crossing?" Blood Thorn asked, staring at the locals in their colorful dress. "You could stock all of Uzachile just on what's available here."

"Wait until you see the capital," I remarked. "It's really four towns, each of which serves a different clan. The Wind Clan, from which the High Sun is descended, occupies Coosa itself. The Cougar Clan has their town just downriver about two hands' walk. There the tastanaki, or Red Chief, holds sway. Were the four towns all built in one place, the thing would dwarf Telemico."

"Are there great mounds with high palaces? Like those at Telemico?"

"Not as high. Mostly because the capital hasn't been there as long. Several generations back, a faction of the Wind Clan overthrew the leadership. At the time they were living down at Etowah. Since most of the Nation's interests lay in the north, they moved the capital."

"Just like that?"

"Well, being more centralized shortened the lines of communication and made Coosa less vulnerable to attack from the Ocute and Tuskaloosa. The new High Sun also took the opportunity to order the other clans to build close to him—a way to better keep an eye on them. Since they'd helped to overthrow his relatives at Etowah, he was afraid someone might use the same trick on him."

Blood Thorn made a face. "Sounds like a viper's nest."

"Isn't that what government is?" I grinned. "And people wonder why I'm just a lowly trader."

"Lowly, all right," Blood Thorn said. "With Horned Serpent's sepaya hung around your neck."

After we crossed the Coosa, Two Packs pushed us harder. As a gentle rain fell we followed a winding trail past farmsteads. I wondered at Two Packs's pace. Maybe he'd been dwelling too much on Pearl Hand's enticing curves.

The rain finally broke, puffy clouds rolling off to the north. Evening gloom settled on the land as the trail we followed split off from the main route and paralleled the bank above the Coosahachi River—so called to distinguish the branch upon which the capital had been built from the main channel to the north. Through the trees we got a glimpse every now and then of the water to our left.

Two Packs's house was built on a terrace overlooking the river. Nestled between its tree-lined banks, the Coosahachi reflected a silver sheen from the evening sky. The odor of smoke carried on the breeze, and here and there, on the floodplain across from us, fires flickered as people in farmsteads cooked their evening meals. Just visible to the southwest was Cougar Town, home of the tastanaki, the war leader, or Red Chief, of the Coosa Nation.

"I'd forgotten how charming it is," I said as Pearl Hand stepped up to wrap her arms around me.

Then I turned back to Two Packs's house, or should I say, houses. Four structures had been built back against the trees. Red Tie and Black Rope were calling orders to the pack of dogs that charged out to greet us. Several children who'd been standing by the fire rushed out to help, crying, "Papa! Papa!" as they rushed forward to clasp at Two Packs's legs. He slung his pack down, dropped to his knees, and enfolded them in his arms.

I slipped my arm around Pearl Hand's waist as the confusion unfolded and ordered my dogs to heel. They did so with obvious reluctance, wishing to go mix it up with Two Packs's dogs.

At that point a woman stepped out, wiping her hands on her apron-like skirt. She shook her head and, striding forward, began calling orders.

Two Packs straightened and gave the woman a hug that should have cracked her ribs. When he released her, she batted him playfully on the shoulder, obviously delighted to see him. Then, spotting us, she came forward.

"Welcome, welcome," she called. "I hope you've something to add to the pot. We didn't make enough for all of you."

I chuckled, "Willow Root, we would never impose upon your supper. Don't worry about us."

She squinted in the gloom. "Black Shell? That you? By the Piasa's balls, it is! You scoundrel! Where have you been all these years? And with a charming woman? Does she know what kind of cur you really are?"

I introduced Pearl Hand and Blood Thorn while Two Packs showed the porters where to place our packs.

By then Willow Root was fawning over her sons, shooing the other children away, sending them on errands to fetch water from a creek just down from the house.

Somehow enough food was scraped together, the fire enlarged, and we threw out our blankets under the starry sky.

Supper was the time for stories, but I could tell Two Packs was antsy, sitting with his arm around his wife. It didn't take long before we called it a night.

The next morning, after breakfast, Two Packs wandered over to squat beside our fire. His broad face was introspective as he hunched, arms braced on his knees, hands hanging.

"I think we should go on to Coosa today." He yawned.

"I'll introduce you to an oreta I've done favors for in the past. He's Wind Clan, a cousin of the High Sun. Since he's in favor, he can take your request for an audience to the High Sun without going through the various yatikas, oretas, and mikkos."

"We would appreciate that." I handed him a cup of tea. "Is there a place we could rent in Coosa, someplace where the trade won't be out in plain view?"

"I have a storehouse there." He glanced at me. "If you don't mind, I'd like to accompany you."

"You would be more than welcome, and besides, it saves me the humiliation of begging."

He grinned. "I always did like you."

"You're notorious for poor taste in friends."

He slapped his knees. "I got that from you. But before we go, have you looked over my dogs?"

"I have. First thing. That black and the brown-and-white look like prospects."

He nodded. "Blackie and Patches, the two I thought you'd pick. Good choice. But don't expect them to go for a couple of trinkets."

"Take a look at my trade. Help yourself to whatever catches your fancy."

"As long as it's not a Kristiano sword, huh?"

"Except that."

A hand's time later, Two Packs was a strand of pearls and an engraved shell cup richer. I laced Fetch's old pack on Blackie. Skipper's I tied onto Patches's brown-and-white body. Having been bred by a trader, they were already broken to the pack and had been living with discipline from the day they were whelped.

Introducing two new dogs to a longtime pack is not

without its trials, jealousies, snarls, nips, and fights. A new pecking order has to be established. But with Two Packs's help we had them on the trail and by midday were passing around cornfields where women and children worked, backs bent to the sun. We encountered a constant stream of people, mostly local farmers who greeted us with a smile, bowing at the sight of our trader's staffs.

The road led us around houses, ramadas, and gardens, past children and dogs, the occasional inconveniently placed basket, and finally to the landing below Deer Town. Set on the Coosahachi's northern bank, the town looked lazy with its low palisade and ditch.

Blood Thorn drew stares as he admired the two high palaces built on adjacent flats atop the single great mound that dominated Deer Town. The surrounding high granaries with their pointed roofs added to the illusion of height.

The canoe landing was crowded with people sitting on the parallel ranks of beached canoes. It was apparent from the crowd that we'd have to wait our turn. I kept the dogs in hand with Two Packs's help; then he merged with the crowd, seeking to arrange our crossing.

A disorganized bazaar had been set up, locals having spread blankets or placed their goods under the few ramadas. Smoldering fires gave the air a smoky flavor, enhanced by the smells drifting off the food vendors' steaming pots. At the periphery, a group of old men played at dice, laughing and talking, and two smiling young women dressed in bright yellow dresses danced to flute music.

Blood Thorn tried to take it all in, oblivious of the people who paused to point at him and whisper behind their hands.

Two Packs managed to buy us crossing for a couple of pieces of shell, and a finger's time later we were across the Coosahachi. Above the landing rose the imposing buildings of Coosa itself. Here, too, people were hawking their wares, children running up to offer us smoked fish, skewers of boiled crawfish, turkey legs, local pottery, and every other ware.

Two Packs, brandishing his trader's staff, waved them back and managed to get us—unscathed—through the crowd. Blood Thorn, however, found himself fascinated by a magician who made things disappear into thin air. Pearl Hand grabbed him by the elbow and had to physically tug him away.

Smoke hung over the valley like a thick mist through which the distant hills could barely be seen. The capital itself was surrounded by a high wall, the portals manned by squads of warriors. Spread around the bastions, in a haphazard and crowded clutter, were various structures, including the one Two Packs owned: a tall granary, built atop eight sturdy poles. I could just reach up and touch the cane-pole floor. Two Packs untied a ladder that he'd hung beneath the floor joists and set it before climbing up to the wooden-plank door.

"Why the heavy door?" I asked, realizing that I couldn't see hinges, so cleverly had it been constructed.

"Thieves," he replied with irritation. "This close to the capital, with so many passing, anything left unattended tends to disappear. See this bit of cane sticking out?"

"Looks like shoddy construction." I shielded my eyes against the sun, watching Two Packs at the top of his ladder, hoping the weathered poles wouldn't snap under his weight.

"It's the latch," he said smugly. "Just lift . . . so. And push."

I saw how he did it and watched him push the door open. He was grinning down at me, quite proud of himself. "Better put your trade in here. Out of sight and safe."

One by one we lifted the packs. After Two Packs disappeared inside, I climbed up, feeling the spring in the ladder.

The inside was uncomfortably warm, stuffy, and dark, but I could see the split-cane roof was tight and the walls had been made of woven willow stems interlaced with shreds of basswood bark.

The packs stowed, we crawled out and Two Packs showed me the trick to relatch the door. Stepping out into the breeze was a welcome relief. We congregated in the shade beneath the granary floor, my dogs growling at their new companions. Blackie and Patches kept wanting to bolt in terror. Pearl Hand took it upon herself to reassure them, much to Bark's dismay.

Dogs can be as complicated as people.

A shabby-looking ramada was attached to the southern side of the granary like an unwanted appendage. An old fire pit was situated in the middle, and sunlight played through the frayed roof.

"I should see to that," Two Packs mused.

In near defeat, Pearl Hand roped Blackie and Patches to one of the poles and firmly ordered the rest of the dogs to lie down in the shade. One by one, the growls died down.

Seeing the porters off, I turned to Two Packs. "All right. How do we do this?"

He considered the warriors guarding the palisade gate,

his broad face thoughtful. "Let me see if I can get a message to the oreta. It might take a while."

We watched him stroll off, his massive shoulders rolling with each step, and seated ourselves in the shade, backs to the thick support posts. Blackie and Patches whined as they watched him disappear, and I knelt beside them, petting their necks, reassuring them.

Blood Thorn stared around. "Coosa's not as grand as I thought it would be, but I can't get over the number of people. It's . . . *busy!*"

I scratched behind Blackie's ear while Pearl Hand kept Squirm and Gnaw from interfering. "Within two days' walk, there are close to ten thousand people."

He nodded, eyes on the high palace, the temple, and the tall granaries jutting from behind Coosa's wall. "That's just Coosa itself. Factor in all the towns we passed up on the Tenasee . . . all the way to Chiaha. That's another thirty thousand, at least."

"And Coosa extends for another fifteen days' travel to the southwest." I pointed. "There are another twenty-five large towns. How many people does that make? Forty, fifty thousand when you figure in the villages and farmsteads?"

"It would take a lifetime just to count them," he whispered, shaking his head. "You seem at home here."

"I did most of my trading out of Coosa. Mostly from here to the west and south."

Pearl Hand arched an eyebrow. "And you have more friends like Two Packs? Big brawny rascals who like to leer at women?"

"As many as I could get."

"What about Tuskaloosa?" she asked. "Is there someone like Two Packs who can smooth the way?"

"Old Half Bear and I always got along." I smiled at the memory. "But if the Coosa High Sun can be talked into it, de Soto might not get that far."

"And what are our chances of that?" Blood Thorn wondered.

"We'll find out when we finally get in to see the High Sun." I sighed, rubbing Patches's back.

Bark continued to growl promises of mayhem at the new dogs. I prayed it wasn't prophetic.

Two Packs came striding out of Coosa's main gate less than a hand's time later. He looked pensive as he walked up, his thick arms swinging. From the set of his wide mouth he was in a serious mood.

"Well?" I asked with unaccustomed anxiety.

He gave me a thin smile, eyes narrowing. "I couldn't find my friend, but a different oreta was more than interested when I mentioned that you came with news of the Kristianos. I told him everything I knew: that you'd been following de Soto up from the peninsula; that you'd been at Napetuca and Cofitachequi. That you'd fought the Kristianos, taken one captive, and been a captive yourself."

He hesitated. "The oreta, Tall Owl, a Cougar Clan man, immediately went to the palace, talked to the yatika, and was given admission to the Coosa High Sun. I waited only a finger of time before Tall Owl was back. He said he'd like you to come just after the evening prayers."

We all glanced at each other.

Two Packs continued. "I told him you were a Chicaza noble, a Chicora, and an Uzachile iniha. I lied through my teeth and said you were all honorable individuals and of a noble bearing."

"Finally telling the truth, huh? Going to make a habit of this, are you?"

He grinned, exposing his few peglike teeth. "I could have told him about the time you put that dead rat in the high priest's water jar down at Talisi town."

To immediately change the subject, I asked, "So we should arrive in full dress?"

"It wouldn't hurt." Then he turned grim again. "But you should also know that messengers have been passing back and forth. Your monster plays the game well. He has sent runner after runner telling the Coosa Sun that his intentions are entirely peaceful, and so far the message has been received with a great deal of satisfaction. What you're about to tell the High Sun? Well, it might not come as welcome news."

He placed a hand on my shoulder. "Be careful, Black Shell. You're about to upset the most powerful man on earth."

And for the first time in days, I felt the sepaya quiver.

THIRTY-TWO

After bathing, we greased ourselves, dug the finest garments out of the packs, and sorted through the various jewelry, copper ornaments, and feathers. Again Blood Thorn and I painted each other's faces. He opted for the traditional white and blue design favored by the Uzachile, while I had him apply white around my eyes with red on each cheek, followed by a wide black band running from my mouth down over my chin. The colors communicated peace at the top and war in the middle, but the black reminded the observer that death lay below it all.

Pearl Hand applied a striking design of black and yellow to her face, as if rays of sun were piercing the night. She left her glossy hair loose to hang down her back and donned a yellow dress that, through clever wrapping, emphasized her curves.

I pinned my hair with the turkey-tail copper pin, added splays of feathers to each shoulder, wore a white apron that tapered to a point between my knees, and laced thick shell necklaces around my neck. On my chest I hung a copper piece embossed with Horned Serpent's image, his wings spread wide. Then I hung the Kristiano sword at my right side, letting the sheath dangle beside my leg.

Finally, as the evening prayers were sung from the palace, the town went silent. The high notes of the Coosa hilishaya carried on the smoky and humid air, followed by the distinctive timbre of a conch-shell horn.

Two Packs gave us a final inspection, his eyes widening as I pulled the old copper mace from its hide wrapping.

With the old dogs ordered to stay and the new ones tied up, we set out across the trampled loam toward the main gate. The soil here was impregnated with old bits of pottery, charcoal ash, discarded flakes from stone tools, and old freshwater clam shells—trash common to any town.

People stopped short during their evening tasks, watching wide-eyed as we passed. I walked with my head up, Pearl Hand at my side. Blood Thorn swaggered along behind us, his right hand perched on the hilt of his Kristiano sword, his hair pom straight up and wavering with each step. We cut a dramatic image. Why didn't I think the High Sun would be impressed?

At the gate, the warriors stiffened as Two Packs bellowed, "Comes now Black Shell, of the Chief Clan of the Chicaza; Blood Thorn, iniha of the Uzachile; and Pearl Hand, matron of the Chicora. They come to have counsel with the glorious Coosa High Sun. Make way! And announce our coming."

We marched straight into the sacred city of Coosa, acting as if we had every right in the world to stroll past the intricately carved charnel house atop its mound. We bowed to the various guardian posts carved in the shapes of Rattlesnake, Cougar, Deer, Raccoon, Vulture, Eagle, and the other Spirit Creatures.

Two Packs led us boldly across the great plaza, past the stickball goals, the *akbatle* basket atop its high pole, and finally to the red-and-white-striped World Tree, a mighty red cedar that towered over all.

I glanced longingly at the chunkey courts—each immaculately groomed—and then we stopped before the long wooden staircase that led up to the palace itself.

The elevated veranda was filled with nobility: clan leaders, subordinate mikkos, oretas, and high-ranking kin belonging to the Wind Clan. The yatika, stepping front and center, called down, "Who comes?"

Two Packs repeated his booming announcement of our identities.

"Let them come, bringing only the white Power of peace and tranquility in their hearts."

I noticed that this time, Two Packs let us go first. Wise man. Why draw attention to yourself when a wrong word could lead to the square?

I climbed the stairs with all the dignity I could muster, reminding myself that it was for moments like these that my uncle had tried so mercilessly to prepare me. And that I was no ordinary man, but one who had faced the most terrifying Spirit Helper of all—and been eaten alive. The sepaya on my chest seemed to thump its approval.

We stopped before the yatika, an old man with white hair and knowing eyes. One didn't live to become an old yatika without having seen just about everything.

"You are Black Shell, of the Chief Clan of the Chicaza?"

"I am." I kept my back arched, head high. "We have business with the Coosa High Sun."

"What business?"

"We would communicate what we know of the Kristianos and their designs on the Coosa Nation. We come under the Power of trade and the White Arrow, and bind ourselves to them."

"Are you here to show your obedience and worship to the High Sun?"

"We are not." That caused a series of whispers among the nobles. "We are here to show our respect as allies—under the White Arrow—and to engage in conversations which we hope the High Sun will find useful given the arrival of the Kristianos."

"Do you come as representatives of the Chicaza and with the blessings of the high minko?"

"We do not. We come as nobles from three nations who have found common cause against the Kristianos. Our purpose is to inform the High Sun of the nature and history of the Kristianos while in our world."

He studied me thoughtfully, then looked at Blood Thorn. In passable Timucua, he asked, "And you are a holata?"

"I am Blood Thorn, son of Bit Woman, of the Fish Clan, and iniha to the council of Holata Uzachile. I have been granted the rank of nicoquadca among the Apalachee and come to converse with the Coosa High Sun under both the Power of trade and the White Arrow."

The yatika turned. "And you, woman?"

She gave him a grim smile. "I am Pearl Hand, of the

Chicora, wife of Black Shell. I have been granted the rank of nicoquadca among the Apalachee, speak the language of the Kristianos, and have lived among them. I have stood in council with the *Adelantado* Hernando de Soto and heard the private conversations of his *capitanes*. If the Coosa High Sun would learn of the Kristianos and what lurks in their hearts, I am willing to tell him."

He considered this, waiting, perhaps to see if we would offer anything else. Blood Thorn and Pearl Hand followed my lead, standing silent, heads up, eyes front. Visiting nobles didn't get chatty with the underlings.

"I will inform the Coosa High—"

"Bring them to me," a soft voice called. "They've sharpened my curiosity."

The Coosa High Sun stood in the doorway. I placed him as in his midtwenties. He was inspecting us with hooded eyes, his face tattooed with a series of zigzagging black lines running down his cheeks from the forked-eye patterns: weeping eyes. Copper ear spools gleamed from his elongated earlobes, and he wore a simple white cloth cape. A beaded breechcloth hung down over his knees, onto which had been embroidered a most striking rattlesnake design. His hair bun was fastened with a copper turkey-tail pin. I thought mine was bigger, but his had been polished to a reflective sheen.

The yatika stepped aside, touched his forehead, and indicated that we might pass. Micos and oretas stepped back, shuffling on the tightly woven cane matting.

Just in front of the High Sun, I dropped to one knee, palms raised, head up, looking him in the eyes. I could hear Blood Thorn and Pearl Hand follow suit.

Again there were gasps. The Coosa High Sun's subjects

were required to prostrate themselves and touch their foreheads to the ground. I tried to take the man's measure by his reaction. After all, he believed he'd been born a god.

The Coosa High Sun's eyes flickered. "Rise. Tell me your purpose."

As I stood, his gaze went to the old copper mace that I held. In a toneless voice, he asked, "Where did you get that?"

"It was given to me by the Apalachee hilishaya as a badge of office in my service to Horned Serpent and Power."

"Such possessions are reserved only for the greatest leaders, those descended from the Beginning Times."

"I am Chief Clan, of the Chicaza. The chosen of Horned Serpent." *And that's all the answer you need, High Sun.*

He studied me thoughtfully, and I could feel my heart begin to pound. I was taking a terrible gamble. My fear was countered by the warming of the sepaya against my breast.

"Of the Chief Clan," he whispered, "yet your younger brother sits on the panther chair. Why would that be, Black Shell?"

He couldn't have missed my surprise. To keep him off balance, I grinned. "Horned Serpent had other plans for my life, great High Sun."

"And what would those be?"

"I have been chosen to fight for our world against the Kristianos."

"And do you have proof of this?"

"Is your hilishaya present?"

He turned, calling, "Hilishaya. The Chicaza wonders if you are present."

"I am, great Coosa." The old priest stepped forward. His eyes were like two white pebbles in his ancient face. He felt his way, one hand out before him. Dressed only in a coarsely woven brown smock, he nevertheless radiated Power.

The High Sun—as if he were discussing the taste of his food—asked, "Can you test this man?"

The old priest tottered toward me, asking, "You serve Horned Serpent?"

"I do."

"What did he demand of you?"

"My life, great Hilishaya."

"And you paid it?"

"I did."

"And what did you receive in return?"

"Let me take your hand, elder. There, that's it." I guided his leathery fingers to the pouch around my neck. At his touch, I could feel the heat.

"Sepaya," the old man whispered. "How?"

"As I was being devoured, I grabbed for anything I could."

"The old stories tell of such things." He almost jerked his hand back. "You have been to the Sky World?"

"I was carried there by Horned Serpent."

"And the Underworld?"

"Piasa doesn't like me."

"Hmmm. Piasa doesn't like much . . . outside of chaos."

"He is afraid, elder."

"What does Piasa have to fear outside of the Thunderers?"

"Abandonment and oblivion should the Kristianos conquer our world and replace our Spirit Beasts, Breath

Giver, and the red and white Powers with their *paraíso* and *dios*."

The old man's wrinkled face became a mask of worry. He stepped back unsteadily, and an assistant hurried forward to take his arm. "I wish you well, Black Shell. The *sepaya* told me your fate. I pray you are strong."

My fate? "So do I, elder."

The High Sun had watched all this, no reaction crossing his face. "Bring them inside. Fetch food. I would hear what they have to say." He disappeared into the dark interior.

Even as we followed, two boys were adding logs to the great central hearth, placing them in the cardinal directions: east, south, west, and north. Additional, smaller logs were added, causing the blaze to spring up and illuminate the room. The place was large, the wall benches ornately rendered as twisting serpents; the support posts rose in carved renderings of striking rattlesnakes, their fangs bared. Beautiful textiles hung from the walls, dyed in bright colors, representing scenes from the Beginning Times: piasas, great ivory-billed woodpeckers, Eagle Man, and the two twins: the orphan—called Facha'seko, or the Wild One—dancing with his brother, Morning Star.

The floor—as was common among the elite—was artfully woven as an entire mat. This one now looked worn, ready for its yearly replacement during the upcoming Busk: the Green Corn Ceremony. On the third day, the matting would be removed and ritually burned. Then its replacement would be installed.

The Coosa High Sun took his seat, a raised chair piled with cougar hides perched atop a tiered clay mound just behind the fire.

To Blood Thorn I whispered, "Whatever you do, do not step between the High Sun and the fire."

"Wouldn't dream of it," he muttered, staring at the embossed copper image of Eagle Man on the wall behind the High Sun's head. The back walls were hung with cattail mat woven into geometric shapes; two doors were at the rear of the room.

I was eyeing the carved boxes, large burnished jars, stacked fabric blankets, and thick buffalo hides beneath the benches. The benches themselves were covered with winter bear hides, the fur gleaming in the firelight.

These were soon obscured by the rush of nobles filing in and taking the seats. Within moments the room was crowded.

At a gesture from the High Sun, a large stone pipe was placed before the fire. One of the priests carefully removed a long stem carved in the traditional image of a snake and inserted it into the rear of the pipe. From a beautifully beaded pouch he shook tobacco into the bowl and tamped it with a wooden dowel. Once lit, prayers were called out, and one by one, Pearl Hand, Blood Thorn, and I took a draw. We exhaled the scented tobacco, calling prayers of blessing for the Coosa Nation. We watched it rise and carry our wishes to the Sky World.

Black drink was ladled, and we each accepted the shell cup—cut from a huge whelk—and drank.

"Now," the High Sun said, "as food is brought tell me your story from the beginning."

We did, each of us in turn. And when it came to Blood Thorn's tale, the yatika translated. Through it all, the room remained silent.

When food was brought and laid out on our side of the

fire, the High Sun propped his head on his hand and said, "Eat. Meanwhile I will consider the things you have told me. Tishu Mikko? You have heard everything?"

"I have." An older warrior, dressed in a stunning crimson apron, approached from the right. A beaded forelock hung over his forehead. He studied me with hard black eyes, his face tattooed, copper ear spools filling his earlobes. "I, too, will have questions when our guests have eaten."

At a gesture from the High Sun, wooden plates—skillfully hollowed from sections of log—were filled with spiced squash, roasted deer, quails, and tasty root breads.

As soon as the repast had been washed down with a delightful raspberry-grape juice and a bowl of water had been passed for our fingers, the High Sun clapped his hands.

He looked around the room. "Here is what we know: The Kristianos come professing peace. I have entertained several runners from Chiaha, and just yesterday, two from Coste. What I have heard is perplexing.

"At Chiaha, the Kristianos seem to have fulfilled their agreement to keep the peace. At Coste, however, due to the arrogance of their men, a battle was narrowly averted. The Kristianos, we are told, tried to raid a granary and became abusive of the clan to whom it belonged. The Kristiano chief—apparently to save his men—beat his own people back, claimed friendship, and talked the Coste mikko into dispersing his warriors. Only after returning to the Kristiano camp did he order the Coste mikko detained and the nobles placed in collars and chains. The Coste mikko has asked me to send forces to kill the Kristianos and free him.

"Finally, this morning, a runner arrived from the Satapo mikko, claiming that all is well and the Coste mikko has been released."

I touched my forehead respectfully. "Understand that the invader uses Nations for what he can get out of them. His preferred method is to arrive in peace and make demands. As long as the mikkos provide food, porters for his supplies, and women to service his men, and there is no attack on his forces, he will not resort to taking mikkos captive or chaining the people."

He considered that. "Then, is it not to our advantage to supply him with these things and send him on to the Tuskaloosa?"

"Cofitachequi tried it that way," Pearl Hand said. "In return de Soto raided the temples for pearls and desecrated the bones of the ancestors. Atrocities were committed by the soldados, people enslaved, and the Cofitachequi mico's nieces were taken captive." She pressed her palms together. "I have heard the Kristianos speak. They are interested only in what serves their purpose for the moment. They have no sense of honor or respect as we know it."

"What is their ultimate goal here?"

I said, "They search for wealth, particularly gold. At Cofitachequi we learned they also covet pearls—even if they have to desecrate the dead to get them."

"And what did the Cofitachequi get in return?"

"Misery and enslavement," I said. "The Kristianos, however, have been known to dispense cloth and *hierro* tools to people who have been helpful."

"What is this *hierro*?"

Pearl Hand pulled her knife from its scabbard and

stepped around to the side, careful to avoid placing herself between him and the fire. She knelt respectfully and offered the blade, handle first.

The High Sun inspected it, almost cutting his thumb on the edge.

"It is a most remarkable metal, High Sun," she said, extending her hand politely to take it back. "Their armor is made of it, as are many of their weapons. It makes them almost invulnerable in battle."

The tishu mikko snorted, an amused smile on his face.

I turned. "With all respect, great Red Chief, you have heard our report of Napetuca and the fighting in Apalachee. While neither of those Nations has the might of Coosa, your army cannot prevail on the field of battle."

"Oh?" he said almost insolently.

I touched my chin to soften my words. "I am Chicaza, Tishu Mikko. A statement that stands by itself. The Kristianos are unlike any warriors who have ever existed. Their cabayeros move like the wind on great armored beasts. And behind them come massed ranks of soldados with terrifying weapons. Only a lucky hit with an arrow to the face, neck, or perhaps legs will bring one down."

Blood Thorn crossed his arms, speaking in atrociously accented Mos'kogee. "Our arrows are no more effective than cactus thorns tossed against a turtle's shell. I have killed them, Tishu Mikko. I stand before you as a nicoquadca. Once I spoke as you do. Then, at Napetuca, I watched them mow through formations of trained warriors the way a flint-edged sickle lays grass low. When it comes to killing Kristianos, a smart warrior hunts them one by one. Only then are they vulnerable."

The tishu mikko asked, "What, then, did you come here to do?"

"Warn you," I almost snapped. "Tell you that there are ways to destroy the monster. But it must be done with cunning and guile. Remove the food stores before his arrival— or burn them if you can't." I heard incredulous gasps. "Evacuate the towns in advance of his march. Send your warriors in small parties to ambush the trails, river crossings, anywhere they can attack from cover and fade away."

"But the country is full of food!" one of the mikkos cried. "The first corn crop is ready to be picked."

"Evacuate the towns?" another almost laughed. "That's ludicrous! What purpose would that serve?"

I shot a hard look around the room. "The Kristianos depend on porters to move their supplies. If the local people aren't there to be captured, the invaders must carry what they eat on their backs. If the granaries are empty, they must forage into the fields to fill their bellies. Scattered so, they can be picked off, one by one."

"And what does that gain us?" the High Sun asked.

"It makes the *Adelantado*'s soldados rebellious." Pearl Hand walked back to join us. "Up until they arrived at Cofitachequi, the soldados were on the verge of revolt. Now, however, with their bellies full, their supplies carried, and women provided for them, they feel content. None are dying. They no longer fear to stray from the protection of the cabayeros. Life is good." She gave them a crooked smile. "Were it up to us, we would make it miserable again."

One of the mikkos snorted his derision, stepped forward, and dropped to his knee. "If I might speak, High Sun."

"Of course, Mikko."

The man rose, giving us a look of utter disgust. "This is ludicrous! Have you listened to what they've said? We should *evacuate* our towns, *empty* our granaries, or worse, *burn* them? Deploy our warriors—and right before the Busk? In short, they want us to loose chaos all across our land and turn our people upside down!"

He stomped over to glare at us as though we were the loathsome insane. "My question is: Why are they here? Who do these people really serve? Is this some ploy by the Tuskaloosa? Perhaps to weaken us? Possibly a means of coring out our hearts prior to some treacherous plot? Disperse our warriors, they say? Send them out in small parties? Why? So our forces can't be assembled should an army of Tuskaloosa or Cherokee raid Coosa itself?"

I met his rabid stare, refusing to rise to the bait. "With the arrival of the Kristianos, your world is forever changed, Mikko. One way you become their servants, and the High Sun is made their captive to ensure obedience. The other, you have the chance to break them. Destroy them. All their *hierro* and fine cloth becomes yours. Coosa is known henceforth as the mighty Nation that destroyed the monster."

He was shaking his head as if I were mouthing nonsense.

In a soft voice I added, "I didn't say it would be easy or without pain, death, and misery. I'm sorry de Soto picked this time to invade Coosa. But that, unfortunately, is the way it is. And he can be beaten no other way."

Another man in back rushed forward, dropped to his knees, and cried, "I beg you, High Sun. Do not listen.

They speak poison! Though they claim to serve the White Arrow, I fear that they sow red chaos among us."

Grunts of assent came from around the room. I could see the High Sun's eyes flicking back and forth, taking note of who was loudest in their dissent.

"We speak the truth," I said, keeping my calm. "We serve no Nation."

A couple of guffaws came in answer.

I turned, trying to send a hard-eyed stare toward the fools. *If you don't act like a high minko, Black Shell, you're dead.*

The High Sun made a hand gesture; the room went silent. "Tishu Mikko, as tastanaki, leader of our military, what do you think?"

"I am inclined to agree with the mikkos, High Sun. What is proposed here is unthinkable. The Kristianos pose a threat, yes. But my advice is to wait and see if there are other actions like those in Coste. If the Kristianos prove untrustworthy, we still have time to assemble a large enough force to defeat them."

Calls of approbation came from around the room.

The High Sun gave us a reproving stare. "I think I have heard enough."

We'd lost. Looking around, I could read the extent of our defeat. Pus and blood, we'd be lucky just to get out of Coosa with our lives. Assuming we didn't end up hanging in a square.

"Great High Sun, a moment please. Hear me," another voice called. I turned to see the old hilishaya being led forward by his assistant. The nobles reluctantly made way.

The old man tottered up, extending a hand toward the fire, as if to feel its heat. He smiled gently and said, "I have investigated this man." He gestured in my direction. "He carries the sepaya. He is Horned Serpent's. And nothing he has said here tonight is false. The sepaya ensures that. A liar would be burned down where he stands. Black Shell carries the word of the Spirit World, and it must be listened to with respect."

I could see doubt for the first time on the High Sun's face.

"And what do you recommend, Hilishaya?"

The old man turned his white-blanked gaze my way. "Did the Horned Serpent tell you why Breath Giver and the Spirit Beasts won't just destroy the invaders themselves?"

I touched my forehead, knowing the old man couldn't see it. But the others could. "Old-Woman-Who-Never-Dies told me that this is a matter to be settled among men. For reasons I do not understand, our Spirit World and the Kristianos' gods are evenly balanced. Neither is superior to the other. With gods and Power equal, the outcome is left to human beings."

"Have you seen anything to support this?"

I laid a hand on the old man's thin shoulder. "I watched the Apalachee hilishaya, Back-from-the-Dead, face one of their priests. As they each called upon their spirits and Power, neither stumbled, flinched, or was struck dead by lightning. This copper mace had no more effect than the Kristiano priest's long-tailed cross. No peals of thunder rent the skies, no great beasts rose up from the earth. It was as if the world were frozen."

"How did it end?"

"With a burning woman's scream and a rush of armored Kristianos."

He nodded, head slightly cocked.

"Hilishaya?" the High Sun asked.

The old man's frown rearranged his wrinkles. "Being blind, I can no longer look into the sepaya's heart to see the future, High Sun. But my ears are fine, and the sepaya whispers many things to me. There is great worry and apprehension in the Spirit World. I also hear these people, sent to us by Power. They do not tell lies but speak with the tongue of Power. As to the course Coosa should take? That, High Sun, I cannot tell." He paused. "But do *not* dismiss these people or their warning lightly."

And with that the old man turned—his assistant steadying him—and was led out of the room.

The High Sun took a deep breath. "Chicaza, it would please me if you and your party would remain in Coosa for the moment. You have my protection under the White Arrow. I will consider your words most carefully."

As he made a gesture, the yatika appeared at my side. Not a word was spoken as we were escorted out.

Two Packs was lingering just outside the door. No smile split his wide face. "That could have gone better."

"At least we're not being hung in a square," I retorted.

Two Packs shot me a dark look. "Yet."

THIRTY-THREE

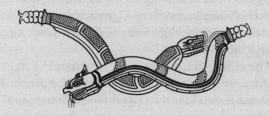

WE WAITED FOR FOUR DAYS. MOST OF THE TIME WAS spent working with the dogs, patiently introducing Blackie and Patches to the pack, addressing canine jealousies and insecurities. Dogs are as narrow-minded, socially obsessed, and incomprehensible as people.

A light drizzle was falling when a man came trotting out from the Coosa gate, splashing his way over to where we had just finished repairing the roof on Two Packs's ramada. A small fire smoked beneath its shelter.

"Tishu Mikko," I said, greeting him as I recognized that tattooed visage, grizzled hair, and muscular walk. A cardinal-feathered cape hung from his shoulders. Water beaded on his copper ear spools.

"Chicaza," the Red Chief answered, a thin smile on his lips. Droplets of water streaked down his tattooed face as he stepped in out of the rain. "Well, you've caused quite a stir."

"Have a seat. Dry off. May we offer you anything?"

He settled beside Blood Thorn, giving the Timucua a slight nod. Then, as I seated myself beside Pearl Hand, he gave me a thoughtful stare, as though trying to see the very quality of my souls.

"Has the High Sun come to a decision?" I asked casually.

"He has." The man fingered the laces on his moccasins. "Coosa is a complicated place. Certain balances need to be maintained, and the High Sun's position is never secure."

We waited.

"The mikkos were right. Had we taken the steps you suggested—evacuate the towns, disperse the people, burn the granaries, send the warriors off in small parties to ambush the trails—it would have ended in disaster."

I gestured for patience as Pearl Hand was about to speak.

The tishu mikko continued. "But not in the way you would think. Rather—assuming the invader could be destroyed—some of the more rebellious mikkos, as well as certain factions of the Wind Clan, would see it as an opportunity."

"Perhaps even leading to the overthrow of the High Sun," I replied, seeing where this was going.

The tishu mikko nodded. "We might indeed be able to defeat the invader through the means you suggest. But doing so would tear this Nation into pieces. Mikkos would seek to settle old scores with neighbors; other elements would act to raise themselves and their lineages to the high chair." He smiled wearily. "What good would it do to win the war against the Kristianos, only to lose everything else in the end?"

"It may end that way anyway," I answered softly, hating the poisonous politics. "The monster might see to it himself. Especially if he decides to stay in Coosa, make it his capital. I told you, he has ships down on the coast. And nothing he's seen in other Nations will compare to Coosa."

The tishu mikko nodded as he continued to finger his laces. "I have served two High Suns during my life. The first was a fool. This High Sun is a remarkably smart man. There's a reason tribute is paid to us from as far away as Chiaha. And lest you think he doesn't understand the risk—given what you told him, and what the messengers have relayed—he knows perfectly well what will happen when the Kristianos arrive here."

Pearl Hand interjected, "Then you must get him out of Coosa. The monster *will* take him captive. And once surrounded by the soldados and cabayeros, there is nothing you can do to save him."

The tishu mikko gave her a faint smile. "Your concern for Coosa and the High Sun is appreciated, lady. The High Sun, however, believes that he can best serve his people by meeting the Kristianos in peace and acceding to their demands."

I patted Pearl Hand's knee. "Then we have no further purpose here."

"That's what I have come to talk to you about. The invader is on his way. While there have been no repetitions of the events in Coste, we are not fools. Your warnings have been heard, Chicaza. And so far, the invader is doing just as you said he would . . . insisting the mikkos accompany him as 'guests.'"

I cried, "The High Sun is not just some local mikko!"

"Get him out of here," Pearl Hand growled.

"And allow some lesser but more ambitious mikko to gain status?" The tishu mikko raised an eyebrow.

"Then, what do you see us doing?" I asked.

He glanced around and lowered his voice. "What would happen if a message were to be delivered to Tuskaloosa? Perhaps one that offered an alliance against the Kristianos should things not go well in Coosa?"

I shot a look at Pearl Hand, seeing her indecision, then said, "Tuskaloosa is a charismatic and very competent leader. His acceptance would depend on a great many things. How much of an alliance are you talking about?"

"As many of our warriors as I dare strip from the outlying towns." He paused. "And the High Sun's niece in marriage."

"That, I'd say, will get his attention." I shot him a look. "You wish to fight here, in Coosa?"

"We'd prefer someplace between our territories. Perhaps in the thickly wooded hill country around Talisi."

I nodded, my heart sinking. I began to understand the High Sun's strategy. "And who would command the Coosa forces?"

"As tastanaki, I would. Assuming, of course, that the Tuskaloosa will accept me and my warriors under the White Arrow."

"The right place for a combined attack would have to be chosen very carefully," Pearl Hand said thoughtfully. "Someplace where the Kristianos would be disorganized, unable to use their cabayeros."

"The Tuskaloosa mikko would know that better than I."

I smiled wistfully at that, a sense of loss sucking at my

gut. "An admirable solution. Brilliantly thought-out." And it took the fighting, the political liabilities, right out of Coosa and made them Tuskaloosa's. Not only that, if the attack went badly, the Kristianos would take their rage out on the Tuskaloosa.

"What do you think?" The Red Chief glanced at each of us.

I hid my disappointment. "A combined force of warriors, in the right ambush, would stagger the monster. And Power would favor the fact that two of the greatest Nations unified to accomplish the task."

"Assuming Tuskaloosa agrees," the tishu mikko added.

I considered the ramifications. "The High Sun . . . If he stays, you do understand he will be made a captive, his life forfeit when the fighting starts."

Blood Thorn whispered, "Your leader will lose everything in the end."

"He knows the risks but has no choice." The Red Chief turned grim. "Are you interested?"

The Coosa Sun was throwing together all the ingredients for a disaster—a series of half measures, compromises, and desperate gambles. I was on the verge of saying no when Pearl Hand reached out, squeezed my knee, and said, "We shall do everything in our ability to serve the High Sun in this task."

What? I shot her a look of incredulity.

Pearl Hand flashed me a warning look.

The tishu mikko smiled. "If we're to be partners, perhaps you might call me by my family name. I am just Tastanaki to my friends." That he had taken the title as his name was indicative of the authority and respect with which he was regarded.

"Tell the Coosa mikko that we will do our best, Tastanaki," I said, wondering why Pearl Hand had committed us to such folly.

For good measure, Tastanaki feasted us that night. We ate deep-pit-roasted elk, smoked turkey, smilax bread seasoned with juniper and bee weed, nut-bread patties, and blackberry cakes. We drank copious amounts of tea, smoked excellent tobacco, and I played Tastanaki two games of chunkey on the High Sun's court. I won the first by a single point, the second by two. Tastanaki, it turned out, was a very good player. Blood Thorn, as a novice, lost miserably and declined further humiliation.

By the time we walked out of the main gates, night had fallen, the heavens a sooty black flecked with stars. Patches of cloud made patterns of deeper black across the dome of the sky.

Fortunately enough fires were burning that we could pick our way among the buildings and make out the faint pale path that led to the river.

I took Pearl Hand's hand in mine, saying, "We need to talk."

"Yes," she said, "we do."

Blood Thorn, catching the undertones, gestured his understanding.

I veered to the left, taking the wide path that led down past the clan houses and several tall granaries. Ahead the river was illuminated by hickory-oil torches atop tall segments of cane that projected over the water. Beneath them young men worked to ply nets, catching fish attracted to the light.

The entire affair was carefully orchestrated, the nets

stretched out on canoes and gently lowered into the water. Then willing hands carefully pulled them in, dragging the catch onto shore. Once the nets were emptied, they were folded and loaded onto the canoes, and the entire process was repeated.

"Coosa is doomed," Pearl Hand said as we seated ourselves on the hull of an overturned canoe.

"I know. So why did you volunteer us for this nonsensical mission to Tuskaloosa?"

She rubbed the back of my hand with her thumb, shook her long hair back, and stared up at the inky sky. "Because the defeated have to go somewhere."

"I'm not following you."

"Here's the thing: De Soto might stay in Coosa. Eventually he's going to figure out that there's no gold here. Coosa is the biggest, grandest Nation of them all. Sure, the Tuskaloosa, the Natchez, the Chicaza, all need to be reckoned with, but Coosa would provide de Soto with everything he and his men need."

"Except gold."

"Like I said, eventually he's going to figure that out, Black Shell. But even if he doesn't, Coosa is doomed."

"If there was just some way to make them understand that these half measures . . ." I gestured my frustration.

"There isn't, so don't waste your time trying to find one. Even if the High Sun believed us, he couldn't order his people to evacuate, burn the food, and attack de Soto. Two-thirds of his northern mikkos would flock to the Kristianos, offering alliances in return for a chance at assuming the high chair. The fact is that Coosa is like a lump of mud. As soon as it gets wet it's going to disintegrate."

"Well, if the High Sun thinks he's got problems with

his mikkos, wait until the *Adelantado* moves into his palace. The man's smart like Tastanaki said, but de Soto brings a whole new kind of politics backed by the sword. Plot as he might, the High Sun is going to do everything de Soto tells him to."

"No question about it. And that's why we need to ensure that Tuskaloosa makes this alliance. Don't you see? If we can make it happen, the disaffected from Coosa have a place to go. From Tuskaloosa they can carry the fight back to Coosa. We can resume the kind of warfare that worked so successfully at Apalachee."

"Assuming Tuskaloosa agrees," I muttered. "He might waffle with the same finesse as the High Sun." I shook my head. "I don't know, wife. Sometimes I wonder if any of our people are smart enough to even understand the threat, let alone make the commitment to destroy it."

The day de Soto finally arrived with his Kristianos, we watched the High Sun's party emerge from Coosa. The spectacle was stunning, with hundreds of brightly dressed nobles, all spouting the finest of feathers, gleaming shell, and reflective copper. Like a great serpent they flowed out from the buildings surrounding the city. Above them all rode the High Sun, carried on his lofty litter. More than three hundred people composed the procession; another couple thousand commoners were watching from the surrounding fields, granaries, and rooftops.

The melodic sound of flute music and singing coupled with the rhythmic rumble of drums carried on the air. Around the peripheries, people danced gaily, unaware of the true nature of the venomous creature they were admitting to their capital.

De Soto's army emerged from the eastern trail, the *Adelantado* himself riding at the forefront of his cabayeros. Their armor was mostly polished, and they formed ranks immediately after emerging from the trees to present a wide front, perhaps eighty animals.

It suddenly struck home: Of the more than three hundred war cabayos that landed at Uzita, only *eighty* remained combat-ready for the vanguard? We were winning! Then came the soldados, forming their ranks behind the cabayeros. They marched out with precision, the clanking of metal carrying across the distance.

"So that is the great threat?" Tastanaki asked softly. "They do look impressive, but we outnumber them by the thousands."

Pearl Hand pointed a slim finger. "In an open field like this the massed cabayeros would slash your largest formations like giant arrows through a stand of cane. With your warriors milling in confusion, the soldados would smash into them, cutting, hacking, and shooting."

The war chief nodded. "I begin to understand."

"Good," I murmured. "Now, let's get in the canoes and be on our way."

"As tishu mikko I should be back there," Tastanaki said insistently. "Beside the High Sun. Just in case anything goes wrong."

"You will do better to convince Tuskaloosa to join forces," Blood Thorn replied doggedly. "You said your High Sun is a smart man? If so, why is he marching out to offer his empire to the monster without a fight?"

Pearl Hand and I glanced at each other, hearing the despair in Blood Thorn's words.

"Come on," I added. "Last time, Antonio almost

caught us. And if he does this time, we could be the spark that sets off a disaster."

We turned to the canoes, sixteen of them, with warriors to man the paddles. Our packs had been stowed, along with the Cofitachequi boxes, upon which the dogs perched, tails wagging with anticipation. Two large trade canoes were filled with Coosa's gifts for Tuskaloosa. And an ornate litter had been packed for Tishu Mikko Tastanaki so appearances could be maintained for his meeting with Tuskaloosa.

Two Packs watched from the side, his curiosity about the Kristianos warring with his desire to see us off.

I clapped him on his thick shoulders. "Be well, my friend. And thank you for everything."

He grinned. "If nothing else, you did a splendid job repairing my ramada."

"Whatever happens, don't be around when the Kristianos need porters. According to plan, the monster will order the High Sun to supply people. When he does, you—and your family—must be far, far away."

He nodded. "I understand. But I want to at least see them up close."

I remembered when I, too, had been so consumed. I pointed to the scars on my neck. "See them quickly, today, and be long gone by tomorrow."

"I need no scars of my own." He clapped me on the back, the impact of his mighty hands rocking me on my feet. "Who knows, I might see you in Tuskaloosa."

"Don't. There will be war and death there."

I clambered aboard as warriors pushed us into the current and promptly had a time with Blackie and Patches. They weren't used to canoes, and we wobbled until I managed to cow them into lying down on the packs and staying still.

One by one the rest of our flotilla launched, and as I looked back, it was to see de Soto riding forth with a man I took to be Ortiz, his translators in tow.

High Sun, it's already too late to save yourself.

We made good time, passing the towns along the Coosahachi River, making its confluence with the Coosa by late afternoon. The warriors—each hand-chosen for the task—plied their paddles with vigor, driving us onward.

Across from us, Tastanaki rode in a long war canoe with the sacred bundle containing the Coosa White Arrow across his lap.

We were gambling, but with how many lives? And while the High Sun was a smart man, he had doomed himself. Would Tuskaloosa prove any wiser? Coosa had been a near thing for us. But for the words of a blind hilishaya, we might have been hanging on squares, dying of torture as Antonio and his poisonous lord entered Coosa.

Our journey carried us downriver for eleven days; we stopped each night at a town, village, or farmstead where the locals immediately bowed to Tastanaki's orders and provided food, lodging, and provisions for the next day.

Where the river entered the narrows, Tastanaki ordered locals to help portage both canoes and packs for the four-day journey downstream to safer waters. As tishu mikko, he was borne in his litter.

Walking along, I couldn't help but notice Blood Thorn's worried expression. Matching his pace, I asked, "Something wrong?"

He glanced at me, a ghost of a smile on his lips. "We're

losing, Black Shell. Not only is the *Adelantado* better than we are at war, he's also smarter."

"I don't think so. It's just that—"

"Forget it, old friend. The Hichiti met him in friendship. That I could understand, after a fashion. They've been our enemies for years. Then, even with the Death, the Cofitachequi could have crippled de Soto's mighty army. Instead, for her own purposes, White Rose surrendered even the bones of her ancestors to him."

I was silent as Blood Thorn continued. "And then we travel to mighty Coosa. And what is the result? The High Sun—descended of a god, no less—hasn't the balls to fight. Oh, no. Taking the battle to the invader might offend some of his mikkos, or maybe lose him the high chair."

Blood Thorn shook his head. "So, old friend, what am I to think? The greatest mikko in our world thinks he can play it safe and pass the problem along to this Tuskaloosa. Why? Because he wants an easy way out. One without risk to himself or his fragile empire."

"Blood Thorn, I know it hasn't gone the way we thought—"

He cut me off with a chop of his calloused hand. "It's not your fault, Black Shell. Nor do I blame Horned Serpent. It's us. A sort of rot in our world and souls, something that eats at our very roots. We're not going to destroy the monster. For the sake of politics, we're going to destroy ourselves."

I was starting to feel the same, but I gave him a smile. "Tuskaloosa is a new Nation, different, with a scrappy high minko." But I wasn't sure I believed it.

Blood Thorn gave me a sidelong glance. "Horned Serpent chose well, my friend. You keep that beating heart of yours thumping away in your chest. But me? I'm starting to see death everywhere. Not like you think, from cabayos and *hierro*. We're just not *smart* enough. That's what's going to kill us all in the end."

"I don't believe that."

His smile was a fleeting, vulnerable thing. "No, Black Shell, I'm sure you don't."

At Talisi, on the Tuskaloosa border, we found the town fortified—a concession to their proximity to Tuskaloosa's nearest town, Caxa, a half-day's journey downriver.

The Talisi mikko, a grizzled old warrior from the Cougar Clan, greeted Tastanaki with a bear hug, turned over his palace, provided a feast, and was anxious to hear news of the Kristianos.

That night, after most had sought their blankets, Tastanaki and I sat up, prodding the fire with a stick. The Talisi mikko sat cross-legged across from us.

"This plan," the old mikko began, "it has merit. But Tuskaloosa is both cunning and skilled."

"How do we approach him?" Tastanaki asked.

"By serving his best interest." The old mikko took out his pipe, tamped tobacco into the bowl, and lit it with our prodding stick. He drew, puffed out an aromatic blue cloud, and added, "Much will depend upon what happens in Coosa. How the Kristianos act."

Tastanaki nodded. "A group of runners has already been assembled. One a day is being sent down the trails, each bearing the latest news. These will all carry the White Arrow, and we will inform Tuskaloosa as they arrive."

The old man glanced at us, eyes evaluative. "And if it

turns out that the High Sun has been made captive, that the Kristianos are acting disrespectfully?"

"Then Tuskaloosa will be more likely to accommodate an alliance."

"What of me?"

"The High Sun may order you to evacuate your town, burn the granaries, and have your warriors harass the Kristiano advance. If relations with the Kristianos remain friendly you may be asked to help lull the invader, carry his packs, and feed his army when it comes through."

I added, "And if the monster believes nothing is afoot, he'll probably leave the High Sun here."

"Let us hope." The old man pulled on his pipe. "But what you are doing . . . it will be dangerous."

Tastanaki gave the old man a thin smile. "More dangerous than being worked to death while chained to a line of slaves?"

The following morning we boarded the canoes and made the trip to Caxa. Nor did we catch the Tuskaloosa sleeping. On a long reach of the river, a sleek canoe launched from the bank, four young men within. Slim of build, with ropy muscles, they wore their hair pinned up, beaded warrior's forelocks hanging down. They paralleled our course just out of bow-shot, calling, "Who are you?"

I raised my trader's staff. "We come under the Power of trade, bearing a White Arrow from Coosa. We are bound by both."

They paddled a little closer. "Where are you going?"

"To take a peace mission to the high minko Tuskaloosa," I called back. "The Coosa High Sun sends his tishu mikko to the capital at Atahachi. We have news of the Kristianos."

The young men conferred for a moment. "Land at Caxa. We will inform the minko there." Then they bent to the paddles, their slim craft literally flying across the water. Our heavier canoes had no chance to catch them.

"Tuskaloosa watches his approaches well," Tastanaki said in admiration.

"Let's hope he receives us with an open heart," I added.

"You worry?" Tastanaki asked.

"But for the hilishaya's keen ear, what would our fate have been at Coosa?"

Tastanaki had no reply, but I could see his expression turn grim. The warriors glanced uneasily back and forth; their paddles kept us to the thread of the river.

And then it began to rain.

At Caxa, a flotilla of warriors launched as we came into view. They were waiting, backing water along the shore, and paddled out to meet us. Behind them, the small outpost town seemed to bristle with warriors. I noticed that none of the usual fishing craft were out with their nets or divers. It probably wasn't due to the weather.

"Greetings," I called, and tried to look noble in the pounding rain.

Tastanki stood, holding his White Arrow high. "I am tishu mikko of Coosa, ruler of the Red Moiety. The Kristianos are in Coosa. Under the White Arrow we seek counsel with High Minko Tuskaloosa."

Their leader—a warrior dressed for battle—stood in his canoe, his shield held to block the pattering rain, his bow strung. "We honor the Coosa White Arrow and will escort you directly to Atahachi town. A runner has been dispatched to the high minko. All will be ready for your arrival."

So saying, they paddled out to meet our small flotilla.

That afternoon, the weather finally broke, with beams of sunlight shooting through the puffy white clouds.

As evening fell, to my surprise, we were ordered not to make shore and camp, but to continue on. This we did, aided by the full moon. Meanwhile, one of the Caxa war canoes pulled ahead, the lead warrior rising to his feet. When snags or shallows appeared, he'd call the location, pointing, guiding us down the black water.

My biggest problem was the dogs. They kept whining, getting up, trying to turn around, desperate to pee. The Tuskaloosa—unimpressed—-refused to stop. I winced each time an "accident" happened on the packs. Coupled with weariness, stiff joints, and an aching butt, it did little to lighten my mood.

Just before dawn we were allowed to camp, our warriors so exhausted they couldn't have committed treachery even if they'd wanted. It seemed as if I'd barely closed my eyes before we were awakened and ordered into the canoes.

Pearl Hand nudged me and pointed. Tastanaki whacked one of his warriors who was yawning, and I heard him say, "Look sharp! Do you want these Tuskaloosa to think we're weak and sleepy? Your honor's at stake."

Four days later we arrived at Atahachi town a little after dawn, exhausted, cramped, and bleary-eyed. The capital lay on the river's southern bank, just off an oxbow below the confluence of the Tallapoosa and Coosa rivers. The town itself was set back from the floodplain atop a low terrace with well-drained soils.

As the canoes were pulled ashore by willing locals, we clambered out, taking steps like old men. The dogs bailed over the sides, wading in, some of them urinating and defecating right in the water.

Nevertheless, a yatika was waiting, his staff of office in hand. I found my trader's staff, while Tastanaki climbed into his litter chair and was lifted. I took the lead, calling my traditional if fatigue-slurred greeting.

Tastanki was carried forward, the White Arrow held high as he cried, "Commanded by the High Sun of Coosa we seek to have counsel with the high minko Tuskaloosa. We bind ourselves under the White Arrow and come in peace with news about the Kristianos."

The yatika raised his arms. "By order of the high minko Tuskaloosa, you are welcomed and received. A house has been made ready for you. You will wish to rest, eat, and refresh yourselves. If you will come with me, your packs will be delivered."

"We are grateful for the high minko's hospitality. But one thing first, good Yatika. Runners are being dispatched from Coosa with updates on the Kristianos and their actions. We ask the high minko to pass these men under the protection of the White Arrow. Their reports are for both of our benefits and will determine the direction of our negotiations."

"Your request will be honored, great Tishu Mikko. Come. Let us see to your comfort, and then, when you have rested, the high minko will be pleased to meet with you."

I glanced around the canoe landing, filled with locals come to watch our arrival. I'm sure we made a spectacle, blinking, stumbling, asleep on our feet. Trade ramadas stood off to each side, and behind them several granaries had been built on high-stilted legs, their floors hopefully above flood stage.

The capital itself was small, consisting of two smaller mounds for a charnel house and temple, and across a plaza, a higher mound that supported Tuskaloosa's palace. While the Coosa warriors played their flutes, we followed the path around irregularly spaced houses, ramadas, mortars, and gardens, and I struggled just to hold my trader's staff high.

Tastanaki's Coosa warriors marched, heads up, backs straight, trying to look as impressive as they could after agonizing days in the canoes. I kept the dogs at heel with Pearl Hand's help and wasn't even enthused at the sight of the plaza with its stickball field and chunkey courts.

The house provided to us was just off the plaza, to the right of the high minko's palace. The place had a wide porch, clay-plastered walls, and a peaked roof constructed of split cane over bark.

We stumbled into the dim interior, finding beds covered with finely tanned deer hides.

Pearl Hand grinned, walking over to the bed and flopping down. I climbed in beside her, hearing the poles squeak under our weight.

"If you're feeling amorous," she murmured, "forget it." And then she was asleep. Moments later, after calling the dogs in, so was I.

THIRTY-FOUR

I WAS AWAKENED FROM DREAMS OF WAR AND DEATH by a gentle voice calling, "Black Shell? Are you going to sleep your life away?"

I pried an eye open to see Tastanaki's grizzled and tattooed face staring down at me. I hoped that I didn't look as used up as he did. I groaned and stretched, wincing.

"What time is it?"

"A little after sunset. The priests just sang the blessing."

I sighed and slid my feet over the edge of the bed. Pearl Hand muttered and shifted, rolling to her other side. I shook her. "Come on, wife. Time to get up."

"Go away," she mumbled, opened her eyes, and stared petulantly at me. "You're serious?"

"Uh-huh."

She shoved me away and kicked her feet out. Then she made a face. "Is that you or me I smell?"

"If it's moldy river mixed with stale sweat, that's you."

"Be as charming as you like. It'll get you nowhere."

Tastanaki straightened. "The high minko will see us in a hand of time. He's apparently very interested in what we have to say."

"Let's hope," Pearl Hand groused; then she yawned.

I winced. "Gods, wife! Don't breathe on me. If it takes all our trade I'll get you a willow-stem toothbrush."

"Two Packs is looking better all the time."

I turned my attention to Tastanaki. "How are the dogs?"

"They've been fed," he answered. "But keep your voices down. The warriors are still asleep."

I rubbed crusty stuff from my eyes. "Today I want to be a warrior. You can tell me how it worked out when I get up tomorrow."

Tastanaki wasn't impressed so I kicked Blood Thorn awake, and like me he winced from stiff muscles as he slipped off the pole bed and stood. With his sleep-puffy face he looked like an overinflated chipmunk.

On the porch we found jars of water and went about bathing. Pearl Hand washed her hair, and we began the ritual of dressing. After Coosa, who knew the sort of reception we were going to get? I felt that old shiver of unease. But for the old priest's words in Coosa, it would have ended in disaster.

I was tired of micos, mikkos, and minkos. Tuskaloosa was known as one tough and salty old boar of a raccoon. Like my Chicaza, he traced his ancestry back to the Sky Hand people and Split Sky City up on the Black Warrior River. Which, perhaps, is why he was so scrappy. His interest was in how he could add to his territory, prestige, and might. As though the ancestral shadow of the Sky Hand insisted he reestablish their glory on this new river where his kin had carved out a Nation.

Perhaps we should just load the dogs and head out . . . To where?

Futility and frustration sucked at my heart. After half a year of disappointment by leaders and Nations, was the fight even worth it anymore? How did one make a high chief see past his own selfish goals? From the time we'd left Apalachee, trying to do so had proven fruitless.

We can't beat the Kristianos when we've already beaten ourselves!

By the time we were ready, night had fallen. Tastanaki climbed into his litter and was lifted by his carriers. Clutching my copper mace, we made our way across the corner of the plaza to the ramp leading up to the palace. The air smelled of wood smoke, latrines, and moldy thatch.

The yatika came down, nodded, and asked if we were ready.

With him in the lead, we climbed the steps to the covered veranda, where Tastanaki was lowered. At the door, the yatika announced us and led the way in.

Like all palaces, this one was opulent—a dwelling fit for a high minko with its wall hangings, carvings, and brightly painted walls.

A gay fire—logs laid in the cardinal directions—crackled and spat sparks toward the lofty ceiling, where smoke escaped through a gap in the roof.

High Minko Tuskaloosa sat on a three-legged stool covered with panther hide. I was back in the west, where each leg represented one of the worlds: Sky, Earth, and Underworld.

Tuskaloosa's claim to fame—outside of being high

minko and a terribly tough character—was his stature. Everything about him was oversized; he towered a full head over the tallest of his subjects. This night he wore a white linen cape embroidered in black with images of falcons. The high minko had chosen white paint for his forehead, the forked-eye tattoos around his eyes darkened with charcoal, his cheeks and chin finished in blue. The man's graying hair had been pulled back into a bun from which a marvelous display of eagle feathers radiated. His massive chest made the huge shell gorget hanging there look small. The piece was decorated with the sun-fire symbol surrounded by a square representing the world— the one with the winds on each side. A monolithic ax— the emblem of his office—rested in his large hands.

To the left stood his two nephews and on the right his tishu minko, Crying Falcon, head of the Raccoon Clan. The *thlakko,* or war chief, was known as Darting Snake, of the Panther Clan, of the Red Moiety.

It was said that being Tuskaloosa's thlakko wasn't an easy job. To my surprise, Darting Snake was a small man, missing his right eye, and his left leg was badly deformed, as if he'd once broken it in several places. He stood braced on beautifully carved crutches that gave him the appearance of being propped up by two rattlesnakes.

Beyond that, only a handful of nobles, kin, and oretas sat on the benches, watching us with sober curiosity.

The usual ceremony of smoking, praying, and drinking black drink was reverently conducted by Snail, the *alíkchi hopaye,* or high priest.

Like his counterpart in Coosa, Snail was an old man, simply dressed. A collection of ratty raven feathers had been poked into his grizzled hair. That he could be mistaken for a derelict indicated that he was considered to be enormously Powerful and without need of ostentation.

Then the yatika called, "Who comes forth with the White Arrow?"

Tastanaki stepped up to the fire, locking eyes with Tuskaloosa. "I am tishu mikko of Coosa, Red Chief, and war leader of the Coosa Nation. I come, bearing the White Arrow, by order of the High Sun of Coosa. I come in peace, blessed by the white Power, to discuss the possibility of an alliance with the Tuskaloosa Nation and its high minko."

"And the particulars of this alliance?" the yatika asked as Tuskaloosa sat erect, his face expressionless. His eyes, however, glinted in the firelight.

Tastanaki extended his arms, palms up in deference. "The High Sun has reservations about the intentions of the Kristianos. He would like to inquire as to the willingness of Tuskaloosa to join in military actions against the Kristianos should they prove treacherous. As a symbol of his intentions, the High Sun offers his niece, the lady Yellow Stem, of the Wind Clan, in marriage to Tuskaloosa."

Tuskaloosa touched his chin respectfully. "We are honored and amenable to further discussions. Does the High Sun request warriors be immediately sent to his aid?"

"Not at this time, High Minko. He will wait and determine the true objectives of the invader. Then—in council with his mikkos—warriors will be gathered and dispatched to a place to be mutually agreed upon. There, we hope that our combined forces will be able to crush the invaders. Spoils to be shared equally."

Oh sure, that's a recipe for disaster! Two armies consisting of old enemies, two war chiefs, and a fortune in Kristiano loot at stake? I met Pearl Hand's gaze, seeing the futility reflected there.

"We will carefully consider your offer, great Tishu Mikko." Tuskaloosa smiled. "And be it known that though we have been enemies in the past, among my people your skill, courage, and resourcefulness are respected"—he smiled thinly—"if not always appreciated. In Tuskaloosa, you are my guest under the White Arrow and will be treated accordingly."

Tastanaki touched his chin respectfully, carefully considering his next words.

Before he could speak, Tuskaloosa turned his attention to us. "So, this is the renowned trader Black Shell? Welcome. The same to you, Pearl Hand of the Chicora. And to you, also, Iniha Blood Thorn."

We must have all been gaping like idiots, surprised by his recognition and interest.

He made a gesture with the stone ax, as though shooing a fly with the heavy stone. "I had hoped that Power would bring you here." He paused. "Tell me, how has your reception been among the mikkos in the east?"

"With respect, High Minko," I said, stepping forward, the copper mace in my hand, "we have been treated honorably."

"But found your reception . . . shall we say, lukewarm at best?"

"That might be an appropriate word, yes." The penetrating look he continued to give us added to my unease. *Pus and blood, tell me he hasn't heard that I am akeohoosa.*

His eyes narrowed. "The stories they tell about you border on the fantastic. Some things I've learned from the local traders, those who either know you or know of you.

And most recently . . . well, it would amuse me to hear in your own words if such incredible feats are true."

I felt my heart fall through my stomach. "My companions and I are here under the Power of trade. You have my word. No matter what my reputation, I would ask that you do not hold it against the tishu mikko or prejudge his embassy. He is an honorable man."

His lips quirked. "You are not what I expected."

I pulled myself up the way a Chicaza noble should when he's about to be lectured. "Who I am, or what I might have done, is not at issue here. The threat posed by the Kristianos *cannot* be underestimated. If my presence here is in any way detrimental to the tishu mikko's embassy, my companions and I will happily remove ourselves."

"Remove yourselves?" He laughed and slapped his thigh. "I expected lightning to flash, thunder to boom, and Horned Serpent to be riding on your shoulder."

"Uh . . . Excuse me?" I think my mouth fell open.

"Black Shell, the Apalachee sing your praises as though you were a hero sent from the Beginning Times. Is that the sacred mace you were gifted with?"

"It is," I answered warily.

"According to the stories, you single-handedly rescued Cafakke's hilishaya from the monster's clutches."

"Single-handedly?" Pearl Hand whispered sourly.

I shot her a sidelong glance. "Yes, well . . . I had a little help."

Tastanaki was inspecting me with renewed interest.

Tuskaloosa asked, "How has your war against the Kristianos progressed since you left Apalachee?"

"Poorly, High Minko. The monster learned a valuable

lesson in Apalachee. Since that time he has approached Nations offering peace. The rulers meet with him, believing that he shares their belief in the white Power. Later they are taken hostage, and he seizes what he wishes. By the time Nations discover what is loosed among them, it is too late."

He nodded, then looked at Tastanaki. "The Coosa High Sun has already surrendered himself, hasn't he?"

Tastanaki looked uncomfortable. "While the High Sun has offered peace, he does not trust the Kristianos, High Minko. Fearing perfidy, he has sent me here."

Tuskaloosa began tapping calloused fingers on the stone ax. "If what I have heard is correct, the *Adelantado* will not stay long in Coosa. The question is: Will he head down to the coast at Ochuse, where his ships are supposed to meet him? Or will he come here?" He saw our surprise. "Oh, yes. The rumors we hear from the Pensacola are that his great boats are scouting the southern bays looking for good harbor."

"He'll come here," Pearl Hand said confidently. "He seems to be traveling from Nation to Nation, emptying their granaries and exploiting their labor. You'll be an inviting target."

Tuskaloosa nodded. "My thoughts exactly." Then he looked at Blood Thorn. "Iniha, you are supposed to have some Mos'kogee."

"A little, High Minko. But I still get confused. Each dialect is a little different." Blood Thorn touched his forehead.

"Tell me of Napetuca. What Holata Uzachile planned, how it all went wrong. Black Shell can help you find the right words."

Blood Thorn told how Holata Ahocalaquen had been captured through treachery and the steps the Uzachile had taken to effect his release.

"And the battle itself?" Tuskaloosa asked.

"But for the trader's dogs, I wouldn't be standing here today, High Minko. The cabayeros cut through our formations like a knife through hot bear grease. Then the soldados arrived and massacred what was left of the shattered squadrons."

Blood Thorn followed up with how war chief Rattlesnake had been captured, how the captive holatas had tried to revolt inside the city using only what they could grab hold of on an instant's notice.

Tastanaki seemed unusually cowed. But Tuskaloosa's thlakko, Darting Snake, was leaning forward on his crutches, listening intently.

Tuskaloosa asked, "Black Shell, you're Chicaza. How would you rate the Uzachile warriors?"

"Very competent, High Minko. Not as disciplined as Chicaza, but in a similar circumstance, no one could stand against Kristianos in the open."

I glanced at Darting Snake. I was used to seeing war chiefs smirk, convinced of their own inherent superiority. Instead the little man nodded thoughtfully.

I couldn't help but add, "High Minko, I am impressed by your understanding of the threat."

In a humorless voice, he said, "I try not to underestimate my enemies. I know the Apalachee. They fight as well as anyone. That they did not march out to be slaughtered teaches me a lesson."

Tastanaki hesitantly asked, "High Minko? About the possibility of an alliance with Coosa?"

"Noble Tishu Mikko, I would march to join Coosa in an instant. My only regret is that the High Sun did not comprehend the threat." Tuskaloosa was tapping his fingers on the stone ax again. "If the invader has him, he has Coosa. My problem now is what to do about it."

I could have fallen on my knees and kissed his feet.

Then he looked at us. "You've followed them, fought them from the beginning. Given the circumstances, I see two options: One, retreat from their path, deny the invader porters and food. Break our warriors into small and mobile groups, then attack from cover as the Apalachee did. Make them pay for every step while we try to wear them down.

"The second option is to see if we can lure the *Adelantado* into a place where we can kill him."

Tastanaki was staring at me as if in shock, probably remembering I'd told his High Sun the same thing. He asked, "What of the High Sun's offer to fight in Coosa?"

Tuskaloosa answered, "Tishu Mikko, unless the High Sun can escape as Cafakke did, Coosa and its territory belong to the Kristianos. I would rather control the ground, the circumstances, and the time to attack."

It was Pearl Hand who said, "If the Coosa people begin to turn against the invaders as they did in Cofitachequi, or if the High Sun somehow manages to escape, I'd say fight them the whole way. If the High Sun remains captive—hoping to get de Soto out of Coosa as quickly as possible—the Kristianos will arrive here with full bellies, primed with arrogance, and trusting the *Adelantado*'s leadership."

Tuskaloosa mused, "Assuming the latter, it would make sense that I do all I can to ensure that they have no suspicions, lead them into the trap myself."

"High Minko," I said, objecting. "That places you at unacceptable risk. At Napetuca, they killed everyone in retribution, even the women and children."

He nodded and gave his nephews an appraising look. "Black Shell, you, yourself, have already vowed to sacrifice your life. That was Horned Serpent's price, was it not?"

Where did you hear that?

He smiled, reading my expression. "Someday soon I will be an old man. We all die, Chicaza. But if I can kill de Soto in the process? How then would I be received among my ancestors?"

"As a hero," Darting Snake answered from the side.

Tuskaloosa gave the man a cunning grin. "But we have time yet." He raised his stone ax in salute to Tastanaki. "And we have allies. Meanwhile, as the Coosa absorb the Kristianos' attention—one way or another—we shall plan, prepare, and be ready when the monster comes. Even at the cost of our lives, he shall not leave!"

The next morning I was up early, too excited to sleep. After all the long trails, the missed opportunities, here was a chance to destroy the monster.

Or so I hoped. Ever since my conversation with Blood Thorn, I'd begun to wonder. Despite Tuskaloosa's enthusiasm, I could see doubt in Blood Thorn's expression. And why not? Since leaving Apalachee, every time we'd had the advantage, it was to watch it slip away and fade into disappointment.

Blood Thorn would just give me his infuriating smile and shrug, saying, "In the end, old friend, there is only death and defeat."

I stepped out into the predawn and took the dogs for a

walk through the fragrant morning mist. Blackie and Patches were coming along nicely, and while they hadn't completely worked into the pack, at least they were accepted.

My path took me through mist-shrouded houses and down to the river. While the dogs sniffed among the parallel lines of dewy canoes, I looked out across the smooth water. Sunrise silvered its surface. On my chest, the sepaya radiated heat, and I swear, at just that moment, a great serpent's back broke the water. I watched it slide, smooth and sleek, only to disappear amid widening rings.

Horned Serpent? Or just an old waterlogged gum tree raised by the current?

Making my way back through the canebrakes and up to the houses, I nodded to women stoking morning fires under their ramadas and smelled boiling hominy.

I left the dogs on the porch, telling them to stay and guard. Then I reached around for my chunkey lances and found my stone. As the first rays of sunlight cleared the trees, I paused respectfully while the hopaye, high on the palace veranda, sang the morning benediction.

I unlimbered my lance and cast my stone down the smooth track. My first cast felt wooden, the lance wobbling in flight.

As I loosened up, my skill seemed to return, and I was surprised when I saw Tuskaloosa emerge from his palace, a lance in one hand, a stone in the other. He strode up as if he owned the place . . . which, well, he did.

"Might I join you?"

"Of course, High Minko. For what shall we play?"

"Whatever you wish to trade for whatever I wish to."

"And your color?"

He gave me a thin smile as I looked up to meet his gaze. He truly was a big man. "Red," he said. "It fits my mood these days."

"To twenty," I replied.

"Done. As a guest, you first."

I took my mark, rolled, cast, and watched my lance embed itself within a hand's distance.

He whistled. "You have a reputation as a chunkey player. I shall need all the skill I have and the blessing of Power to win."

He rolled and cast, the lance a forearm's length away.

As we retrieved our pieces, he shot me a measuring look. "I am sending the White Arrow, along with gifts, to all the surrounding Nations. I hope to gain as many allies as I can, even if I have to give away my mace of office to do it."

"You won't have to," I told him. "We've got two boxes of trade—the best Cofitachequi had to offer. It was meant to fight Kristianos. Use it. And anything else of ours that you need."

"I thank you." He paused, a pensive look in his eyes. "Have you talked to your brother recently?"

"I am akeohoosa, High Minko."

He fingered his stone as we headed back to the marks. "Does that bother you?"

"It did. Once. Long ago. These days I am Horned Serpent's." I touched the sepaya.

He smiled slightly. "I would send the White Arrow to your brother. I think that the more allies we have, the better our chances. And, if it doesn't go well here, others should have a stake in the monster's destruction."

"I do not brag when I say there are none better than the Chicaza when it comes to a fight."

He grimaced. "Don't I know. I have made an alliance with the Albaamaha at Apafalaya. I would just as soon not have it destroyed any time soon."

"I've heard."

"Would it be wise to mention you when I send the White Arrow to Chicaza?"

"High Minko, I was branded a coward. Mentioning me might not be conducive to ensuring their heartfelt co-operation."

He watched me with hooded eyes as I rolled and cast. Seeing my lance land just beyond the stone, he said, "I have known many cowards in my life, Black Shell. You are not one."

"Thank you, High Minko." *Do I owe him an explanation?* "The day it happened . . . it was in a fight. I'll freely admit I was scared down to my bones. Then Horned Serpent's voice told me to run. I saw him . . . as if through a haze. And run I did."

"Did you ever learn why he called to you?"

"He said he was saving me."

Tuskaloosa cast, beating me by a finger's length.

"Perhaps he did." He looked at me. "When I think of the things you have done, survived, and the woman who has decided to share your life, I can think of no greater man alive."

"I am just a common trader, High Minko."

"That sepaya on your chest belies your words, Chicaza."

"It came at a terrible price." I fingered the pouch containing the sepaya.

The lines tightened around his mouth, then he changed the subject. "What do you think of the High Sun's plan to choose a place in Coosa and attack the Kristianos?"

"It's a disaster in the making—the needless death of hundreds. By now he and his nobles are captive. How could his warriors be induced to fight, knowing their High Sun would be killed the moment they attacked?" I gave Tuskaloosa a solemn look. "And if you go to de Soto as you are planning, become his captive, how can you motivate your own warriors to attack?"

He gave me a cunning smile, as if he were way ahead of me. "I'm thinking about Mabila."

"Mabila?" I was trying to follow his direction.

"You've been there?"

"It's downstream from here, a Pensacola town in one of the upland meadows, two days' journey beyond Piachi town."

"The forests are close by should things go wrong. The fields around the town could be cleared, and the palisade could use some work, but the houses are large, sturdy, and packed close. A lot of warriors could be hidden inside them, arms stockpiled. If we do this right, the Kristianos would have no clue anything was amiss until the last moment."

"Why are you telling me this?"

"Because there will be no battle in Coosa. His politics are too fragile. His lineage came to the high chair by overthrowing their predecessors in Etowah three generations ago. The Wind Clan has a long memory, and heirs to the old leadership still live, chafing over the fact that one of them no longer sits in the high chair. Nor can the Coosa trust his subordinate mikkos. Too many want to break away. The High Sun will do anything to rid himself of the Kristianos as fast as he can."

I nodded. "We think alike."

"And this tishu mikko?"

"A good man. Solid. And, I think, coming to realize the error of his ways."

"How do you think the Kristianos will treat Coosa?"

"As if they owned it. The High Sun is in trouble. He's smart and adept, but only as long as he can use his authority. He expects to manipulate the Kristianos by the same subtle finesse and intricate sophistication he employs with his council. Unfortunately the Kristianos are as direct and blunt as a swung club."

He thought about that, leaning on his long lance, the chunkey game forgotten. "I hear your words, Chicaza, and take them to heart."

"You have already made your plans, haven't you?"

"Mabila," he said, straightening.

"Why there?"

"Because I don't want to wage a war of attrition like the Apalachee did. I want to kill the monster and his *capitanes* in one blow. Then, as they flee, we can hunt down his demoralized soldados." He stared thoughtfully down the chunkey court. "Tell me, Black Shell, what would the outcome have been if *five thousand* fully armed warriors had been hidden in Napetuca instead of several hundred disorganized survivors?"

I paused, seeing it all in my head. "Five thousand warriors, in such close quarters, and the Kristianos without the tactical advantage of cabayeros . . . ?" I felt a spear of excitement.

He read it in my eyes. "Had that been the case, de Soto's forces would have been dealt a terrible blow."

"One they'd never have recovered from!" I cried, seeing the implications.

Tuskaloosa said, "My job will be to get him to Mabila without his suspecting that he and his army are walking into an ambush."

"And how will you escape before he kills you?"

"That's up to Power." He gave me a curious look. "And where will you be when the day comes?"

"Mabila," I answered. "Killing Kristianos."

THIRTY-FIVE

OUR PREDICTIONS AND FEARS FOR THE FUTURE OF Coosa were confirmed as the first runners began to arrive. De Soto had moved into the capital, occupied the palace, and taken over the fortifications.

The High Sun spent those first days as an honored and appreciated chief . . . until de Soto's forces—assured that no vast army was hidden in the surrounding forests—began to scour the country for women and loot.

The first atrocities were reported by local leaders, appealing to their oretas, mikkos, and lineage elders. When these made their way to the High Sun, he demanded de Soto make restitution or discipline the miscreants.

I could imagine the monster's reaction as he lounged about the palace, fingering the High Sun's wealth. I visualized his long face and droopy eyes; he would have yawned, deepening the lines running down from that thin nose to his small mouth. Turning lazily to his *capitanes,* he'd have said, "Place this filthy *indio* and his subordinates in confinement."

Nor were the High Sun and his local leaders the only ones who ran afoul of de Soto. From all over Coosa, mikkos came in a rush, anxious to have an audience with the invader and elevate their status under the new conditions.

They, too, ended up as "guests" of the Kristianos. Within a quarter moon, most of the nobles in Coosa were issuing unhappy orders to their people to provide food, porters, and women for the conquerors.

Keep in mind, our understanding of events was delayed by the weeks it took for runners to travel from Coosa to Atahachi. Then came the day when we were sitting in the shade of our porch. A messenger came trotting in, accompanied by several of Tuskaloosa's men.

I could see the sudden worry in Tastanaki's eyes, and sure enough, we were called to the palace.

The runner—another long-legged young man—was weary, haggard, and exhausted from his long journey. We hurried to meet him on the palace veranda.

Tuskaloosa stepped out as Tastanaki knelt by the runner, asking, "What news?"

The young man lowered his eyes. "Trouble, Tishu Mikko." Then he glanced up suspiciously at Tuskaloosa.

"You may speak. We are among allies." Tastanaki gave him a reassuring smile.

"The atrocities have continued, but the people have had enough of their wives being raped, their possessions taken, and the young people made to work. In violation of the High Sun's orders, they picked up in the middle of the night and ran into the forests, fleeing every which way."

"Go on."

"The Kristianos reacted immediately, sending out sweeps of cabayeros and soldados, rounding up anyone they could find. These were driven like hunted deer into the fields, where they were chained by the neck." His eyes were anguished. "They are made prisoner in *their own Nation!*"

"And the High Sun?" Tuskaloosa asked.

The young man blinked, lowering his head. "He, too, has been chained and paraded around Coosa as a symbol. Surrounded by Kristianos, he orders the people to do as the Kristianos tell them and to make no trouble."

"But not everyone is obeying?" I asked.

The young man shook his head. "I heard of an attack. A group of warriors—angered by the actions of the invader—ambushed a party of soldados on one of the forest trails. One of the Kristianos was slightly wounded. That's all. The warriors escaped, but the *Adelantado* has ordered that if anyone so much as threatens a Kristiano in the future, an oreta or mikko will be taken from among the captives and burned alive. If a large force marches on Coosa, the High Sun and his family will be burned."

"He would do that?" Tastanaki cried.

Tuskaloosa beat me to the punch. "He did it in Apalachee. Why would he treat Coosa differently?"

Tastanaki swallowed hard and lowered himself to the matting, eyes vacant. "Then there is no way Coosa can mass its forces and free our High Sun."

"No," I replied gently. "Your High Sun has been played like a fish in a net. If there is a fight, it will be here, in Tuskaloosa."

He nodded, the look of defeat about him.

"Mabila," Tuskaloosa whispered. "But in case events in Coosa miraculously change, we still need to be able to evacuate our people, burn the towns and granaries, and fight his advance." He turned. "Thlakko?"

"Yes, High Minko?" Darting Snake clomped up on his rattlesnake crutches, his mangled leg swinging. He arched his brow over the gaping socket of his right eye. The effect was chilling.

"The towns of Caxa, Casiste, Hamata, Uxapita, and the other upriver settlements must prepare for one of two eventualities. In the first, women and children must be ready to evacuate, but tell the minkos that any able-bodied men must remain. I want the towns to appear lived-in should I have to go there and meet with the invaders."

"And the second?" Darting Snake asked.

"If Coosa miraculously rises against the Kristianos, and the invaders fight their way here, the towns are to be burned at the last moment and the men are to flee. In that event, the trails must be blocked with trees, ambushes laid at any narrow protected place. Our warriors must be told that any Coosa war parties will be treated with the greatest respect and added to our own forces."

"I understand, High Minko. As per our prior conversations, I've already taken such steps."

Tuskaloosa looked at me. "How many porters will he demand?"

"Four hundred at least."

Tuskaloosa glanced at Darting Snake, who simply nodded.

"Meanwhile, what of Mabila?" I asked.

Darting Snake hunched on his crutches. "Work has already begun on the fortifications; excess food is being removed from the granaries and hidden in surrounding towns and in the forest for our use—with sufficient left in Mabila to feed the arriving warriors. I have figured the number of baskets against the expected number of warriors to leave a thirty-day supply. Should anything go wrong, we can still burn Mabila and the surrounding towns at the last minute without starving the people."

"And the plans for Atahachi?" Tastanaki asked.

Darting Snake's expression didn't change. "As soon as the invader approaches we will evacuate all families, leaving only enough men here to serve as porters. Food stores, and the upcoming harvest, will be removed to the forests pending our return."

"Good." Tuskaloosa looked down at the runner. "And in the meantime, brave Coosa, may Power protect your High Sun."

After a week of drenching rains, we learned that de Soto was on the move. True to form, he kept the High Sun and the nobles, taking them with him to Etowah, where the swollen river delayed his march.

"Etowah?" Pearl Hand asked. "That's *south* of the Coosa capital. You don't think he's headed back to Toa, then down to Apalachee again, do you?"

"And leave Tuskaloosa unmolested?" Blood Thorn scoffed. "No, he'll come. He's bringing death here. I can feel it."

The next messenger related how the Ulibahali town mikko had—of his own accord—rallied his warriors, defended his city, and laid out a line of battle before the advancing Kristianos.

"At the last moment," the latest runner told us, "the

High Sun himself was carried out. He ordered the Uliba-hali mikko to lay down his arms and disperse his warriors. It broke people's hearts, but they did as ordered. The *Adelantado* slept that night in the mikko's palace. And now the poor mikko's wives and nieces are passed from one soldado's bed to the next. The mikko is chained among the slaves; he carries a heavy box full of *hierro*."

Tuskaloosa sat back thoughtfully. "And there, my friends, is our answer: There will be no fighting in Coosa. The High Sun will ride in his litter to the Talisi towns." He looked to Darting Snake. "Inform the Caxa minko to begin the evacuation of the women, children, and elderly."

He next turned to his younger nephew, Bluebird. "Prepare your things. From Caxa you will journey upriver to the Talisi towns and meet with the invader. Your duty will be to greet de Soto, ask him politely to release the High Sun, and inform him that I will be waiting in Caxa town with porters to carry his supplies to Atahachi."

"Yes, Uncle." The young man straightened, very full of himself.

Tuskaloosa gave Tastanaki a smile. "Would you send a runner to the Talisi mikko? I need him to get word to the Coosa High Sun any way he can. Tell the Coosa that we will value any warriors he can spare. Have them travel by the back routes to Mabila. Darting Snake has seen to establishing provisions along the trails to ensure that they are fed along the way."

Tastanaki gathered himself, a new, flintlike edge to his resolve. "It will be my honor, High Minko." In his mind, he was already killing Kristianos.

Pearl Hand asked, "Can you be certain that this is the best way, High Minko? Going among them yourself?"

He smiled at her. "Great lady, you have told me everything you know about Kristianos." Then he reached out, placing a large hand on her shoulder. "No one but I can successfully lure them into the trap. I have learned from the mistakes others have made before me, so I am prepared and know the game I must play. As their captive, I will trick them into believing all is well."

"I should go with you," Pearl Hand stated matter-of-factly, "as your wife or servant. I can listen in on their conversations . . . tell you exactly what they are planning."

"What?" I cried, jerking around to stare at her.

"No," Tuskaloosa said solemnly, "you should not. As much as I would value your advice and skills, this Antonio has recognized you every time. By now they know that Concho Negro tried to warn the Coosa. They undoubtedly know you came here. Perhaps they even know of the tishu mikko's involvement. Why else would they have insisted that the High Sun's niece Yellow Stem accompany them, if not to deprive me of a reason to ally with Coosa? Should they recognize you, they will know I am leading them into a trap."

"Are you always this smart?" Pearl Hand asked, irritated that she'd been outmaneuvered.

"Were I not, my cousin would be high minko today. Alas, he's with the ancestors, and I sit atop the high chair." Then he turned serious again. "Your place is at Mabila with your husband. No one has killed more Kristianos than you. So, once there, you will lecture my warriors on how to kill more."

"They will listen to a woman?" she asked.

"Oh yes," Darting Snake called from his crutches. "And with rapt attention after I persuade them to."

Tuskaloosa stood, stretching to his amazing height. "The Kristianos are on the move to Talisi. We don't have much time. Thlakko?"

"Yes, High Minko."

"I would appreciate it if you would accompany Black Shell's party to Mabila. Show them what we have in mind and seriously consider any criticisms they make about our defenses."

"It will be my pleasure, High Minko." He turned his single eye on us. "Let's figure out how to really kill Kristianos."

Tuskaloosa gave everyone a bitter smile. "It has fallen to us to make an end of this. May the Power of the three worlds be with us."

"Akasam," I whispered. "May it be so."

The evening after that final meeting with Tuskaloosa, we were on the river, part of a flotilla of thirty canoes—most filled with warriors—heading down the oxbows toward Piachi town.

We didn't see Tuskaloosa's departure from his capital; accompanied by several hundred warriors he started upriver, riding high in his ornate minko's chair.

Pushing hard, we arrived at Piachi on the fall equinox, just after dark. The town—founded by a group of disaffected Pensacola from the south—stood atop a high bluff overlooking a loop of the river. We landed, grounded our canoes, and made the long hike up to the town gates.

There we were greeted by the minko—an irascible and independent-minded young man. Only at Darting Snake's insistence did he finally order food to be brought, a house prepared, and camping facilities for the warriors accompanying us.

"He doesn't seem at all cowed by Tuskaloosa's authority," I noted during supper.

Darting Snake gave us a thin smile. "Our Nation is composed of many different peoples. The eastern talwas are descended from Coosa, the central ones from Sky Hand—relatives to your Chicaza—and the western talwas from the Pensacola. To the northwest lie the Albaamaha talwas governed by Apafalaya Minko. The secret of Tuskaloosa's success is that he doesn't interfere with local politics or traditions. But when it comes to security, he's the first one there with warriors, or canoes full of food should a crop fail." He smiled grimly. "No one challenges his authority. More than once, he has challenged a rebellious minko to single combat."

"And when his nephew finally ascends the high chair?" I asked mildly.

Darting Snake's inscrutable expression didn't change. "Then we shall see if he's learned his uncle's courage and if Power has given him the intelligence to rule."

I began to appreciate and respect Darting Snake. The little man was no one's image of a warrior as he stumped about on his crutches. In most Nations he would have been discounted immediately. He'd killed no enemies, claimed no valiant combat honors, but when it came to war, no detail eluded his quick attention.

"How many Nations are sending warriors?" I asked.

"Some Coosa have already arrived. The Albaamaha towns at Apafalaya have volunteered warriors. We have almost a thousand Pensacola. Word has come that the western Yuchi and the Chicaza are sending forces." Darting Snake smiled wickedly. "Everyone is looking for Kristiano spoils."

"And there have been no problems?"

"My deputies have strictly enforced the White Arrow." He ran a hand down his twisted leg. "While old grievances smolder below the surface, the chance for glory and booty outweighs them."

He studied us with his dark eye. "Blood Thorn has told me that shooting at Kristianos is like pitching cactus spines at a turtle."

"Even a turtle is vulnerable if you know where to aim," Pearl Hand replied.

From Piachi we traveled overland, Darting Snake borne on a litter. For two days the trail took us west through upland forests of chestnut, oak, and pines. Isolated meadows were studded by mulberry trees. It was raining when we entered the first of the black-clay meadows, and the sticky soil clung to our feet with each step. The trail crossed lush grasslands, and stands of tall cane grew in the low spots.

The town of Mabila sits on a wide plain surrounded by forest. Within a couple of hands' walk to the east, west, and north are smaller towns, and the entire area is filled with farmsteads, granaries, and fields.

I could see why Tuskaloosa picked the place. Mabila had a relatively new palisade made of thick logs interlaced with vines and saplings; the whole of it had been plastered over with the hard local clay. Bastions jutted out every fifty paces, allowing archers to loose arrows on attackers.

Within the walls were eighty-some buildings, consisting of a couple of charnel houses, granaries, clan houses, men's and women's houses, and ordinary dwellings. Though tightly packed, the houses were spacious inside. The narrow spaces between them were shaded by occasional giant hickory trees that rose from their midst. Mazelike passages—so close the heavy cane roofs almost touched overhead—ran between the densely packed houses.

Dancing Snake's deputies had already been at work. Holes had been cut through each building's plaster walls. Defenders could shoot point-blank at enemies in the narrow confines between buildings. Once in the maze, the Kristianos couldn't mass their forces or employ their mixed weaponry. They'd be confused, cut off, and ripe for slaying.

An elongated plaza sporting a World Tree and chunkey courts ran from the main gate to the centrally located palace. Atop a low mound no higher than my waist, the palace rose two stories, and a covered veranda fronted its entire width.

As we walked through the town, Dancing Snake took reports from his deputies. I glanced inside one of the houses. Stacks of bundled arrows and bows, along with several wicker shields, had been placed atop the sleeping benches where they abutted the walls. Even as I stood there, a young man shouldered past with an armload of war clubs.

Dancing Snake had taken seriously the lessons of Napetuca.

As evening fell, I took my wife's hand, and we walked through the camps of warriors. Individuals filtered through the soft fall light, calling in search of friends, while deputies trotted out to meet them, giving directions to various encampments.

We walked out from the town walls to the barrow pit, where clay was dug to be mixed with grass as plaster or turned into pottery. Rain had filled the excavation to create a moderate-sized pond. Along the edge, evidence of recent digging could be seen where clay had been extracted for use on the walls.

Staring out at the placid water, its surface golden in the sunset, she said, "Well, here we are, ready to spring the final trap."

"It's been a long time coming," I replied, giving her hand a squeeze. "What if the Hichiti had planned this instead of greeting de Soto like a long-lost friend? What if they'd trapped him between the might of their warriors? Or—even after the Death—we had been able to muster Cofitachequi's warriors to ambush the remnants as they stumbled out of the forest?"

"You'd be White Rose's husband? . . . With me as your willing concubine?"

"Now, that would have been a match, wouldn't it? Like Piasa and a Thunderer sharing the same bed."

"I don't know. You're a talented lover. What you couldn't persuade her to do through logic might have tumbled to the magic you keep in that hard shaft of yours." She bumped me playfully with her hip.

My eyes on the water, I said, "Cofitachequi is dying. When White Rose seats herself in the high chair, she'll just bring rot to the corpse."

"And Coosa?"

I watched a fish jump, rings widening. "De Soto is a black cloud of disaster blowing across the land. Where he goes, ruin follows."

"What about Tuskaloosa?"

I rubbed my forehead. "He's going to die. I don't know enough about his heir to guess at the future, but if he has half of Tuskaloosa's abilities, perhaps it will work out all right."

"Provided we kill the monster here." Her gaze narrowed. "My biggest concern is the open ground around the town walls. The cabayeros will find it perfect."

"The plan is to kill the *Adelantado* and his *capitanes* behind Mabila's walls. Leave the cabayeros leaderless."

"And you don't think the surviving Kristianos will take offense to that?"

I tilted my head to give her a questioning look. "What would you do? Stay and fight, or try to head south to rescue?"

She chewed on that for a while. "The soldados have wanted to get out several times in the past. Recently life's been good. But take that away? You could be right."

"Our warriors will chase them all the way to the coast. That armor they wear, the very scalps on their heads, will ensure that. A warrior who kills a Kristiano gains great prestige and wealth."

"If we kill de Soto," she said. "Everything hinges on that."

"And High Minko Tuskaloosa's trap."

Across the pond the far bank had taken on an orange glow. There, perched on a snag overhanging the pond, sat an anhinga, the first I'd seen in so long.

Even as our eyes met, the bird dove. To carry what message to the Underworld? Staring at the water, I wondered if the Piasa was down there, staring back. The notion sent a shiver down my spine.

THIRTY-SIX

As we waited, fall—like a harbinger of the world's impending death—came to Mabila. Great vees of geese, herons, loons, and ducks winged overhead on their way south. Each morning the sun edged its way farther down the horizon. A chill crisped the mornings, and the first fruits of the harvest found their way to the warriors' camps.

Rather than dwell on the coming cold, darkness, and storm, Dancing Snake made sure our days were fully occupied. We taught warriors where to aim in order to make a killing or wounding shot on an armored soldado.

Every night, by the light of crackling fires, we told our stories. We lectured on Napetuca and what went wrong there. They heard of the battles around Apalachee and how to successfully ambush cabayos.

Each time before we were introduced the young men

grinned and elbowed each other, joking about Pearl Hand's beauty and whispering rude things into their friends' ears.

But when Dancing Snake fixed the miscreants with his single eye and introduced Pearl Hand as a nicoquadca, they lifted their eyebrows. After Pearl Hand began to speak, telling them of how many Kristianos she'd killed, they sat up respectfully.

Runners came each day, and we learned that Tuskaloosa had met de Soto in Caxa town. Together they were proceeding to Atahachi. Apparently Tuskaloosa relished his role: De Soto had given him a cabayo to ride. Nevertheless, the monster's *capitanes* rode in advance to scout the trail.

"Does that mean he doesn't trust Tuskaloosa?" Blood Thorn wondered one night.

"Or else they know we are here." Pearl Hand—sitting on the bench—propped her chin on one hand.

"Give the high minko time," I told them. "Even if they are suspicious, Tuskaloosa's not in chains yet."

"But surely they are suspicious," Blood Thorn said insistently. "They can't help but notice that the women and children aren't in the towns they pass through."

"Patience," I told him. "So far there has been no trouble. Tuskaloosa planned for this. No women means no chance for angry relatives sneaking up to shoot arrows at wandering soldados."

"He's right," Pearl Hand added. "The important thing is that de Soto's belly is full, his packs are being carried, and he's got Tuskaloosa at his side being a good little minko."

"You call him little?" I arched an eyebrow.

"All right, so he's a big little minko."

"And"—I made a face—"the *Adelantado* has given him a cabayo to ride?" I tried to form an image of the giant Tuskaloosa on a Kristiano cabayo. "Never, dear wife, has the mighty *Adelantado* given a chief a cabayo of his own. That tells me that Tuskaloosa is playing his game well."

The next day word came: De Soto was in Atahachi. The monster was only days away.

The runner arrived by swift canoe, trotting overland with great haste.

The hollow sound of the conch horn called all deputies to the palace. We arrived ahead of most, and Dancing Snake motioned for us to come up onto the veranda.

When the others had assembled, the thlakko asked, "What news?"

"Possible trouble," the runner told us. "The Piachi minko placed a formation of his warriors before the town. Tuskaloosa ordered him to desist, and he did. But the damage is done.

"Then, to make matters worse, two of the Kristianos wandered away into the forest to pick chestnuts. Apparently a party of passing Coosa—headed here—ambushed them. Both Kristianos were killed, ihola'ka taken, and their bodies mutilated."

"And the high minko? Is he all right?"

"He is," the runner said. "The Kristianos were enraged. They demanded the guilty warriors be turned over to them. The high minko remained calm, saying he didn't have them but would dispatch warriors to chase them down. They are to be delivered here, to Mabila. If they are not, the *Adelantado* promises to burn the high minko alive in the plaza."

Growls went up from the warriors.

"Enough," Dancing Snake said. "What else?"

"The Kristianos have ordered the high minko to provide them with women. They are growing more suspicious with each town they pass, finding no women or children. The high minko informs them that here, at Mabila, women will be provided to lie with the Kristianos."

"Oh, yes." Dancing Snake chuckled. Accented by the missing eye, his smile was nothing nice.

"The high minko orders that you find twenty slave women, bring them here, and have them ready to dance upon the Kristianos' arrival at Mabila. There must be music, an almost festive atmosphere. Can you do this?"

"You!" Dancing Snake indicated one of the deputies with his chin. "Find the women. See to locating a drummer and men who can play the flute. That is your responsibility."

"Yes, Thlakko." The deputy pivoted on his heel and raced off across the plaza.

The crippled thlakko turned back to the runner. "When are they expected to arrive?"

"The morning after tomorrow. And there is one other thing: Upon their arrival, the Mabila minko is expected to greet the Kristianos outside the gate. Men are to be dressed in feathers and good clothing. The reception is to look authentic, festive. This is to allay the *Adelantado*'s fears and to mask the presence of any warriors foolish enough to show themselves."

"It will be done," the Mabila minko agreed. He was a middle-aged man, lacking in charisma and imagination but awed by the knowledge that a great battle was going to be fought in his town.

"Anything else?" Dancing Snake asked.

The runner smiled wearily. "Only that Power bless us."

That day was frenetic, squads of warriors being moved into specific houses, weapon stocks checked, and shooting angles inspected.

Anything loose, like baskets, large pots, pestles, and mortars, was removed to leave the paths and passages clear of things Kristianos could hide behind. Latrine screens and flimsy ramadas were torn down. Tours were made by the newest warriors so they knew their way around the labyrinth of houses.

Pearl Hand oiled her crossbow and carefully sharpened the metal tips of her weapons. Blood Thorn and I polished our swords. Locked in our heads was the knowledge that we would finally strike a blow for all of the dead, mutilated, raped, and murdered souls. Here, at Mabila, the decisive battle for our world would be fought.

All that day, the sepaya seemed to burn from an energy all its own.

De Soto comes!

The monster had left Piachi and was marching overland toward Mabila. The good news was that Tuskaloosa still hadn't been chained and, from the scouts' observations, was being carried by his litter bearers. Evidently, after Piachi, the *Adelantado* had taken away his cabayo. Given what I knew about the beasts—which was nothing good—I wasn't sure if this was a blessing or not.

We spent the day making sure that all was prepared. That afternoon the conch horn sounded, and all deputies assembled at the palace. Darting Snake and the Mabila minko stood atop the low palace veranda. The little thlakko called for attention, his leg hanging impotently.

"This is the plan," he shouted. "Look behind you down the plaza. At the far end is the gate through which the high minko will lead the Kristianos. He and the Mabila minko will bring them here, to where you are standing. After greetings, they will probably dismount and relax. Food will be brought. Those of you chosen for the honor will be here, lining the plaza sides, your weapons just out of sight. You job is to keep any Kristianos from wandering away from the plaza and looking into the houses. Stand in a line, shoulder to shoulder, smiling the entire time. Bring some kind of gift with you. A feather, a pot, I don't care what. When you are approached by a Kristiano seeking to pass, hand this to him and smile, as if giving him a present.

"We will continue this for as long as we can, keeping up the illusion that all is peace. At some point—as we all know—one of the Kristianos will figure it out. When that occurs, you will run for your weapons and attack."

People shifted, glancing at each other, some winking, others grinning, still others becoming uneasy.

Darting Snake gestured with his arm. "This is the major killing ground. Here, in the plaza. Your first targets are the leaders and—remember this—the cabayos."

Warriors nodded.

Darting Snake made a gesture. "When the fighting begins, *the gates must be closed*! Immediately. This is delegated to Wild Cat Mankiller of the Albaamaha. The gates must be guarded to the last man to trap the Kristianos inside.

"Meanwhile, the rest of you will be facing hardened, armored warriors. Expect them to push you back. When they do, fall back among the houses. Let them chase you through the narrow passages where warriors can shoot them through the house loopholes at close range. They should become disoriented, confused in the maze.

"Others of you have been given the job of securing the walls, manning the shooting towers. Your job is to ensure that the soldados outside do not come to the rescue of those we have trapped."

He resettled himself on the crutches. "When the *Adelantado* and his *capitanes* are killed, their bodies will be carried to the walls and thrown over. This is to dishearten the Kristianos outside, break their spirit."

Nods of assent passed among the warriors.

Finally, Darting Snake shouted, "Many of us will die. Those who do will be honored among their ancestors, granted passage to the Land of the Dead. Your descendants will sing your praises."

Shouts of "ahoo"s and "hau"s were called out.

"Does everyone understand?"

More "ahoo"s and "hau"s answered.

"All right." Darting Snake slumped on his crutches. "Go, and make your medicine, prepare yourselves."

The assembled warriors slowly trickled away. I could see Tastanaki leading his Coosa toward the temple, where huge pots of black drink had been boiled.

"What do you think?" Blood Thorn asked.

It was Pearl Hand who said, "It will be paid for in blood, but by this time tomorrow, de Soto's fate will be sealed."

"Providing nothing goes wrong," I muttered.

We had a private supper that night, me, Pearl Hand, and Blood Thorn. We carried our food to the banks of the barrow-pit pond and watched nighthawks give way to bats as the sun set in the southwest. What began as a brassy yellow sky darkened to orange, backlighting scattered clouds, then turned to a radiant crimson before fading to a deep purple.

Insects clicked and chattered in the grass around us, and far off, an owl hooted from the trees.

We shared pit-roasted venison, corn cakes seasoned with raspberries, and dried plums. Finally we finished off with mint tea.

"It's been a long trail," Blood Thorn said as he sat cross-legged, staring out over the sky-silvered pond. "Though it is just over a year from the day the Kristianos marched into Ahocalaquen, it might have been another lifetime—one more dreamed than lived."

I followed his gaze, seeing a small fish surface to send fading rings over the pond. Frogs croaked from the rushes that grew on the opposite side. The first stars had flickered into existence in the eastern sky.

"A dream life?" I mused, trying to think back to who I had been before de Soto. "Yes. One lived in another world."

Pearl Hand looked off to the east, flicking her long hair back with one hand, the gesture refreshingly feminine and vulnerable. "And to think he's just over there, camped but a short run away."

"Which means he'll be here early tomorrow." I started to reach for my pipe where it lay in my belt, but we had no fire to light it.

Blood Thorn said, "The scouts will tell us when he's on the road." He paused thoughtfully. "Even if we trap him in the plaza, it won't be as easy as Darting Snake thinks. These warriors have never fought Kristianos."

Pearl Hand and I both nodded, sharing the skepticism in his voice.

"What do you think?" Blood Thorn asked. "Even if everything works just the way Darting Snake has planned, what are our chances?"

Pearl Hand took my right hand and held it tight. "We've seen them fight their way out of ambushes time after time. Were this ambush sprung on anyone but Kristianos, it would be a massacre."

I sighed. "Somehow, they always have a trick, some advantage to fall back upon. I wonder what it will be tomorrow?"

We pondered that in silence, watching the stars emerge, some obscured by patches of cloud. Cool air had begun to descend, and the songs of warriors could be heard on the still night air as they sang to Power to bless them with skill and courage. How many of those voices would be silenced by this time tomorrow?

Later we picked our way back in the dark, seeing to the dogs and finding our beds. Pearl Hand looked around the crowded house. Warriors shifted uneasily in their blankets where they lay on sleeping benches and every open spot of floor.

Bending close, she whispered, "Let's take our blankets. Go somewhere we can be alone."

I gave her a smile, and moments later we'd rolled our bedding and walked quietly through the town and out the gate.

That night we shared each other over and over, sometimes with a passionate desperation that left us panting and exhausted, other times with a soft and gentle caring that implied we had all of eternity before us.

With Pearl Hand locked in my arms, I finally surrendered to sleep—only to enter a world of dreams filled with fires and death and the endless screams of dying men.

THIRTY-SEVEN

AS THE SUN CLEARED THE TREETOPS TO THE SOUTHEAST, Mabila was a hive of activity. Darting Snake made one last tour of the town, pointing out anything that might trigger de Soto's suspicion. Hobbling on his crutches, he issued orders to his deputies as if he were Breath Giver himself.

Pearl Hand and I had dressed in feathers, painted our faces, and donned good clothing; the jewelry we left behind. Ever tried to draw a bow with strings of beads draping your neck?

Blood Thorn had painted his face black, his expression grim. He told us, "Today I offer my life to Power. If I am alive come nightfall, it is because de Soto is dead. It's his life or mine."

"See that it's his," I said, clapping him on the shoulder.

The look he gave me—a haunted one, made piercing by his dark eyes—shook me down to my bones. "I had a dream last night. Water Frond hovered above the palisade, her body illuminated as if by a great fire. Her hair was blowing around and her dress flapping. She seemed to spread her arms wide, as though trying to draw me in."

"Telling you that this day you will avenge her ghost," I stated with false assurance.

"Today," Blood Thorn repeated, "de Soto will die, or I will."

We were placed at the side of the plaza, our house just behind us. The dogs—along with all of our weapons—were waiting just inside. When the trap was sprung, we would leap for the door, grab our bows, and unleash Bark and the rest of the pack on any Kristiano war dogs.

I took a moment, hugging each dog around the neck, petting him, telling him how brave I knew he was. When I got to Skipper, I took an extra moment, wishing he were somewhere else.

"You don't take risks," I told him. "You've too many aches, and you've already done your part."

He wiggled in my arms, trying to lick my face, as if to say, "Hey, I'm good for one last fight."

Then the sound of the war drum came from the palace. The Kristianos were coming.

Pearl Hand and I gave each other one last hug. "I'll be making love to you tonight," I told her, nervous like I had never been.

"And I to you, my beloved." She tightened her hold on me, nuzzling my neck. "You be careful today."

"You too." I pushed her back, taking the moment to stare into her dark and magical eyes. "Kill all you can, but remember, I'd prefer that you let a couple go rather than lose you."

"You can't lose me," she said, chiding me. "You'd die of boredom."

We walked out, taking our places. A solid line of warriors, dressed in their finest, created a cordon around the now empty plaza. Excitement filled their eyes, energy near to bursting in their tense bodies. On legs as springy as saplings, they rocked back and forth, joking, uttering barks of laughter, anything to vent the rising anxiety.

"This is the hard part," Pearl Hand told me. "Once the fighting starts, you don't have time to worry."

Blood Thorn nodded, his pom swaying with the motion. "Life or death. The gaming pieces are cast. My beloved Water Frond awaits."

Assuming his ghosts could find her. But I wasn't going to bring that up.

A conch horn sounded from the distant forest.

The Mabila minko was raised on his litter and borne down the plaza toward the gate. Wild Cat Mankiller and his Albaamaha touched their foreheads respectfully as he passed. Everything depended on that gate being closed at just the right time.

"Here we go," I whispered, staring up at the morning sun, now a hand's breadth above the palisade wall.

What had we forgotten? What had we done wrong?

Blessed Power, tell me that this time there is no traitor anxious to whisper into de Soto's ear. Tell me that he suspects nothing!

Thinking back, it had to have taken at least a hand of time for the monster's party to ride out from the forest, more time for the ritual greeting of the Mabila minko just beyond the gates. What should have been an eternity felt like the blink of an eye.

And then everyone stiffened, frozen in the moment, as the conch horn sounded, hollow and melodic.

Moments later the Mabila minko's litter was carried in through the gate. Then came Tuskaloosa atop his litter. To my relief he wasn't chained but looked regal, a tall feather headdress rising from a copper headpiece.

Behind him followed de Soto and his *capitanes,* all mounted, their cabayos prancing, sun shining off their polished armor. The warriors gasped at their first sight of men on cabayos wearing colorful cloth and shining *hierro.* The Kristiano banners fluttered from long poles. The invaders looked splendid and deadly as they clattered and clopped down the plaza.

De Soto rode in the lead, two war dogs trotting at his cabayo's side. He glanced around arrogantly, and I got a good look at his thin and bearded face. Those sleepy eyes were dismissive as they took in the long line of us, standing so obediently at the sides of the plaza. A derisive smile lingered on his thin mouth.

Soon, monster. Soon.

Ten, twenty, forty, or more of the *capitanes* rode their beasts in. I saw Ortiz, followed by Ears, and my eyes narrowed. *I owe you for Napetuca, you piece of two-legged filth.* The Southern Timucua wore his big wooden cross bouncing on his chest as he strode forward in a fine Coosa-made hunting shirt.

Antonio followed in the rear, still wearing the oversized armor he'd never fully grow into. His beard seemed a little fuller, his *puerco*-like eyes just as mean.

De Soto, Ears, and Antonio! Perfect! Power willing, I'd kill them all.

Finally the servants, dressed in reds, yellows, whites,

and blues, filed through the gate. Some of these carried packs bristling with swords and shields. I gaped in amazement: Many of the riders were unarmed; De Soto expected no ambush! The long months spent encountering submissive *indios* had lulled his suspicions.

I gave the *Adelantado* a fierce glare, fixing on the spot on his chest where I would drive my arrow.

Finally a squad of twenty additional soldados marched onto the plaza, their long spear-axes over their shoulders, and I counted four of the thunder-stick shooters mixed in among their ranks. To my delight, the long cords that set the weapons off were not smoking and would have to be lit before they could shoot.

I took the measure of our surrounding warriors, trying to read their expressions through the thick war paint. Each was identifiable by the distinctive designs on their aprons, and the way they fixed their hair. The majority had recovered from the initial shock and amazement and now looked eagerly at the packs that were being laid to the side of the plaza.

"Fools," Pearl Hand whispered, noticing their attention. "They've got to kill the Kristianos before it's theirs."

"They can have it," Blood Thorn growled. "I just want the monster himself."

Both the Mabila minko and Tuskaloosa were carried up onto the palace veranda, their litters lowered. My heart hammered like hail against my chest.

De Soto gave an order and dismounted. The lesser nobles, Antonio among them, collected the cabayos and led them off to the side. The leaders climbed onto the low veranda.

"Let there be dancing!" the Mabila minko called out.

Flute music and soft drumming signaled the dancing girls. They trotted out in a line, forming up before the dismounted Kristianos. Anyone who knew women could read their discomfort and fear. Kristianos obviously knew nothing of women. They just smiled, attention fixed on the female forms. I watched the men pointing, grinning, a gleam of anticipation in their eyes.

I dared a glance at Pearl Hand and saw her eyes, half-lidded and promising mayhem.

Heaping plates of food were brought around from the fires behind the palace and placed on the edge of the veranda.

"It's working," Blood Thorn whispered hopefully. "They don't look like they suspect a thing."

"It's early yet," Pearl Hand muttered from the side of her mouth.

And then, unbelievably, the soldados began to remove and stack their weapons off to the side. They were laughing, gesturing at the dancers, and some even dropped their helmets onto the pile and began to undo their chest pieces.

Yes! Take it all off.

Meanwhile the warriors surrounding the plaza had begun to sing and dance in time to the music. I wondered how the Kristianos would have reacted if they'd known it was a war song calling on the red Power—a promise of death and dismemberment.

I shot a worried glance at Ortiz where he stood behind de Soto, his line of translators so busy carrying on a dialogue that they didn't have time to so much as listen to the song.

The cabayos had been led off and tied, some to the

World Tree pole, others to the stickball goals. I smiled in anticipation as most of the cabayeros began stripping the saddles from the beasts, laying them to the side. Others were even removing the animals' armor. Giddy anticipation filled my breast.

Tuskaloosa stood beside de Soto and two of the *capitanes*. Ortiz—with Ears behind him—continued to dicker between the minkos and de Soto.

Kristianos flocked to the food and began serving themselves, dipping from the wooden trenchers, laughing, slapping each other on the back.

Several of the *capitanes* had seated themselves on the veranda. Meanwhile, other Kristianos walked over, inspecting the line of warriors, wondering, perhaps, why we were staring straight back.

Here, I realized, was where things would snap. What if they tried to push past and one of ours pushed back? The deputies interspersed along the line kept shouting "Hold!" between the words of their song, reminding the warriors to wait.

At the first opportunity, Tuskaloosa stepped off the side of the veranda and passed the line of warriors. As he ducked into one of the houses, de Soto stood thoughtfully, his sleepy stare fixed on the house. He said something to one of the *capitanes* and Ortiz. They, too, looked at the house.

That structure held at least eighty warriors, all crammed in the back, waiting for the horn call that would initiate the battle. I could imagine the high minko painting his face, arming himself.

Ortiz spoke to Ears, who spoke to one of his translators, who in turn trotted over to the house and peeked inside. The man lost no time hurrying back to Ortiz. Ortiz said something to de Soto, and a *capitán* started down off the step, his hand on his sword hilt. He shoved rudely past the line of warriors, reached the doorway, looked in, and called something to de Soto.

Pearl Hand translated, "He says Tuskaloosa refuses to leave . . . and the house is full of armed men."

"This is it," I murmured, and Blood Thorn tensed.

At that precise moment, Tastanaki—painted in red— appeared from behind the palace, heading for Tuskaloosa's doorway. De Soto shouted, "*¡Traiga le aquí! ¿Quién es?*"

Tastanaki glared insolently at the *capitán*, and the Kristiano grabbed the war chief's arm.

One doesn't offhandedly grab the Red Moiety war chief, let alone the one from Coosa. Tastanaki flung the *capitán* off the way a bear does a junebug. The *capitán* staggered, almost fell, then ripped his sword from the sheath. The blade flickered in the sunlight, arced, and I stared in amazement as Tastanaki's severed arm dropped in the dirt.

The war chief let out a bellow that became a blood-curdling scream.

Any need for the conch horn vanished.

Arrows hissed from Tuskaloosa's doorway and the loopholes cut in the house wall. Warriors were rushing out, screaming, bows clenched in their hands. Others held war clubs high.

"Let's go!" Pearl Hand shouted, and we raced for our house, our weapons, and the dogs.

Those first moments of the battle of Mabila were a blur of activity as we fought our way past warriors streaming from the house. Inside, we grabbed the weapons we'd stacked by the door, Pearl Hand cocking her crossbow. The dogs were barking, bouncing around, and outside was a cacophony of screams, shrieks, and bellows.

Emerging on Blood Thorn's heels, I saw that the plaza was a chaos of charging warriors and panicked Kristianos. Sunlight glinted from the shafts of flying arrows and gleamed off Kristiano armor. The dancing girls were scampering this way and that like quail before a bobcat.

I caught sight of de Soto; his nobles had gathered in a tight knot around him. As a unit they waded into the thick of the fight, slashing this way and that. By the time Pearl Hand and I made it to the plaza, the Kristianos were in the fight of their lives.

The dogs were right behind us. Bark wasted no time, launching himself at the first of the Kristiano war dogs. Blackie and Patches looked confused, but they came from good stock. They were on the first war dog Bark knocked off its feet.

Instinctively we ran for de Soto. He and his *capitanes* were surrounded by a flurry of warriors. Hate the man all you want; when it came to war, he was an awesome fighter. I could see no fear on his face, just a vicious half smile as he cut and thrust with his sword. A desperate excitement animated his eyes, as if the entire weaving of his life came down to this one final thread.

The lessons on aiming we'd taught so assiduously might have blown away with the wind. Warriors shot for the center of the chest, only to curse as their stone points shattered on *hierro* or their arrows thunked impotently into cloth batting. I watched a war-club-wielding warrior hammer a Kristiano repeatedly in the helmet, over and over, the force of his blows staggering the foe but never bringing him down.

Cabayos were loose, bolting this way and that in panic. As the terrified animals crashed around, warriors shot them full of arrows. The beasts screamed horribly as they toppled and died.

As if by dint of will alone, de Soto and his core group fought their way down from the palace to the center of the plaza. If I could just get close, de Soto was mine. But I'd come face-to-face with a Kristiano, blood streaming from a scalp wound. As the man lifted his sword to split my head, I shot an arrow into his open mouth. Stepping over his thrashing body, I nocked a second and found a target. One of the Kristianos had managed to mount and was slashing his way toward de Soto. The cabayero's head and chest were armored, but his legs appeared clad only in cloth. I drove the barbed point into his hip, seeing it sink to the fletching.

Beside me, Pearl Hand's crossbow twanged, and the iron-tipped point drove into the man's side. He swayed, staring down at his wounds, and someone leaped up, dragging him off the beast. The man, screaming his fear, vanished under a mass of warriors.

De Soto managed to rally his men, and as a unit they fought their way toward the gate.

The gate!

I stared in disbelief. It remained open, a beacon for the trapped Kristianos. Where, in the name of bloody pus, were Wild Cat Mankiller and his Albaamaha?

"Close the gate!" I bellowed, unheard in the din of screams, whoops, and clattering weapons. Blood Thorn heard me, turning, and, cursing under his breath, charged off for the gaping portal.

Antonio had vaulted onto a cabayo's back and was hacking his way for the gate, fleeing for his life. Unlike so many of the others, he hadn't had time to remove his armor, and even in the brief glance I had, I could see arrows bouncing off his breastplate like twigs off a stone.

Among warriors seeking to close with de Soto, Pearl Hand and I struggled to get a shot in the jostling crowd. Arrows were flying from all directions; the man beside me stopped a shot loosed by one of our people across the way.

De Soto had so many arrows stuck in his armor, they hindered his ability to fight. I watched him curse as he broke off the stubborn shafts he couldn't pull free.

Somehow, the Kristianos fought their way to the still-open gate, and there, dragging their wounded behind them, they spilled out into the open.

What had happened to Blood Thorn and his quest to shut it? I had no time to search for his body among the corpses and dying we stumbled and tripped over as we tumbled out in pursuit.

Had they not worn that wonderful armor, they'd have never made the gate. As it was, many looked as if they'd been slapped by a porcupine. Shafts stuck out of them like fur. As they fought their way into the field, most were limping, supported by their fellows. Blood soaked their legs or arms. Best of all was the terror shining from those once-arrogant bearded faces. Surrounded on all sides by a horde of screaming warriors, the Kristianos understood there was no escape. Eventually, despite their armor, an arrow would find a crack or exposed neck.

Shouts from behind surprised me, and I threw a glance over my shoulder. The throng of porters, slaves, and captives—their burdens laid on the ground before them—stood cheering and waving. They'd been left in long lines beneath the town walls. The guards, abandoning their charges, ran like frightened rabbits, casting whips, swords, and clubs aside. The hideous attack dogs milled, watching their masters flee, then glancing back uncertainly at the dancing, leaping, and shouting slaves.

When I looked back, the outcome was apparent. Cut off from further retreat, de Soto's small force was faced with the inevitable. One by one the defenders were falling, the ring of *hierro* ever smaller.

Fate, however, can change in an instant.

A trumpet sounded, and a squad of cabayeros emerged from the distant trees, dashing across the cornfields. It looked to be about sixty of them, lances held low. As fast as cabayos ran, they'd be here in moments.

THIRTY-EIGHT

"Pearl Hand!" I shouted as she recocked her crossbow and placed an arrow. I wasted another look at the charging cabayeros and cried, "The captives!"

She glanced at the long rows of them leaping and shaking their chains beneath the high town walls. Their heavy packs lay forgotten on the ground.

"But de Soto's getting away!" she shouted angrily.

"It's too late!" I pointed, and she followed my finger to the closing cabayeros. The bright anticipation in her eyes went dull. Together, we raised heels, sprinting toward the captives.

"Inside!" I shouted to the nearest. "Pick up your loads! Carry them inside the gate! You're rescued! Saved! Carry your loads into Mabila!"

They fell all over themselves, tangling in the chains, grabbing up boxes, bales, casks, heavy jars, you name it.

Nor were they alone. Not all of the warriors streaming out of Mabila were interested in pursuing de Soto's harried party. Loot creates a remarkable distraction. The slaves had plenty of help carrying the hundreds of packs and crates through the gate.

Even as we urged the last of the captives through the gate, their chains clanking, the arriving cabayeros slammed into the warriors boiling around de Soto's beleaguered party. My gut went cold. The result was as predictable as that of dropping a heavy stone onto a hickory nut.

For a moment, the deputies tried to hold their warriors, keep them in the fight, only to be lanced through the chest or cleft by a swinging sword.

"*Fall back!*" I shouted, trotting forward. "Fall back to Mabila!"

Granted, I could have bellowed my lungs out for the good it did. Another cabayero charge rid the remaining warriors of any desire to stand and die. In the ensuing panic, what they saw was me, waving my arms, gesturing for the gate. That, at least, they could understand.

I stepped to the side of the rush, waving them back through the gate.

The cabayeros could have killed another hundred of us had they followed up. Instead, once the attack broke, they formed up in a protective ring around de Soto.

All but one. I saw him race his cabayo into the stragglers, slashing this way and that with his sword: Antonio.

It made sense, of course. Someone was surely going to mention that he'd been the first one out the gate, leaving his leader to his fate. But even more were going to witness the string of dead warriors he was leaving in his solo charge.

"Antonio, you shit-eating maggot," I muttered under my breath, hurrying forward. I nocked a war arrow, drew, and waited as he thundered forward. Maybe I hadn't killed de Soto, but driving a shaft into Antonio would be a wonderful consolation.

Warriors fled before him like rabbits in a drive. I held my aim, trying to follow his face as he guided his cabayo back and forth.

Closer, closer. That's it.

I filled my lungs and bellowed, "Antonio! ¡Es el Concho Negro!"

He heard, pulling his cabayo up, glancing around until his eyes met mine. I saw a smile on his bearded face, a killing delight in his eyes. His heels slammed into the cabayo's sides; he galloped straight for me. I held my position, muscles tense as I watched him over the point of my arrow.

We were no more than five paces apart. His left arm lifted, the sword high for the killing stroke, and I released. Hitting such a small moving target as a human face is a tough shot under any circumstance. I watched my flashing arrow cut his left cheek, saw his helmet twist sideways as the shaft impacted against it.

Antonio jolted, his swinging sword forgotten. I threw myself sideways as he thundered past. I grabbed for another arrow as he spun his cabayo around, and I shot it into the animal's belly.

The cabayo stiffened, almost pitching Antonio from the saddle. Somehow he kept his seat, clawing at the shaft wedged between his head and helmet. The way he angrily jerked it out might have done more damage than the impact. He tossed it violently aside as I nocked another arrow. When he turned toward me, I could see blood streaming down the side of his face. An expression of fear mixed with anger gave him a savage look. He forced the cabayo forward, screaming curses, raising his sword again.

I readied myself. Time to finish this. But he lowered his head, watching me from under the brim of his helmet as he beat his cabayo right for me.

He's going to run me down.

I drove my arrow into the cabayo's chest, leaping sideways at the last moment. Antonio had anticipated this. He turned the great beast, heeling it around before I could recover.

Moving in close, he masterfully drove me this way and that. Scrambling for my life, I clawed for another arrow and dropped it as I jumped away. The whistling sword cut empty air a finger's width from my head. My own sword kept slapping my leg, constantly in the way as I tried to duck.

He's going to kill me.

Antonio kept the horse close, turning with each move I made, crowding me. Again his blade swished half a heartbeat behind me. My fate was but a matter of time.

The beast hit me in the shoulder, rolling me. I lost hold of my bow as I scrambled to one side on all fours.

Catching sight of the gate—no more than thirty paces away—I scrambled to my feet, desperate to escape. I ran for all I was worth, hearing the terrible beast closing.

I ducked right as Antonio thundered past. When was the accursed cabayo going to bleed out? The thing had two arrows in its guts.

"*¡Tú mueres, pieza de mierda!*"

I looked up, panting, to see him raising his sword for the final stroke.

Skipper came out of nowhere. I barely caught the image of light brown, his blue eye gleaming. Lunging through the air, Skipper sank his teeth into the cabayo's front leg, the weight of his body slinging around, ripping hide as it went.

The cabayo screamed, rearing, Skipper hanging on with all his might.

Cabayo, dog, and man crashed backward to the earth. Even as Antonio rolled away, I ducked the flying hooves and charged forward, ripping the sword from my side.

I swung—mindless with rage—only to have the edge clang off Antonio's armored shoulder. He grabbed up his own sword, blocking my next swing. He was on his back, braced on his right arm, awkwardly blocking each blow I sent his way.

Behind me, Skipper yipped and whined in pain. Like I said, I'd lost my wits. I stepped back to look, and in that instant, Antonio was on his feet. He almost had me, but I managed to get enough sword up to take the blow.

I'd carried the weapon long enough, practiced with it, combining my skill with the lance and war club with what I'd learned from Antonio during his captivity. We went at each other, the *hierro* ringing as we thrust, cut, and blocked.

He's using his left hand! Before, he'd used his right. Had the wound I'd given him at Napetuca permanently injured it?

One of his slashes cut my arm, and he grinned through the bloody mess of his face.

"*Por mi padre,*" he hissed.

"*Gusano con un pene blando,*" I growled back. I'd have called him other things but my *español* wasn't good enough.

He ran at me, beating me back, slicing the top of my thigh as I leaped away. Any time I managed to sneak past his guard, his armor blunted the blow. He'd begun to grin, knowing full well the eventual outcome. His armor made the difference.

With a skillful feint, he knocked my blade aside and pushed close where I couldn't swing. His arm went back, a crazy glitter in his eyes, when something hit his back with a thump.

Surprise flashed across his bloody face as I leaped away. He'd grasped his blade by the middle, seeking to thrust it like a knife. I used his momentary confusion to slash my blade across his face. The helmet took most of the blow, but I cut him across the bridge of the nose.

"Black Shell!" Pearl Hand screamed. "Run!"

I drew back for another stroke.

"Run!"

Pearl Hand's scream penetrated my rage. Without thinking, I pelted for the gate.

She was there, waving with all her might, panic shining in her eyes. Her crossbow hung impotently from her right hand. Seeing I was coming, she turned and charged through the opening.

I heard the cabayos as they thundered closer. They were just behind me as I bolted through the gate, panting, bleeding, my heart racing in my chest.

Even as I passed through, the heavy wooden gate was pushed closed behind me, warriors bent to the task.

Pearl Hand turned, throwing her arms around me. "I thought I'd lost you."

"Almost did," I rasped. "But for Skipper." I stiffened. "He's still out there."

Pearl Hand clasped my shoulder, staring me in the eyes. "He's gone, Black Shell. Or he will be soon. I think the cabayo kicked him. He was on his side, blood running from his mouth. I barely had a chance to see. My concern was keeping Antonio from killing you. His armor stopped the arrow I put into his back. But it was distraction enough for you to get away."

I blinked, trying to understand. The thump in Antonio's back? It had been Pearl Hand's arrow? Skipper was dead?

I stood dumbly, trying to comprehend.

"Blood Thorn?" I asked.

"I haven't seen him." Pearl Hand avoided my gaze.

In the plaza around us, the warriors were hammering on the slave chains, setting porters free, handing out bows and quivers of arrows. Other warriors were gleefully looting the Kristiano packs, pulling out cloth, odd pieces of *hierro*, mirrors, strings of beads; opening packs of corn; lifting Kristiano chairs; unrolling tents; donning bits of armor; slashing with swords; and inspecting one of the thunder sticks. The atmosphere was like a festival as they plundered the Kristiano baggage.

I saw one walk by, a Kristiano saddle in his arms. Before the palace, Tuskaloosa was waving de Soto's colorful banner by its tall pole. Warriors were whooping, singing, and dancing as if they'd just conquered the world.

I watched one of the Kristiano corpses being carried naked around the plaza, the entire head stripped of ihola'ka.

"You're bleeding." Pearl Hand inspected the long cuts.

I looked down. "I don't have time to bleed. They'll be coming."

She nodded, reaching out to test the cuts. I finally had time to feel the sting of them. When I looked down at the gaping slice in my thigh, my stomach turned.

"We'll sew them up later." She turned, grabbed a quiver of crossbow arrows from a complaining warrior, and led the way to one of the ladders leading up onto the walls.

I made a face, feeling each step pull the various cuts. The one on the top of my thigh looked the worst—a hideous, bloody smile that leaked crimson in a sheet down my leg. Any deeper and I wouldn't have been able to walk.

At the platform atop the palisade, we found Darting Snake. I wondered how he'd made it up there with his mangled leg. He was propped with his arms on the wall, staring out at the Kristianos.

I could see Skipper lying beside Antonio's dead cabayo. Hope as I might, he made no movement, the breeze toying with his light brown hair.

I swallowed against the lump in my throat, then followed the line of dead and dying warriors back to where Antonio—surrounded by cabayos—was stumbling back to the main party of Kristianos. He had both hands to his face, and what a pretty sight that must have been.

"Well," I growled, "between the gash my arrow cut and the sword slash that cleft his nose, he'll remember me forever."

"As you'll remember him," Pearl Hand muttered, glancing at my arm and leg.

Movement caught my eye, and in the distance beyond the congregated Kristianos, just shy of the tree line, a cabayero was weaving his mount back and forth. Before the cabayo, two shapes darted and dodged: Gnaw and Bark. There could be no mistake. Then I saw them dash headlong into the trees and safety. But where was the rest of the pack? Worry began to set in. My dogs were my life, my family. And one was already dead.

Please, Breath Giver, keep them safe.

"Something's happening," Darting Snake said, pointing.

De Soto had been given a horse. Now he was riding out shouting orders, pointing this way and that. Soldados were forming squads, and cabayeros were riding out in a sweep around the town walls. We watched them ride down parties of warriors who had left the safety of Mabila.

"Looks like they want to surround us," I noted, trying not to wince at the pain in my souls or body.

"And when they do?" Darting Snake asked.

"That depends," I said, my heart dropping. "But being Kristianos, I'm sure they've an idea about how to deal with a walled town."

Darting Snake nodded. "I suppose so. And I'm willing to wager that the monster is ready for a little revenge."

THIRTY-NINE

A GROUP OF PENSACOLA WARRIORS TRIED TO LEAVE, marching out the north gate, singing, rattling their bows against their cane shields. Darting Snake sent warriors to call them back, but believing the fight over, they refused.

The Kristianos allowed them to make it halfway to the forest before the cabayeros hit them, killing them to the last man.

The lesson was sobering.

Meanwhile the remainder of de Soto's army began appearing from the east, marching in lines. Obviously they'd been scouring the countryside since they carried pots and baskets looted from farmsteads.

In trickles and streams, we watched de Soto's ranks growing.

Then the Kristianos split into four groups, one for each side of the town. Marching into position, they just waited. Our warriors gave them a show, waving bits of their colorful clothing, captured weapons, and the thick fabric flags that hung from long poles. Down the way, a Chicaza warrior swung the golden cross carried by their priests, and beside him, I saw an Albaamaha brandishing the precious golden cup the Kristianos drank out of when they worshipped. I chuckled to myself, realizing de Soto was actually *losing* his gold.

During this time I kept looking for Blood Thorn, worried about his fate. I kept expecting to see his bobbing hair pom, his gleaming eyes triumphant as he approached and lifted ihola'ka. Nowhere did I see him among the hundreds of warriors being hurried back to positions in the town.

"What are they waiting for?" Darting Snake asked.

Instinctively, I said, "At the sound of the horn, they'll attack from all four sides, seeking to penetrate the palisade."

Pearl Hand added, "And they'll do it."

Darting Snake turned to one of the deputies. "Call the Tuskaloosa and the remaining Pensacola warriors to the palisade to repel the attacks. Keep the others hidden in the houses. When the Kristianos breach the wall, I want the wall defenders to fall back to the houses. Lure them into the maze. Shoot through the loopholes. Each one of those worms has a face, so *hit* him there."

"Yes, Thlakko." The man leaped down the ladder, disappearing into the town.

I looked out at the packed houses with their overlapping roofs. The passages between them were small and crowded. The original plan had been to cut off escape to the gate and then use the maze of passages between the houses to kill the Kristianos. Get them into that maze, confused, and we could kill a great many more. Maybe enough to make de Soto think twice about risking the rest of his army.

"It's going to be bloody fighting in there," I declared ominously.

"But they can't use the cabayeros against us the way they did the Pensacola." Darting Snake fingered his chin. "And in the confines between the houses, they can't bunch up like they did in the plaza this morning." He smiled, the action pulling at the socket of his missing eye. "Our warriors will be shooting from mere paces away. They can't miss."

"Why don't I like this idea?" Pearl Hand wondered.

In Timucua, I whispered, "Because we don't have an escape route?"

The signal wasn't a horn. Instead a thunder-stick shooter walked out opposite us, leveled his tube, and shot at our palisade. The heavy ball fell short, smacking the wall an arm's length below us.

"You missed, you hoobuk wakse!" I bellowed.

We said nothing more as the soldados formed up, holding their shields up over their heads. They marched forward that way, shoulder to shoulder, shields overlapping like some perverted, flat-backed tortoise.

A sense of terrible dismay started to chew at my gut. The first arrows clattered off the impregnable formation like hail off boulders.

"They always have a way," I said sickly.

"Even if they get in," Darting Snake said reassuringly, "they can't use that tactic among the houses."

When the massed soldados reached the walls, they

pressed up, hunching under their shields. The sound of *hierro* axes could be heard chipping at the plaster, smacking hollowly at the underlying cane, vines, and posts.

Darting Snake motioned to one of his deputies. "As soon as they cut a hole, have our warriors shoot through it. Arrow after arrow, right into their faces."

"Yes, Thlakko!"

The attacks on the walls, it turned out, were mostly a diversion. Their real objectives were the town's wooden gates. The *hierro* axes chopped through in no time, and within moments, the soldados came spilling in.

They were met with a barrage of arrows that clattered on their shields and stuck in their batting. Here and there a soldado pulled up, screaming, as a barbed shaft found a crack or pierced a foot or leg.

According to plan, our warriors melted back to the houses, calling taunts, bending over and slapping their buttocks.

But the Kristianos didn't take the bait. Instead they formed up in a protective wedge, waiting while other soldados ran up from outside, each carrying a clay jar. Then the formation advanced. From my high perch, I clutched my sword, wishing fervently that I'd had the sense to collect a bow. Any bow.

Pearl Hand leveled her crossbow, took aim, and fired at a soldado. He gave a gratifying shriek and clutched his side, but the formation didn't break until the last moment. In a rush, the soldados charged in among the houses.

I watched impotently as the screams, shrieks, and bellows of combat mixed with the clatter of arrows off armor and the chopping sounds of men killing each other.

Several spotted us on the bastion and broke away. Hidden behind his shield, the one in the lead started to climb the ladder. Pearl Hand fit one of her arrows in the crossbow and took aim.

"Wait," I called, stepping off to the right with my sword. "When I get his attention, you step left and shoot under his shield."

She gave me a worried look but nodded.

I waited until the top of the shield rose above the platform, the soldado's spear-ax ready to thrust. I leaped forward, clanging my sword across his shield. Instinctively he turned to follow me, and Pearl Hand drove an arrow into his side from an arm's length. The man cried, tried to shift, and I reached out with a foot and kicked his shield. Off balance, he fell like a rock, snapping a couple of rungs out of the ladder on the way down.

His companions picked up his limp body and, under the cover of their shields, drew back.

In the process, we missed what the others had been up to. The Kristianos should have been advancing into the town as our warriors fell back. Instead, the line of battle had stalled at the first line of structures.

"Fools!" Darting Snake screamed. "Someone go to the deputies, tell them to fall back! Lure the Kristianos in!"

"They're not following!" a deputy down the wall called back.

"Not following?" Pearl Hand said, wondering. "They always follow when they're winning."

At that moment a horn blared, and the Kristianos began to pull back, soldados scurrying out of the houses they'd invaded.

"Scurrying" might not be the appropriate word.

Granted, they were in a hurry, but to my eye, every single one of them was limping, cut, holding an arm, dragging a leg, with a dozen feathered shafts sticking out of them. From all sides, our warriors advanced, literally raining arrows on them.

Forming up as well as they could, shields held side by side, the soldados backed into the plaza. For a moment our warriors surrounded them, only to have the Kristianos break through and withdraw orderly through the shattered gate as arrows clattered off their helmets and armor.

"That's it?" Darting Snake asked. "We pushed them back so easily?"

"It doesn't make sense." Pearl Hand knotted a fist, worry creasing her face.

I was staring at the dead, dying, and wounded left in their wake. What had begun as a pristine plaza was now littered with bodies, the clay ground clotted here and there with drying gore.

"Pus and blood," Pearl Hand whispered, staring at the houses they'd just left. Blue smoke rose in curling streamers, like dancing, airy serpents, from around the eaves. And no, it couldn't be explained away as cooking fires. Within the period of a few short breaths, the streamers turned to puffs, and flames crackled through the roofs. First two, then a third and fourth. All along the line of attack, houses began to burn.

"The jars they carried," I said softly, ". . . filled with hickory oil. Splashed on the bedding, all it took was shoveling the coals from the fire pits onto the fabric."

On the far side of town, shouts went up, and there, too, distant houses leaped into flame.

I lifted a hand to check the breeze coming up from the

south. "We've only moments before the entire town goes up."

Pearl Hand looked sick. "They're doing to us what the Apalachee tried to do to them at Anhaica."

Cries of dismay rose from the warriors in the plaza. Some of them immediately fled for the ruined gate. I stepped over to the wall. As they spilled out into the open, cabayeros wheeled their mounts where they covered the retreating soldados. They gleefully charged the refugees, lancing some, driving the others back into the gate.

I turned toward the line of burning houses. "We have several thousand men hidden in those houses. We've got to get them out!"

"We've got to get off this wall," Pearl Hand said grimly. "A shift in the breeze and the fire will cook us alive up here."

I glanced down at the ladder with its broken rungs.

"You go on," Darting Snake whispered softly, a look of defeat in his single eye. He watched the flames spreading from house to house. The overlapping eaves carried the fire with a relentless efficiency. Warriors by the hundreds were screaming, fleeing north into the maze of houses, unaware that another line of fire was already burning there, blocking their retreat.

I slipped the sword into my scabbard, bodily picking Darting Snake off the platform. "Arms around my neck. Hang on." Then I looked at Pearl Hand. "You first." I grinned. "Catch us if I fall."

She shot me a disapproving look. Slinging her crossbow over her shoulder, she grasped the uprights and disappeared over the edge.

"I'm down," she called. "Use your feet on the outside of the uprights in the missing places."

I stepped onto the ladder, finding the first rung, feeling it sag under the combined weight. I did my best, sliding the tops of my moccasins down the missing sections, my fingers straining to keep a grip on the poles.

"There!" Pearl Hand called. "There's a rung under your foot."

Somehow I managed to find the rung, and with Darting Snake cutting off my air, I scrambled down to the earth. His crutches were there, and by the time we had him situated, the heat was like a wall beating at us.

"This way!" Darting Snake picked the shortest path toward the plaza.

Pearl Hand and I ducked—bent like land crabs—as we scuttled between the narrow walls of the closest houses. Then we were clear, joining the others who had made it to the plaza.

I looked around, guessing that perhaps two or three hundred stood aimlessly, staring in horror at the roaring wall of fire that shot flames half a bow-shot up into the clear blue sky. A keening howl carried through the crackling roar, and I wondered, having never heard such a thing before.

Then it hit me: the intermingled screams of men burning to death. How many? We'd had nearly four thousand warriors hidden in Mabila before the battle. And we'd freed nearly a thousand slaves.

"We've got to get out!" a burly Coosa warrior cried.

Pearl Hand pointed at the gate. "It's swarming with Kristianos out there. They'll kill you."

"Better to die a warrior than a cooked turkey." The warrior gripped his war club, turned, and ran for the gate. The rest followed him just as a shift in the breeze curled a thick pall of smoke around us.

I choked, reeling from the stench of burning flesh, and instinctively grasped Pearl Hand to me. We crouched there, embers dropping around us, until a wisp of wind twisted them away. No, not wind: a draft. As the fire grew, the draft that fed it became a gale. Fingers of dust streaked across the hard-packed plaza, then bits of debris. Pieces of looted Kristiano clothing were sucked up, twisting and flapping, only to catch on the bodies of dead warriors and flutter like broken flags.

Darting Snake hunched in his crutches, his eyebrows singed, his hair curled and prickly. He kept coughing, then spat to the side.

"What do we do?" Pearl Hand asked.

"The palace," Darting Snake cried. "Look! There's the high minko."

"It's burning." I blinked at the great structure, now a roaring inferno. Tuskaloosa staggered along the edge of the mound, blood seeping from a puncture in his belly. He stopped, wavering on his feet, silhouetted by the fire engulfing the palace.

I could see little round kegs, the ones that held powder for the thunder sticks; three of them had been placed on the palace veranda. Flames were licking around them. Then the veranda just vanished in a yellow flash. Tuskaloosa's body was flung up, somersaulting through the air. The concussion blew us off our feet, hammering us against the ground. Bits of burning cane, wood, and splinters shot past us, then Tuskaloosa's body fell from the sky.

I blinked and stared, my ears ringing. As a great pall of blue smoke rose, I could see the entire front of the palace was missing, the interior a raging inferno.

What in the name of the ancestors just happened?

A handful of warriors came staggering back in through the gate. One was bleeding, his arm hanging, a sword stroke having cleft his shoulder just above the arm.

I turned to Darting Snake. He sat, propped on one arm. His mouth gaped stupidly, his single eye glassy; a splintered section of post had been driven like a giant skewer through his chest. Even as I blinked, he collapsed backward, the skewer rolling his torso sideways.

The roof collapsed in the closest house, a fountain of sparks shooting up into the sky to mix with billows of smoke and burning debris.

Pearl Hand and I crouched among the bodies in the center of the plaza, batting out sparks as they twisted down from the sky. The dancing girls appeared as if out of nowhere. And from the smoky haze, Blood Thorn staggered like an apparition. His face was soot streaked; an insane glaze filled his eyes. A handful of warriors appeared behind him, coughing, bewildered, half their hair burned away.

I staggered to my feet, ears still ringing, and clapped him on the shoulders before I noticed the blisters. He barely winced. "Death," he whispered. "Nothing but death. The girls make it?"

I pointed to where they'd thrown themselves facedown on the plaza, desperate for the clean air that rushed along the ground to feed the voracious flames.

"We're going to find a way out," I called.

"There is none," he bellowed back. "Just death."

I watched another batch of warriors—some crying, others shouting insanely—turn and dash for the gate. When I turned to Pearl Hand, she remained crouched, filth in her draft-tangled hair, an empty madness in her vacant eyes.

Tears were streaming down my face as I turned, staring at the roaring inferno of the palace. The rush of air being sucked into the fire was carrying dust and debris like a tornado's wreckage toward the mountain of flame. At the foot of the mound lay a Kristiano's body, untouched and fully dressed; the man's hair and beard fluttered in the rushing vortex feeding the fire.

Terror is a curious thing, beyond the scope of time. We waited for an eternity that, looking back, might have been but a few heartbeats. What was left of the palace was quickly consumed, the roof falling in and, finally, the walls collapsed.

When I looked up at the sky, I was amazed to see the sun slanting in the west. Blood Thorn hunched with the three remaining warriors. I blinked idiotically. Where had the rest gone? When I looked around, all I saw were the dead sprawled where they'd fallen. The dancing girls were lying among them, their hair in disarray. From their streaked faces, I could tell they were crying, terrified.

Blood Thorn tottered back, his shoulders slumping. He bent to pluck up a dead warrior's quiver. "I'm going out there."

"They'll kill you."

He gave me a crazy man's smile. "There is only death. Like Napetuca. Like Water Frond. Don't you get it, Black Shell?" Tears were streaking down his soot-coated face. *"Our world is dead!"*

"There are only four of you."

". . . You and Pearl Hand come, it's six."

Pearl Hand gave him a hollow smile and began to laugh as the draft jerked tears in zigzag lines down her filthy cheeks.

Blood Thorn smiled as if at a silly joke. "They won't ride the girls down. We'll send them first."

"Give them to the Kristianos?" I cried.

His half-crazy eyes met mine. "They're *already* the Kristianos' women! Look around you! Tomorrow, or later tonight, when the fire burns down, they're coming back. This way the girls serve red Power. And I can kill another couple of Kristianos."

I stared back at the burning town. One of the mighty hickory trees—green with leaves and heavy with nuts that morning—could be seen through billows of smoke. Spectral, naked black branches now clawed impotently at the tortured sky.

Nothing left.

"You coming?" Blood Thorn asked.

"You'll die," I told him.

He chuckled, which made him cough. After spitting dark goo onto the ground, his soot-blackened face lined. "I died at Napetuca." Then he turned, walking toward the three warriors.

We watched as they prodded the girls to their feet. They formed up the young women, driving them like a flock toward the gate. Then, just like that, he was gone.

FORTY

A CRASH SOUNDED BEHIND ME AS A HOUSE COLLAPSED.
Perhaps I was too shocked to think, the horror of
Mabila numbing my mind. Blood Thorn was gone. I
stared absently at the broken gate, then at Darting Snake's
body, at Tuskaloosa's crumpled corpse, and at the rest of
the sprawled dead—so many of them—their clothing flut-
tering in the fierce draft.

"Come," I said as I felt the sepaya tugging against my
chest. Was it pulled by the draft? Or was the sepaya urging
me toward the wrecked palace? I took my wife's hand; she
followed mindlessly, gaze vacuous. The roar had died
down, the rush of wind relaxing. Where a wall of flames
had been, billows of inky black smoke now rose.

I stared down at the dead Kristiano as we passed;
the man's sightless eyes were coated with dust. He'd
been a soldado, killed at the last. No one had even

bothered to pick up his helmet or strip the armor from his body.

Following the sepaya's tug, I limped onto the low palace mound. Heat radiated from the still-burning timbers. The pouch bounced on my chest, leading me left . . . to a wooden disk, barely exposed where the dirt had been blown away: a storage pit lid. It sat on the southwest corner of the mound, the wooden cover charred but otherwise intact.

I bent down and pried up the lid, finding the hole full of freshly harvested squash. I climbed in, handing squash, one by one, out to Pearl Hand, who tossed them into the burning remains of the palace. As the wind played tricks, we ducked, scurrying away from the searing heat, and returned to the task when we could.

"That's good," Pearl Hand called, staring uneasily out toward the ruined gate. "There's room."

My cuts stinging, I lowered myself onto the remaining squash. Then Pearl Hand dropped over the edge, giving me a faint smile. She was coming back to her old self, the shock wearing off. Together, we pulled the charred cover over us and sat on the bumpy squash. Normally I'd have groused over the uncomfortable condition of my rear. Now we just sat in shocked silence heavier than the darkness that pressed around us.

Sometime later, I heard voices calling in *español*. We stared at each other in the inky black. I found foul humor in the notion that if they looked in, as soot-blackened as we were, they'd never see us.

Pearl Hand finally shifted; standing on the uneven squash, she lifted the lid. No light slipped in, and she eased it to one side, raising her head.

"No one is in sight."

I poked my head up next to hers, staring around. The fires still burned with enough illumination to see that the plaza was empty.

"What time is it?" she asked.

I studied the few stars visible between the black blotches of cloud and smoke. "A couple of hands after sunset, I suppose."

"We'll wait," she said.

"To do what?"

"Escape."

"They'll be guarding the gates."

We ducked as a couple of armored Kristianos appeared at the gate, swords in their hands. Our eyes above the rim of the pit, we watched them wander around, kick bodies, point at the piles of charred corpses in the smoldering houses, and talk.

Finally they left. Over the popping of logs and the crackle of flames, we barely heard them call to someone beyond the gate.

A finger of time later, another group of Kristianos entered. When they, too, saw the piles of charred corpses among the burned houses, they stared in fascination before hurrying away.

"I have an idea," Pearl Hand said. "Lift me out of here."

I boosted her up to the rim, stifling a cry as my wounds tore. She slipped to the edge of the low mound, then over.

I winced at the pain, tears trickling at the corners of my eyes.

Pearl Hand scrambled up the side of the mound, a bundle of clothing in her arms. I almost shrieked from the pain as I crawled out.

"What are you doing?" I finally whispered.

"Saving us." She offered the clothing. "Put these on."

I stared up at the night, my wounds hurting, blisters on my shoulders stinging, my souls weary to the point of collapse. Then I really got a good look at the still-burning remains of Mabila, realized what I was seeing . . . smelling. The charred piles of dead lay like weird stacks of driftwood around the burning circles of collapsed house walls. Above them, the heat played games with the air, shimmering, wavering, and dancing over the blackened thickets of arms and legs.

Pearl Hand helped me don Kristiano clothing. I gasped at the pain as cloth slid over my cut thigh. When I tried to walk, I could only limp, agony shooting up from my now stiff leg.

Pearl Hand pulled a dress—something she'd found— over her shoulders and helped me down to where the dead Kristiano lay. Leaving me to wobble and fight the pain-tears, she bent down to the corpse.

Mind numb, I watched as she undid laces and yanked the Kristiano's armor from his stiff body. Straightening, she dropped the cloth batting over my shoulders.

"What are you doing?"

"Turning you into a Kristiano."

"I don't have a beard."

"You will."

Her *hierro* knife sliced around the Kristiano's skull. Expertly she peeled the man's scalp off, then followed the bones of the face, severing the skin just below the man's chin.

I shied back when she straightened and tried to slip the hideous hide over my head.

"Stop it!" she hissed. "What's a dead man's face after you've been eaten by a Spirit Beast?"

She had a point.

I shivered, sucking in a deep breath as she laid the cold, bloody skin over my head. My Chicaza souls began to scream as she used bits of torn cloth to tie the dead man's face onto mine. At the end she clapped the man's helmet over my head—pressing the gore onto my scalp—and aligned the eye holes.

"You've got to trust me," she told me, brooking no argument. "Lean on me. Play like you're wounded. If anyone speaks to you, simply say, '*Hay dolor.*'"

"*Hay dolor,*" I answered, chilled by the notion that my words were passing through a dead man's mouth. Then she made me repeat it a couple of times to get the pronunciation right.

"This is insane." I blinked, feeling my eyelashes rasp the dead man's skin. His face didn't fit me well.

"Come on." Pearl Hand placed herself under my good arm, taking my weight. Then we started, winding our way around the dark shadows of bodies as we made our way to the gate.

I didn't even flinch when a Kristiano called, "*¿Quien es?*"

Pearl Hand answered, "*Mi hombre está muy herido. ¿Donde están los médicos?*"

A sudden shiver went through me as the guard leaned close in the night, staring. Then he straightened and pointed. "*Están por alli. ¿Necesitas ayuda?*"

"*No, pero gracias. Tienes un encargo.*"

We started to hobble away when he called behind us, "*Bueno suerte, mujer.*"

Pearl Hand said nothing as we limped our way into the

darkness, veering wide around the winking Kristiano campfires that dotted the night.

Twice more voices called from the dark, and at Pearl Hand's reply, the moonlight reflecting from my armor, no one hindered our passing.

FORTY-ONE

In the dream I stood at a sprawling canoe landing, the roiled surface of the Black Warrior River at my back. I knew this place, had been brought here as a boy by Uncle. He had come—accompanied by a party of Chicaza nobles—bearing the bones of his older brother, the recently deceased high minko of the Chicaza Nation. Uncle had just been confirmed—made the new high minko—and, as a gesture of respect for his dead brother, had brought his remains here, to Split Sky City, the ancient home of the Chicaza.

How old was I then? Five? Six? I had clambered out of the canoe and followed the long procession up from this very landing. The dead high minko's bones had been carried to the top of one of the mounds, a hole dug, and there, among the emblems of his office, he'd been laid.

I remember the bed of colorful feathers they laid him on. A chipped-stone mace, a copper headpiece, and a wealth of shell necklaces had been placed beside his cleaned bones. After prayers and offerings, the earth was blessed and shoveled atop him. All the while, the hopaye had sung, sending him on to the Path of the Dead.

Now I stood alone on the landing, the river at my back. A terrible weariness weighted my souls, which were plagued by the horrors of Mabila.

I turned my steps to the trail, wondering what Split Sky City must have looked like before it was abandoned to the ghosts. Here traders would have spread their wares; thousands of people had trod this very soil. This city had housed the heroes Old White, Green Snake, and Morning Dew.

I made the long climb to the high terrace, winding past abandoned mounds where the charred remains of temples resisted the invasion of grasses that waved in the breeze.

Skirting the deep gullies, I walked to the palace mound and scrambled up the steep ramp; the rotting remains of steps turned under my feet.

At the top, I looked north, where the river made a great loop, washing at the foot of the city. At the base of the mound I could see the collapsed remains of a great earth lodge sinking back into the soil. There, my ancestors had once met in council with the Chicaza clans.

Where the high minko had been buried, goldenrod, daisies, and sunflowers sprouted. I searched for any sign of the dead minko's ghosts, feeling only the warm wind blowing up from the gulf.

"There are no answers here, Black Shell."

At the sound of the voice, I turned, startled by Horned Serpent's appearance. His scaled body reflected the iridescent colors of the rainbow, and his mighty wings were folded along his back. The Spirit Beast studied me through crystalline eyes that seemed illuminated from within. Atop his scale-armored head, great red antlers forked and rose. The tip I'd broken off had regenerated.

His tongue flicked, sensing the air, and I stared at the Spirit Beast's mouth, remembering how it had once crushed my body.

"We lost everything at Mabila," I told him. "Maybe five thousand warriors."

"Mabila is the turning point."

I stared my disbelief. "Did you hear me?"

Was that a smile at the corner of that serpentine mouth?

I stepped forward, filled with a desperate anger. "We had *them!* The monster walked straight into the trap, only to fight his way out. Then, incredibly, he destroyed us!"

"Did anyone promise you it would be easy?" Horned Serpent's head rose from the coil of his body, slipping silently toward me. "De Soto is a master of war, perhaps the finest in all the world. But you have wounded him. Mabila is the turning point."

"How?" I cried. "Time after time, we are outthought, outfought, and defeated."

"Yet you win." The great shining eyes fixed on mine.

"Tell that to the thousands upon thousands of dead."

"They know what they have done with greater clarity than you."

That set me back.

"Under their armor, Black Shell, what are Kristianos?"

"Men," I countered. "Unlike any our world has ever seen."

"You watched their banners burn at Mabila. But in killing so many, they have destroyed themselves."

"I don't understand."

"You're smarter than that. The turning point has come."

"It has? Where? In all the fighting, I saw perhaps twenty Kristianos dead. I wore the skin of one to escape."

He actually smiled. "Pearl Hand is incredibly clever, isn't she?"

"My souls are polluted beyond cleansing. I spoke through a dead man's mouth, saw through his eyes." I winced. "Skipper is dead."

The glow behind the giant snake's eyes increased, as if lit by the sun. "His souls romp with Fetch's. He is honored among the dead."

I felt a swelling within my chest, a single tear escaping my eye. "Bless him, Horned Serpent. I don't even know if I'll ever see any of my dogs again."

"You will." He paused. "Provided you choose to continue the fight. And as to the pollution of your souls, the dead cannot harm you or dilute your Power. You have been purged, protected, and given a cleansing that will *remain with you forever. No hopaye, hilishaya, or minko will ever doubt you. The sepaya is proof of that."*

I felt the bit of brow tine tingle in its pouch.

"So, what will you do, Black Shell? See this to the end? Or will you rise from here and find your way to the ancestors?"

I would see my dogs again? Spend my last days with Pearl Hand? "You said Mabila was the turning point?"

"The proof lies in the fires of Mabila. In the process of destroying the Tuskaloosa, they have dealt themselves an irreparable blow."

"How?"

"You will figure it out . . . provided you go back." His scaled mouth seemed curved into a mocking and reptilian smile. "Or you may begin the journey that will take you home to the ancestors your people have buried here. The choice is yours, Spirit warrior."

I frowned, thinking, They have dealt themselves an irreparable blow? *The image of de Soto's long face, his sleepy eyes and arrogant smile, hung between my souls.*

What would I give to see that man dead?

Anything.

"Black Shell?" Pearl Hand called, intruding into the dream.

Pain came as I tried to stir. Blinking my eyes, I stared out at leaf mat, stems, and bushes. Birds were singing, a breeze rattling the leaves overhead. I could smell moldy leaves . . . and the stench of smoke.

"Horned Serpent?" I asked, my throat dry and rasping.

"Sorry. No," Pearl Hand muttered caustically, "but I'm more fun to sleep with."

I gasped as I tried to straighten, turning to see her crouched beside me. Her face was soot blackened, her singed hair in a wild tangle; the scavenged dress—covered with leaves and twigs—clung to her curves.

Bark and Gnaw were lying among the leaves, watching me with serious brown eyes. They had new wounds, but Gnaw's white-tipped tail was patting the leaves as he wagged it. Bark was panting and looked oddly satisfied, his pink tongue lolling.

"Spirit Dream," I whispered. "I was at Split Sky City. Horned Serpent was there."

"And now you're back here," she added. "And you stink. Not only that, we've got to wash out those wounds. Find something to stitch them up. They're festering."

I glanced down at the Kristiano armor and clothing that I still wore. I reached up and prodded my face, feeling caked blood. Gods, I'd worn a dead man's face!

But your souls are not polluted.

The cut in my arm opened and stung as I sat up. The sun hung low in the west, slanting its light through our hideout.

"Horned Serpent told me Mabila is the turning point. Something to do with the fires."

She arched her eyebrow, studying me. "All is not lost?"

"Not according to Horned Serpent."

She gave me a grin. "Then let's crawl out of here. Squirm, Patches, and Blackie are out here somewhere." She sighed. "But I'm afraid our packs burned. We're no better off than the Kristianos when it comes to that."

"The packs?"

"All of our trade. Our supplies. Gone."

I grinned for the first time. "Packs, saddles, weapons and armor, clothing, bundles of crossbow arrows, lots of *hierro,* trade goods, leather, axes—they lost it all! Everything the slaves were carrying."

She nodded. "All they've got left is what's on their backs."

The fires of Mabíla! They'd burned all those precious supplies. Harnesses, tools, the chairs and furnishings, even the gaudy flags had been consumed. Their precious golden cup would have fallen to the flames. How much more, things beyond our comprehension, had been lost?

"There's something else," Pearl Hand said, eyes unfocused. "Did you see those camps we passed last night?"

"I was wearing a loosely fitted dead man's face, remember?"

She continued, ignoring my sarcasm. "They've got wounded everywhere. They were lined up by the tens, moaning, their legs and arms bound with rags. I caught a glimpse of a couple of soldados trying to pull an arrow out of a man's thigh by firelight."

"And your point is?"

"My point, husband, is that the armor may have saved their accursed lives, but every one of those wounded men is going to realize he can die. Just like the ones we killed in Mabíla." She smiled to herself. "Their confidence is going to erode like beach sand in a hurricane."

"The turning point," I whispered. "Come on. I need to drink, get out of this dead man's clothes, and wash." I hoped I wouldn't faint at the sight of my leg.

If there was any consolation, it was that Antonio couldn't have been looking much better.

EPILOGUE

I'D AS SOON FORGET THE WAY PEARL HAND TREATED my wounds. Suffice it to say that her "thorough cleansing" made enough sweat pop out on my forehead that it trickled down in rivers. I sank my teeth into a chokecherry stick against the pain.

She made sympathetic cooing noises.

I made whimpering sounds that would have shamed a five-year-old. Then I made worse ones while she used a thorn and flax thread to sew the gaping edges of the wounds together.

She said she was taking her time to do a good job. I said she was as heartless as a Kristiano in search of a gold nugget.

Over the next couple of days, the stitches held, though the cuts oozed pus and turned red.

At night we hobbled as close to Mabila as we could,

and I whistled for Squirm, a stony anxiety in the pit of my gut. The second night he appeared, ghosting out of the dark forest to leap onto my chest. A small melee burst out as Bark and Gnaw pounced on him in sheer delight.

Patches and Blackie—to our surprise—were waiting in our hidden camp one morning when we returned, having sniffed us out. That they were smart enough to avoid the hungry Kristianos was a fortuitous surprise.

Perhaps it was the Power of the sepaya, but I healed quickly, and one evening, I managed to climb one of the tall oaks in order to spy on the Kristianos.

They remained camped on the Mabila plain, though in the distance, we could see columns of smoke rising where the surrounding towns had been. Talking to a couple of local Albaamaha who sneaked through, we learned that the Kristianos had burned every standing structure they could find in the area.

And it was true: The fires of Mabila had destroyed their valuables, including medicines for the wounded. As a cure, they'd even used fat cut from the bodies of our dead warriors as a poultice. How disgusting and inhuman can they get?

The difference in their demeanor could be seen, even from the distance over which we watched. They no longer swaggered. The laughter and smiles had been replaced by a sullen weariness, and the lines of wounded were long. But even better, nearly to a man, they wore a bandage, had an arm in a sling, or hobbled along on crutches.

Their little herd of *puercos* had feasted on the dead and were swarming around like the vermin they were. I'd offer good riddance when the last one died.

But even more to the point, I could count no more

than a hundred cabayos left of the three hundred that had landed at Uzita.

One of the dancing girls—who managed to escape after a week—informed us that Blood Thorn had fought bravely to the end. We prayed for his souls. She also said the Kristiano *médicos* had tallied up over seven hundred wounds among the soldados and cabayeros. De Soto himself had taken an arrow to the hip that left him disabled for weeks.

She related these things with a dullness behind her eyes. And I could only guess at what she'd endured, given the anger and anxiety in the Kristiano camp.

"They are eating up what is left of the food," she told us. "And they have heard that Pensacola warriors are waiting in the south to ambush their travel should they try to reach the sea."

"What else have you heard?" Pearl Hand asked, a sympathy in her eyes.

"That they will try to head north," the broken young woman replied. "They have heard that the northern Albaamaha have stores of food at Talicpacana, Mosulixa, and Zabusta towns."

"I know those towns," I said. "The Albaamaha might feed them for a moon, maybe more. They don't have enough surplus to feed his army through the winter."

Pearl Hand turned her eyes on me. "Then where would they head?"

I gave her a humorless smile. "The Albaamaha will send them to Chicaza. Or at least—given their long history of abuse at Chicaza hands—that's what I'd do if I were one of their mikkos."

Pearl Hand gave me a level stare. "Chicaza? Do you want to go there?"

I kept my humorless smile. "After what we experienced in Mabila? No. But if any nation can finish this, I would like for it to be my own."

I reached up, fingering the sepaya. Eleven long years had passed since I'd fled in disgrace. That Black Shell had been a frightened and angry youth. I wasn't really sure who this man who called himself Black Shell had become.

A Spirit warrior? The chosen of Horned Serpent? Or the reincarnation of the Orphan—the Wild One of legend? Where I went, death would follow.

The Kristianos feared my name.

The Chicaza despised it.

So, brother, you are the Chicaza high minko now. This will be a most interesting homecoming.

And if Mabila had truly been the turning point, the monster would rue the day that he even considered turning his feet toward Chicaza.

I smiled in anticipation.

BIBLIOGRAPHY

Adair, James
    2005 *The History of the American Indians.* University of Alabama Press: Tuscaloosa.

Anderson, David G.
    1994 *The Savannah River Chiefdoms: Political Change in the Late Prehistoric Southeast.* University of Alabama Press: Tuscaloosa.

Bense, Judith A.
    1994 *Archaeology of the Southeastern United States: Paleoindian to World War I.* Academic Press: New York.

Brose, David S.
    1984 "Mississippian Period Cultures in Northwestern Florida" in *Perspectives on Gulf Coast Prehistory,* edited by Dave D. Davis. University Press of Florida: Gainesville.

Brown, James, and David H. Dye
    2007 "Severed Heads and Sacred Scalplocks: Mississippian Iconographic Trophies" in *The Taking and Displaying of Human Body Parts as Trophies by Amerindians,* edited by Richard J. Chacon and David H. Dye. Springer Press: New York.

Brown, Robin C.

1994 *Florida's First People.* Pineapple Press: Sarasota, Florida.

Chacon, Richard J., and David H. Dye

2007 *The Taking and Displaying of Human Body Parts as Trophies by Amerindians.* Springer Press: New York.

Clayton, Lawrence A., Vernon James Knight, and Edward C. Moore, eds.

1993 *The De Soto Chronicles,* vols. I and II. University of Alabama Press: Tuscaloosa.

Duncan, David Ewing

1995 *Hernando de Soto: A Savage Quest in the Americas.* Crown Publishers: New York.

Dye, David H.

1995 "Feasting with the Enemy: Mississippian Warfare and Prestige Goods Circulation" in *Native American Interactions: Multiscalar Analyses and Interpretations in the Eastern Woodlands,* edited by Michael S. Nassaney and Kenneth Sassaman. University of Tennessee Press: Knoxville.

Ewen, Charles R., and John H. Hann

1998 *Hernando de Soto Among the Apalachee: The Archaeology of the First Winter Encampment.* University Press of Florida: Gainesville.

Granberry, Julian

1993 *A Grammar and Dictionary of the Timucua Language.* University of Alabama Press: Tuscaloosa.

Grantham, Bill

2002 *Creation Myths and Legends of the Creek Indians.* University Press of Florida: Gainesville.

Hally, David J.

2008 *King: The Social Archaeology of a Late Mississippian Town in*

Northwest Georgia. University of Alabama Press: Tuscaloosa.

Hann, John H.

1988 *Apalachee: The Land Between the Waters,* Ripley P. Bullen Monographs in Anthropology and History: No. 7. The Florida State Museum/University Press of Florida: Gainesville.

Hudson, Charles

2003 *Conversations with a High Priest of Coosa.* University of North Carolina Press: Chapel Hill.

1997 *Knights of Spain, Warriors of the Sun: Hernando de Soto and the South's Ancient Chiefdoms.* University of Georgia Press: Athens, Georgia, and London.

1990 *The Juan Pardo Expeditions: Exploration of the Carolinas and Tennessee, 1566–1568.* Smithsonian Institution Press: Washington, DC.

1979 *Black Drink: A Native American Tea.* University of Georgia Press: Athens, Georgia.

1976 *The Southeastern Indians.* University of Tennessee Press: Knoxville.

Hutchinson, Dale L.

2006 *Tatham Mound and the Bioarchaeology of European Contact.* University Press of Florida: Gainesville.

Jacobi, Keith P.

2007 "Disabling the Dead: Human Trophy Taking in the Prehistoric Southeast" in *The Taking and Displaying of Human Body Parts as Trophies by Amerindians,* edited by Richard J. Chacon and David H. Dye. Springer Press: New York.

Knight, Vernon James, ed.

2009 *The Search for Mabila.* University of Alabama Press: Tuscaloosa.

Lankford, George E.

    2008 *Looking for Lost Lore: Studies in Folklore, Ethnology, and Iconography,* University of Alabama Press: Tuscaloosa.

Larson, Clark Spencer, Christopher B. Ruff, Margaret J. Schoeninger, and Dale L. Hutchinson.

    1992 "Population Decline and Extinction in La Florida" in *Disease and Demography in the Americas,* edited by John W. Verano and Douglas H. Ubelaker. Smithsonian Institution Press: Washington, DC.

Larson, Lewis H.

    1980 *Aboriginal Subsistence Technology of the Southeastern Coastal Plain During the Late Prehistoric Period.* University Press of Florida: Gainesville.

Laudonnier, Rene

    2001 *Three Voyages.* Translated by Charles E. Bennett. University of Alabama Press: Tuscaloosa.

Lewis, David, and Ann T. Jordan

    2002 *Creek Indian Medicine Ways: The Enduring Power of Muskoke Religion.* University of New Mexico Press: Albuquerque.

Lewis, R. Barry, and Charles Stout

    1998 *Mississippian Towns and Sacred Spaces: Searching for an Architectural Grammar.* University of Alabama Press: Tuscaloosa.

Lewis, Thomas, and Madeline Kneberg

    1946 *Hiawassee Island: An Archaeological Account of Four Tennessee Indian Peoples.* University of Tennessee Press: Knoxville.

Martin, Jack B., and Margaret Mauldin

    2000 *A Dictionary of Creek Muskogee.* University of Nebraska Press: Lincoln.

McKivergan, David A.

    1995 "Balanced Reciprocity and Peer Polity Interaction in the Late Prehistoric Southeastern United States" in *Native American Interactions: Multiscalar Analysis and Interpretations in the Eastern Woodlands,* edited by Michael S. Nassaney and Kenneth Sassaman. University of Tennessee Press: Knoxville.

Milanich, Jerald T.

    1996 *The Timucua.* Blackwell Publishers: Cambridge, MA.

    1995 *Florida Indians and the Invasion from Europe.* University Press of Florida: Gainesville.

Milanch, Jerald T., and Charles Hudson

    1993 *Hernando de Soto and the Indians of Florida.* University Press of Florida: Gainesville.

Moore, David G.

    2002 *Catawba Valley Mississippian: Ceramics, Chronology, and Catawba Indians.* University of Alabama Press: Tuscaloosa.

Morgan, William N.

    1999 *Precolumbian Architecture in Eastern North America.* University Press of Florida: Gainesville.

Myers, Ronald, and John J. Ewel

    1990 *Ecosystems of Florida.* University of Central Florida Press: Orlando.

Nelson, Gil

    1994 *The Trees of Florida.* Pineapple Press, Inc.: Sarasota, Florida.

Peregrine, Peter

    1995 "Networks of Power: The Mississippian World System" in *Native American Interactions: Multiscalar Analysis and Interpretations in the Eastern Woodlands,* edited by Michael Nassaney and Kenneth Sassaman. University of Tennessee Press: Knoxville.

Purdy, Barbara A.

1991 *The Art and Archaeology of Florida's Wetlands.* CRC Press: Boca Raton, FL.

Reilly, F. Kent, and James F. Garber, eds.

2007 *Ancient Objects and Sacred Realms: Interpretations of Mississippian Iconography.* University of Texas Press: Austin.

Scarry, John F.

1996 "Stability and Change in the Apalachee Chiefdom" in *Political Structure and Change in the Prehistoric Southeastern United States,* edited by John F. Scarry. University Press of Florida: Gainesville.

1992 "Political Offices and Political Structure: Ethnohistorical and Archaeological Perspectives on the Native Lords of Apalachee," in *Lords of the Southeast: Social Inequality and the Native Elites of Southeastern North America.* Archaeological Papers of the American Anthropological Association, no. 3.

Smith, Marvin T.

2000 *Coosa: The Rise and Fall of a Southeastern Mississippian Chiefdom.* University Press of Florida: Gainesville.

Smith, Marvin T., and David J. Hally

1992 "Chiefly Behavior: Evidence from Sixteenth Century Spanish Accounts" in *Lords of the Southeast: Social Inequality and the Native Elites of Southeastern North America.* Archaeological Papers of the American Anthropological Association, no. 3.

Swanton, John R.

2000 *Creek Religion and Medicine.* University of Nebraska Press: Lincoln.

1928 "Aboriginal Culture of the Southeast" in *42nd Annual Report of the Bureau of American Ethnology,* 673–726.

United States Government Printing Office: Washington, DC.

1928 "Social and Religious Beliefs and Usages of the Chickasaw Indians," *44th Annual Report of the Bureau of American Ethnology,* 169–274. United States Government Printing Office: Washington, DC.

Townsend, Richard F., ed.

2004 *Hero, Hawk, and Open Hand: American Indian Art of the Midwest and South.* Art Institute of Chicago in Association with Yale University Press: New Haven and London.

Ubelaker, Douglas H.

1992 "North American Indian Population Size" in *Disease and Demography in the Americas,* edited by John W. Verano and Douglas H. Ubelaker. Smithsonian Institution Press: Washington, DC.

Vega, Garcilaso de la

1998 *The Florida of the Inca.* Translated by John and Jeanette Varner. University of Texas Press: Austin.

Williams, Mark, and Gary Shapiro

1990 *Lamar Archaeology: Mississippian Chiefdoms in the Deep South.* University of Alabama Press: Tuscaloosa.

Read on for a sneak peek at

A SEARING WIND

Book Three of Contact: Battle for America

Kathleen O'Neal Gear and W. Michael Gear

Coming in February 2012 from Gallery Books!

Essence

The screams are deafening. Pain, agonizing pain, squeezes tears from her clamped eyes. Terrible heat sears her skin until it curls and bubbles. Smoke clogs her nostrils, carrying with it the smell of burning bodies.

I'm back!

She keeps her eyes shut, terrified to open them lest, once again, she see Mabila burning around her. The sound of the houses erupting in flames, the shrieks as men and women burn alive—the sizzling of human fat—are bad enough. She can't stand to see the town, the whirling dust, or the billowing smoke. . . .

Please, Breath Giver, make it stop!

"Elder?" *a soft voice intrudes from another world.*

The horror recedes, the smells fading from her nostrils, the sounds whimpering away into a familiar silence.

Mabila slips painfully into the past. . . .

"Elder?" *the voice asks again.*

She wills herself to open her eyes, blinks, and finds herself lying on the packed red clay of the plaza. Around her, people are hovering, staring down like curious vultures. They whisper to one another behind their hands. The worry expressed in their wide eyes unnerves her.

"Elder?"

She places the voice; it belongs to the Hopaye, the high priest of Chicaza. His face intrudes, hovering reassuringly between her and the distant sky. He gives her a concerned smile and asks, "Are you all right?"

"Mabila," she says, voice hoarse.

"What about Mabila?"

"I was just there."

The Hopaye nods, and the concern in his eyes shades into curiosity. "The people say you were walking across the plaza when you collapsed. Your souls have been flying outside of your body, Elder. I was called. Just in case . . ."

She waits, glancing past him to the warm summer sky—blue, with patches of fluffy white cloud. The sun is casting hard white light at an angle. The sensation of heat, she realizes, is the baking sun. Not the fires of Mabila.

". . . In case I was dead," she finishes what he will not speak.

"You were in Mabila," he states, intent dark eyes on hers. A bead of sweat trickles down the side of his face. There are beads of it in the pores on his nose. He smiles. "You are here now, with us. Mabila . . . that was years ago. When you were young."

"Yes." She is aware of the people crowding forward, confusing her memories with a Spirit Dream.

Fools.

"What about Mabila?" the Hopaye asks.

"The essence," she whispers, hoping her voice will carry to the past. Black Shell needs to know this.

"What essence?" the Hopaye asks.

She smiles, letting her souls float back into the past. For some reason they settle on the night she and Black Shell went back to Mabila. What was she thinking that night?

Ah, yes.

Lost in the moonlit night, so long ago, she tells Black Shell, "The battlefield renders existence down to a crystalline clarity. This bloody and smoking ground compresses everything into purity. Hatred, fear, compassion, exaltation, love, misery, euphoria . . . any human quality is experienced to its full-

est. Words are poor things when trying to convey the triumph or tragedy, the glee or desolation, or the fear, pain, or desolation of the souls. Those things must be lived in battle to be truly understood."

Limping ahead of her, Black Shell says nothing, his broad back swaying with each step as he avoids the rotting corpses—the sprawled dead of Mabila.

From a distant future, the Hopaye's voice asks, "Do you understand, Elder?"

Black Shell continues to limp away from her as if she's rooted. She watches in panic as he disappears through the shattered and splintered wooden gate. It gapes like a perversely broken mouth—a charred wound in Mabila's once formidable defensive walls.

"Understand?" she whispers to the past. "Had you asked me the morning before the battle of Mabila, I would have told you I was prepared for the horror, the desperation, and the ensuing pain. I would have told you that the chance to kill Adelantado Hernando de Soto was worth the coming blood and misery. After all, we were fighting to save our world."

"Elder?" The Hopaye's face swims into her vision, as if through clear water. "Let us help you up. We need to move you to the shade . . . get you to drink something."

Hands reach out. She feels her bony body raised, the dank odor of sweaty people who press too close replaces the stench of Mabila.

Absently, she says, "Black Shell? Oh, Black Shell, the question still lingers: How many lives is a world worth?"

ONE

ACROSS THE FLATS, I COULD SEE THE MOON-BATHED walls of Mabila standing silently in the night. In the soft light, accented by white-rimmed clouds in the east, the town seemed eerily peaceful. The bastions still stood, casting triangular shadows onto the high palisade. Charred plaster added false patterns of darkness to the town's fortifications.

Odd, isn't it? Moonlight, still air, and mass death can create the eerie illusion of tranquillity.

I grunted at the irony.

My wife, Pearl Hand, cast a worried look my way. "Are you all right?"

I snorted and ignored the pain in my left thigh as I limped across the trampled grass. The occasional corpses we passed had already been rendered to bone by crows, maggots, vultures, and the accursed Kristiano *puercos*. Rib cages reflected as shell-white lattice. Partially fleshed skulls seemed to stare at us through black-hollow pits, now empty of eyes. Sometimes the cold white light gleamed on a bow stave, or the polished handle of a forgotten war club.

The dead lay everywhere.

Are they the lucky ones?

De Soto's Kristianos had killed them quickly, lancing many of them in the back, slicing others with sword strokes. Most had bled out within a hundred heartbeats. Others, lanced through the guts, had died more slowly. Put in perspective, they'd watched their world die in moments.

As a survivor of Mabila, I would spend the rest of my life as a witness of the inevitable.

I am Black Shell, of the Chief Clan, of the Hickory Moiety of the Chicaza Nation. Once—not so many turnings of the moon past—I would have introduced myself as *akeohoosa*, an exile dead to my people. In the terrible aftermath of Mabila, concerns as petty as a man's identity seemed disgustingly vain.

I paused to ease my smarting leg and stared down at a sprawled corpse; partially skeletonized, it lay on its back, one arm thrown wide, the forearm bones exposed, fingers missing. Chewed away no doubt.

"Why are you stopping?" Pearl Hand hissed from behind me.

I studied the nameless corpse, and wondered who he'd been as a man. Not even a half-moon past, his heart was beating, blood rushing in his veins. His souls had been full of plans, concerns, courage, and fear.

Cocking my head, I searched for any hint of spiritual essence remaining in the bone, the dried gristle, rotting muscle, and leathery tatters of skin. Extending a hand, I tried to feel for the spirit's presence, as if it might have some temperature the way a campfire did.

"Who was he?" I wondered, thinking back to the thousands of excited men who had streamed into Mabila before the battle. They'd come, dressed in their best, bearing polished bows, brightly feathered arrows, engraved war clubs, and decorated shields. Anticipation had sparkled in their eyes, their supple bodies—bursting with life and vigor—had literally danced as they trained. Memory of their anxious smiles, the echoes of their rising and falling voices, remained . . .

Dead.

All dead.

Looking closer, I could see through the scavenged ribs to the place where a Kristiano lance had been thrust through the man's back. Like so many he'd been run down from behind by a cabayero, skewered, and left bleeding and broken on the field before Mabila.

I straightened and turned my attention to the town's high walls; they rose tall, plastered, and true. Moonlight buffered the black soot, softened and smoothed the outlines. The smashed main gate gaped black and empty, as spiritually vacant as the empty eye sockets hollowing the dead man's skull.

I took a deep breath, aware of the stench: Rot and death carried on the cold night wind. "What is the price of a world?" I shot a glance at Pearl Hand.

Her eyes looked like glowing black stones in her perfect, triangular face. The moon accented her straight nose, but turned her full lips into a black slash. Her hair might have been an extension of midnight where it was pulled back into a long braid.

She wore a dark fabric blanket over a long hunting shirt that fell to her knees. Her feet were clad in moccasins tightly laced to her calves. Darkly dressed as she was, she might have been but another shadow, one to be carefully massaged from the night around us.

"Whatever we have to pay, husband," she replied firmly. "It's the only world we have."

Over five thousand men . . . variously burned, cut, pierced, and butchered. Skipper, my dog. Blood Thorn, my friend. Tastanaki, Red Chief of the Coosa Nation. Tuskaloosa, the High Minko, supreme chief of Atahachi. The thlakko, Darting Snake, war chief of the Tuskaloosa Nation. And so many more . . .

"And for what?" I wondered as I glanced anxiously toward where the campfires of the Kristianos winked in the distance. Unable to travel, with over two hundred of their men wounded, they'd made camp as far from Mabila as they could, and upwind from the thousands of burnt and rotting corpses.

"Come on," Pearl Hand coaxed. "We don't have all night. Morning's too close as it is."

I nodded, picking up my limping pace, making for the gate as quickly as I could. She was right: We didn't want to be caught anywhere in Mabila's vicinity come morning.

As we neared the gate, we passed the place where my dog, Skipper, had been killed. He'd saved my life, appearing out of nowhere in the middle of the battle. He'd attacked the cabayo—the great round-hoofed beast Kristianos rode to war—just as Antonio was about to split my skull with his *hierro* sword.

Pearl Hand, bless her, had previously retrieved Skipper's body while I lay half-fevered from my wounds. Together we had prepared him, painted his brown hair with colored clay, and laid both food and water in his grave. As we'd covered him in a low mound of soil, we'd prayed his life soul toward the Spirit path that led west to the edge of the world. There, come spring, he would make the leap over the abyss and through the Seeing Hand—the constellation that marked the opening to the Sky World. As valiant as he had been, I had no doubt that he'd be honored by the Sky Spirits and escorted to the Land of the Dead.

I hesitated as we passed the place where Antonio had nearly killed me. As it was, he'd cut a deep slice into my leg—hence the limp—and a lesser one still festered and burned in my left arm.

"What are you looking for?" Pearl Hand asked, casting a nervous glance toward the distant Kristiano camps.

"My bow."

"I told you, I already looked."

I had a habit of losing my bow after battles. I'd had to go searching for it after the fight at Napetuca, too. That time I'd hidden it in willows as I ran for my life. This time I'd lost it while fleeing Antonio and his vile cabayo. I stepped over and kicked the animal's great skeleton, happy to have at least managed to kill it.

Cabayos are hornless creatures with round hooves, flowing hairy tails; and they run like the wind. Kristianos, known as cabayeros, ride them to war. Mounted thus, cabayeros can smash the most disciplined formations of infantry. Had I not killed Antonio's cabayo that day, Antonio would have killed me. Fortunately I was able to drive a couple of arrows into the animal's chest.

That it was now nothing but bones was no surprise. The Kristianos had come the next day and stripped the cabayo's carcass of its meat. Kristianos will eat anything. Even their vile *puercos* after the beasts have feasted on human dead.

What's a *puerco*? Another of the funny animals they brought from across the ocean. It's a mostly round, hairless, short-legged, flat-nosed, floppy-eared beast with a curly tail. De Soto had originally off-loaded three hundred of the things down by Uzita. He had special boys to herd them along in the wake of his army.

Nowhere could I see my bow, though several of my arrows lay trampled in the grass.

"Black Shell," Pearl Hand reminded, "if we're going to do this thing, let's be about it. I'm worried enough as it is. Let alone coming here without the dogs."

She referred to the rest of my dog pack: Bark, Squirm, Blackie, Patches, and Gnaw. To a trader like me, dogs were as essential as legs. Big and strong, they carried the trade packs. Or at least they had before Mabila.

I winced as I hobbled through the town's splintered gate and stopped short to stare at the carnage. Everywhere were ruins—even the great trees, black-charred and dead.

I hadn't been on the plaza since the night Pearl Hand had tied a dead man's face over mine and led me—wobbling, bleeding, and hidden under a dead Kristiano's clothing—toward escape.

Perhaps I haven't mentioned that my wife is incredibly clever and innovative when it comes to keeping me alive? That she is half Kristiano and speaks their language is another blessing. She's also beautiful and talented at the arts of love. And did I mention that she's killed more Kristianos than any other warrior, or that she's known among the Apalachee as a *nicoquadca*—the highest ranking of their warriors?

I could go on and on when it comes to Pearl Hand.

For the moment, however, I just stared at the corpses littering the plaza. On either side, the charred wreckage of houses merged with the night. Misshapen lumps inside the blackened walls would have defied identification had I not known that they were the piled bodies of men—warriors trapped when the Kristianos fired the town. They'd burned alive by the thousands, hemmed in by the town walls, unable to flee between the tightly packed houses that roared fire and belched smoke. Clumps of incinerated corpses could be seen beneath the collapsed ash of houses. Others were piled atop one another where they'd been trapped in narrow passages. Even now, weeks after the holocaust, the stench caused my stomach to tighten.

"Let's hurry," Pearl Hand suggested hoarsely. "I don't want to be here a moment longer than necessary."

Me either.

Mabila reeked of death. But the worst part was the great hickory trees. Once they'd provided the town with refreshing shade. Now they rose as skeletons in the moonlight. Bare branches, like piteous imploring arms, reached out forlornly to the silent moon. Like everything in Mabila, they had died, tortured and agonized.

Making a face, I hobbled forward, picking my way around the sprawled bodies. The Kristiano dead were missing, collected by the survivors to be prayed over, their single souls sent to the boring afterlife they called *paraíso*. As Antonio had once explained it, there were no animals or plants, no hunting, no feasting, just singing in the company of other Kristianos.

And these people wanted us to convert to their god?

I hobbled around a burned pack, seeing, of all things, a pile of Kristiano boots. They'd obviously been picked through, but the scorched and curled leather couldn't be mistaken for anything else. Nor could the remains of one of their heavy-cloth tents, gaping holes burned in the fabric.

Just beyond lay another charred bale of what had once been fabrics, the gay Kristiano colors now mostly ash. We passed some of their big jars, green things that had held oil. Borne on slaves' backs all the way from the gulf, they'd ended here, shattered and broken as their contents ignited and exploded.

So, too, were the incinerated remains of a Kristiano saddle, one of the ones I'd seen stripped from the cabayos the morning of the Mabila battle.